A GRAVE
DENIED

Also by Dana Stabenow

The Kate Shugak Series

A Fine and Bitter Snow
The Singing of the Dead
Midnight Come Again
Hunter's Moon
Killing Grounds
Breakup
Blood Will Tell
Play with Fire
A Cold-Blooded Business
Dead in the Water
A Fatal Thaw
A Cold Day for Murder

The Liam Campbell Series

Better to Rest
Nothing Gold Can Stay
So Sure of Death
Fire and Ice

The Star Svensdotter Series

Red Planet Run
A Handful of Stars
Second Star

A GRAVE DENIED

Dana Stabenow

www.minotaurbooks.com

Library of Congress Cataloging-in-Publication Data

Stabenow, Dana.
    A grave denied / Dana Stabenow.—1st St. Martin's Minotaur ed.
        p. cm.
    ISBN 0-312-30681-4
    1. Shugak, Kate (Fictitious character)—Fiction.   2. Women private investigators—Alaska—Fiction.   3. Alaska—Fiction.   I. Title.

PS3569.T1249G73   2003
813'.54—dc21

                                                            2003050605

First Edition: September 2003

10 9 8 7 6 5 4 3 2 1

For
Glenn Winklebleck,
Virginia Parks,
Ken Cash,
and
Tom Sexton,
teachers all,
and for all teachers everywhere.
You make the difference.

Acknowledgments

My thanks to the Danamaniacs, who will know why by the end.

What the grave says,
The nest denies.

—Theodore Roethke

A GRAVE
DENIED

Friday, May 2

Ms. Doogan wants us to keep a journal this summer for freshman English next fall. What we write about is up to us. Great, no pressure there. She says she wants a page a day from each of us. Glad I don't have to read them all.

I didn't know what to write at first, I mean I'm just not that interesting. But I was over at Ruthe's cabin the other afternoon, looking through all the pictures she has of animals in the Park. I told her about the journal and she gave me a copy of *My Family and Other Animals* by Gerald Durrell, this kid who lived on an island off the coast of Greece way back before World War II. This kid never met a bug he didn't like, plus animals and birds. Plus his family was crazy. I can relate. It's kind of fun, or it would be if every time I put it down Kate didn't pick it up and start reading it. I don't mind living with her but I wish she'd keep her hands off my books. At least till I've finished reading them.

So anyway, this journal. I'm starting it even before school is out, that ought to get me extra points. I'm going to be like Gerry, I'm going to write about the birds and animals I see every day on the homestead. Like today I watched a moose cow have a calf in the willows out back of the cabin. Talk about disgusting, he sort of oozed out in this gooey sack and then his mom licked it off him. The calf is so tiny, I've never seen a moose so small. He was totally gross at first, all bloody and icky from being born. The cow kept licking him until he was clean and his hair was standing up in cowlicks (now I know what that word means) all over his body and finally she nudged him to his feet. His legs were so skinny they looked like pick-up sticks. He couldn't stand up straight on them, one always kept bending out from under him and down he'd go on his nose. I couldn't tell if he was a boy or a girl at first, I had to go get the binoculars to see if he had a penis. He did.

Kate keeps warning me not to get too close to the animals already, she'd probably freak if she knew I was going to write a whole journal about them. Vanessa says Kate's probably afraid a bear is going to rip my head off. If one smells that calf it could happen I guess. I'll be careful.

Van and I are looking for jobs for the summer. We both want to make some money, Van doesn't even get an allowance. I was thinking maybe we could find someone who lives in the Park who fishes in Prince William Sound who needs help picking fish. There's an old woman named Mary who's some kind of relative of Kate's who has a setnet site on Alaganik Bay. That would be cool.

1

"Yuck!" The pool of slush covered the road from snow berm to snow berm and thirteen-year-old Andrea Kvasnikof had just stepped in it up to her ankle and over the tops of her brand-new, white on white Nike Kaj. "Ms. Doogan! Ms. Doogan, my shoe's all wet!"

"This is where the leading edge of Grant Glacier was in 1778," Ms. Doogan said, standing in front of a signpost surrounded by the seventeen students of the seventh and eighth grade classes of Niniltna Public School. "Who can tell me what else happened in Alaska that year?"

"The Civil War started!" cried Laurie Manning, a redheaded virago who seemed always to be on the verge of declaring war herself.

"No, the Revolutionary War!" yelled Roger Corley, a dark-browed eighth-grader who wasn't going to let some little old seventh-grade baby go unchallenged.

"Not a war, stupids," Betty Freedman said calmly. Betty always spoke calmly, an unnerving quality in an adolescent. She didn't peer over the tops of her glasses only because she had twenty-twenty vision and didn't need them, but it was impossible not to imagine two round lenses perched on her nose, magnifying her big blue eyes and increasing her resemblance to an owl. With all that fine white-blond hair, a great snowy owl. She even blinked slowly. "That was the year Captain Cook sailed to Alaska, wasn't it, Ms. Doogan."

It wasn't a question, it was a statement of fact. "Yes, it was, Betty," Ms. Doogan said.

"He anchored in Turnagain Arm on June first," Betty said.

Ms. Doogan made a praiseworthy attempt not to grit her teeth. It didn't help that Betty knew as much history as her teacher did, and sometimes more. Ms. Doogan glanced back to see Moira Lindbeck, the one parent she'd managed to coerce along on this field trip, roll her eyes. She faced forward quickly—it would never do to laugh—and continued up the trail, moving to the gravel shoulder to miss an ice overflow rapidly liquifying in this warm spring morning. Bare green stalks of wild rice clustered together in the ditch, loitering with intent, waiting for the temperature to get high enough to burst into bud. She paused next to another signpost and waited for the class to catch up. "This is where the leading edge of the glacier was in 1867. What happened that year?"

They all knew this and they said so in chorus. "The United States bought Alaska from Russia!" Somebody turned a cartwheel, kicking muddy water all over Andrea Kvasnikof's lime green down jacket. Andrea did not suffer this in silence.

Betty Freedman waited for the furor to die down. "For seven point two million dollars."

Ms. Doogan, the breeze soft on her cheek and the heat of the sun on her hair, felt suddenly more in charity with the world and smiled down at Betty. Besides, she knew that behind her back Moira Lindbeck was rolling her eyes again. "Yes."

"Seven cents an acre."

Ms. Doogan transferred the smile to Johnny Morgan. The tallest boy in the class, with a serious brow beneath an untidy thatch of dark brown hair that fell into deep-set blue eyes, Johnny seldom volunteered information. He seemed older than the other students, and every now and then Ms. Doogan caught an expression on his face that she thought might indicate something between tolerance and scorn. She had the feeling that he was only putting up with her until the end of the school year. Indeed, he seemed merely to be marking time until the day he turned sixteen, when he could legally quit school. Which would be a pity, as Johnny Morgan was one of the brightest students she'd ever had the privilege of teaching. She'd tried to reach him all year, but while he was unfailingly polite, he remained aloof. He did his work well and got it in on time in more or less readable shape, or as readable as you could expect from a kid living in a log cabin with no electricity. He was attentive and respectful, but she was always conscious of the shield he had erected around himself, high and wide and, by her, impenetrable.

"Seward's Folly," a small voice said. Ms. Doogan looked down in some surprise. Vanessa Cox, short, slight, dressed year round in Carhartt's bib overalls with a turtleneck beneath in winter and a T-shirt in summer. It was economical, Ms. Doogan supposed, and even a practical solution to dressing a child to go out in any weather in the Alaska Bush, but every time she saw the girl she had to repress an urge to break out the crinolines, or even just a lipstick. If it weren't for the delicate features of her face and the braid of thick fine dark hair that hung to below her waist, it would have been hard to tell that Vanessa was a girl. "That's right, Vanessa," she said, smiling. "Alaska proved them wrong on that, though."

Vanessa, rarely seen to smile, gave a solemn nod. She exchanged a glance with Johnny Morgan. Here, it seemed, was one person who had managed to reach through the shield. Good for both of them, Ms. Doogan thought. Johnny Morgan was only fourteen, but if her instincts were right, here was a young man with the ability to remind any young woman, no matter how deliberately neutered by her foster parents, just how female she was. And anyone as young as Johnny was all the better for a friend. Especially given that his father had been murdered a year and half before, and that he was estranged from his mother.

Ms. Doogan moved up the trail about ten feet. It was starting to get steep and the snow on either side of the trail to get higher. At the same time they could hear the sound of running water. "The glacier was here in 1898. What happened in 1898?"

Betty opened her mouth but Vanessa beat her to it. "The Klondike gold rush."

"Very good, Vanessa," Ms. Doogan said. "Have you been reading ahead in your history book?"

Vanessa gave her solemn nod.

"And you're remembering what you read. Good job."

Betty was much too mindful of the might and right of authority to do anything so lèse-majesté as to pout, but Moira Lindbeck was close to dancing in the street. Ms. Doogan fixed her with a quelling eye, and led the way to the next signpost. "In 1914, the glacier was—"

"World War One!" shouted Laurie Manning, capering up and down in excitement. Laurie had yet to master middle-school cool. "World War One! World War One!"

There was a soldier or soldiers in Laurie's future, Ms. Doogan thought with an inner sigh, but she smiled and said, "Yes, Laurie, World War One. Eric Kizzia, if you pinch Mary Lindbeck one more time, I'm going to pinch you myself, in the same place and just as hard. Knock it off."

Eric tucked prudent hands into the pockets of his corduroy jacket and did his best to look as pure as the driven snow. His grin was impudent and dimpled and it was hard not to grin back. He'd had a crush on Mary Lindbeck since the second grade, only temporarily sidetracked by luscious upperclassman Tracy Drussell last year. Eric's plan had been for Tracy to flunk until Eric made it into her class, but Tracy's family had moved to Anchorage instead, and in the interim Mary had grown breasts, which had effectively cut short Eric's mourning for Tracy. It also made it difficult to keep his hands to himself. If he'd tried to hold her hand, Mary would have shoved him into the ditch with the wild rice. Ignoring her was not an option. A pinch had seemed a safe compromise.

Mary, whose awareness of the male sex had undergone a sea of change in the last year, left her nose in the air but let the corners of her mouth indent in a tiny smile. Eric saw it and it was enough. Moira Lindbeck saw it, too, and was struck dumb with terror.

Teenage hormones were bad enough, Ms. Doogan thought, as she led the class around a corner, hopping from dry spot to dry spot on the trail as they went. Teenage hormones and spring was a lethal combination. Add in a parent who had just been made aware of her child's burgeoning sexuality and Ms. Doogan thought she felt the earth tremble a little beneath her feet, in either anticipation or apprehension, she could never decide. On the whole, she thought she might skip the planned lesson on the Romantic poets. They could do with rather less talk of young men and spring at Niniltna Public School at this time of year.

The trees opened up and the snow berms melted away and a small lake filled with icebergs dissolved into weird and wonderful shapes spread out before them. Between the bergs the lake was like a mirror, reflecting the bank and the trees and the bergs and the Quilak Mountains and the sky above. She dropped a curtsy. "My class, meet Grant Glacier. Grant Glacier, allow me to introduce the seventh and eighth grade classes of Niniltna Public School."

This time the whole class rolled its eyes. She'd made them walk all the way up here, that was bad enough, but curtsying to glaciers? What next? Ms. Doogan was always doing weird stuff like that.

But she was kinda cool weird, Vanessa Cox thought. At least Ms. Doogan cared enough to get excited about what she was teaching. Vanessa shrugged out of her daypack to pull out her lunch. She sighed a little over the PB&J. Sometimes she thought it was the only sandwich Aunt Telma knew how to make. But there was also a cranberry-raspberry Snapple and a Ziploc bag full of Thin Mints, so lunch wasn't a total loss.

Ms. Doogan paced up and down at the edge of the water, talking and gesturing with what looked like a tuna fish sandwich. Her students were sprawled on the bank facing her and the lake, eating and trying to look interested. Her light olive skin was already starting to tan in the spring sun, and her short bob of fine dark hair was beginning to frizz from proximity to the glacial lake. She looked like a poodle, Vanessa decided. Moriah, her best friend back in Ohio, had had a standard poodle, a huge black dog named Matisse. Matisse was interested in and excited about everything, especially after he'd eaten a sixty-ounce bag of Nestle's semi-sweet chocolate chips Moriah's mother had bought for Christmas fudge. Vanessa wondered if Ms. Doogan ate a lot of chocolate.

"Grant Glacier descends from what ice field?" Mrs. Doogan said. "Come on, guys, we talked about this in geology."

Vanessa knew the answer, but her teeth were a prisoner of peanut butter and she couldn't suck them clean in time to beat Betty Freedman to reply. "The Grant Ice Field."

"Correct. The Grant Ice Field, like the largest glacier descending from it, also named for Ulysses S. Grant, the nineteenth president of the United States."

"The eighteenth president," Betty said.

"The eighteenth, then," Ms. Doogan said amiably, "you got me, Betty. It was so named by a couple of Army lieutenants on a survey mission back in, oh, 1880, I guess it was, after the purchase anyway. They had served under Grant in the Civil War and they were probably hoping that if they named an ice field this big after their commander-in-chief that they'd get promoted."

Betty looked suspicious. She hadn't read that anywhere, and she doubted any information she had not seen laid out in columns in a textbook.

Grant Glacier was a wide ribbon of ice winding out of the Quilak Mountains, white higher up and black lower down with a blue layer sandwiched between the two. "Why's it black lower down?" Peter Mike said.

"Who remembers what happened on March twenty-seventh, 1964?" Ms. Doogan said.

There was a blank silence.

"Come on," she said, and sang, " 'Rock and roll is here to stay, it will never die'—come on, you guys, you know this. Unless you've been propping your eyes open with toothpicks in class."

Johnny Morgan finally opened his mouth. "Earthquake." Anything to keep Ms. Doogan from singing again. Sheryl Crow she wasn't.

"That's right, Johnny," Ms. Doogan said, beaming, "the Good Friday Earthquake of 1964. Nine-point-two on the Richter scale. One hundred and twenty-five people were killed, some by the resulting tsunami as far away as Oregon and even Hawaii. The biggest earthquake ever felt in the United States in recorded history. And, by the way, eight of the top ten biggest quakes in U.S. history have had their epicenters in Alaska. Little bit of trivia there for you."

They knew better. Ms. Doogan's trivia had a way of showing up on tests. Once more Johnny threw himself into the breach. "How's that make the glacier black on the bottom?"

"That same quake caused the mountain right next to it to shake into pieces."

"There is no mountain next to it," Alan Totemoff said.

"Exactly," Ms. Doogan said. "The resulting debris fell onto Grant Glacier, in a layer that was three feet thick." She demonstrated with a hand at midthigh.

Even Betty Freedman was impressed.

Like any good performer, Ms. Doogan had them from that moment and she was quick to press her advantage. "The edge of a glacier is a case study in giving birth."

Johnny thought of the baby moose and cringed inwardly.

"During the last ice age, glaciers advanced over much of the known land masses of the earth. They are now in recession. Look," she said, pointing. "Glaciers leave rocks behind, every size from sand to boulder. What's easiest to grow on rocks?

Come on, we were talking about this on the hike up."

"Lichens," Betty said.

"Mosses," Vanessa said thickly, wrestling the peanut butter into submission.

"Very good. Yes, mosses and lichens, which begin the process of breaking down the rocks to form soil. Not much, at first, but some, enough for—what, to take root?"

"Flowers!" cried Andrea Kvasnikof.

"And grasses," Johnny Morgan said.

"Like lupine," said Andrea, who had her eye on Johnny Morgan, if only Vanessa Had-no-right-to-exist Cox would get out of her way.

"Yes, like lupine," Ms. Doogan said. "Talk to me about lupine. Anybody."

"They're purple," Andrea said after a brief pause.

"They're members of the legume family," Vanessa said.

"Which means?"

"Legumes fix nitrogen in the soil."

"And?"

"Nitrogen makes the soil more habitable for more complex plants," Betty said.

"Like?"

"Like shrubs."

"Give me an example of shrubs."

"Willows."

"Alders."

"Cottonwoods!"

"Cottonwoods are trees, doofus."

"And after the shrubs, what?"

"Trees!"

"Spruce trees!"

"Hemlocks!"

"Birches!"

"Christmas trees!"

Ms. Doogan waited for the laughter to die down. "Think about this, boys and girls," she said, waving a hand at the glacier.

"Seventy-five years ago? This little strip of beach we're picnicking on was under the glacier. That's right, under a big slab of ice just like that one. Your grandmas and grandpas couldn't have had a school picnic here." Eyes widened, measured the distance between the face of the glacier, a wall of ice a hundred feet high, and their beachfront picnic site. "Mother Nature doesn't waste time in the Kanuyaq River basin. How many of you remember last summer, when Grant Glacier thrust forward right over the lake?"

Blank looks all around. Ms. Doogan tried not to let her exasperation show. These kids were living in the middle of a geological experiment in progress. If only she could get some of them to notice, they could go on to make a living from it one day.

They finished lunch and set out to explore. Ms. Doogan insisted that they go in groups of two or larger and stay in sight of her at all times, but beyond that they were free to wander as they chose, which added to the sense of it being more like a day off. Eric Kizzia ripped pages from his notebook and made paper sailboats to float in the lake, gathering other students to make a regatta out of it. Mary Lindbeck sat with her hands clasped around her knees and her face turned up to the sun. Others stretched out, some making notes, some napping.

"Hey, look, here's a trail," Johnny said. "It looks like it goes around the lake to the mouth of the glacier. Want to go?"

"Sure," Vanessa said.

"I'll go, too," Andrea said.

"And me," Betty said.

Andrea scowled.

Betty blinked.

Johnny and Vanessa exchanged martyred looks. Johnny led off, with Vanessa behind. Somewhere along the route Andrea elbowed Vanessa to the rear. She tried to walk next to Johnny but the trail was too narrow, so instead she relied on tripping and slipping a lot. "Thanks," she said, the third time it happened. She smiled up at him as she used his hand to pull herself upright.

"Sorry to be so clumsy." She turned the smile on Vanessa, who looked more than usually wooden of face.

The next time Andrea tripped, Johnny stepped nimbly out of reach and Andrea went down on both knees. She didn't mind bleeding as much as she minded getting blood on her brand-new Gap khakis. Her language was unladylike.

"Sorry about that," Johnny said, only he didn't sound sorry at all. "Hey, Van, look at this. Is this a lupine?"

Betty shoved past both of them and peered at the slender green shoots, comparing them to the copy of Pratt's *Field Guide to Alaskan Wildflowers* she held open before her on the palms of both hands, like a priest consulting a sacred scroll. *"Lupinus arcticus,"* she announced in the manner of one handing down a prophecy. "Of the pea or *Fabaccae* family. A perennial, which means it comes back every year."

They gazed at her, stunned into silence by an oblivious self-assurance that allowed Betty to be convinced that they were as spellbound by the subject as she was. "The arctic lupine grows ten to sixteen inches tall, prefers dry slopes, fields, and roadsides, and is not to be confused with the Nootka lupine, which grows in Southeastern, Southcentral, and on the Chain." She frowned down at the plants. "I can't tell which this is. The pictures only show them in bloom." She displayed the book accusingly.

"Yup, that's lupine," Johnny said, and Vanessa quickly followed his lead. "Lupine, definitely."

Once more Andrea brushed ineffectually at the knees of her khakis and muttered dire imprecations to the fashion gods. Johnny watched her for a moment, and said, "Want to get closer to the glacier?"

"Sure," Vanessa said, measuring the distance. "Can we?"

"Sure, the trail looks like it goes right up to it."

"It could fall on us," Andrea said.

"We won't get that close," Johnny said. Andrea hesitated, and he shrugged and turned, saying over his shoulder, "Stay behind if you want."

Vanessa and Betty swung out onto the path behind him. Andrea bit her lip, and followed.

It was rough and rocky going, with treacherous bits of ice cleverly hidden by glacial silt only revealing themselves when trodden upon. A faint, translucent fog seemed to be rising up out of the face of the glacier, looming large and blue in front of them.

They heard a faint cry, and looked around to see Ms. Doogan waving at them from the beach. "Did you hear her?" Johnny said.

"Hear who?" Vanessa said.

"We'd better go back, we could get in trouble," Andrea said.

Betty, caught between a natural inclination to succumb to authority and a congenital compulsion to amass scientific data, wavered.

"Come on," Johnny said. "We're almost there."

In the end the four of them approached the foot of the glacier together. Where the moraine ended, the leading edge of ice had eroded into a yawning black cave, shallow, dark from the silt and dirt embedded in it, an enormous, engulfing shadow in ominous contrast to the bright, sunny day a few feet away. It was melting so fast that the runoff sounded like rain. The gravel beneath, rounded smooth by millennia of glacial erosion, was wet and shiny. The cold and the moisture hit their faces like a slap.

"It's like standing in front of an open refrigerator," Andrea said.

Johnny didn't look at Vanessa, the same way she didn't look at him. Andrea lived in Niniltna, where they had electricity coming out of every wall plug. She didn't live on a homestead, like he did, or on a defunct roadhouse site like Vanessa, or in the middle of a bison farm like Betty. Townies just had no clue.

Johnny peered into the interior. "Whoa," Betty said. "You don't want to get too close." She pointed. "The face is calving all the time. Look at all that fallen stuff. Some of those pieces are pretty big. You don't want to get hit."

"Darn right we don't," Andrea said tartly. "Okay, we've been here, done that, let's go back."

"There's someone in there," Johnny said.

"Oh, come on," Andrea said with a playful slap at his shoulder. "Stop kidding around."

"I'm not kidding," Johnny said, "there's somebody inside, under the glacier."

"What?" Betty and Vanessa crowded next to him, peering into the gloom. "Where?"

"Right there."

They followed the direction indicated by his pointing finger, and out of the dim a figure coalesced, a dark outline, vaguely human, sitting bolt upright with its back to the ice where the ice curved in to meet the gravel. The figure appeared to be clothed. At least no flesh was gleaming whitely at them.

It also wasn't moving. "Um, hello?" Johnny said.

It didn't move. "Hello, you there inside the glacier," Betty said in an unconscious imitation of Ms. Doogan's authoritarian accents. "You need to come out from under the glacier. It could fall on you."

At that moment a shard of ice roughly the size of a brontosaurus calved from the face of the glacier and smashed to the earth outside in a thousand pieces, one of which narrowly missed Andrea, which, after her own heart settled down, Vanessa thought was a darn shame. They all jumped and bumped into each other. Johnny swore. Andrea, of course, screamed. "You guys are nuts, you're all going to get squished! There's no one in there, no one would be crazy enough to go in there! I'm going back to the lake!"

The other three heard the sound of rapidly receding feet. The opening into the ice was still free. "Hello?" Johnny repeated. "You need to come out of there, whoever you are."

There was no response.

"Maybe they're dead," Vanessa said, articulating the thought uppermost in all their minds. "We should check." She stepped inside the open mouth of the cave. After a momentary hesitation, Johnny and Betty followed.

As they approached the sitting figure, their eyes adjusted to the darkness. It was a man, dressed in worn jeans and a Carhartt's jacket. His face was the blue-white of the face of the glacier, veined and mottled.

The hole in his chest was the size of a basketball.

2

"ou were idiots to go inside the mouth of the glacier in the first place," the trooper told them in a stern voice.

"That's what I said," Andrea said. She was fully aware of Jim Chopin's many and manifest charms, and she smiled up at him, using all of her own fledgling ones.

"But you did good when you didn't touch anything, in getting Ms. Doogan to make sure no one else went inside, and in getting Mrs. Lindbeck to come for me."

"It was Johnny," Vanessa said. "Johnny did it all."

Johnny's shoulders had slumped beneath the trooper's stern words. Now they straightened.

Jim grinned at him. "You must have picked up some crime scene smarts from your dad."

They had to step to one side when Billy Mike and his son, Dandy, shuffled by with the body. A nervous titter that must have been equal parts amusement and horror was quickly suppressed. The body was frozen into a sitting position. Billy and Dandy had draped a tarp over the body but the shape itself looked lumpen and grotesque. It didn't help that the tarp kept slipping, and that the face of the corpse kept peeping out at them, like a child playing hide-and-seek.

"Do you know who it is?" Johnny said. "Was."

"It's Mr. Dreyer," Vanessa said.

Jim looked at her. "What?"

"It's Mr. Dreyer, the handyman," Vanessa said. She was pale but resolute. "He came last spring to rototill our garden."

"You're sure?"

She nodded. "His face wasn't . . . I could see his face. It's Mr. Dreyer. He helped Uncle Virgil build our new greenhouse, too, so I really do recognize him, sir."

Billy Mike slammed the door of his Eddie Bauer Ford Explorer, new the year before and now looking as if it had been driven through the eruption of Mt. St. Helens, and walked back up the trail in time to hear Vanessa's words. "Yeah, it's Len Dreyer all right," he said.

"Len Dreyer," Jim said, writing it down in his notebook. "Vanessa says he's a handyman?"

"Oh yeah," Billy said. He pulled out a bright blue bandanna and mopped his forehead. "He does everything. Did everything. Wasn't a machine he couldn't run, from a Skil saw to a D-6. Or fix, if it was broken. He cleared my land so I could build my house, and then he installed the kitchen cabinets and appliances for me." Billy shuddered. "I don't mess with any kind of gas, not even propane. He did some work on the Association offices, too."

"So, mostly construction work?"

"No, I said everything and I meant everything. He worked the sluice a while back for Mac Devlin out at the Nabesna Mine. He did some guiding for Demetri, or at least some packing, and Demetri said he was a hell of a cook. He fished when somebody needed a deckhand for a period. He installed the new bleachers in the school gymnasium, and did the electrical for the Native Association's building. He was all over the Park."

"Was he married?"

"Don't think so."

"Girlfriend?"

"Don't think so."

"Kids?"

"Don't think so."

"Where did he live?"

Billy brightened, glad to have a question he could answer definitively. "Got a snug little cabin up the Step road, about two miles north of the village."

"How long had he lived in the Park?"

Billy shrugged. "Twenty years? Thirty? Like I said, he's been around a while." He gave Jim instructions on how to get to Dreyer's cabin. "So?"

"So, take the body into town and get it on the first plane to Anchorage. Tell George the state's buying."

Billy grinned. "He'll like the sound of that. Especially when he can probably strap this body into a seat."

Jim became aware of Ms. Doogan standing at his elbow. "Sergeant Chopin?"

"It's Jim," he told her.

"Jim," she said, "I'd like to get my kids back to town." She indicated the huddle of students halfway up the slope from the beach. They looked subdued. "You know the way the Bush telegraph works. The parents will start showing up any minute now."

Ms. Doogan was right, and if the news had reached Bobby Clark, chances were it had probably already gone out over Park Air. The last thing Jim wanted was an exercise in crowd control, especially a crowd consisting of anxious parents, who were by definition never on their best behavior. He looked at Johnny. "Only you,"—he consulted his notes—"Vanessa, Andrea, and Betty went anywhere near the ice cave, is that right?"

Johnny and Vanessa both nodded solemnly.

The rest of the class sat huddled together. Jim closed his notebook and raised his voice. "Okay, kids, listen up. Most of you already know me, but for those of you who don't, I'm Sergeant Jim Chopin of the Alaska state troopers. As you all know, the body of a man was found inside the mouth of the glacier. It looks like he's been murdered." He kept his voice matter-of-fact, and waited for the ripple of shock to settle. Andrea had broadcast the news in full voice, according to Johnny, so it wasn't news to them but it was still a shock to hear the words out loud. "He was probably killed somewhere else and brought here, which means his killer could have dropped something that might give us a clue as to who he or she is. Did any of you find anything while you were wandering around?"

Jim waited long enough for the following silence to get a little uncomfortable. "Okay, then. Anybody who remembers anything later on, doesn't matter how small or insignificant or downright silly it seems, doesn't matter when, I want to hear about it. You're all deputized for the duration, okay?"

"Lame," somebody muttered.

Jim ignored it. The effective practice of law enforcement required an aptitude for selective hearing. "I'll go over the ground, but twenty pairs of eyes are always going to be better than one. Chief Billy knows how to get in touch with me." He stepped back and nodded at Ms. Doogan, and she shepherded her charges to the trail and into a fast clip down the hill.

Jim sat on a convenient boulder, facing into the sun, and went over his notes. Len—Leonard?—Dreyer was a white male in his mid to late fifties. He hadn't had a wallet but that wasn't unusual in the Park, where there weren't any ATMs requiring cash cards and where barter was the major method of exchange of goods and services anyway. A driver's license might be needed once you hit Ahtna and the Glenn Highway, so you wouldn't necessarily carry it around in your pocket unless you were making a special trip outside the Park. Some Bush rats didn't bother getting a license at all because they didn't drive anything bigger than a four-wheeler or a snow machine.

There was a roll of bills totaling $783 and sixty-seven cents in loose change—bet Dreyer didn't have a bank account, either—a moly bolt, three Sheetrock screws, one metal washer, half a roll of Wintergreen Lifesavers, and one of those miniature screw-drivers with interchangeable heads. There was a well-used Leath-erman clipped to his belt.

Whoever had killed him hadn't gone through his pockets, or the money would have been gone. Or they didn't care, which made the crime personal. But then when was it ever anything else in the Park. Sometimes Jim thought he'd sell his soul for just one random, faceless welfare mugging, instead of the inter-mittent internecine warfare practiced by the denizens of the Park. With varying levels of enthusiasm and at different levels of in-tensity, true, but it was there in every clique, group, and gang nonetheless, white, Native, old, young, male, female, subsis-tence, sport, or commercial.

Except Bobby. Good old Bobby Clark, a minority of one, a majority of mouth.

And Kate Shugak, a photograph of whom could be found in Webster's after the word "loner."

He didn't envy the medical examiner the task of determining how long Dreyer had been dead. The body had been cold and stiff, but then it had been sitting under a glacier for who knew how long. Rigor set in after twelve hours, held on for another twelve, and passed off in the next twelve, and Jim had a feeling that the body had been there longer than thirty-six hours. He hoped the medical examiner who drew Dreyer liked mysteries, because he was pretty sure finding a time of death wasn't going to be easy.

Well, if Dreyer was a handyman, he had to make appoint-ments. Jim just hoped Dreyer's memory was bad enough that he'd had to write them down, and that an appointment book was to be found in his cabin.

"Len Dreyer?" Kate said.

Johnny nodded. "Did you know him?"

To the educated eye Kate would appear to have drooped a little in her chair. "He was the guy."

"Which guy?"

"*The* guy. The go-to guy. The guy everybody calls when they need help with a job."

"What kind of job?"

"Any job. Construction, mechanics, fishing, farming, mining, guiding. He could turn his hand to anything." She sighed heavily. "I was going to get him to help us build your cabin."

Johnny's voice was stern. "Somebody killed him, Kate."

She pulled herself together. "Yes, of course. Horrible thing to have happen. Awful. Shot, you said?"

"With a shotgun," Johnny said, not without relish. "In the chest. At point-blank range," Jim said.

"Jim was there?"

Johnny nodded. "I wouldn't let anyone else go into the ice cave until he came."

"Good for you," Kate said.

"That's what Jim said. He said I must have picked up some stuff from Dad."

She looked up to see a smile tucked in at the corners of his mouth, and felt an answering smile cross her face. "He's right about that," she said. If nothing else.

He opened a notebook. "I have to write in my journal now."

"Okay," she said. "Moose burgers for dinner?"

"Sounds good."

"Good, because it's your turn."

"Kate!"

She laughed but shook her head. "We agreed we'd trade off on the cooking. I cooked last night." She nodded at the package of ground meat wrapped in butcher paper on the counter. "I got it out of the cache this morning, it's thawed. But finish your journal first. I've got some stuff to do in the yard."

He made a token grumble, but his head was bent over the journal before she had her jacket on. Mutt had all one hundred and forty pounds pressed up against the cabin door, and she exploded outside as if she had been shot out of a cannon, arrowing across the yard with her nose to the ground, tail straight out behind her like the needle of a compass. She vanished into the brush at the edge of the clearing like wood smoke into a blue sky.

The weather had hit the big five-oh two weeks before and it had stayed warm ever since. Kate stood for a moment in the center of the yard, face raised to a sun that wouldn't set for another six hours. She loved spring. The May tree her father had planted was now thirty feet high and the dark green branches of the spruce trees were tipped with new, lighter green growth. A lilac and a honeysuckle were budding even as she watched, and a tamarack, the only evergreen to shed its leaves in the fall, was preparing to put forth new needles and cones. Her father had been a lover of trees, and she was still discovering species not indigenous to the Park that he had planted all over the 160-acre homestead. So were the moose, of course, but Stephan Shugak had planted enough trees to keep a step ahead even of their big bark-stripping teeth.

Forget-me-nots and chocolate lilies and western columbine and shooting stars and Jacob's ladder and monkshood clustered thickly at the edge of the clearing and around the walls of the semicircle of buildings—cabin, cache, garage, workshop, out-house—fat with the promise of a colorful month to come. It was going to be one of those summers, she could feel it, a lot of sunshine, just enough rain to keep the garden watered, just warm enough for the wildflowers to run riot, just hot enough to go skinny-dipping in the creek out back.

She'd felt that way during previous springs and been proven wrong. Not this year, though, she was sure of it. She walked around behind the cabin, pausing to tap each of the six fifty-five-gallon drums stacked in a pyramid on a raised stand, connected to the oil stove of the cabin by a thin length of insulated copper tubing. They were all low, but it was coming up on warmer weather and it wouldn't matter until fall, when the fuel truck made its last runs to Park cabins, businesses, and home-steads. The stand was getting a little rickety with age, and she added replacing it to the mental to-do list that got longer and longer at this time of year.

A trail behind the drums led to a rock perched at the top of the steep path. The path climbed down to the creek below and the swimming hole the creek had carved in the bank. The rock was an erratic dumped there by some itinerant glacier and instead of putting it into orbit with a stick of dynamite, her father had left it where it was, a four-by-six-by-eight-foot misshapen lump of weathered granite. It was streaked here and there with the odd vein of white, glittering quartz that sparkled when the sun got high enough in the sky. The top of the rock was worn smooth from three generations of Shugak butts, into which groove Kate's fit comfortably. Due to a judicious thinning of trees and the precipitous nature of the cliff, the sun made a comfortable pool of golden warmth in which to sit and contemplate one's navel, a pastime to which Kate was addicted.

The thinning of trees around the stone seat had been done by Len Dreyer. He'd done a good job of it, had taken just enough trees to let the sun through, not so many as to look as if someone had come through with the blade of a Caterpillar tractor. Stumps had been cut to the ground, drilled and filled with an organic stump-rotting powder, with the result that they were already being overgrown by raspberry and blueberry bushes and wild roses and of course the inevitable fireweed, with horsetail, forget-me-nots, and lupine fighting over what ground was left. Usually the trees and the brush formed a dark undergrowth impenetrable by eye or foot, close, confining, to some even claustrophobic; when Len Dreyer was done, the sun dappled a landscape of trees, shrubs, and flowers that, if it hadn't been tamed, was at least open to be admired.

That was the last big job Len had done for her. She'd been able to tend to other chores as they cropped up on her own, until Johnny Morgan had appeared on her doorstep and indicated his intention to embrace permanent Park rathood. Her one-room cabin with its sleeping loft was roomy enough for one person. With Johnny, it was getting a little crowded. They'd made it through the winter amicably, more or less, and now it was spring with summer hard on spring's heels. They'd be spending most of their time out of doors, but autumn would come, when they would be driven back inside, first by rain and then by snow and then by the bitter cold of the long Arctic winter night.

And the Park was rife with stories of lifelong friends, entire families, and couples married and unmarried splitting the blanket over the effects of that long night on the psyche. Kate wasn't about to let that happen to her and Johnny.

Initially, the plan was to have added a room on to her cabin. The winter together had changed her mind. Or, truthfully, Johnny's. "Why not my own cabin?"

She didn't have a lot of experience raising kids, so she said unwisely, "Because I said so."

"That's not good enough," he told her, and, impressed by the lack of temper in the statement, she shut up and listened. They had been sitting across the table from one another, Kate sprawled back with her hand wrapped around a mug of cocoa, Johnny sitting up straight, torso precisely perpendicular to the edge. Kate was beginning to recognize Johnny's body language. This posture meant business.

"You're kind of solitary," he said. "You like living alone or you wouldn't be here on your dad's homestead in the middle of twenty million acres of national park, with the nearest village twenty-five miles down an unpaved, unmaintained road." He wasn't being confrontational or accusatory, exactly. It was more like he'd adopted the impartial air of the scholar. A sociologist, perhaps, come to the Park to examine non-mainstream socio-economic systems, about which he would then write his thesis, which would then earn him a doctorate, followed by a publishing contract, followed by a visiting chair at UC Berkeley, a college in a state which celebrated alternative lifestyles.

Johnny had continued to tick off items on his list, and Kate had reined in her imagination. "Even Dad only visited, or you visited him in Anchorage, you never lived together. Right?"

"Right so far," she said obediently.

"I want to stay here with you. I'm not going back to Anchorage to live with her, and I'm sure as hell not going back to Arizona to live with my grandmother. I don't want to be anywhere else but here, so if I'm smart I'm going to annoy you as little as possible."

She couldn't help laughing a little. "You don't annoy me, Johnny."

He grinned. "Thanks, Kate. That's so sweet of you," and then had to duck when she'd thrown a spatula at him. "To tell you the truth, Kate, I'm feeling a little cramped myself."

Amused, she said, "Oh, you are, are you?"

"Yes. It's why I couldn't stand Arizona, too many people. Which is why I think I need a cabin of my own."

She raised an eyebrow.

"It doesn't have to be as big as this one," he said quickly. "No loft. Just room enough for a chair, a woodstove, a sink, and a bed. Maybe a desk where I can study. Look," he said, and pulled out a notebook. "Like this."

He'd drawn a floor plan that bore a strong resemblance to the cabins at Camp Teddy, and showed signs of having been influenced by Ruthe Bauman, the camp's owner. Kate had to admit they had done a good job of it.

He took that as an opening. "It'd be a lot easier, a lot less labor-intensive to build a new, separate cabin than to add on to this one," he said.

"It'll cost more in materials," she said, more to test him than to contradict him.

"Not really," he said. "Look, I found a book on construction in the school library," and he hauled it out. "You add on, you gotta mess with stuff like the foundation, and then there's the roof." He slapped the book shut. "And think about having to live in the mess while the construction's going on. If we build me my own cabin, we can just live here until it's done, like we are now. I figure we could get it done this summer, and I could move in in the fall, when school starts."

He made a good argument. Still. "Johnny, I don't like this idea of a fourteen-year-old boy living by himself."

"I'll only be thirty feet away. I measured it last night, come on, take a look," and he dragged her into the yard. He'd been busy with strings and pegs, laying out a neat square on the other side of the outhouse, and had taken advantage of the mud to draw in the floor plan.

He watched her as she paced it out. She looked up to see the determined expression on his face, the sun slanting across it, making his blue eyes narrow, highlighting the untidy thatch of thick dark hair falling over his forehead, the stubborn chin. The strong resemblance to his father didn't hurt anymore.

Well. Not as much.

Snow was melting inside the tops of her tennis shoes. "Let's go back inside."

They sat down at the kitchen table over new cups of cocoa. "I don't know," she said. "Kids are supposed to live with their parents."

"Not this kid," Johnny said.

"Yeah, yeah," she said, "let's not go there, okay?"

"I'm not living with her, I don't care what she does or says."

"I know, I know, calm down." *Her* was Jane Morgan, Jack's ex-wife, Johnny's mother and Kate's sworn enemy. Jane had placed Johnny with his grandmother in Arizona when his father had died, and he had liked it so much that he had hitchhiked all the way back to Alaska the previous fall. Kate, who had worked as a public investigator specializing in sex crimes for five and a half of the longest years of her life, knew exactly and precisely every awful thing that could have happened to a young boy on that journey. She still couldn't think of it without a chill running down her spine. He'd shown up in August with Jane hot on his heels. Somehow Jane had learned the location of Kate's homestead, so Kate had tucked Johnny away with Ethan Int-Hout, but Ethan's wife had returned with their two daughters and had returned Johnny to Kate with more haste than grace, citing a wholly imaginary lack of space. Johnny would have had hurt feelings had not the antipathy been wholly mutual.

Kate, deciding that running from Jane was not the answer, had settled him in on her homestead and prepared for a probably legal and undoubtedly expensive siege. Unskilled at saving money, nevertheless she had made an obscene salary the previous year working security for an election campaign. She was prepared to spend it all if necessary to get and keep custody of Johnny. *"Look out for Johnny for me, okay?"* his father, her lover, had asked her the day he had died in her arms. It never occurred to her to do anything else.

In this, she had the tacit approval of the law in the Park, in the person of state trooper Jim Chopin, who was currently involved in a building project of his own. Yes, the troopers were opening a post in Niniltna, staffed by the aforesaid Chopper Jim, an event that in Kate's eyes drastically shortened the twenty-five miles of road between the village and the homestead. It seemed to have a distinct effect on the regularity of her heartbeat and respiration, too, so she tried not to dwell on it.

"Okay," she had said. "We'll build you your own cabin."

Johnny had been prepared for everything but capitulation. "What?"

She grinned. "But," she said, and she leveled a forefinger for emphasis, "you eat here, you hang mostly here, and I'm consulted if and when there are any overnight guests."

"That works both ways," he replied smartly.

She got up to rinse out her mug in the sink. "Dream on," she said to the window, and had hoped that he hadn't noticed the flush beneath the brown of her skin. The only downside to Johnny living with her was that now she had a witness when she embarassed herself.

She was recalled to the present by the sun going behind the tops of the trees. The stone seat had gone cold, and she slid to her feet and walked back to the cabin. With Len Dreyer dead, she was going to have to put Johnny's cabin up herself. This would require a rearrangment of her summer to-do list, some of which might have to be put off until the following year. She'd like to catch whoever killed Len Dreyer herself, and roast him—or her—over a slow fire.

She was on the doorstep, kicking the mud from her shoes, when a movement caught the corner of her eye. She looked up and saw a tall man enter the clearing. "Oh shit," she said beneath her breath.

Mutt burst from the clearing and launched a joyful assault. The man laughed, trying to dodge out of the way of an enthusiastic tongue. When Mutt liked, she *liked*.

"What?" Johnny said, appearing in the doorway, a pen behind his ear, one finger marking his place in his journal.

"We've got company," she said, and opened the door wide.

The far-too-familiar shark's grin flashed out at her. "Hey, Kate."

"Jim," she said.

The grin, if anything, widened. "Your lack of enthusiasm is duly noted," he told her. "Hey, Johnny."

"Hey, Jim."

Kate, noticing the answering smile on Johnny's face, thought sourly that Johnny was still young enough to be impressed by the crisp blue and gold of the state trooper uniform, not to mention the Smokey the Bear hat. Although, come to think of it, she hadn't seen Jim in his Smokey hat since before . . . well, since before last summer in Bering. He was wearing a dark blue ball cap with the trooper insignia on the crown and a noticeable lack of gold braid. And while he wore the uniform shirt, it was tucked into a pair of faded blue jeans, and the shiny half boots had given way to shoepacks, scuffed and muddy.

She looked up and saw him watching her. One dark blond eyebrow raised ever so slightly. She couldn't help it, the flush crept right up her neck, over the thin white roped scar stretching almost from ear to ear, and into her face.

For some reason, it didn't amuse him. The smile faded from his face and he said briskly, "I've got a job for you, if you've got the want ads out."

3

At minimum, Bush courtesy required that no visitor be turned away without refreshment, and it was, unfortunately, time for dinner. Jim accepted Kate's less than enthusiastic invitation and settled in on the L-shaped built-in couch, long legs stretched out in front of him with the air of a man entirely at home. Johnny was shaping moose burger into patties. Kate, having drained the fries and put them in the oven to keep warm, and having set the table and otherwise occupied herself in the kitchen half of the cabin, which after all was only twenty-five feet on a side, and having been the recipient of an ungentle elbow when she got in Johnny's way, twice, found herself with nothing better to do than pour two mugs of coffee and offer one to their guest.

Jim blew on the steaming liquid, a small smile in his eyes.

Kate cleared her throat and sat down on the couch as far away from him as was physically possible. "What's the job?"

The smile didn't go anywhere but he answered readily enough. "You hear about Len Dreyer?"

She nodded at Johnny. "Got my very own personal town crier."

Johnny looked over his shoulder at the two of them, a fragment of ground meat adhering to his cheek, and grinned.

"He did a good job there," Jim said. "Kept everybody out, kept them from contaminating the scene."

"Was Len killed there?" Kate said.

Jim shook his head. "I doubt it. He caught a shotgun blast through the chest at point-blank range. There wasn't enough blood at the scene for it to have happened there."

Kate thought about it, about the physics of a body left beneath the overhang of a glacier. "How long had he been there?"

"I don't know. He was stiff, but given the location, I don't think we can put that down to rigor."

"No. Did you talk to Dan O'Brian?"

"Why would I? Did he know Dreyer?"

Kate hunched an impatient shoulder. "Everybody knew Len. No, I was thinking about the glacier. It's receding."

He raised that eyebrow again, the one that made his expression shift from shark to Satan.

"Yeah, I know," she said. "It just seems an odd place to hide a body."

"If you wanted to hide it," Jim said. "Maybe the killer wanted Dreyer to be found."

"By whom? Who the hell walks around inside glaciers?"

The eyebrow stayed up. They'd been conversing in low voices, so as not to break the concentration of the glacier trekker making hamburgers ten feet away. She smiled in spite of herself, and it was a rare enough occasion to make Jim's breath catch.

Alaska state trooper Jim Chopin wasn't the only man who had found Kate Shugak to be beautiful, not least the father of the young man currently beating moose burger into submission across the room. From anything Jim had been able to discover, there had been no one else for Jack Morgan from the moment he'd set eyes on Kate Shugak, what would it be, nine, ten years before? No, more like twelve. Kate had taken a degree in justice from the University of Alaska Fairbanks, done a year at Quantico, and had gone straight to work as an investigator for the

Anchorage district attorney's investigative arm, of which Jack Morgan had been head. From all accounts, the future was pretty much set in stone from that moment forward, and it wasn't a future when those two were not together.

Of course, that didn't include the eighteen-month period following Kate burning out on working sex crimes and moving back to this very homestead, after which Jack arrived at this very door, FBI in tow, to hire her to find a missing Park ranger. That had marked the end of Kate's self-imposed seclusion and the beginning of her career as a, pardon him, consultant. Jim had tossed her cabin the previous summer when she had gone missing, and he had run across her tax return. That was what she had put in the space marked "Your Occupation": Consultant. It was the only real smile he remembered getting out of the exercise. She was still pissed at him for tossing the place, too. Among other things.

He looked at her now, the smile lighting her narrow eyes, eyes sometimes hazel, sometimes a light brown, sometimes verging on a mossy green. He'd never been close enough for long enough to figure out which was the one true color. Her hair was thick and black and as shiny as a raven's wing, and had once hung to her belt in a neat French braid. Now it was cropped short, brushed straight back from a broad brow, falling into a natural part over her right temple, the ends apt to curl into inky commas around her ears. Her cheekbones were high and flat and just beginning to take on that bronze tint he had noticed during previous summers, all gifts of her Aleut heritage, although the high bridge of her nose was all Anglo and the jut of her chin as Athabascan as it got.

She seemed tall but wasn't, reaching a neat five feet on a lithe, compact frame. She had a tall personality, he decided. There were curves, plenty of them, from which the inevitable T-shirt and jeans did nothing to detract, but they were sheathed in a deceptively smooth layer of muscle, firm and well-toned, that gave her a grace of motion that could fool the eye into thinking she wasn't as strong as an ox and as quick as a snake. She was both.

She became aware of his steady, unblinking scrutiny, and the smile went out like a light. It was replaced with a wary expression, shuttered, watchful. Vigilant, perhaps, was the most appropriate word. The watch was set, bayonets fixed, ready to repel invaders. He hid a grin. It suited him to have her on her guard around him. She wouldn't have been worried if he didn't constitute a threat. And Jim Chopin wanted very much to be a threat to Kate Shugak. If only in the most horizontal meaning of the word.

Their eyes met, and he smiled at her, a long, slow smile filled with memory and purpose.

The sizzle of moose burgers hitting olive oil filled the room, followed by the inviting smells of charred meat and garlic.

"Tell me what you know about Len Dreyer," Jim said over coffee. They had remained at the table following dinner, which had been received with healthy noises of appreciation, to the chef's great pleasure.

"He was good at just about everything," Kate said. "Mechanics, carpentry, fishing. He worked for everybody in the Park, I think, at one time or another. I think he helped Mandy out one year on the Iditarod when Chick was still drinking. He could turn his hand to pretty much any task."

"I know all that. What else? Was he married? Divorced? Girlfriend? Children? How long had he been in the Park? When did he get here? Did he have any fights with anyone? Anybody mad at him? You know the drill, Kate."

She did, indeed. "I haven't heard anything like that. I knew who he was, he did work for me on the homestead, but we weren't friends."

"You didn't like him?"

"It's not that," she said, taking refuge in a mouthful of coffee. He waited.

Johnny was on the couch, feet up, scribbling something into a notebook, earphones on, the so-called music he was listening to mercifully the faintest of annoying buzzes. Even in the Park, you couldn't get away from Britney Spears. If Duracell ever stopped making batteries, every kid within twenty million acres would rise up in revolt.

"Len was kind of reserved," Kate said. "He was polite, even friendly, but he didn't volunteer information about himself. I don't remember him hooking up with anyone, but that doesn't mean it didn't happen. Sometimes I only go into town to pick up my mail. Ask Bernie, he'll know."

"Yeah," Jim said. "That's the problem."

"What is?"

"I've got a hit-and-run outside Gulkana, one dead, one in critical condition in the hospital in Ahtna. I've got an aggravated assault in Spirit Mountain, where the husband's screaming attempted murder but it's looking more like battered wife syndrome and self-defense and I need time to find out for sure. I've got a guy busted for dealing wholesale amounts of coke out of a video store in Cordova, who says the owner was the dealer and so far as he knew he was just renting out movies, and I need to get into that."

"There's no mystery about Len Dreyer," Kate said sharply, "you know he was murdered."

"Yes, I do. Until the ME tells me different, I'm also pretty sure Dreyer wasn't murdered recently, which lessens not only my chances of finding who killed him but—and that's another thing. Why didn't anyone notice he was missing? Why didn't any flags go up?"

Kate shook her head. "That's not unusual. Len probably holed up in the winter, like most of us do. You don't see a lot of the Park rats from September to March, if you don't count the regulars at Bernie's. Even if someone went looking for him and didn't find him home, they would figure he was out on a trap line or hunting caribou for the cache, or hell, even Outside on vacation. I hear Hawaii's big with the crowd that has money."

She added, "Or in Len's case, doing a job for somebody. MIA isn't a red flag offense in the Park. It doesn't set off any alarms." She gave him a hard look. "Usually."

Jim had been primarily responsible for finding Kate when she had deliberately gone missing the previous year. "So?"

"So what?"

She bristled, and he repressed a grin. Betraying amusement would only irritate her further, and he needed her on the job. "So will you check out Len's background for me? I'm going to be in the air most of next week, between Gulkana, Spirit Mountain, and Cordova."

She wanted to say no, and he knew it. He watched her look over at Johnny, oblivious beneath his headphones, and he could almost hear the ka-ching of the cash register between her ears. Raising a kid was an expensive proposition, especially if you were anticipating a custody battle with his birth mother, and his birth mother hated your guts enough to be willing to spend every dime she could beg, borrow, or steal on getting her son back. Which reminded him of something else Jim had to talk to Kate about.

She looked back at him. "Usual rates?"

He only just stopped a satisfied smile from spreading across his face. "Of course. Keep track of your hours and expenses. I've got your Social Security number on file, and we'll cut you a check when you submit your bill."

The words were brisk and businesslike, but she examined them suspiciously for hidden meaning anyway. This time he did allow himself a full grin, a wide expanse of perfect teeth in a face tanned from exposure to sun and wind, crinkles at the corners of his eyes from staring through a windshield five thousand feet above sea level at an endless horizon, laugh lines fighting for space with the dimples on both sides of his mouth.

She caught herself staring at the dimples, bolted the rest of her coffee, and got to her feet in the same motion. "If that's all, I've got some work to finish before dark."

He rose with her. "Walk me out." He jerked his head at Johnny.

Outside and far enough up the trail for Kate to feel that they were safely out of earshot, she said, "What?"

"Jane's contacted a lawyer in Anchorage. He called me."

She folded her arms across her chest, pushed out that Athabascan chin, and waited, her mouth a grim line.

"She hasn't filed suit yet, but they are what he called 'exploring the possibilities.' He says he thinks they can go before a judge and get an order remanding Johnny into Jane's custody."

She snorted. "Get Johnny to tell his story before that same judge and he'll be thinking something else."

"Kate, there was no abuse."

"Depends on what you define as abuse," she shot back.

"Kate."

She shook her head angrily. "I promised him, Jim. I promised him."

He didn't make the mistake of thinking she was referring to Johnny. "I know you did."

"Will they make you enforce the order?"

"They haven't got it yet."

"Will they?"

"They'll try." He pulled his cap on, settling it firmly down over thick dark blond hair cut neat and short. "But I believe my footwork is a little fancier than theirs."

She looked up quickly. He smiled at her, and vanished up the trail. She was still standing there when she heard the distant sound of a truck door opening. The engine started, gears shifted, and the sound receded into the distance.

When she became aware that she was straining to hear it, she turned abruptly and went into the garage, where her big red Chevy pickup sat, hood open, waiting for a tune-up after a winter's inactivity. Nuts and bolts, spark plugs and oil pans and ball joints. Now there were things a woman could make sense of.

She found a ⅝" open-end box wrench and waded in.

"Is he going to make me go back?"

She jerked, banging her head on the hood. "Ouch. Damn it!" She peered around the hood.

Johnny's figure was outlined against the bright evening. His face was in shadow. "What?" she said, rubbing her head.

"I heard him telling you that she got a lawyer. Is Jim going to make me go back to her?"

So much for speaking out of the hearing of the children. She stepped down from the chunk of railroad tie she used to bring engines into arms' reach and found a rag to wipe her oily fingers. "No one's going to make you do a goddamn thing."

"That's not good enough, Kate." His voice rose. "I won't go back. I won't!"

She tossed the rag into the rag barrel. "Johnny—" When she turned back to him, he was gone.

"Great," she said out loud. "Just great."

Mutt, sitting like a sentinel in the doorway, cocked an inquisitive ear, disliked the quality of the vacuum Johnny had left behind in the air of the garage, and padded off.

"*Et tu*, Mutt?"

Monday, May 5

So this journal writing isn't so bad. Ms. Doogan kinda leaves us alone if we're doing it in class, which is a plus. It's not that I don't like her or that she's a bad teacher. It's just that the textbooks are so boring. If they could get Greg Bear to write our science textbook I could stand to read it. Or Robert Heinlein, except he's dead.

Speaking of the dead. Jim Chopin came out for dinner on Friday, partly to talk to me about the body we found. I didn't remember anything I hadn't told him before but I remember from Dad how cops always like to check everything over again. Plus I think he might have been a little worried about me finding the body.

Finding the body was weird. First time I've ever seen somebody dead. The other kids either, I guess. I thought Andrea was going to hurl. Betty was pretty calm but then she never gets excited about anything. Except maybe Eric. Van was scared but she held it together.

I don't believe in god or ghosts or anything like that. Still, that body was weird. There used to be somebody home and then there wasn't. So there is something that makes us all us.

Mostly I think Jim came to see Kate. He practically walks into the wall when she's in the room, always looking at her, always smiling at her. Probably wants to sleep with her. Dad did, it was Mush City when she was around. I remember once Dad made her get dressed up to go to some party or other when she was staying with us in town. Man, she was gorgeous, she had this sparkly red jacket on and her hair was all stylin', she looked as good as anyone you ever see watching the Oscars on TV, and Kate can shoot a moose, too. She's got two guns in a rack over the door, a .30-06 rifle and a twelve-gauge pump action shotgun. She says we'll take the shotgun with us when we go duck hunting down on the Kanuyaq River delta in the fall and I'll have a chance to shoot it then. She says I have to know how to protect myself in case something happens to her. I can't imagine anything ever happening to Kate Shugak. But then I couldn't imagine anything ever happening to Dad, either.

Saw two eagles on Sunday on the way back from the out-house. They looked like they were fighting. Kate said they were mating. They'd fly real high and then they'd sort of smoosh together and fall, and then before they got too close to the ground they'd break apart and fly up again. Kate says she knows where their nest is, downstream in the top of an old dead cottonwood tree. She says she'll take me to see it in a week or so, after the eggs get laid. I drove the four-wheeler to Ruthe's in the afternoon and she told me it can take an eagle nine or ten days to lay two or three eggs. She had some cool pictures, one of a raven stealing a salmon right out from under an eagle who was eating it. I like ravens, too, but eagles are the coolest. I remember when I stayed on the river with Kate's aunties I saw an eagle swoop down on the surface of the water and snatch up a salmon in its claws. Red salmon weigh an average of eight pounds, Ruthe says. That's a big load for something that only weighs fourteen pounds, even if it does have wings eight feet across. What's delta vee for an eagle, I wonder?

I like the way Kate is never embarrassed to talk about stuff. Van didn't even know where babies came from until I told her.

She's fourteen, the same age as me, and she's hanging with me, you'd think the Hagbergs would have told her. But then maybe the Hagbergs don't know. They don't have any kids of their own, maybe they haven't figured out how it works. Maybe the eagles will give them a clue. Showing is better than telling anyway.

I've figured out a plan to stay in the Park. I haven't told Kate. Showing her is better.

4

Kate surveyed the charred remains of Leonard Dreyer's shack and said one succinct word: "Shit."

It had been a small cabin made entirely of peeled spruce logs, and it had burned like one. She waded gingerly into the wreckage and found ice beneath the first layer of debris.

Mutt, lifting her lip, retreated to the far edge of the clearing and sat down to wait out Kate's investigations with an expression of saintly patience on her face. Mutt had learned from a forest fire two years back that she didn't like cleaning between sooty toes with her tongue.

There was nothing to be found beyond the square bulk of a small woodstove, upon which rested a cast-iron skillet. A lump of metal might once have been a coffeepot. Kate kicked a hole in the pile and bent over to sniff without much hope. She straightened up without having smelled anything except the memory of a fire of which the coals were only an old, old memory. "Damn it," she said out loud.

And there was no sign of any kind of transportation. No truck, no four-wheeler, no snowmobile, there wasn't as much as a bicycle or a pair of snowshoes. A handyman had to have something to haul tools around in. Dreyer must have gone to his death, as opposed to death coming to him.

Or not. Someone could have come here, shot Dreyer, and driven him to Grant Glacier in his own vehicle. Thinking of the rolling hills of moraine that surrounded the mouth of Grant Glacier, much of it covered in impenetrable stands of alder and birch and spruce and all of it an excellent hiding place for anything up to and including a belly dumper, she might have whimpered a little.

She drove up the road to talk to Howard Sampson, the next neighbor north of Dreyer's. Howard, mending a net in his shop, had spent the winter in Anchorage and hadn't seen Dreyer since the previous spring. "He ever do any work for you?" Kate said.

Howard tongued the wad of Copenhagen in his right cheek over to his left and spat a blob of brown fluid directly between Mutt's forefeet. Mutt's yellow eyes narrowed and her ears went back. "I do for myself," Howard said.

Kate got Mutt out of there before Mutt did for both of them. Howard never had been what one might call neighborly.

The Gette homestead was on the downhill side of Dreyer's cabin. It had been deserted for four years, but as Kate came up to the driveway she noticed a thin plume of smoke curling into the air. The drive in was challenging, as the brush and tree roots had been allowed to reclaim a greater part of the road, but she emerged into the clearing eventually to find two men standing in front of the cabin. One of them was holding a shotgun.

"Whoa." She hit the brakes and rolled down the window. "Hello."

The man with the shotgun peered suspiciously into the cab of the truck and recoiled when Mutt lifted her lip at him. "Jesus! Is that a wolf?"

"Only half," Kate said.

"Jesus!"

"Don't worry," Kate said, lying with a straight face. "She's harmless."

"Well." The man with the shotgun swallowed hard, and exchanged an apprehensive look with the other man. "Just keep her in the truck, okay?"

"Okay," Kate said, and took that as an invitation to get out. She mistakenly didn't tell Mutt she was supposed to stay in the truck. Mutt was out and standing next to Kate, shoulder to hip, yellow eyes fixed unwinkingly on the man with the shotgun before he could lodge a protest. He swallowed again instead, audibly this time.

Kate smiled at the other man. "Hi. I'm Kate Shugak."

He smiled back. "I'm Keith Gette. The Neanderthal with the artillery is Oscar Jimenez."

"Oh," she said. "You must be the long-lost heir. Lotte and Lisa Gette's cousins, am I right?" Lotte and Lisa Gette having been sisters who had inherited this homestead from their parents. Lisa was dead and Lotte long gone. At least Kate hoped she was.

Keith nodded. "That's us. Or me. Oscar's my partner."

"Heard the lawyers had found an heir. We've been wondering when you'd show." If ever. "Where are you from?"

"Seattle."

She surveyed the cabin behind them. Four years of neglect lay heavily on it, but it had good bones. The greenhouse behind it was twice the size of the cabin and showed signs that it was being restored first. To the right of the greenhouse an area was being cleared of the heavy brush that always moved into cropland in the Arctic when people stopped tending to it. "How long have you been here?"

"Since last summer."

She smiled. "You made it through your first winter."

He grinned then. "Sure did. Although we did have a couple of interesting encounters with the wildlife."

"Bears?"

"One." He slapped his neck. "Although I'm thinking the mosquitoes are going to be worse than any bear."

"Yeah," she said, "you can shoot a bear."

"And the moose." He shook his head. "Do they eat everything, or just the stuff on our property?"

Kate laughed. "Whatever you particularly like that's growing on your land, they'll eat. They're kind of perverse that way."

Keith laughed, too. "Can we offer you some coffee?" he said.

"Sure, but another time. I'm kind of on a mission." She looked directly at Oscar for the first time. "Could you point that thing somewhere else, please?"

Mutt, ever the diplomat, chose this moment to plump her butt down on the ground and scratch vigorously. Oscar took this as a sign of good faith and swung the double barrel maybe four inches to his left. "Sorry," he said. "I'm a little spooked. And she sure does look like a wolf."

"Only half," Kate repeated. It had little or no effect on Oscar, who continued to regard Mutt with an uneasy eye.

"What can we help you with?" Keith said.

"When you guys came last fall, did you introduce yourself to your neighbors?"

"The one up we did. What's his name, Carnation, no, Breyer, Dreyer—that's it, Dreyer."

"When?"

Keith looked at Oscar. "We got here the middle of July. The greenhouse roof had caved in and about half the glass was broken. When we went down to the post office we asked the postmistress, uh—"

"Bonnie Jeppsen?"

"That's right, Bonnie. We asked her if she knew of anyone who could repair it." His smile was rueful. "Neither of us is much good with a hammer. She told us to talk to Mr. Dreyer. He did a good job of it, too."

"Had to pay him in cash, though, he wouldn't take a check," Oscar said. "There isn't a cash machine in Niniltna, did you know that?"

"No, I didn't," Kate said.

"I had to write a check and have that pilot guy fly it into Ahtna and cash it for me at the bank and bring the cash back."

"Imagine," Kate said gravely. Oscar was oblivious but Keith gave her a sharp look, which she met with an innocent stare. "About Len Dreyer," she said. "Did he mention any family or friends, or where he came from? Any arguments he might have gotten into with another Park rat?"

The men looked at each other, and gave a simultaneous shrug. "I don't remember anything like that," Keith said. "He showed up, and when he did, he worked. I was so grateful, I wasn't about to ask any questions. We needed that greenhouse up and running."

"Before winter?"

"Sure. We installed a couple of propane stoves at either end, and grew stuff straight through the year."

"You must have laid in one hell of a lot of propane," Kate said.

"Yeah, our biggest expense," Oscar said gloomily. Gloom seemed to be key to his personality. "We'll be lucky if we break even this year, even if we don't draw salaries."

Kate almost asked them what they were growing, but thought better of it just in time. "So you don't remember any personal information about Len Dreyer."

"I didn't even know his first name was Len," Oscar said.

"He's good with corrugated plastic, though," Keith said. "That roof is watertight."

"He was good," Kate said. "He's dead."

"What?"

"He was shot. With a shotgun." She looked at Oscar, still holding what upon closer inspection proved to be a very old side-by-side with some very fancy silver work.

Oscar gulped and paled beneath his dark skin. "Well, I didn't shoot him."

"Didn't say you did," Kate said.

"Who are you, again?" Keith said.

"I'm Kate Shugak. I'm—assisting Jim Chopin, the state trooper posted to Niniltna, in his inquiries into Dreyer's murder."

Keith put a comforting hand on Oscar's shoulder. "It's all right, Oscar. I don't think Ms. Shugak—"

"Call me Kate."

Keith smiled. "I don't think Kate is going to clap us into irons just yet."

"Do you remember any shots fired near here last fall?" They shook their heads. She nodded at the shotgun. "Have you fired that lately?"

Oscar proffered it mutely. Kate broke it open. It was unloaded, and dusty with disuse.

"It was my father's," Oscar said. "I don't know what the right shells for it are. I don't even know if it still shoots."

Kate handed it back, thanked them for their time, and left.

"Burned down?" Bobby said. "Recently?"

Kate shook her head, earning a thwack from Dinah. She sat on a stool, enveloped in a sheet, while Dinah trimmed her hair. Katya slid from her knee and headed for the open door at flank speed. Her mother downed scissors long enough for an intercept and deposited Katya in a floodplain of toys in the living room. "It's cold and wet, and I found some ice when I kicked around a little. I'd say somebody torched it last fall."

"You sure somebody torched it?"

"Absent conclusive forensic evidence, no, I suppose not. However, considering that it was Len's cabin, and that Len's body has just been found under Grant Glacier, and that Len underwent a radical lungectomy with a shotgun sometime in the past year, yeah, I'm pretty sure."

Unperturbed, Bobby said, "Where did he live, anyway? When I got him to do the roof, I got him through Bernie."

"He hung out at the Roadhouse?"

"Who doesn't? Where was his cabin?"

"Okay, you're done, thank god," Dinah said, whipping off the sheet. "Are you absolutely sure you don't want to let your hair grow out again, Kate?"

The note of quiet desperation in Dinah's voice was not lost on Kate but it failed to illicit the response Dinah was hoping for. "I'm absolutely sure," Kate said. She wriggled away the stray hair that had insinuated itself inside the neck of her T-shirt and poured herself a cup of coffee.

Bobby had thwarted another of Katya's escape attempts, and Kate followed them both into the living room to sprawl on a couch, of which there were two, parallel to each other across the vast expanse of hardwood floor, both wide enough for Kate's Auntie Balasha and long enough for Chopper Jim. A huge rectangular window overlooked the yard that sloped down to Squaw Candy Creek. The Quilaks jutted up behind, rough-edged peaks still covered in snow. "He had a cabin up the Step road," she said. "Just past the Gettes'."

"Oh yeah?" A broad grin spread across Bobby's face. "Been up there lately?"

"I told you, I was just there."

"No, not Dreyer's place, the Gettes'. Been there lately?"

"Yes, as a matter of fact. Why?"

"The heirs showed up."

"I know, I met them."

"And?"

"And what? They're babes in the woods, but pretty harmless, I thought. The Hispanic one is upset that there isn't a cash machine in Niniltna. The Anglo one seems a little more relaxed. How long had Len Dreyer been in the Park, anyway?"

"You don't know?"

She sighed. "What Abel didn't teach me to do for myself, he did for me, carpentry, plumbing, mechanics, you name it. I never needed to hire on someone else until after he died, so I don't have a clue how long Dreyer was here. Auntie Vi might. How about you?"

"Beats me. He nailed one hell of a shingle, I'll say that for him. I hired him to fix the roof last October. He was finished the last day before the first snowfall. It was tight as a drum all last winter, not to mention which, warm as toast." He hooked a thumb over his shoulder and grinned. "Not easy, after I punched that hole in it."

She followed the direction of his thumb to the post running up the center of the large A-frame, almost invisible beneath the lines of black cable linking all the electronic equipment on the circular console with the antennas hanging off the 112-foot tower outside. Bobby was the NOAA observer for the Park, or at least making daily reports to the National Weather Service in Anchorage was his excuse to the IRS every time he bought a new receiver. He also ran a nice little pirate radio station, hosting Park Air every evening, or whenever he felt that Park rats were in need of some gospel according to the Temptations. Or someone bribed him with a package of moose T-bones to air a for-sale ad.

Bobby had appeared in the Park the year Kate had graduated from high school, carrying a worn duffle bag with his name stenciled on it in big black letters, and a deed from the state of Alaska to forty acres on Squaw Candy Creek. He'd built this A-frame, installed enough electronic hardware to run JPL, and had copped the NOAA job right out from under Old Sam Dementieff. To top it off, he was the first black man many of the Park rats had ever seen.

Three things worked in his favor. He'd hired locally to build his A-frame. From the first day of broadcast he had traded want ads on Park Air for moose meat and salmon. And he'd lost both his legs below the knee to a Vietcong land mine.

"I think the men folk thought I wouldn't be able to run after their women," he'd told Kate years before. They'd been in bed together at the time. He'd grinned and reached out an arm to pull her in tight. "They were wrong about that, but by then it was too late."

They were indeed, and it was, far too late, and when Dinah Cookman showed up in the Park three years earlier he'd taken one look and wedded and bedded her, not necessarily in that order. Dinah was white and twenty-five years younger than Bobby was, but so far as Kate could tell neither one of them had noticed. The result was the going-on-two tornado currently making her proud parents' lives a living hell. "Don't touch that!" Dinah said, leaping forward to catch the end table next to one of the couches from tilting forward and landing on her daughter's head. Katya's face puckered up and everyone held their breath. Precious little Katya had a yell that could frighten a bear into the next county.

Katya's eye fell on Mutt, who knew the signs as well as everyone else and who was poised to rocket through the door as soon as the siren went off. She didn't move fast enough. "Mutt!" Katya said, pointing.

"Mutt!" Dinah said gladly. "Come play with Katya! Come on, girl!"

Mutt looked at Kate, mute misery on her face, and slunk toward Katya, her tail as close to being between her legs as it ever got. She flopped down and Katya launched, landing on Mutt's side with a force that caused a "Woof!" of expelled air and a wheezing, pitiful groan.

"Goddamn, woman, you're letting the kid play with the wolves!" Bobby bellowed at Dinah.

Dinah raised an eyebrow. "Handing over to you, Dad," she said, and retired behind the central console to her computer, where she was editing a twenty-minute video for the community health representative on the practices of safe sex, to be shown that fall to health classes at Niniltna Public School. She was trying to keep the opportunities for snickering to a minimum but the local high schoolers were a precocious bunch and it was hard going. The Niniltna Native Association was footing the bill, however, so she waded in with a light heart.

Bobby, deprived of a husband's legitimate prey, shifted his sights. "And you," he bellowed at Kate, "I keep telling you, no fucking wolves in the house!"

Kate tried not to wince away from the volume. Katya was truly a chip off the old block. She heard a low moan and looked around to see Katya pulling mightily on one of Mutt's ears.

Hard-heartedly, she turned her back. "So Len Dreyer reshingled your roof?"

"Yeah."

"Before the first snowfall, you said. When was that?"

"Lemme look." He wheeled over to the console and pulled down one of a row of daily diaries from a shelf. "Let's see. October twenty-third. Late last year." He closed the diary and replaced it. "His cabin's really burned down?"

"It really is."

"Anything left?"

She shook head. "No. No papers, nothing. And he didn't have much ID on him. Any, actually. The only reason we know his name is he worked for everyone."

Bobby nodded. "Not much need for ID in the Park." He cocked an eyebrow. "Although, now we're going to have our own resident trooper, might pay to keep a driver's license handy."

She tried to look down her nose but it wasn't long enough. "It might." She jerked her head at the radio. "Call Anchorage for me?"

He grinned. "The game's afoot!" he said. He turned on one wheel and docked into the radio console like a ship nosing into port, flipped switches and turned knobs without looking, and said over his shoulder, "Who'm I calling?"

"Brendan McCord. Got his number?"

"Babe, I got everyone's number."

A snort came from the other side of the console, followed by a long, lupine moan from the living room. Both were ignored.

"Brendan? Kate Shugak here."

"Kate!" Brendan's rich, full tenor rolled off the airwaves like an aria. "Long time no talk. What're you up to, girl?"

Kate, mindful of the thousand ears listening in from Tok to Tanana, said, "I'm working a case. I need some information."

"Oh. Ah. Well," he boomed cheerfully, "I live to serve. What do you need?"

"Anything you can dig up on a Len Dreyer."

"Got a Social Security number?"

"Nope."

"Got a date of birth?"

"Nope."

"Got a driver's license number?"

"Nope."

A brief pause. "Well, if it was easy, everybody'd be doing it."

"Jim shipped the body to the ME yesterday. It was stuck in a glacier. His prints ought to be fairly well preserved."

"Freeze-dried," Brendan said respectfully. "Who do I call?"

Bobby nudged Kate to one side. "Brendan, this is Bobby."

"No offense, Bobby, but I'd rather be talking to Kate."

Bobby laughed. "You and me both, bubba. I'm on-line nowadays. When you get what she wants, email it to Bobby at parkair-dot-com. That way I can print it out for you," he told Kate.

Kate, who liked computers, said, "Just like downtown." She raised her voice. "Thanks, Brendan."

His voice sank to a lecherous purr. "Come to town and you can thank me in person."

Kate laughed. "I'll be on the next plane."

"You're cutting into my action, McCord, I'm cutting you off," Bobby said, and cleared to the sound of Brendan's laughter. He cocked an eyebrow at Kate.

"Cut it out," she said. "You're starting to sound like Dolly Levi."

"I didn't say a word," he said virtuously. "You working for Jim on this?"

She nodded, careful to keep her expression neutral. "Usual rates."

She waited grimly for the ragging to start, but all he said was, "Hmmm. Didn't you owe me some money?"

When the door closed behind her he checked on Katya, who had fallen asleep with her head beneath the coffee table, her little butt stuck up in the air, which inspired him to scoop his wife out of her chair and into his lap. The kiss that followed was long and enthusiastic. She squirmed halfheartedly before giving in.

He pulled back to look down at her flushed and smiling face. "Promise me you'll never leave me."

She laughed. "Where's that coming from?"

He jerked his head at the door.

Her laugh faded. "You mean her and Jim?"

"Who else?"

"Ethan's totally out of the picture?"

"What I hear, his wife's got him on a leash so short he hardly ever gets off the homestead anymore."

She was silent.

"What?"

"I don't want Kate hurt," she said.

"Hurt? Kate?" It was his turn to laugh.

She shoved herself off his lap and sat back down in front of the computer. Even the line of her spine looked angry, so he wasn't surprised when her voice was curt. "You're such a moron, Clark. You think Kate's invulnerable?"

He took a chance and rolled over to slide his arms around her waist. He nuzzled her ear and whispered, "I think she can handle herself. Meanwhile, back at the ranch, I'd like to handle you."

She tried to shrug him off, and only managed to shrug off her clothes and into their bed. A while later he said, "Got some news."

"Good or bad?" She raised her head to see if Katya was still out, and was reassured by the mound of little behind beneath the baby quilt the four aunties had made.

"Bad."

She rolled up on an elbow. He was staring at the ceiling, his face set. She let her hand wander to afford some distraction from whatever it was that was making him unhappy.

"Cut that out," he said without force.

"Tell me or I'll quit."

"All right, all right, Jesus! Some women." He pulled her back down for a fierce kiss.

"Forget it," she said, grabbing his hair and pulling. "Talk."

"Ouch! Damn it! Jeez, you're always beating up on me. You think you'd take it easier on a poor, helpless cripple with—"

She pulled harder. "Tell me."

He sighed. "My brother's coming."

"Your brother?"

He nodded.

"You have a brother?"

He winced. "Yeah."

"We've been married, what, going on two years, we have a child, and this is the first time you tell me you have a brother?" A murmur from Katya in the living room made her lower her voice. "Older or younger?"

"Older."

"Does he have a name, this older brother?"

"Jeffrey."

"Any other siblings I need to know about?"

"No."

"This is like pulling teeth," she said. "Talk to me, Clark. Why is it bad news that your older brother Jeffrey is coming to visit?"

"He's not coming to visit. We don't visit."

"Then why is he coming?"

"He didn't say, he just said he was coming."

"Did he write, call, what?"

"I got a letter yesterday when I went into town to check the mail."

She digested this. "When?"

"Tomorrow."

She took a deep breath. "I appreciate all the advance notice there, Clark."

"I didn't get much either, Cookman, like I said, I just got the letter yesterday. I don't even know how the hell he found me. I haven't spoken to anyone there since before I joined up."

Mistaking her silence, he added, "Don't worry, he's not staying here. I got him a room at Auntie Vi's. With luck, you won't even have to meet him."

"I don't mind if he stays with us, Bobby. Half the Park's on the couch every other night as it is. Besides which, you're his brother. Why wouldn't he stay with us?"

"Because I wouldn't invite him to." When she would have said more, he said, "Let it alone, okay, Dinah? He has nothing to do with me."

"He's your family."

There was a moment of silence so fraught that Dinah could feel the hairs on the back of her neck stand straight up. "Jeffrey Clark is not my family," Bobby said, enunciating each word with exaggerated care. "That he is my brother is strictly an accident of birth. You are my family. Katya is my family. And Kate. Nobody else, and in particular no one from inside the city limits of Nutbush, Tennessee!"

She flinched a little at the volume of his response. He saw it and took a deep breath. When he spoke again his voice was lower and more controlled. "If I could have gotten away with it I never would have told you he was coming at all, but the way the Bush telegraph works, you'd have heard about the only other black man in the Park two seconds after he got off George."

Dinah was the only child of two only children and her parents had died young, and the most family she'd known was beneath the roof she was living right now. To whistle family of any kind down the wind seemed to her the height of foolishness.

On the other hand, she knew something of the circumstances surrounding Bobby's departure from Nutbush, Tennessee, which had resulted in him lying about his age to get into the army. It had also led, indirectly, to his residence in the Park, which was where she had found him, and she was inclined to regard whoever had helped make that happen with a benevolent eye.

On the whole, however, she thought that this might be one of those times when a smart wife stayed quiet.

He'd rolled to one side, his body so tense she could hear him glaring. She leaned over and kissed his spine. "Were you thinking you wanted dinner anytime soon?"

He looked at her over his shoulder and must have been reassured by what he saw on her face. "Hell, yes, I want dinner!" he said, the familiar bray back in full force. "You just worked ten pounds off me, woman, I need fuel!"

"Then get your butt into the kitchen and peel me some spuds."

She took her time getting back into her clothes, knowing he was watching, and knowing too that Bobby was never so ready as when he just had. She was rewarded when a hand grabbed her elbow and tumbled her back into bed.

The last thing she thought before giving herself up to his single-minded possession was, "I'll ask Kate to check this brother out. Then we'll see." And then she stopped thinking, because only a fool would not pay attention when Bobby got her horizontal, and Dinah Cookman was no fool.

5

I don't think I've seen Dreyer since last fall," Bernie said. "September, maybe? Maybe later."

"He stop in for a drink?"

"He was working for me. Hauled and laid gravel on the paths between the cabins and the outhouses, and the Roadhouse and my house. They were starting to get a little boggy."

The Roadhouse was one big square room with exposed beams, a bar down one side, tables around two others, and a small dance floor covered with Sorel scuff marks. A thirty-two-inch television hung from the ceiling, blaring a basketball game.

"Isn't basketball season ever over?" Kate said unwisely.

There was a sign behind the bar that proclaimed FREE THROWS WIN BALL GAMES, and Bernie, in his spare time the coach of the Kanuyaq Kings, swore to the precept with a fervor only previously matched by medieval saints. "Basketball?" he said, politely incredulous. "Over?"

"Sorry," Kate said. "I forgot myself there for a moment. I'm all better now. About Dreyer."

"Basketball is never over, Kate," he said. "Basketball is the one true thing. Basketball is the only game where brains and brawn are equal. Basketball—"

"Bernie—"

"Not to mention which, basketball is the only sport where the ball is big enough you can actually keep your eye on it. I mean to say, have you ever watched a football game? Or baseball? Now there's a ball you could shove up a—"

"Yes, yes," Kate said hastily. "You're absolutely right. Couldn't be righter if you were the governor. But about Len Dreyer—"

Bernie, deciding he'd ridden that horse long enough, capitulated. "Like I said, last time I saw him was August, shoveling pea gravel. I think I paid him off around Labor Day."

There was a note in his voice she couldn't identify. "Check or cash?"

He gave her a look.

"Right," Kate said, "of course cash, what was I thinking." She was thinking a check was traceable and that cash was not, and that she'd like to have just one piece of paper with Dreyer's prints on it. "Probably didn't make him sign a W-2, either," she said with no hope at all.

"What, you're working for the IRS nowadays?" Bernie inspected an imaginary spot on the glass he was polishing. "Is it true he caught a shotgun blast to the chest?"

"That news already out, is it?"

"Well, hell, Kate, there were a few kids around when the body was found."

"And some of them play for you," Kate said. "Yeah, I get it. Anyway, yes. Front and center."

"Ouch."

She frowned. "You know him well?"

He shrugged. "Well as anybody, I guess."

He met her eyes with a look of such studied indifference that she stiffened. "He hang with any particular Park rats?"

"Didn't have many friends that I noticed." Somebody yelled

for a refill, and as he moved down the bar Kate thought she heard him say, "Not a big surprise."

She watched him pull a tray full of beers and amble over to the table in front of the television, where sat the four Grosdidier brothers and Old Sam Dementieff, taking turns calling the play-by-play and not hesitating to revile the ancestry of the referees every time a whistle blew.

She heard a song she liked, a woman singing about sweet misery, and she wandered over to the jukebox to see who it was.

"Play a song for you, Kate?" George Perry appeared next to her, smoothing out a bill in preparation for feeding it into the slot.

"I like this one," she said.

"Yeah, Michelle Branch, great album. Want me to pick up one for you next time I'm in Ahtna?"

"Sure. George, did you know Len Dreyer?"

"Len? Yeah, sure. Well." He shrugged. "He did some work on the hangar for me last August, after that idiot from Anchorage tried to taxi through the wall." He fixed her with an appraising eye. "This an official interrogation?"

She made a face. "I'm asking some questions for the trooper."

"Working for Jim, huh?"

"Yes."

The flatness of the syllable warned him to go no further down that road, and unlike Bobby, George Perry was a man who liked a quiet life.

"Did Dreyer ever talk to you about friends, his birthday, his parents' names, his hometown, anything? Maybe you needed his Social Security number to make his payroll deductions?"

He grinned at the hopeful note in her voice. "Nope, sorry. Len worked on a strictly cash basis. For me, anyway."

"For everybody, is what I'm hearing," Kate said glumly.

At that moment Brenda Souders walked in, all tits and ass and big hair, and George deserted Kate without a backward glance.

"Hey, girl," someone said. "Looking for a job?"

"I've got one, damn it," Kate said, and turned to face Old Sam. He wasn't any taller than she was and he probably weighed less, but in this case size didn't matter. Old Sam Dementieff had a personal authority that sprang directly from the unshakeable conviction that he was right. All the time. The annoying thing was that he usually was.

"You hear about Len Dreyer?" she asked him.

"Who hasn't?"

"The trooper wants me to ask around."

Old Sam raised an eyebrow, which made him look even more like a demented leprechaun. "Len Dreyer, huh? Hear he got it point-blank with a shotgun."

The Bush telegraph, contrary to form, was keeping it right. Usually by now the weapon should have been metamorphosed into a Federation phaser. "Yeah."

"I didn't know him much. Him and Dandy came to Cordova to help me tear down the mast and boom on the *Freya* when I put her in dry dock last September. I was wanting to get the job done before the first snow. Good worker."

"You didn't like him?" Kate said, replying more to the feeling behind the words than the words themselves.

Old Sam drained his beer and looked sadly at the empty bottle.

"Come on, Uncle, I'll buy you another." She led the way back to the bar and got him a refill. "Tell me about Dreyer."

"Not much to tell," Old Sam said. "Showed up on time, knew enough about hydraulics so's I could trust him with the winch, kept showing up until the job was done. Smiled a lot."

"That's it?" Kate said.

"He smiled a lot," Old Sam repeated, "and he didn't seem interested in women."

"He was gay?"

"Didn't say that," Old Sam said. "Just I remember one day young Luba Hardt came sashaying by, you know like she does."

"Young" Luba Hardt was fifty-five if she was a day, but then Old Sam was about a thousand. Everyone looked young to him.

"It was July, and hot," Old Sam said with relish. "She had her jeans cut up to there and T-shirt cut down to there." He smacked his lips, and shook his head. "Dreyer barely looked up to say hi."

It was an exercise in self-control to keep her face straight. "I suppose he could have been playing hard to get."

Old Sam shook his head. "Don't think so."

"Just because he didn't look at women doesn't mean he didn't like them."

"Didn't say he didn't like them," Sam said. "Just wasn't interested. Saw it happen a couple of other times, although I admit I mighta been looking for it after that. Can't be too careful these days, Kate. Guy was gay, he mighta made a pass at me."

This time Kate resorted to prayer to maintain control. "Thanks, Uncle," she managed to say, and he took his beer back to the game just in time.

Dandy Mike was in one corner, nuzzling at the neck of a pretty girl, Sally Osterlund, if Kate was not mistaken, Auntie Balasha's granddaughter. She looked around for a calendar. It was Monday. Quilting night at the Roadhouse was Wednesday. Sally was safe from her grandmother, if not from Dandy.

Well, Sally was of age or Bernie wouldn't have allowed her to set foot inside the Roadhouse door. Still, Kate wasn't averse to throwing a monkey wrench into the situation. Dandy Mike spread it around a little too generously for safety's sake. She walked over to the table. "Hey, Dandy."

Dandy's right hand, caught in the act of sliding up the back of Sally's T-shirt, descended again to a more discreet level. He didn't dump Sally out of his lap onto the floor, though. "Hey, Kate. You know Sally."

"Hey, Sally."

"Hey, Kate." Sally sprawled back in Dandy's lap and gave Kate a companionable grin.

So much for the monkey wrench. "Dandy, did you know Len Dreyer?"

"Sure," Dandy said. "Everybody knew Len." He caught on. "You checking into his death?"

"I'm asking a few questions is all."

"Jim ask you to?"

Since Jim Chopin had moved his base of operations to Niniltna, Dandy's father Billy had been after Jim to put Dandy to work as his assistant. Billy was Niniltna's tribal chief and not someone Jim wanted to irrevocably piss off, so he was ducking the issue by saying he wanted a bona fide VPSO, or village public safety officer, one trained in criminal statute and procedure at the state trooper academy in Sitka, to back him up. Not, he didn't say, a rounder of epic proportions whose penchant for partying was only exceeded by his passion for gossip. Although the latter quality could be considered an asset in the law enforcement line of work, Jim absolutely did not want the details of whatever case he was working made known all over the Park. If he hired Dandy Mike, he might as well get Bobby to broadcast them nightly over Park Air.

Jim had in fact been so circumspect that Billy now regarded the situation as a done deal, with the result that Dandy, used to his father fixing little things like DUIs and unplanned parenthood for him, regarded himself as Jim's de facto right-hand man. It followed that he did not look kindly upon Kate when she infringed on what he considered to be his territory.

He was in for a serious reality check in the near future, Kate thought, but that was Jim's job, not hers. "Yes, Jim wants me to find out what I can about Len, who his friends were, the jobs he worked lately. What can you tell me?"

The hand on Sally's waist regained the ability to move. Sally squirmed. Dandy bent his head and whispered something in her ear, and she giggled.

Kate pulled over a chair from another table and sat down, crossing her legs and folding her hands in her lap. She kept her gaze steady, and she said nothing.

Dandy threaded his hand through Sally's hair, artfully styled into a mop to look like she'd just gotten out of bed, and kissed her. It took a long time and involved a lot of tongue accompanied by, Kate had to admit, some very nice hand work. His technique, though somewhat lacking in spontaneity, appeared effective. Sally's eyes were glazed and she whimpered a protest when Dandy raised his head. He gave Kate a challenging look.

She yawned, covering her mouth politely with one hand.

He looked exasperated. "Jesus, Kate, you could give us a little room."

"You should get a room," Kate said. "Right after you tell me anything you know about Len Dreyer."

He sighed and looked down at Sally. "How about you get us a couple more beers, honeybunch?" He kissed her pout away and got her started toward the bar with an encouraging pat on the behind. "I didn't know Len well," he said. "We worked a couple jobs together, some construction up on the Step for Dan O'Brian, some fixer-upper stuff for Gary Drussell, some foundation work for the Hagbergs."

"Old Sam says you did some work on the *Freya*, too."

"Oh yeah, forgot about that. Last September, maybe? Old Sam had her in dry dock. He flew us both down." Dandy grinned. "I like Cordova. It's a great little town."

Translated into Dandyspeak, that meant one or more willing women per block.

"Did Len socialize any?"

"Not that I noticed. He was always on time for work, I remember that. It got to be really annoying after a while." A sly grin appeared. "I oversleep a lot."

The grin creased his cheeks and lit his eyes and displayed a full set of white, even teeth to best advantage. He was a good-looking, well-spoken man, and not for the first time Kate wondered why she'd always been immune to his charm. She hadn't even had a crush on him in high school like all the other girls. He had no focus, she thought, and no ambition beyond the next beer and the next girl.

She wondered if there was any White Anglo-Saxon Protestant in her background. Certainly some ancestor had hardwired her with a respect for the work ethic that wouldn't quit. The jury was still out on how grateful she was for it. "Anything else you can tell me?" she said. "What'd he do for fun? Who did he hang with? He ever married? Have a girlfriend? Did he read? Did he listen to music? What did he spend his money on?"

"He never mentioned a wife or a girlfriend. Hell, I never saw him with a man friend. He didn't like Megadeath. He did like Poison, or at least he liked 'Something to Believe In' when I played it. Asked me to play it again. He didn't smoke. Never saw him drunk." Dandy thought. "I don't know, Kate, when it comes right down to it, Len Dreyer could've taught dull to a brick." He looked over her shoulder to where Sally was standing at the bar, waiting on beer and flirting with Bart Grosdidier. "Now if you'll excuse me, I have a previous engagement."

"Dandy." She restrained him with one hand. "There's nothing else you can tell me?"

"No," he said. "Nothing."

You're lying to me, you miserable little shit, Kate thought. Should she warn him to keep his nose out of it, or not? Not, she decided. Riding herd on Dandy Mike wasn't her job, and he wouldn't listen to her anyway.

She made it back to Bobby's just as Dinah was pulling steaks off the barbecue.

Bobby shoved a fistful of paper at Kate. "Brendan came through."

She looked at the first page. "Great," she said with a sigh. "There are eleven Dreyers in the system. None of them are named Leonard."

"It would certainly be easier on you if he was on the lam, with a rap sheet a mile long," Bobby agreed.

Kate mumbled something that might have been "Oh, shut up," and turned the page. "Okay," she said after a minute. "This is weird. According to Brendan, Dreyer never had a driver's license." She paged through more of the pile. "And I don't see a vehicle registration, either." She looked at Bobby. "He must have had transportation. Any handyman has to have something to haul his tools around in." She thought. "I seem to remember, what, a pickup, maybe?"

Bobby frowned. "Yeah, he had a truck. Old Chevy, I think it was, a V8 crew cab with a long bed. A 1981, maybe? Maybe 1982. It might have been silver originally, but that might just have been the primer he was using to patch the rust."

Kate looked at Dinah. Dinah grinned. Men couldn't tell you the color of a woman's eyes they'd spent the previous night with but they never forgot a vehicle. She looked back at the paperwork. "He never applied for a hunting or a fishing license, either. No moose permits, no bear tags."

"Doesn't mean he didn't hunt and fish, Kate," Bobby said very dryly.

"No, but still."

"Not everyone hunts and fishes, either. Even in Alaska. Hell, I let everyone else do my hunting and fishing for me. What?" he said, when Kate looked too long at the page.

Kate read the entry for the third time, and it wasn't because it was hard to read, as Bobby's printer was working fine. "He never applied for a permanent fund dividend."

"What!" Bobby roared. "Even a hermit like Dreyer knew enough to stick his hand out for free money!" He would have said more, but the concept of not applying for the permanent fund dividend shocked him into what for Bobby was speechlessness, and well it might. The permanent fund dividend was paid out to each Alaska resident every year from interest earned on oil pumped from the Prudhoe Bay oil fields, which sat on leased state lands. The annual dividend over the past twenty years had varied from $300 to almost $2,000, and no Alaskan, whether you agreed with the program or not, failed at the very least to apply for it.

Bobby gave her a shrewd look. "You know what this means, don't you?"

"I know exactly what it means," Kate said. "It means his name wasn't Leonard Dreyer."

"Dinner," Dinah said, bringing in a platterful of steaks from the porch, "is served."

"I got to thinking after you left," Bobby said, handing Kate a plate to dry. The dinner dishes had been cleared away, and Dinah was readying Katya for bed. "I think maybe Dreyer was in 'Nam."

"Yeah?" She put the plate away and got handed a bowl.

"I was working in the yard the day he was working on the roof, and I had the portable CD player on the porch with CCR on. 'Run Through the Jungle' was playing, and he sang along to it. Hell, we both did. When it was over he looked down at me and said, 'Lord it was a nightmare,' and I said 'The devil was on the loose,' and he said, 'Got that right,' and I went back to my bonfire and he went back to stapling shingles."

"That's all?"

"If you were there, that's enough." He pulled the plug and let the water gurgle down the drain.

Kate thought about it as she hung the dish towel on the handle of the refrigerator. The only other personal information on Dreyer she had discovered was that he'd liked a song by another band, who was it . . . Poison, that was it. It rang a bell with her but she couldn't place it. She'd have to look through her tapes when she got back to the cabin.

"Kate?"

She looked around to see Bobby jerk his head toward the porch. Dinah was billing and cooing to Katya and didn't notice them leave, or pretended not to.

Kate perched on the porch railing and inhaled spring air. It had been another sunny day, temperatures in the mid to upper fifties. That was one thing she liked about living in interior Alaska, it warmed up faster and got hotter than the coastal communities. "What?" she said.

Bobby rolled the tires on his chair back and forth some. He radiated an aura of deep discomfort. Kate wondered what was coming. Was Dinah pregnant again? If so, why the long face? Was he finally, at long last, low on cash? She did a mental calculation, figuring out how much she could spare from what she needed to keep in reserve to wage a custody fight.

"It's about my brother," he said, the words bursting out of him like champagne following a cork, only not quite as effervescent.

Kate stared at him, mouth slightly open.

"What?" he said defensively.

She got her jaw back up and her voice working again. "You have a brother?"

He scowled. "Why does everyone keep saying that? Yes. I have a brother. And he's coming to town. Tomorrow."

"Oh." For the life of her, Kate couldn't think of what next to say.

Bobby stewed for a moment. "Name's Jeffrey. Not Jeff, not Jeffie, Jeffrey."

"Okay."

"Jeffrey Washington Clark. Washington was my mama's family name. It's my middle name, too."

"Okay," Kate repeated. "So," she said, venturing out cautiously, "great, your brother's coming. Be the first time he's visited the Park, right?" Oh no, she thought, realizing suddenly what was in the wind. He wanted her to give his brother the dollar and a quarter tour. She remembered what had happened the last time she'd toured a friend's relatives around the Park, and shuddered.

"When's the last time you saw a black man in the Park besides me?" he snapped.

Never.

"So yeah, it's his first trip in." He fixed her with a piercing gaze. "This won't be pleasure, Kate. It'll be business. Family, yes, but business. He wants something."

"What?"

"I don't know. He didn't say."

Kate looked over his head to see Dinah standing on the other side of the screen door. She raised an eyebrow. Dinah shrugged her shoulders and shook her head. Kate looked back at Bobby. "So your brother's coming and it won't be fun. Sounds like your ordinary, run of the mill Park family to me."

He gave a short bark of laughter. "I wanted to warn you," he said, and she thought she saw an unusual trace of color beneath his skin. Robert Washington Clark might just be embarrassed, for probably the first time since Kate had known him.

She might have paused to savor the moment had he not been so obviously uncomfortable. "Warn me about what?"

He shifted in his chair. "He's a bigot, Kate. A bad one. He's my father all over again. He doesn't know where I live, who I live among, who my friends are, or—"

"Or, perhaps, to whom you are married?" Kate said delicately.

Bobby cast an involuntary look over his shoulder, but Dinah had moved away from the door. "That, too. I didn't even know he knew where I was. I don't know how the hell he found me. God knows I've had no truck with those people since I joined the army."

Kate detected some Tennessee in Bobby's speech, which only appeared in times of acute stress. "What do you need me to do?" He looked up and she gave a faint smile. "Anything, Bobby. You want me to run him out of town the minute he gets here? I'll meet his plane."

He laughed again, but this time it was genuine. "What I wouldn't give to see that, old Jeffie hustled back into a plane by an unblack female half his size." He sighed. "Much as I'd like that, no."

"Then what?"

"I've got him over at Auntie Vi's. I don't want him here. The man has no manners."

Kate understood. Bobby had a lot of good will going on in the Park. He was afraid his brother was going to step all over that, and he wanted her to make sure it didn't happen. "No problem," she said, sliding to her feet.

He looked at her, worried. "Sure?"

"I'm sure," she said, and looked at him affectionately. There wasn't much she wouldn't do for Bobby Clark.

"No," he said, "I meant are you sure you can keep it together when he starts insulting the slant of your eyes and the color of your skin."

She laughed. "Oh Bobby," she said, still laughing as she went down the steps, Mutt at her side. "If a whole country full of white folks hasn't managed to irretrievably piss me off, one lone black man isn't going to, either. I'll spread the word."

"Thanks, Kate," he said, raising his voice as she climbed into her truck. "I owe you one."

"Don't kid yourself, Clark, you owe me all!" she yelled out the window, and headed down the road.

The Hagbergs' homestead was one of the oldest in the Park, though the Hagbergs themselves were relatively new to it, having moved there only in the late '70s. It was the old Barker place, Kate remembered as she drove down the narrow track from the road. The Barkers had originally come north in the gold rush, taking the route up and over from Valdez via mule train, and by the time they got to what would become the Park they'd gotten tired. Mrs. Barker, according to legend, had tied up her skirts to show a prettily turned ankle and served pancakes hot off a griddle she'd hauled to Alaska from San Francisco. Mr. Barker played the squeeze box and sang sea chanties. By the time the rush had dwindled to a trickle, they'd amassed a sum large enough to homestead. They'd been good pioneers, so it was said, until Mrs. Barker decided seven children were enough and ran off to Fairbanks, where it was said she and her ankles prospered on the Line. Mr. Barker held down the home fort, raised the kids, and on his deathbed enjoined his daughters to be true to their husbands and his sons never to trust a woman. Two of the sons joined Castner's Cutthroats and both died on Attu in World War II. The third son stayed home to marry off his sisters. This wasn't difficult, as women were in even shorter supply in Alaska during the war than they were in normal times. The third son, name of Ezra, stayed single and made a living trapping beaver and wolf. He'd died suddenly of pancreatic cancer in 1976, and his sister, Telma, who had married a Norwegian fisherman from Valdez, moved in that same summer with her husband, Virgil.

Virgil and Telma Hagberg were in their fifties now, although Kate thought they looked older, especially Virgil, with his stooped shoulders and his thinning strands of ash gray hair. He didn't talk much. Telma spoke even less than Virgil. She smiled a lot, though, which held within it the memory of a once-startling beauty, now faded, almost overgrown, as if the weeds had overtaken the rose too soon.

Virgil was known for the wooden toys he carved from birch and spruce, models of airplanes and trucks and bulldozers and the like, finely crafted with moving parts, sanded to a deep, satiny finish, and sold to Park rats at the school's Christmas bazaar for next to nothing. Telma, so far as Kate could remember, sat in the background and never sold anything.

Situated on a south-facing slope on the opposite side of the road from Kate's homestead, it was about halfway between Kate's place and Niniltna and the sun was still up, so it seemed efficient to stop there on her way home. Kate knew the Hagbergs to say hi to at the post office, but that was about it. It was one of the Park's greatest attractions, the ability to disappear into the undergrowth if you wanted to. It was also, Kate reflected on the doorstep of the Hagberg home, one of the greatest disadvantages to the practicing detective.

"Kate," Virgil said when he opened the door to Kate's knock.

"Hi, Virgil. How you been?"

He was surprised to see her but his manners were too good to ask her what she wanted. He invited her in. She told Mutt to wait on the porch, and followed Virgil inside. They passed a room with two workbenches and a set of shelves filled with hand-carved objects. "Still working at the carving, I see," she said.

He stopped and smiled. "Oh, yes. I make the toys for the children. They like them, and it makes a little money for Telma."

He led the way into the kitchen and Kate took the chair offered at the kitchen table. "Telma," he said, raising his voice. "We have company."

Telma came in and smiled at Kate. "Hello, Kate."

"Hi, Telma."

"Would you like some coffee and cookies?" Telma's voice was perfectly normal but her eyes were off, just a little, exactly how Kate couldn't quite figure. They were a washed-out blue and placid as a pond, but unlike the pond they were all surface and no depth.

"Sure, Telma, I'd love some," Kate said, and cringed to hear the note of false heartiness in her voice. Just so did one speak to the simpleminded.

Virgil seemed not to notice. He kissed Telma's cheek, a quiet salutation in the manner of one making willing, worshipful obeisance to a god. It might not have grated so much if Kate hadn't just come from Bobby and Dinah's, where the kisses were loud and lusty and generally led to something horizontal, or looked like they would as soon as the kissers got rid of their company. Virgil's kiss was just too damn reverential for Kate's taste.

She thought back to the last time Jim Chopin had kissed her. Nothing reverential about Jim's kisses, nosireebob. But best not to think of it, or of what happened after, and who was she to dictate how people kissed one another, anyway? She shook her mind free and settled herself to being as pleasant as she could possibly be.

While Telma brewed the coffee and got down mugs, Kate and Virgil talked about the coming fishing season, and how the dip netters and the sports fishermen and the subsistence fishers were cutting into the commercial fishing action. From there they moved on to hunting, and the gay abandon with which the rangers opened and closed the moose, deer, and caribou seasons. "I was talking to a man in Ahtna," Virgil said, traces of Norway still present in his slow, deliberate speech. "He tells me there are more deer on the Kanuyaq delta than he has ever seen. What happens if there is no managed harvest, if they are allowed to eat up all their food supply?" He gave his head a solemn, mournful shake. "I am glad that I can afford to buy beef in Ahtna, Kate, because I do not believe I can support us any longer with my rifle and my shotgun."

They agreed that hunting to eat in Alaska as it had been traditionally practiced was very probably doomed. Telma relieved their mutual despondency with coffee and peanut butter cookies produced from a large ceramic jar cast in the shape of Sylvester the Cat's head.

Kate swallowed and said, "Great cookies, Telma."

Telma smiled her thanks.

"I was wondering if the two of you could help me with something."

"If we can, sure, Kate," Virgil said.

"I don't know if you've heard about Len Dreyer."

"Dreyer?" Virgil said slowly.

"The guy who used to fix things. Houses, trucks, snow machines, boat engines." Virgil still looked blank. "I understood that he and Dandy Mike did some work for you last summer."

Virgil's brow cleared. "Oh. The handyman."

"Yes."

"He helped me build our new greenhouse." Virgil nodded several times. "What about him?"

"Well." Kate fortified herself with a sip of coffee, which was dark and rich and laced with just the right amount of evaporated milk. "To start with, he's dead."

"Oh." Virgil looked at Telma, putting a hand over hers, as if she needed comforting after the shock of Kate's announcement. "I did not know that. I am sorry to hear it."

Telma smiled her sympathy.

Clearly trying for politeness, Virgil said, "Were you friends?"

"No. I was like you, he did some work for me, and beyond that I didn't know much about him personally. The thing is, the trooper has asked me to ask around about him."

"The trooper? What for?"

"Well." There was something so civilized about the Hagbergs' house, a neat log cabin, exterior logs freshly oiled, interior Sheetrock freshly painted, floors freshly scrubbed, that made it difficult to utter the word "murder" within its walls. "It appears that Mr. Dreyer was a victim of homicide."

Virgil stared at her. "Well, for gosh sakes." The expression would have sounded quaint coming from anyone except Virgil Hagberg. It also added ten years to his age.

"Yes."

"What a terrible thing to have happen to someone."

"Yes," Kate said.

Virgil cast around looking for something else to say. "Who did it?"

"That's just it. We don't know. His body was discovered inside the mouth of Grant Glacier."

"Well, for gosh sakes," Virgil said again.

"So the trooper has asked me to trace Mr. Dreyer's last movements. And Dandy Mike said he and Dreyer had done some work for you last summer."

"Of course, of course," Virgil said. He made an obvious effort to gather his thoughts. "It was in July, around the middle of the month, I think. Mr. Dreyer and Dandy Mike came out and put in the foundation and did the framing and the roof. I wanted to put in some tomatoes." His chest puffed out a little. "We got ourselves a daughter to feed now, you know."

At that moment a thin girl with a pale, solemn face came into the kitchen. "Have you met Vanessa? Vanessa Cox, this is Kate Shugak."

Woman and girl exchanged nods.

"Our cousin's only child," Virgil added in a hushed voice, as if Vanessa wasn't standing at the counter directly behind him. "There was a tragedy, you know. Both her parents were killed."

He raised his voice. "Did you want something, Vanessa?"

"One of Aunt Telma's cookies," Vanessa said.

"Sure, go on, help yourself." Virgil turned back to Kate. "Her grandparents were dead, and she was all alone in the world. It looked like she was going to have to go into foster care until we said we would take her. I would not put a dog into foster care."

He patted Telma's hand. Telma smiled her agreement.

Vanessa reached into a drawer and pulled out a Ziploc bag. She proceeded to fill it with cookies from Sylvester's head. Both Telma and Virgil had their backs to her and her movements were noiseless and efficient. When the bag was full, Vanessa vanished again.

"A lovely girl," Virgil said. "And so quiet around the house. Is it not so, Telma?"

Telma smiled her agreement.

"Johnny . . ." Kate said, and then she was stumped at what to call Johnny. He wasn't her son, he wasn't even a relative. "Johnny Morgan, the boy who is living with me, is in Vanessa's class. He's talked about her some." In fact, Kate thought, Vanessa was with Johnny when he discovered the body. Had Vanessa not told the Hagbergs about it?

"All good things, I hope," Virgil said, smiling at Telma.

Telma smiled back. Telma smiled a lot.

"Of course, all good things," Kate said, and shifted into investigator mode. She asked the usual questions and got the usual answers. No, Dreyer hadn't mentioned family or friends. No, he hadn't said where he was from. He'd showed up when he was called, and he'd done what he'd hired on to do and that well, he'd been paid in cash, and then he'd left.

The ideal handyman, Kate thought. Why on earth would anyone want to kill him? She drained her mug and got to her feet. "Thanks for the coffee and the cookies, Telma. Virgil."

"Kate. I am sorry we could not help more."

"You and everybody else," Kate said.

She climbed into her truck and sat in thought for a moment. Bonnie Jeppsen had sent Keith Gette and Oscar Jimenez to

Bobby. After to the Roadhouse, and particularly for those who didn't, couldn't, or wouldn't drink, the postmistress was the next best contact point for the Park. Everybody got mail.

The most conversation Kate had had lately with Bonnie Jeppsen was "Hi" when she picked up and dropped off her mail. Perhaps that should change.

Of course, there were reasons why Bonnie Jeppsen might be perfectly happy to live out the rest of her life on a "Hi, how've you been" basis with Kate.

"But she's probably forgotten all about that by now," Kate said out loud.

Mutt stuck her cold nose in Kate's ear. Kate fended her off. "All right, all right, we're going." She started the truck and set off.

They got home at nine o'clock to find Johnny gone.

6

"Dear Kate," the note on the kitchen table began.

I'm not going back Outside to live with my grandmother. I'm not going to Anchorage to live with my mom. I'm staying in the Park. No judge who doesn't know me or you or my mom is going to make decisions about my future. It's my "—'my' was in capitals and underlined—" future. Don't worry about me, I'll be fine. I'm in a safe place, I brought my sleeping bag, and I have lots of food.

Kate sighed. "Oh, hell."

There was a P.S.

I'm sorry, but I took the .30-06. I left you the shotgun so you should be okay. I promise I'll pay you for any ammunition I use.

Kate's blood didn't exactly run cold but she could feel frost forming on her veins. "Okay," she said, letting the note fall to the table.

She stepped to the door. The clearing was void of life. She stepped outside and took a deep breath.

"MUUUUUUUTT!"

It took Mutt precisely seventeen seconds, trotting back and forth with her nose to the ground, to pick up Johnny's scent from the T-shirt Kate held out to her, to where the boy's smell from it led into the bushes. It took them forty-six minutes, Kate on the four-wheeler with Mutt loping ahead to track him down to his camp in the entrance of the Lost Wife Mine. Kate didn't know what that was in regular time but she felt she'd aged at least a year door-to-door.

Mutt got to him before Kate did, and by the time Kate killed the engine and climbed off, Johnny was prone beneath an on-slaught of sandpapery tongue. "Off! Help! Mutt! Yuck! Get off me!"

Mutt backed off, tail wagging furiously. Johnny got up and brushed pine needles from his jeans. "Traitor," he told Mutt. She heard what he meant instead of what he said and woofed again.

"Good girl," Kate said with a laudatory scratch behind the ears. "Go ahead. You've earned it."

In response to a signal, Mutt launched herself into the brush and flushed a bunch of rabbits from a peaceful browse. She wasn't really hungry, but they didn't know that and scattered in a starburst of white tails.

Johnny was the first to regain his composure. "Would you like some coffee?"

Kate, now that she could see Johnny had not, after all, shot his eye out with the .30-06, decided firstly that Johnny could live, and secondly that she must retain rights to the grown-up in this situation. As such, she would not lose her temper. She chanted that six or seven times to herself, and when it finally took replied, "Sounds good."

It was after ten o'clock and the sun was as near to setting as it ever got in May at that latitude. The mine entrance was high on a hill and commanded a sweeping view of the valley leading up to the plateau known as the Step, and the Quilak Mountains beyond. The sky was without color, neither the blue of day nor the black of night, and no stars shone save the faint golden glow of the one setting behind the hill the mine tunneled into.

The camp, Kate had to admit, was a cozy affair. Johnny had built up a sleeping platform on spruce boughs, cushioned with a tarp, a Thermarest, and a sleeping bag, set just inside the overhang of the cave out of the dew and the rain. A little fire pit was lined neatly with flat rocks he must have hauled up from the creek in back of the homestead. Canned goods were lined up like soldiers on a shelf made from two weather-stained Blazo boxes, both of which Kate recognized as having been salvaged from the dwindling stack behind the shop. He'd brought his CD player and a carrier full of CDs. Kate saw a bargain pack of batteries for the player and for his book light, which had been folded into the paperback copy of *A Civil Campaign* that sat on his sleeping bag.

No way had he moved this much stuff up here in one day. He'd been planning this for some time.

Mutt had interrupted him in the middle of writing in a notebook, which lay open on the ground. Kate picked it up along with the pen she found a few feet away, only to have Johnny remove both from her hands. He wasn't abrupt about it, or embarrassed, just polite, and firm.

She took a deep breath and reminded herself again that she was the grown-up here.

"Here," he said, "take my seat." Gravely, he proffered a rough but recognizable chair, with back, sliced out of a round section of tree trunk with what had probably been her chain saw.

Kate's sense of humor got the better of her at this point. "Thank you, Mr. Crusoe," she said. She sat down. Her butt overlapped both sides but it got the job done. She waited while the water boiled in a saucepan, and didn't offer to help measure coffee into the filter. The resulting brew threatened to remove the enamel from her teeth, but that was okay because that was how she liked it. She added some evaporated milk from a can and sipped. He did, too.

She wondered when he'd moved on from cocoa to coffee. "Nice camp," she said.

"Thanks," Johnny said.

"You've been planning this for a while."

He nodded. "Ever since she showed up in the Park last fall."

"That long? I'm impressed. But then your father was quite a planner, too."

"He told me patience was the most important thing when you wanted something. He told me not to rush, that rushing just got you nowhere faster."

Kate thought of Jack Morgan, of all the time he'd served for her after she'd left Anchorage, and him. Eighteen months he had waited, until exactly the right event had drawn her back into his orbit, by the time when she'd been willing to allow herself to be drawn. It had worked, too. "Smart man, your father."

"I think so."

Mutt came padding back up the hill and flopped down next to Kate with a sigh of satisfaction. Kate let her hand drop down into the thick gray coat. As always, the warm, solid bulk pressed against her side was comfort and consolation, reassurance and support. Mutt was her alter ego, her backup man, her sister, her friend. Her savior, on more than one occasion.

Kate wished Mutt could save her now. She felt as if she were walking through a mine field, that wherever she put a foot down there was the possibility of an explosion that would destroy forever what fragile relationship she had managed to build with Johnny Morgan. She didn't mind making him mad, but she didn't want to alienate him. "I've been talking to some people today," she said.

"Yeah? Who?"

"People who knew Len Dreyer."

He'd all but forgotten the body in the glacier under the pres-

ward for a while. Weeks, I think. Maybe even months."

"But it's a place to start." Kate sipped more coffee. "Not bad, Morgan. We'll make a detective of you yet."

He grinned, looking very young in the reflected glows of the setting sun and the campfire. "Thank you."

"You're welcome." She was sorry to erase the grin from his face but there was no helping it. "So how long were you thinking of staying up here?"

And there went the grin, to be replaced by a straight, stubborn line with a chin very much in evidence. "As long as it takes."

Kate nodded. "I see. Well, you'll be eighteen in four years and no longer a minor, at which time you can tell your mother to take a hike." She looked around at his camp. "I guess you could stay up here that long."

He looked annoyed. "I won't be up here for four years. I just have to hide out long enough for her to get bored and leave me alone."

Kate laughed a little, and held up a hand when she saw his expression change again. "I'm not laughing at you, Johnny. But I have to say that one thing you inherited from your mother is a whole lot of stubborn. You never let anything go." She leaned forward. "Johnny, neither does she. For whatever reason, she hates my guts, and the thought of you living with me just fries her to a crisp."

"She thinks you broke her and Dad up."

"I didn't."

"I know that. She and Dad were way over when he brought you home that first time. You didn't have anything to do with them. I know that, Kate. I don't know why she doesn't know it, too."

They contemplated the fire together in silence for a moment. "She's not a monster, Johnny," Kate said. "She's a human being. She's got the same amount of human failings as the rest of us." And maybe a few more, she thought but didn't say. "I think so long as your dad wasn't with somebody else that she was fine."

sure of more important affairs. "Len Dreyer?" He caught himself. "Oh. Yeah. The dead guy."

Kate nodded, and took a sip of coffee.

"So," Johnny said, curious in spite of himself. "What did they say?"

"Not much," she said. "It's weird. Everybody knew him but nobody really knew him. Near as I can figure, he worked at one time or another for pretty much every Park rat with a building or a boat. They all paid him in cash. All of them were referred to him by either Bernie or Bonnie."

"Who's Bonnie?"

"The postmistress."

"Oh. Mrs. Jeppsen."

"Yeah. Nobody can remember him having a girlfriend. Nobody remembers him having a friend-friend. Nobody can remember him mentioning family. Nobody knows where he came from. Every single person I've talked to so far says he showed up when he said he would and he did the work well. Nobody's complained about him overcharging, so I'm guessing he worked for a reasonable rate."

"What about where he lives? Have you checked that out? There might be papers and stuff."

"There might have been, if his cabin hadn't burned down."

"Oh. Ohhhhh," Johnny said, and his eyes brightened, so that he looked more like fourteen calendar years old and less like a wary fourteen going on forty. "You mean someone burned it down so you wouldn't find out anything about him?"

"Maybe," Kate said. "I don't like coincidences. I find someone shooting Len Dreyer and his cabin burning down coincidental in the extreme."

"Yeah," Johnny said, his brows knit. "When did the cabin burn down?"

"From the look of what's left, I'd say last fall. No later than early this spring because it got snowed on after it burned. I found ice when I kicked at the debris."

"You think the killer burned it down?"

Kate shrugged. "It's the simplest answer. And in my experience, the simplest answer is usually the correct answer. Not always, of course. But usually."

"There must have been something there that the killer didn't want us to find."

Kate warmed to the "us." "Or thought there was," she said.

Johnny wrapped his hands around his mug. The air was growing chilly. It was still May, after all, no matter how long the sun shone and how far inland they were. "Do you think the killer put the body in the glacier to hide it?"

"Not unless the killer was the dumbest person who ever lived. All glaciers are receding. It's a geologic fact. I think I learned it from Mr. Kaufman in sixth-grade science."

"But according to what Ms. Doogan was telling us, last year Grant Glacier thrust forward."

"What?"

"She told us it pushed forward last year, I think a couple of hundred feet."

"But what about all glaciers being in recession?" Kate said, feeling cheated. Mr. Kaufman, a strict disciplinarian with no sense of humor, had let her down.

"They are, mostly. Except sometimes, one isn't. You heard about Hubbard Glacier?"

Kate's brows knit, then cleared. "Oh yeah, Yakutat Bay. The glacier closed off the neck of some fjord."

"Russell."

"Whatever." Kate grinned. "I remember now, I read about it." Jack Baird's air taxi in Bering fell heir to newspapers carried by passengers on their way from Anchorage into the Y-K delta. As holed up as she had been the previous summer, she couldn't help but notice some of the headlines. "The greenies were all bent out of shape because a bunch of, what, seals got caught behind the ice, and the Tlingits in Yakutat were saying, 'Not a problem, the freezer's a little empty anyway.'"

Johnny grinned. "Really?"

"Really. So why did Grant Glacier thrust forward?"

"No one knows why it happens. Last year all of a sudden Grant pushed forward, right over the top of Grant Lake, you know the lake at the edge of the glacier? Ms. Doogan said you couldn't hardly see the lake at all."

"When did it move forward?" Kate said.

"July." Johnny thought. "The first week of July? I don't know the exact date."

"Dan O'Brian would," Kate said. "When did it move back?"

"When did the glacier start receding again, you mean?" Johnny said. "I don't remember."

"Dan would know that, too," Kate said.

Johnny said, "You think whoever killed Len Dreyer put the body in front of an advancing glacier? Thinking maybe it was the super-duper deep freeze, that nobody'd ever find it?"

Kate shrugged. "It's a theory. A crevasse somewhere up on the surface would be better, but I'd guess humping the body of a full-grown man up on top of a glacier, no matter how small that glacier is, wouldn't be all that easy. Or exactly inconspicuous. How big a deal was it when the glacier jumped forward? Did everybody know about it? Did people in the Park go up to gawk?"

"I don't know." Johnny was quick, though. "You're thinking they did, that everybody knew and went up there. So whoever shoved the body in front of it, maybe he was thinking the glacier would keep coming forward. If he thought that, he must have done it at the same time it actually was moving forward."

"And you're thinking that puts a date on when the body was left there," Kate said.

"Why not?" Johnny said, his eyes wide and excited.

"And you're also thinking that the murderer wouldn't have waited too long after he or she had killed Dreyer to dispose of the body."

"Uh-huh."

"So what you're saying is, we could narrow down the time of death if we looked up the dates the glacier was moving forward."

"It wouldn't be exact," Johnny said, frowning. "It moved for-sure of more important affairs. "Len Dreyer?" He caught him-self. "Oh. Yeah. The dead guy."

Kate nodded, and took a sip of coffee.

"So," Johnny said, curious in spite of himself. "What did they say?"

"Not much," she said. "It's weird. Everybody knew him but nobody really knew him. Near as I can figure, he worked at one time or another for pretty much every Park rat with a building or a boat. They all paid him in cash. All of them were referred to him by either Bernie or Bonnie."

"Who's Bonnie?"

"The postmistress."

"Oh. Mrs. Jeppsen."

"Yeah. Nobody can remember him having a girlfriend. No-body remembers him having a friend-friend. Nobody can re-member him mentioning family. Nobody knows where he came from. Every single person I've talked to so far says he showed up when he said he would and he did the work well. Nobody's complained about him overcharging, so I'm guessing he worked for a reasonable rate."

"What about where he lives? Have you checked that out? There might be papers and stuff."

"There might have been, if his cabin hadn't burned down."

"Oh. Ohhhhh," Johnny said, and his eyes brightened, so that he looked more like fourteen calendar years old and less like a wary fourteen going on forty. "You mean someone burned it down so you wouldn't find out anything about him?"

"Maybe," Kate said. "I don't like coincidences. I find someone shooting Len Dreyer and his cabin burning down coincidental in the extreme."

"Yeah," Johnny said, his brows knit. "When did the cabin burn down?"

"From the look of what's left, I'd say last fall. No later than early this spring because it got snowed on after it burned. I found ice when I kicked at the debris."

"You think the killer burned it down?"

Kate shrugged. "It's the simplest answer. And in my experience, the simplest answer is usually the correct answer. Not always, of course. But usually."

"There must have been something there that the killer didn't want us to find."

Kate warmed to the "us." "Or thought there was," she said.

Johnny wrapped his hands around his mug. The air was growing chilly. It was still May, after all, no matter how long the sun shone and how far inland they were. "Do you think the killer put the body in the glacier to hide it?"

"Not unless the killer was the dumbest person who ever lived. All glaciers are receding. It's a geologic fact. I think I learned it from Mr. Kaufman in sixth-grade science."

"But according to what Ms. Doogan was telling us, last year Grant Glacier thrust forward."

"What?"

"She told us it pushed forward last year, I think a couple of hundred feet."

"But what about all glaciers being in recession?" Kate said, feeling cheated. Mr. Kaufman, a strict disciplinarian with no sense of humor, had let her down.

"They are, mostly. Except sometimes, one isn't. You heard about Hubbard Glacier?"

Kate's brows knit, then cleared. "Oh yeah, Yakutat Bay. The glacier closed off the neck of some fjord."

"Russell."

"Whatever." Kate grinned. "I remember now, I read about it." Jack Baird's air taxi in Bering fell heir to newspapers carried by passengers on their way from Anchorage into the Y-K delta. As holed up as she had been the previous summer, she couldn't help but notice some of the headlines. "The greenies were all bent out of shape because a bunch of, what, seals got caught behind the ice, and the Tlingits in Yakutat were saying, 'Not a problem, the freezer's a little empty anyway.' "

Johnny grinned. "Really?"

"Really. So why did Grant Glacier thrust forward?"

"No one knows why it happens. Last year all of a sudden Grant pushed forward, right over the top of Grant Lake, you know the lake at the edge of the glacier? Ms. Doogan said you couldn't hardly see the lake at all."

"When did it move forward?" Kate said.

"July." Johnny thought. "The first week of July? I don't know the exact date."

"Dan O'Brian would," Kate said. "When did it move back?"

"When did the glacier start receding again, you mean?" Johnny said. "I don't remember."

"Dan would know that, too," Kate said.

Johnny said, "You think whoever killed Len Dreyer put the body in front of an advancing glacier? Thinking maybe it was the super-duper deep freeze, that nobody'd ever find it?"

Kate shrugged. "It's a theory. A crevasse somewhere up on the surface would be better, but I'd guess humping the body of a full-grown man up on top of a glacier, no matter how small that glacier is, wouldn't be all that easy. Or exactly inconspicuous. How big a deal was it when the glacier jumped forward? Did everybody know about it? Did people in the Park go up to gawk?"

"I don't know." Johnny was quick, though. "You're thinking they did, that everybody knew and went up there. So whoever shoved the body in front of it, maybe he was thinking the glacier would keep coming forward. If he thought that, he must have done it at the same time it actually was moving forward."

"And you're thinking that puts a date on when the body was left there," Kate said.

"Why not?" Johnny said, his eyes wide and excited.

"And you're also thinking that the murderer wouldn't have waited too long after he or she had killed Dreyer to dispose of the body."

"Uh-huh."

"So what you're saying is, we could narrow down the time of death if we looked up the dates the glacier was moving forward."

"It wouldn't be exact," Johnny said, frowning. "It moved forward for a while. Weeks, I think. Maybe even months."

"But it's a place to start." Kate sipped more coffee. "Not bad, Morgan. We'll make a detective of you yet."

He grinned, looking very young in the reflected glows of the setting sun and the campfire. "Thank you."

"You're welcome." She was sorry to erase the grin from his face but there was no helping it. "So how long were you thinking of staying up here?"

And there went the grin, to be replaced by a straight, stubborn line with a chin very much in evidence. "As long as it takes."

Kate nodded. "I see. Well, you'll be eighteen in four years and no longer a minor, at which time you can tell your mother to take a hike." She looked around at his camp. "I guess you could stay up here that long."

He looked annoyed. "I won't be up here for four years. I just have to hide out long enough for her to get bored and leave me alone."

Kate laughed a little, and held up a hand when she saw his expression change again. "I'm not laughing at you, Johnny. But I have to say that one thing you inherited from your mother is a whole lot of stubborn. You never let anything go." She leaned forward. "Johnny, neither does she. For whatever reason, she hates my guts, and the thought of you living with me just fries her to a crisp."

"She thinks you broke her and Dad up."

"I didn't."

"I know that. She and Dad were way over when he brought you home that first time. You didn't have anything to do with them. I know that, Kate. I don't know why she doesn't know it, too."

They contemplated the fire together in silence for a moment. "She's not a monster, Johnny," Kate said. "She's a human being. She's got the same amount of human failings as the rest of us." And maybe a few more, she thought but didn't say. "I think so long as your dad wasn't with somebody else that she was fine."

"I don't want you to learn that running away is an acceptable response to trouble." She looked at his mutinous expression and laughed a little. "Johnny, you haven't seen trouble like it's going to come at you in your life. Everyone runs into trouble sooner or later, if they're breathing, if they're conscious, if they're in the world. How you handle it, when it comes, is what makes you."

The silence hung heavy over the campfire. Kate let it. At last Johnny stirred and said in a painful rasp, "You think I ran away from Dad dying?"

His words struck at her like a sledgehammer. "I don't think you ran away from your Dad's death," she said when she got her breath back. "I did. I ran away, as far away as I could get, to a place where hardly anybody knew me, and I hid out. All the while pretending I was fine, just fine, when I wasn't. I could have stayed there the rest of my life, keeping my head down, drifting through life."

"What happened?"

What the hell had happened? She still wasn't sure. "Someone who knew me saw me. And there was a . . . thing. A case. I helped solve it. Sort of. Anyway, it reminded me." She shrugged. "It's what I do. Find things out."

"Catch bad guys," Johnny said.

"Yeah."

"Like Dad."

"Yeah. A lot of people aren't lucky enough to find that one thing they're good at. But if you do, I think you should do it. Practice it. Make a living at it if you can. Make a difference, if you can."

"I don't have a thing."

"You will," she said. "Don't let it be running away."

Mutt had been resting her head on her paws, bright eyes traveling back and forth between her two humans. One of her ears twitched toward home. She raised her head and looked in that direction, both ears testing the air like elongated insect antennae.

"What is it, girl?" Kate said, and then she heard it, too, and got to her feet.

It was another four-wheeler. Vanessa Cox was driving it.

A smile spread across Johnny's face.

Vanessa killed the engine and dismounted.

Johnny got to his feet. "Hey, Van."

"Hey, Johnny. Hello, Kate."

"Hi," Kate said.

"Want some coffee?" Johnny said.

"Cocoa," Vanessa said, and unstrapped a sleeping bag and a pack from the back of the four-wheeler.

Our girl Friday has arrived, Kate thought. "You bunking out here, too?" she said.

"Uh-huh." Vanessa unrolled the bag, folded it in thirds, and sat down on it cross-legged. She pulled her pack into her lap and produced a Ziploc bag full of peanut butter cookies. "Have one?" she said to Kate. Her gaze was wide and clear and without a trace of embarrassment.

"Thanks," Kate said, "I had one earlier." She finished her coffee, mostly to give herself time to think. "Virgil and Telma know where you are?" she said finally.

"They're not worried about me," Vanessa said.

The light from the fire flickered over her face. She looked and sounded tranquil, so much so that Kate decided not to point out that Vanessa hadn't answered her question.

So Johnny had told someone where he would be. That was good. That someone was a child. That was bad. But now Kate knew where they both were. That was good.

Chances were Vanessa had snuck out of her house without permission. That was bad. They were obviously close friends. That was good. Just how friendly were they?

That could be seriously bad. They had school tomorrow. Ah-hah. "You've got school tomorrow," she said.

"We'll go from here," Johnny said.

Vanessa nodded. "I brought my books with me."

Kate wondered what would happen if she ordered them to strike camp and follow her back to the homestead.

There was an old attorney proverb, something about never

asking a witness a question to which you didn't already know the answer.

She tested the air, trying to estimate the sexual tension between the two. She didn't sense any, but that didn't mean diddly. Adolescents were past masters at hiding things from adults, it came with the job description. She'd had the Talk with Johnny the previous winter, so it wasn't like he didn't know where babies came from.

She remembered something she'd heard Emaa tell the mother of a teenaged boy who was worrying over sending him to college Outside. "You bring them up good, you teach them all the right things, and you let them go. Nothing else to be done."

It all came down to trust. She got to her feet and dusted off her jeans. "Thanks for the coffee," she said to Johnny. "And the consultation." She was rewarded by a look of surprise on Johnny's face, and had to suppress a smile. What did he think she would do, yell and carry on? Tackle him and carry him home over her shoulder? Aside from the fact that she wasn't sure she could, it would cause permanent damage to everyone's dignity, and Kate didn't think such an extreme sacrifice was, as yet, called for.

If and when she did, she'd come back with a rope.

She handed him the mug. "Will you think about what I said?"

"I am thinking about it."

"Where's the rifle?"

He looked as if he might protest, and then gave in and fetched it from where it was leaning inside the entrance to the mine. It was loaded. The safety was on.

"I told you," he said, watching her. "Dad taught me."

"I know he did," Kate said, shouldering the rifle. "Mutt. Stay."

Mutt ducked her head and sneezed.

"Oh no, Kate." For the first time, Johnny showed dismay. "You don't have to leave Mutt here."

"Yeah, I do."

Mutt gave a soft whine when she saw Kate climb on the four-wheeler. "Stay," Kate repeated. To Johnny she said, "You can send her home in the morning when you leave for school."

"Kate!"

She caught a glimpse of his expression as she turned the four-wheeler, and waited until she was facing away from him to let the grin spread across her face.

Kate was never without Mutt. Mutt was never without Kate. It was the only other given in the world besides death and taxes, and Johnny was well acquainted with it. Kate didn't want to leave Mutt with him, but she was doing it because she'd taken back the rifle. Kate would be alone on the homestead. And Mutt, bless her melodramatic heart, was adding to the effect as she gazed yearningly after Kate as if her last hope of heaven was vanishing down the hill before her very eyes.

Kate felt smug as she put-putted her way home through the dusk. Not for nothing had she learned at the knee of that champion layer-on of guilt, Ekaterina Moonin Shugak.

Later, she would berate herself for being so self-involved that she hadn't noticed the glow of the flames against the sky.

Later she would curse her failure to hear the crackle of the fire.

Later she would not be able to understand how she had not felt the sheer heat of it radiating outward, that she hadn't even smelled smoke.

All this she would think and more, later and all too late, but when she rolled into the clearing and saw the interior of the cabin filled with a hungry, red-orange glow, heard the angry snarl of the flames, felt the vicious heat upon her face, felt the sharp sting of smoke in her nostrils, all she could think was "Johnny!" and all she could feel was a sharp spear of terror so abrupt, so visceral, and so overwhelming that her legs buckled beneath her when she tried to dismount.

She staggered and nearly fell before reason reasserted itself. No, she thought, in one of the few clear thoughts she was to hold dear that night, no, Johnny, wonderfully, marvelously pre-scient Johnny was safe and whole and unburned, tucked into his bedroll at the entrance to the Lost Wife Mine, kept company by an equally wonderful Vanessa and guarded by even more wonderful Mutt. She knew a moment of absolute relief as overwhelming as the moment of sheer terror that had preceded it, and her legs did give way this time, pitching her forward onto her hands and knees, utterly undone, vulnerable as she had never been in her life. She stared, dumbstruck, unable to move, struck motionless by disbelief.

There was an ominous creak and a small *pop!* of sound, and through the window she could see the flames lick higher, higher, tickling at the ladder to the loft and then the loft itself.

This was her father's house. He had built it and brought her mother home to it, Kate had lived there all her life, and now it was going, eaten alive by a ravenous, red-maned beast.

The next thing she knew she was on her feet and moving forward.

"No," she said out loud, and she was at the door.

"Don't do this," she said, and the door, already open, swung wide.

"Stop right now, you idiot!" she screamed, and she was inside.

Monday, May 5

It's late, almost midnight here at the mine camp. I let the fire burn low so it's just coals. The stars are out but very faint. Pretty soon, with the sun up all the time, I won't be able to see them at all.

Van's asleep across the fire from me, all curled up in her sleeping bag. I wonder what the deal with her folks is. They don't seem to worry about her a lot, she pretty much comes and goes like she wants. They're some sort of cousins of her parents, I think. She doesn't talk about her real parents at all. I asked her where they were and she said they were dead and that's it. I asked her where she lived before the Park and she said Outside and that was that. I like her, though. Maybe because she doesn't talk much. She's different from other girls that way. Except for Kate.

There was a rustle in the bushes a little bit ago and Mutt went off to check it out. She came back without any feathers or fur around her mouth, so I guess whatever it was got away. I saw a bear this evening, a brown, I think. Its skin was all loose, like it hadn't eaten in a while, but the fur was really long and shiny. I think it was a sow although I didn't get a close look. I didn't see any cubs. She was eating horsetail. Ick. Kate told me bears will eat anything when they first wake up from hibernation, they're hungry and there's no salmon up the creeks or any berries on the bushes yet. Dad told me he shot a bear once that had an unopened can of tuna fish in its gut. And Ruthe told me that male bears will eat bear cubs if the female bear isn't watching. I guess protein is protein. Ruthe told me bears are different in different places in Alaska. Like salmon don't get all the way up the rivers and creeks in Denali Park and so the bears there eat mostly plants, with every now and then a marmot to supplement the fat they need. Plus maybe an occasional tourist, Ruthe said, although I think she was joking. I think.

I wonder what it's like to sleep a winter away. I wonder if you dream when you do. If I was still stuck in Arizona with Gram, I wouldn't mind sleeping the year away.

I won't go back. I don't care what anyone does or says. I won't go back.

I didn't tell Kate about the bear.

She didn't make me go back with her. She wasn't mad, either. Instead we talked about how the dead guy got in the glacier. She went all over the Park today talking to people about him.

I like the way she talked to me, like I was a grown-up, too. I almost am.

Kate's thirty-five. Twenty-one years older than me. Sometimes it doesn't seem like that much.

7

It could be two totally different things," Jim said, handing Kate a mug of coffee.

She wasn't cold. She didn't understand why she was shivering so violently that the coffee theatened to spill over the rim. Reaction, she thought, clinging to the thought, and clamped her teeth together so they wouldn't chatter.

"We could have a firebug loose in the Park," Jim said.

She managed to control the shivering enough to sip at the coffee. Made by Annie and poured from Billy's thermos, it was strong and creamy and very sweet. Annie had laid on the sugar with a lavish hand. The shivering began to subside.

"We could be looking at someone going around starting fires for kicks," Jim said.

Kate, wrapped in a blanket and ensconced in her red pickup with the engine running and the heater going full blast, finally found enough composure to where she was sure she wouldn't stutter when she spoke. "One"—she held up one finger—"Len Dreyer was murdered, near as I can figure sometime last fall. Two. Len Dreyer's cabin was torched, sometime after fall and before spring. Three, I've been asking questions about Len

Dreyer all over the Park. Four, somebody torches my cabin."
She looked through the windshield.

It was seven o'clock according to the digital readout on the
dash, and the light of the newly risen sun was merciless. The
cabin wasn't much more than a crumpled, smoking ruin. With
difficulty, Kate said, "My father built that cabin when he home-
steaded this land."

"You could have been inside it when they torched it," Jim
said.

"He brought my mother to that cabin when they were married," she said. Her voice was husky from the scar to begin with,
and the smoke hadn't helped.

"Johnny could have been inside it, too," Jim said.

"They lived their whole married life in it. I was born in it.
I've lived most of my life in it."

"Don't you get it!" he bellowed, grabbing her by the shoulders
and shaking her, hard. The coffee went everywhere, unregarded.
"If you'd been sleeping inside when they torched it, you'd be
dead!" He stared at her, furious, and then he kissed her, hard,
his hand at the back of her head so she couldn't move. Faced
with two hundred-plus pounds of thoroughly pissed off male,
she was smart enough not to try. Besides, she wasn't sure she
was capable of forming a fist.

Billy Mike raised an eyebrow.

"Don't look," his wife chided.

"Like hell," Bobby said, and then gave in to the insistent tug
of Dinah's hand.

The four of them formed a semicircle, drinking coffee to ward
off the morning chill and eating chunks of heavily buttered bread
fresh out of the oven, also made and brought by Annie, who
had kept baker's hours all her life and with the advent of an
adopted child into her home had neither the time nor the inclination to start changing things now. "Where are they going to
stay?" she said.

"They can stay with us," Bobby said, looking at Dinah.

"Sure, if they will," she said. "They won't. Kate for sure won't."

Johnny might." She looked around. "Where is Johnny, anyway?"

"Kate said he was camping out with a friend overnight. He's okay." Bobby looked at the pile of rubble, embers glowing red. "Or he will be until he sees this. Probably melted all his Aerosmith CDs. Darn."

Dinah carefully avoided Annie's eyes. Bobby's abhorrence of any rock and roll recorded post–Credence Clearwater Revival was well-known.

"We could get her a trailer, or a camper," Billy said. "Maybe an RV." He thought. "Kenny Hazen's got some big-ass Winnebago he goes fishing with down on the Kenai in August. He likes Kate. I bet he'd loan it to her, maybe until she gets a new cabin built."

"Sounds like it might be a plan," Bobby said, thinking it over. "How's the road?" He was referring to the gravel road leading into the Park. It was graded twice a year, once in the spring and once in the fall, and the rest of the year left to fend for itself. In spring, it was death on the transaxel.

Billy winced. "They haven't graded it yet. They want to wait until they're sure it won't snow again."

Bobby snorted. "So basically we're waiting until Memorial Day, like usual. Well, hell. I guess we could do the convoy thing, have a truck with a come-along on it before and another behind."

Billy nodded. "That'd probably work."

"Sounds like a good idea," Dinah said. "But ask Kate first." She sneaked a glance over her shoulder. Ah. Things had regressed from kissing back to yelling.

"How'd you do this?" Jim said, grabbing a wrist and forcing her hand from her sleeve, to reveal what seemed to his horrified eyes like third-degree burns on the back. Blisters had already formed.

Kate mumbled something.

"What?" Jim said, managing to infuse the single word with enough menace to back down George Foreman.

Her wide mouth set in a mutinous line. "The cabin wasn't all burned down when I got here. I went inside to get some things."

"I see," Jim said. "You went inside a burning building. To 'get some things.' *Are you out of your friggin' mind?*" He had her by the shoulders again, and he was shaking her, again.

She wrenched free this time. "Will you knock it off! I'm okay!" She stared at him haughtily, very much in princess of the Park mode, and hoped that he couldn't see she was about to burst into tears.

His face was brick red and he was literally speechless with rage. He took a few gulping breaths, glared at her for a moment, and then slammed out of the truck and stamped over to Bobby, who surveyed him with interest. "Count to ten," he told the trooper.

Jim expressed his opinion of Kate's intelligence in a few well-chosen phrases that commanded the admiration of everyone present.

Bobby, careful to keep his back to the truck in which Kate still sat, grinned. "Scared you, did she?"

"Up yours, Clark," Jim said, and with a mighty effort, forced the door closed on his rage and locked it, tucking the key away for a time when he could get Kate alone and bring her to a realization of the error of her ways. He didn't hold out much hope of succeeding but he was eager to try. He reached up to pull off his cap and noticed his hand was trembling. He swore again and slapped the cap against his knee. "What time did she show up?" he said to Bobby.

Bobby checked Dinah's watch. "About four hours ago, give or take. I called you and we came right back out."

Jim nodded and pulled the cap back on, screwing it down over his ears. "An hour to get to your house. So she left the fire about five hours ago, give or take. She wouldn't have left until she was sure it was gone. So it was probably torched around midnight. Maybe. Unless it was something more sophisticated than a match."

"You know anything about arson?"

Jim shook his head. "Fuck all."

"They've got specialists for that back in the world, don't they?" Bobby said.

"Yeah, sure, but I doubt that I can get the state to fork out the airfare for one when said arson doesn't involve either extensive property damage or multiple deaths."

They turned as one to look at the wreckage, and the smoke had cleared enough now to see the handle of the old-fashioned water pump that had once presided over the sink sticking up out of the rubble like a forlorn sentinel. The loft was pretty much intact, having fallen almost as one piece as the walls below had burned. Jim suspected that the falling loft had had something to do with smothering some or all of the fire, and wondered when it had come down. Probably right about the time Kate decided to rescue her "things."

The rage started hammering at the locked door. Never had self-control seemed more elusive. One of the first things taught in trooper school was how to establish authority at a crime scene. If he'd had to take that test this morning he would have failed miserably. For the first time in his career, he wished he had someone else he could hand off a case to.

Thinking out loud, he said, "Log cabin, sixty-odd years old. Probably would go up like tinder once it was torched. Small, too, so it wouldn't take long." He looked around the clearing. The outbuildings were intact, although the roofs of shop and outhouse had some scorch marks. The wooden stand beneath the half dozen fifty-five-gallon drums of fuel oil stacked in a neat pyramid had burned and collapsed, and the drums had broken free of their strapping and rolled into a haphazard scatter into the brush.

Billy cast a wary eye over his shoulder. "This have something to do with Dreyer's death?"

Jim hooked a thumb over his shoulder at the red pickup. "She thinks so," he said.

Bobby grinned again. "Feeling guilty?" he said, entirely without sympathy. Dinah nudged him, and Jim saw it, which was the only thing that saved Bobby from instant annihilation.

He walked over to the cabin. The heat from the still-smoldering embers was warm on his face. He walked around the perimeter, looking for the line of copper tubing leading from the fuel oil into the cabin. It was still there, and as near as he could figure by eyeballing it, it hadn't been tampered with.

He heard a footstep and turned to see Kate. "Did you lock your door last night?" He saw the answer on her face. "Of course you didn't. Who does, in the Park? So it was probably just a matter of someone opening it and pitching a lit firestarter inside. Probably knew you sleep in the loft. Probably knew hot air rises. Probably figured you'd be dead of smoke inhalation before you woke up enough to get to the ladder. Do you get it, Shugak? Somebody tried to kill you last night."

"I got it, Chopin," she said tightly. "I've had longer to think about it than you have."

For the first time he was able to look beyond his own fear and rage and see hers, and the sight only exacerbated his own. "You're fired," he said tightly.

She looked confused. "I'm sorry?"

"You're *fired!*" he bellowed. "Canned, sacked, riffed, laid off! I don't want you anywhere near this case from now on! You will talk to no more people about Len Dreyer, do you hear me! Not one! You will collect *no more evidence!* If the murderer kneels at your feet and offers you a signed confession sealed by a notary public, I want you to walk away! Walk *away*, do you *hear* me?"

"I think they can hear you in Canada," Bobby said.

"Shut the fuck up!" Jim said furiously, rounding on him.

"Okay," Bobby said, hands patting the air. Billy, Annie, and Dinah backed up a step in unison.

"And stay the fuck out of police business!"

"Anything you say, buddy," Bobby said. Billy, Annie, and Dinah backed up another step, and Bobby lowered his hands just long enough to roll the tires on his chair back, just so he wouldn't be hanging it out in front all alone. None of them could remember seeing Jim angry. Jim Chopin didn't get angry; in fact, they had thought that he couldn't, that maybe he didn't know how or that it had been trained out of him in trooper school and on the job. Their mistake.

Their reaction went a long way toward restoring Jim's composure. "Okay," he said more calmly. He turned back to Kate. She had something big and square clamped beneath an elbow. "What's that?"

"My photograph album," she said. "The one I put together from the pictures in Emaa's kitchen."

Another wave of fury almost swamped him. He battled it back, and managed to ask in a reasonable tone of voice, "That what you went back for?"

"Yes. And the otter." She pulled out the little ivory carving with two fingers, wincing. She nodded at the pickup. "And the guitar. Johnny wants to learn to play."

As she spoke they heard the sound of a four-wheeler, and Mutt came arrowing into the clearing. She saw Kate and in the same smooth motion knocked her flat on her back. Front paws on Kate's shoulders, crooning a constant anxious whine, she licked Kate's face, hands, every part of her she could get to, and then nosed her over on her face like she was flipping a pancake and examined her backside with the same attention to detail.

"I'm all right, Mutt," Kate said, exasperated, and got to her feet just in time to see Vanessa and Johnny drive into the clearing on their four-wheelers. Johnny vaulted off his before it stopped moving and headed for Kate. "What happened? Are you all right? Mutt was worried this morning, she woke me up and wouldn't let me go back to sleep. She made us come home early." He looked at the cabin and his face went white. "What happened to the cabin?"

"It's okay," Kate said.

"No, it's not, your cabin's burned down!" He rounded on her, his face dark with suspicion. "Did she do this?"

"What? Who? Oh." Kate pulled herself together. "No. No, I don't think so, Johnny, I don't think it had anything to do with her. We don't know if it was deliberate, anyway, it could have been an accident."

"Yeah, right," Johnny said, "like I've ever, ever seen you leave the fire door open on the stove, or not turn the lamps off when you were going to be gone. Give me a break."

"Her who?" Jim said.

Kate scowled at him. "It's not important."

"It is, too," Johnny said hotly, and looked at Jim. "My mother could have done this."

"Jane?" Jim said.

Johnny nodded vigorously. "It's just the kind of thing she would do if she was smart enough to think of it. Kate has to prove she can provide shelter for me, doesn't she? So I can live with her?"

Jim looked at Kate. "Yes. She does."

"Well?" Johnny pointed at the rubble. "Now we don't have a place to live. What's some judge going to say about that?"

The boy could have a point, Jim thought, and tried to ignore how much he'd like to believe it was Jane who had tried to burn Kate alive and not Len Dreyer's killer. "I don't think so, Johnny," he said gently. "She knows you're living here, too, and I don't care how bad things are between you, I don't think she'd try to burn down a house you were sleeping in."

That rocked Johnny back. Vanessa dismounted, paused at Johnny's four-wheeler to kill the engine, and came to stand shoulder to shoulder with him, staring at the remains of Kate's cabin with wide eyes.

Her eyes got wider when yet another four-wheeler shouldered its way into the clearing, ridden by Virgil Hagberg. Virgil had a hard, anxious look on his face. He spotted Jim first, towering over the other heads, and started forward. "Oh god. Oh god, Officer Chopin, what . . ." His voice trailed away when he looked beyond Jim to the smoldering ruin that was once Kate's cabin. "What . . . oh my god." He looked as if he might throw up right there. "What happened?"

"Somebody burned down Kate's cabin," Jim said.

"Oh my god," Virgil said. "Oh my god. Bobby, Dinah, I'm

so sorry, I know you were good friends. Oh my god. This is awful. This is just . . . awful, I—"

"What are you doing here, Virgil?" Jim said.

A fine tremor ran through the older man's body. "I am looking for Vanessa. She must have gone out after we went to bed, Telma went to get her up for school and she wasn't there. We are worried sick, and then I remembered Kate telling us that that boy who is staying with her was friends with Vanessa, and I thought . . ."

"It's okay," Kate said, stepping from behind Jim's bulk. "Vanessa's right here." She propelled the girl forward.

Virgil went gray, his knees gave out, and Billy had to catch his arm so he wouldn't go all the way down. "Oh my god," he said weakly. "Oh my god."

Kate nudged Vanessa. The girl walked forward to stand next to Virgil. "I'm all right, Uncle Virgil," she told him. "I wasn't even here when it burned down. Johnny and I were camping out at—"

She stopped when Johnny nudged her.

Virgil laid a heavy hand on her shoulder. "Oh thank god," he said, "oh thank god. I don't know what I would have told Telma. Oh thank god." He used her shoulder to regain his feet, moving like the old man he looked to be.

And not for the first time that morning, since she had seen the glow against the sky, since she had rolled into the clearing to see flames through the cabin windows, since she had with almost inconceivable stupidity walked into that fire to grab the photograph album off the shelf and the one-pound Darigold butter can off the kitchen table and the ivory otter from the windowsill and the guitar off the wall, since she had given up the cabin for lost, since she had backed the pickup and the snow machine and the four-wheeler out of danger, and watched fearfully for a spark to set one of the outbuildings on fire, since she had watched the flames consume the old dry logs and her lifelong home collapse in on itself, since she had driven the longest twenty-seven miles of her life to Bobby and Dinah's house, since the even longer drive back, Kate thought of how terrible it could have been had Johnny been inside the cabin, asleep on the couch, when it had been torched.

She looked at Johnny, pale and stricken and looking much younger than he had when he was laying down the law to her up at the mine, and she knew exactly what Virgil was feeling, and a fine trembling seemed to move from his knees to hers.

A warm, steady grip took her by the elbow, and she heard Jim say in a far gentler voice than she had yet heard that morning, "Sit down a minute, Kate."

She didn't remember anything clearly for a while after that.

She woke up on a couch in Bobby and Dinah's living room much later that day, to be greeted by a blinding smile and another tug on her hair. "Kate," Katya said with immense satisfaction. "Kate waked up! Kate play now!"

"Ouch?" Kate said.

"Shhhh, Katya," Johnny said, coming around the corner at a dead run and scooping Katya up in his arms. "Come on, let's go outside and play."

"It's okay," Kate said, sitting up. "I'm awake." She stretched and yawned. "What time is it?"

"About three."

"In the afternoon? Man, I must have been tired." She rubbed at the sore patch on her scalp where Katya had been pulling her hair. She smiled at the toddler beaming at her from Johnny's arms. "You little monster. Come here and let me pull your hair."

"You're better," Johnny said, relieved.

"Better?"

"You were practically comatose when Jim carried you in here this morning."

"Jim carried me in?"

"Yeah. You went out in his front seat on the way here."

"Oh."

Dinah peered over the divider. "Ah, Kate Van Winkle awakes. Want a shower?"

Kate became aware of the sooty and smelly condition of her clothes. "I'd love a shower," she said with feeling.

"Good. I've got a change of clothes in the bathroom for you."

Kate had taken too many snowmelt baths in galvanized wash-tubs to take a hot shower for granted, and she stood with her face in the stream of water until she felt parboiled. Dinah's shirt, a pale blue button-down affair, was too tight across the chest and her jeans were too loose in the hips, but they were clean and she was grateful. She came out of the bathroom refreshed. "I'll need to get some new clothes," she said, rolling up the sleeves of the shirt. "For me and Johnny."

"Want to order them over the Internet?" Dinah nodded at the computer.

"Don't you need a credit card to do that?"

"Yes."

"I don't have a credit card."

Dinah smiled. "I do." She shepherded Kate to the computer and Googled up the Eddie Bauer and Jockey websites. From there they went to Niketown, where they searched for Lady Cortez, except that the style was now called Cortez Basic and cost $35 more than the last time Kate had bought them. It took her a few profane moments to cope with the news, but they had them in size seven so she ordered her usual six pair and had them sent priority mail. "That takes care of me," Kate said. "What about Johnny?"

Johnny had more fashion consciousness than Kate and he knew a lot more about surfing the 'Net, so it took them until dinnertime to fill out his wardrobe. Dinah assured them both that they weren't anywhere near her credit limit. Kate suspected she was lying, but by then Bobby had returned with Jim in tow, and they all sat down to eat chicken-fried caribou steaks and baked potatoes and a cherry pie baked by Bobby the day before.

Halfway through the meal Jim said, "You look fine."

It was almost an accusation. "Why wouldn't I?" Kate said,

forking up another bite of steak. There was nothing like a near-death experience to make food taste better than it ever had. There were other human experiences it enhanced, too, but she wasn't going anywhere near there.

He regarded her with a thoughtful expression. "No reason," he said at last, a statement everyone at the table with the possible exception of Katya recognized as a bald-faced lie.

Dinner was finished in relative tranquility. Coffee was served in the living room. Everyone kept fussing around Kate. She accepted their attentions graciously, which made everyone nervous. Jim, pushed to the limit, was finally goaded into saying, "Don't you want to ask me anything?"

She smiled at him, which expression made Bobby sit up with a jerk that rolled his chair back a few feet. "What about?"

"I mean what I said, Kate. Stay out of this investigation." She smiled again, and his voice rose. "I fired you. I have terminated your contract with the state. You are no longer employed. Go back to the homestead and rebuild your cabin."

She drank coffee. "You're the boss."

"Oh, Jesus God," Bobby breathed, closing his eyes in a momentary lapse into belief.

Katya beamed from his lap. "Yeezuz god!"

Later, when Bobby, Dinah, and Katya had retired to bed, when Johnny was fast asleep beneath an afghan on one couch, Kate sat up next to a lamp on an end table next to hers, ostensibly reading Louise Erdrich's latest novel, about a priest who was really a woman and who wasn't really a priest, either. She liked the book except that one of her all-time favorite Erdrich characters got married to some rich white guy and left the Objibwe to live in the city. The upside was that the irritation this caused was enough to keep her awake until she could hear everyone breathing deeply and rhythmically in sync. She exchanged the book for a notepad and pen and started a list.

In early June Len Dreyer had repaired Keith Gette and Oscar

Jimenez's greenhouse, as confirmed by Keith and Oscar.

Sometime during that same month he and Dandy Mike had helped Virgil Hagberg build a greenhouse, as confirmed by both Dandy and Virgil.

In August he had repaired George's hangar, according to George.

Around Labor Day he had regraveled the paths around the Roadhouse's cabins, according to Bernie.

She regarded that last entry. Bernie had been uncomfortable talking about Dreyer. Could be Dreyer had done a lousy job, although that contradicted what everyone else said about his work, and Bernie wouldn't have been shy to say so anyway. There was something, though, and she put a question mark next to Bernie's name.

In mid-September Dreyer had done some repairs and main-tenance on the *Freya*'s engine, according to Old Sam.

In October he had worked on Bobby's roof, according to Bobby finishing the job the day before the first snowfall, which would make it October 22nd.

She flipped the page and drew a freehand map of the Park. The twenty-five miles between her homestead and Niniltna. The turnoff in Niniltna, left up to the Step, right to the Roadhouse, village between the two forks of the Y and the river. Dreyer's cabin on the Step road, the Gettes' next door. The *Freya* had been in dry dock in Cordova when Dreyer worked on it, so Kate put a notation at the bottom of the page. She put stars where Dreyer had worked, with dates next to them.

She flipped a page and started another list.

She had to ask Bernie if and what Dreyer had done to piss him off. She'd known Bernie a long time and she didn't think he had killed Dreyer, still less that he'd torched her cabin, but there was something there to find out, and the more she learned about Dreyer, the closer she would be to finding out who killed him.

She had to reinterview everyone she'd already talked to and find out how much they had paid Dreyer. He'd had seven hundred plus dollars in his pockets when he'd been found. What if there had been more in his cabin? What if his cabin had been burned down before Dreyer was killed, in an attempt to hide the crime? What if Dreyer had found out and gone after the robber? There was motive for murder right there, although she didn't see why the money found on Dreyer's body hadn't been stolen as well. Still, murder often led to haste and haste led to mistakes, especially unpremeditated murder. If Dreyer's death came down to what would have been basically a mugging if he'd lived, there would be someone with a powerful motive to discourage someone else from looking into the matter. However it worked out, there were some gaps in his work history that needed filling in.

Which led her mind to Bonnie Jeppsen, the postmistress. Kate decided to talk to her first thing in the morning. Any Park rat who'd been in the country for more than five minutes could have recommended Len Dreyer's services to someone who needed a jack-of-all-trades, but Bonnie would see more people any given day than any other single person in the Park, with the exception of Bernie.

Johnny had asked some smart questions about the movements of Grant Glacier. Kate needed to talk to someone who knew about glaciers. She didn't know if Chief Ranger Dan O'Brien knew squat about glaciers but if he didn't, he'd know who did. She might luck out and find some nerdy scientist type who had measured the thrust and retreat of Grant Glacier to the last inch, which would give her a better idea of when the body had been dumped in it, which would give her a better idea of time of death.

Maybe she should go see Dan first the next morning, because she was going to have to discover the time of death on her own, without access to the case file even now being filled in in Anchorage. Jim hadn't been joking. She had been thoroughly, comprehensively, and most definitely fired.

There were various options available to get hold of a copy of the autopsy report. Brendan McCord would help, but she didn't want to go to any one well too often, and she had another task in mind for ex-marine Brendan anyway. Didn't one of her cousins once or twice removed work as a clerk in the state crime lab in Anchorage? And didn't the state crime lab share space with the state medical examiner? She made another note. She might have to fly into Anchorage which, as the killer was most likely still in the Park, might not be a bad idea. She'd take Johnny with her. She could hit Twice Told Tales and Metro Music while she was there, start replacing her music and books.

Her lips compressed into a thin line. She raised her head and stared out the window. The brute bulk of the Quilak Mountains squatted like chained beasts against a steadily lightening eastern horizon, ready to attack on command.

Kate liked lists. She liked tackling a list in the morning, and enjoyed the warm sense of accomplishment she got at the end of the day when most or even all of the items on it had been crossed off. Undone tasks at the end of the day got added to another list, and the previous list sat on the table for a few days longer, silent testimony to its compiler's industry and efficiency.

This list was different. This list was a ruthless, relentless compilation of facts and series of tasks that could lead to only one outcome. Anger was a great motivator, and Kate wasn't just angry, she was enraged. Her eyes dropped from the mountains to the awkward, adolescent lump on the opposite couch that was Johnny Morgan, his face barely visible, eyes screwed shut, mouth open, one arm twisted beneath him and one leg hanging over the side of the couch to the floor.

Someone had burned down her cabin, her home, all her belongings, her clothes, her music. Her books.

But all that was only by-product. Someone had snuck up to her house in the middle of the night with intent to commit murder, and it wasn't their fault that they hadn't been successful twice over.

Johnny snorted and shifted into another impossible position. People had made attempts on her life before. It came with the territory. Stick your nose into someone else's business, especially in Alaska, where maintaining one's privacy came somewhere between a vocation and a religion, you ran the danger of getting that nose lopped off. It was an acceptable risk, but it was a risk of which she was always aware and one she had been willing to take for the sake of the greater good.

But this time, Johnny had been put at risk. Her eyes narrowed. Putting a child's life in danger was not allowed. Someone must be brought to a realization of the error of his ways. Someone must be swiftly and surely punished for it, punished so severely that they knew just how badly they had transgressed, punished so memorably that no one else ever got the idea they could behave the same way.

But first she had to find them. She bent her head back over her task, and not even the creak of bedsprings and the whisper of wheelchair tires distracted her.

The long black arm reaching around and snatching the notepad out of her hands did. Bobby, face like a thundercloud, rifled through the pages and tossed the notepad back in her lap. "Somebody already tried to kill you once," he said in a furious whisper that had Johnny stirring. "You gonna keep at this until they get the job done?"

Kate picked up the notepad and shook the pages into place without replying.

"Jim fired you off this case, Kate. I heard him. Dinah heard him, Johnny heard him, I think the whole fucking Park might have heard him. He's not going to be happy when he hears you didn't stay fired."

Kate looked him straight in the eye and said calmly, "I find who killed Dreyer, I find who burned down my cabin. You really think I'm going to bother telling Jim when I do?"

She turned back to the list, and Bobby, recognizing a hopeless cause, returned to bed. He lay awake a long time, listening to the scratching of pencil on paper, and didn't sleep until the light in the living room clicked off.

Dawn came far too early for everyone.

8

D r. Millicent Nebeker McClanahan ignored Kate to focus on Johnny. "Yes?" she said encouragingly.

It was the next morning. They were up on the Step, a narrow ledge between valley and plateau that supported a cluster of prefabricated buildings and a skinny airstrip that stood in constant danger of either sliding over the side or being overrun by mountain hemlock. This was Park headquarters for the U.S. Park Service, and they were just down the hall of the man who ran it and who was standing next to Kate at respectful attention. Dan O'Brian was a boyish-faced, burly man with bristly red hair and blue eyes so innocent they aroused instant suspicion in those meeting him for the first time.

"Don't bat those baby blues at me, young man," Dr. Mc-Clanahan told him.

Dan, somewhere in his late forties, said meekly, "No, ma'am."

"I know every thought that's going on in that intellectually challenged pea-sized organ you call a brain," Dr. McClanahan said, not without relish, "and there isn't a one of them worth repeating."

"Yes, ma'am." Dan had the temerity to grin at her.

She laughed. "I see you're listening as hard as you always do." She turned back to Johnny. "Well?"

Dr. Millicent Nebeker McClanahan was five-eleven, maybe 130 pounds, with short, thick white hair indifferently cut, and large gray eyes. She wore jeans, a white turtleneck beneath a ratty fleece pullover that had once been dark green, no makeup, and no jewelry except for small plain gold hoop earrings and the worn gold band on the fourth finger of her right hand. She was constantly in motion even when she was standing still, tucking hair behind an ear, tugging on her earlobe, stuffing her hands in her pockets, taking them out again, fiddling with her collar, shifting from one foot to the other as if impatient to be on the move. She didn't quite give off sparks, but one imagined she might if any attempt was made to restrain her.

She was a geologist specializing in glaciers, and by good or ill fortune was currently headquartering on the Step as she completed a study for which, Dan informed Kate in a low voice, she seemed to have unlimited funding because she gave every indication of settling in for the summer, and Dan had been instructed by his masters in D.C. to give her every assistance.

The thing was, Johnny was seriously into it. He hung on every word that fell from Dr. McClanahan's lips. He followed her forefinger intently as it traced a line of glacial moraines on a map. He asked questions. He should have been in school but had insisted on accompanying Kate to the Step, a place in the Park he had yet to visit, and now Kate was glad she had acquiesced.

Dr. McClanahan answered him sensibly, as one equal to another, with no hint of "Run away and play, little boy" in her manner. She was currently describing the state of glaciers in general globally and in Alaska in particular, and Johnny said, "That's why we're here, Dr. McClanahan, we—"

She smiled and said, "Why don't you just call me Millicent, Johnny."

He flushed with pleasure. "Sure. Millicent." He stumbled a little over the pronunciation.

She laughed. "See if Millie works better."

He grinned. "Okay, Millie. Anyway, like I was saying, that's why we're here. We need to talk to someone who knows about Grant Glacier."

"Grant Glacier, hmmmm." Dr. McClanahan tilted her head to examine the map through the half-glasses perched at the tip of her long thin nose. The map covered most of one wall of the conference room and it was a large room. It was done to a 1/50,000 scale and detailed down to the shallowest bend of the smallest creek. Kate located her creek without difficulty, only to be reminded of the ruin on its bank. She wrenched her attention back to Dr. McClanahan, who was pointing at tongues of white on the map and naming them off one at a time. "Washington, Adams, Jefferson, Jackson, Lincoln, here we are, Grant Glacier. Hmmm, yes. That was the glacier that thrust forward last summer, wasn't it?"

She tossed the question over her shoulder at Dan, and Dan snapped to attention. "Ma'am, yes, ma'am."

She grinned. "Do you keep a personal log of Park events?"

"Ma'am, yes, ma'am." He escorted them back to the cubbyhole that was his office and selected from a shelf a daily diary the twin of Bobby's. He paged through it. "Here we are," he said. "Suddenly, last summer, on June twenty-eighth to be exact, Grant Glacier was noticed to be going the wrong way."

Dr. McClanahan's nose twitched. "Any seismic activity in the area prior to the event?"

Dan paged back. "I don't think—oh, wait a minute. Yeah, there was a shaker that week. But—"

"What?"

"Well, it was four days before. And it was just a baby, five point two according to the Tsunami Warning Center."

Dr. McClanahan's nose twitched again. "Hmmm."

Dan waited. When she made no further noise he said, "Hmmm what?"

"We've discussed my paper," she said.

"You've discussed your paper," he said, "I've just been towed unwillingly in the wake of your fanaticism."

"Nicely put," she said, complimentarily. "However, enthusiasm would be a more apt description."

"I was actually thinking zealotry," he said dryly.

They laughed, and it occurred to Kate that Dan's social life had been settled on for this summer. She cleared her throat. "So who reported it?"

Dan looked at her, startled, as if only now remembering she was in the room, and his ears got red. "Who," he muttered, looking back at the diary, "right. Um, yeah." He flipped back and forth. "Okay. A bunch of ice climbers were on a three-week camping trip up the valley. I think a couple of them were actually on the glacier with axes and pitons when it started moving forward. Scared the hell out of them, especially as they were camped out on the edge of the lake at the mouth. They said it sounded like the world was coming apart beneath their feet." He showed them the quote. "Anyway, they got the hell off the glacier, struck camp, and headed for Niniltna. George dropped in on his way home from flying them back to Anchorage."

"When did it go back into recession?" Dr. McClanahan said.

"I don't know the exact date," Dan said, and at least appeared crushed when Dr. McClanahan looked disappointed. "I checked on it as often as I could, and I alerted the geologists at the University of Alaska, but no one was all that interested. It wasn't like when Hubbard thrust forward. Tidewater glaciers are more interesting than piedmont, I guess. The Grant wasn't cutting off any seals from the open ocean. And let's face it, the Grant is pretty small potatoes compared to the Hubbard."

Dr. McClanahan nodded. "And it's not like watching glaciers is your only job."

"I got George to drop a flag on the face and mark the position on his GPS. Whenever he had a paying passenger for Tok, he'd do a flyover and take a bearing on the flag."

"Oh, excellent!" Dr. McClanahan said.

"When did he report it was going into recession again?" Kate said, losing patience.

"Oh." Dan's ears got red again and he dove back into the diary. "Uh, yeah, here it is. He first told me it looked like it had started back in late September. Could have been moving slow enough that he didn't notice it until then."

"How far did the flag move down altogether?" Johnny said, and earned an approving smile from Dr. McClanahan.

"From the time he dropped it until the first snowfall when he couldn't find it again, down over five thousand feet."

"Going on a mile," Johnny said, awed.

"Don't forget, last September was pretty warm. A lot of that was melt off."

"Did you tell anyone that it had started receding again?" Kate said.

Dan shrugged. "Like I said. After the initial excitement, people weren't that interested. I kept track in the diary until the snow covered up the flag and George couldn't take any more readings."

So no one would have known that the glacier wasn't still moving forward, Kate thought. And someone who wasn't glacier ept might have thought the mouth of a glacier a great place to hide a body for a long, long time.

"Let's take a look," Dr. McClanahan said.

"She needs to be studying something that moves faster than a glacier," Kate said, panting.

Johnny was too winded even to nod.

Dr. Millicent Nebeker McClanahan bounded up to the mouth of Grant Glacier like a mountain goat, no hands, hopping nimbly from berg to berg. Her voice floated behind her as Kate and Johnny tried to keep up. "You want to be careful near the mouth of a glacier, especially at this time of year. The face may calve at any moment as soon as it begins to warm up and the insulating layer of winter snow melts off."

Kate looked up at the wall of ice in front of which they were currently standing. "Johnny, maybe you better go back to the truck." That was where Dan had stayed, to lean against the grille and watch them through binoculars, the grin on his face visible even from this distance.

Johnny shook his head. "She's here, and besides, it calved when we were here the other day," he said, and went after his new hero.

"It what?" Kate said, staring after him.

"What's the matter, Shugak, can't keep up?" Dan yelled.

Kate promised retribution with a look and heard him laughing. She followed Johnny, and she did use her hands. By the time she got there, McClanahan and Johnny had vanished inside the mouth. "Johnny, damn it," she said through clenched teeth, and went after him.

It was dark and cold in the ice cave, and noisy with dripping, trickling, running, and rushing water. It felt like being inside a frozen waterfall that was going to melt away completely at any moment. The tall figure of the geologist and the smaller figure of the boy were standing in the center of the sloping floor of the long narrow cave, following the beam from the flashlight the geologist held as it played over the ice. It wasn't clear or even white, but dark with the debris it had picked up on its millennial journey down the mountain.

The gravel crunching beneath her feet had been crushed and rolled to a smooth uniform size. Kate tried not to think about the same thing happening to her. "Is this a good idea, Millie?" she said.

"Probably not," Millie said, not moving.

Kate repressed an urge to get the hell out of there. She would not be outdone in foolhardiness, even if it meant dying in the collapse of a glacier.

"Where was the body?" Millie asked Johnny.

He walked to where the ice left the gravel and began to curve overhead. "Right here."

"Right in the middle," Millie said. She knelt down and ex-

amined the ice directly behind the spot Johnny indicated in ex-
cruciatingly minute detail. Kate tried not to shift from foot to
foot. Catching who killed Len Dreyer and burned down her
cabin seemed suddenly less compelling.

"The body was upright?"

"Uh-huh."

"With his back to the wall?"

"Uh-huh." Johnny's voice sounded tinny against the surrounding ice.

"Hmmm, yes," McClanahan said, peering and prodding at the
ice. "Yes, well, I think that's all we're going to find here."

She got to her feet and clicked off the flashlight. Stygian
gloom fell like a blow. Kate wasn't especially claustrophobic
and even liked the dark, but when she felt rather than saw
McClanahan brush by she nearly levitated off the ground. She
waited until they were up the slope of gravel and back out into
the sunshine before she trusted her voice enough to ask, "What
did we find there?"

McClanahan propped one foot on a chunk of ice, clasped her
hands on her knee, and frowned down at them. "It's the first
week of May. From anecdotal reports we know that the glacier
stopped thrusting forward in September of last year. My guess
would be that the cave has not altered in any substantial way
since last fall. The winter temperatures and the insulating layer
of winter snowfall would have maintained the interior surface of
the cave. Further." Very much the learned lecturer condensing
specialized information for consumption by an amateur audi-
ence, she held up one finger to forestall Kate's comment. "Had
the body been placed there this spring, the difference in temperature between the ice and the body would inevitably have left
some mark."

"An outline?" Johnny said.

Kate, remembering the sound of melting water that had surrounded her in the cave, said, "It wouldn't have melted?"

McClanahan considered this. "Given the difference in temperature between solid ice and human flesh, no matter how

dead, and with the temperature outside the cave steadily rising, I believe I would have been able to detect some mark. If, on the other hand, the body had been placed there late last fall, with temperatures already falling steadily, perhaps also with the body already chilled itself, very little impression would have been left, easily erased during spring melt off."

"So, bottom line," Kate said. "Was the body placed there last fall or this spring?"

"One cannot say for sure," McClanahan said. "Or at least this one can't. But my best guess would be earlier than this spring. Well before breakup, let's say. How deep was last winter's snow-fall?"

"Why?"

"How long would it take given this spring's ambient temperatures to melt that much snow, so that the cave would be revealed and someone could deposit a body inside it?"

Kate looked back at the open slash of the cave mouth at the foot of the wide, dirty wall of ice, and had an unwelcome vision of the body of Len Dreyer propped up against the back of the ice cave, sightless eyes staring toward the snow-filled entrance, waiting out the winter until spring and Johnny's class came to find him. "So, last fall," she said.

"It's only a guess," Millie said, "but I'd say yes."

Plus, so far no one reported seeing Dreyer after October, Kate thought. Bobby might have been the last one to see him alive.

"What's your paper going to be about, Millie?" Johnny said.

" 'The Effect of Seismic Events and Meteorological Transformation on Glacial Geomorphology in Interior Alaska,' " McClanahan replied promptly.

Johnny gulped. "What does that mean?"

"You know about earthquake faults?"

"Sure. Everybody in Alaska knows about earthquake faults."

"You know about the Alaska-Aleutian megathrust subduction zone?"

"Uh, where the two main faults butt up against each other?"

"Not bad," McClanahan said. "There may be hope for you,

Mr. Morgan. My paper examines what effect that zone may or may not have on the thrust and retreat of Alaskan glaciers. With a sidebar on the weather, including global warming."

"Oh," Johnny said, and hesitated. "Maybe . . ."

"Maybe what?"

"Well, maybe I could read it?"

She laughed and cuffed his shoulder. "Sure. I'll even give you an English/geology dictionary to help you in the translation."

At that moment the entire face of Grant Glacier seemed to shudder and shift. A second later an immense *boom!* rocked them back and a piece of ice the size of Gibraltar came crashing down to shatter into a million shards all over the entrance of the ice cave. A splinter whizzed by Kate's face, and to her everlasting shame she yelped and ducked out of the way.

"Magnificent, isn't it?" McClanahan said.

Steady employment was more the exception than the norm in the Alaskan Bush. Most Park rats lived a subsistence lifestyle, eating what they caught or killed, fishing in summer for money to buy food and fuel. Some trapped, but the competition was stiff and the wildlife not as populous as it used to be, and Dan O'Brian was a fierce enforcer of quotas. A few lucky guys had signed early on to oil spill response training, funded directly by the partial settlement coming out of the RPetCo oil spill in 1989, which made them members of a permanent on-call team, for which they drew a stipend that wasn't much but was better than nothing. George Perry ran Chugach Air Taxi Service out of the Park, and Demetri Totemoff led hunts for moose and caribou and deer in the fall and bear in the spring, and any help they needed was strictly seasonal. There were a few fur trappers left, and even fewer gold miners.

But by far and away the most jobs were generated by the government, state and federal, and the support services thereof. Auntie Vi started a bed-and-breakfast out of her home in Nin-iltna because of the need for temporary housing for the fish hawks who came and went with the salmon, and when word got around was inundated with rangers, sports fishermen, hunters, poachers, and the occasional pair of lovers who couldn't find any privacy in Anchorage. To Auntie Vi's ill-concealed horror, the word seemed to have spread to the tourists. She tried to discourage them by doubling her rates, but they only went home and told all their friends about this quaint little Eskimo woman who ran a B&B out in the middle of Alaska and who made great fry bread. Kate didn't know if Auntie Vi was more disgusted at being called an Eskimo, being called quaint, or having to hire two maids to help out, which put her on the wrong side of the Social Security Administration but which also made for two more jobs for the Park.

The previous year the pressure on her kitchen had been so great that Auntie Vi had coerced the Niniltna Native Association into fronting the money for a little café on River Street, not that the street was identified as such by anything so unParklike as a street sign. Laurel Meganack was the chief cook and bottle washer, and her menus ran heavily to hamburgers and French fries, but her fountain Cokes were good and, well, there wasn't really anywhere else to eat out in Niniltna since Bernie refused to get into the selling of any food that didn't come already shrink-wrapped. That first winter the high school kids took to hanging out there, so they left it open year-round. The fact that Laurel was Niniltna Native Association board member Harvey Meganack's niece probably had a lot to do with her getting hired in the first place, but it didn't hurt that she was an extremely nubile twenty-three, had a glimmer of big-city sophistication from having gone to high school in Cordova (a vast metropolis of some two thousand people), and was an Association shareholder herself. Art Totemoff was hired as kitchen help, and so there were two more full-time jobs that hadn't been there before. There was also a receptionist/secretary position at the Association headquarters, generally filled by a descendent of whoever was the current tribal chief.

But the best full-time, year-round job in Niniltna was that of postmaster. It had more pay and better benefits than any other job within a hundred miles, and the competition for it was fierce. There were families still living in the Park who weren't speaking because a son of one had beat out the daughter of another for the position, and there were always dark mutterings of nepotism and influence whenever it went to one person over the other.

Bonnie Jeppsen, the current officeholder, had won the job over next-door neighbor Kay Kreuger, from which tiny seed a memorable breakup had grown like chickweed, leading to not one but two shootouts at the Roadhouse involving live ammunition. Kate had been instrumental in the altercation's resolution, commandeering a D-6 Caterpillar tractor in the process, and she was never quite sure of her welcome when she darkened the post office's doorstep. Bonnie was unfailingly civil and so far as Kate knew she got all her mail, so she approached the post office now in the hope that enough time had passed that Bonnie would be willing to talk to her about something other than postage.

The post office was a brand-new building prefabricated at a shop in Anchorage and freighted in on a flatbed the summer before, yet another new addition to the scenery to which Kate had to accustom herself. It was small, brown-sided, and roofed with what might have been corrugated metal but was probably some kind of plastic. It had two windows in front, a small loading dock in back, and a handicapped-accessible ramp leading to the door. The ramp was probably great for wheelchairs but it was going to be one hell of a slippery slide for feet come winter.

Inside, the building was divided by a counter and mailboxes. Kate heard the faint thuds of mail being slid into mailboxes. "Bonnie?"

Bonnie was a tall, plump blonde, with silky, flyaway hair and pale skin in a constant state of flush. She wore glasses in large bright red frames that framed her sometimes brown eyes like stoplights. She dressed oddly for the Park, in neither jeans nor Carhartts but in loose, flowing dresses with pin-tucked bodices, dropped waists, and tiny flowered prints, draped about with long multicolored scarves made sometimes of silk and sometimes of wool, all fabric she dyed and wove herself, much of it painted with brightly colored flowers. She sold the scarves out of a corner of the post office, probably in defiance of every rule and regulation of the United States Postal Service, and she was eager to explain that all the flowers were indigenous to the area, from the Sitka rose to the forget-me-not and including the wild geranium, the lupine, and the Western columbine, all of which grew in profuse and undisciplined splendor in back of the post office. Kate had a vague notion that Bonnie might make her own dyes from roots and berries of various and also indigenous plants, but that was going far beyond her own ken and she wasn't interested enough to get it right anyway.

In addition to the painted scarves, Bonnie also sold jewelry and sculpture made from beads, most of it free-form, very little of it representational, and none of it traditional. It was original and striking, looking more like it had grown into existence as opposed to having been created, and even Kate had caught herself spending time in front of the shelf, looking at pieces that didn't look at all like a wave-washed beach caught midtide, a tidal pool full of finned, clawed, webbed creatures, a driftwood fire mimicking the sunset behind it, a smoking volcano. The rumor was that Bonnie's pieces were on display in the museum in Anchorage, and Kate, viewing a piece made mostly of what looked like freshwater pearls and a matte beige bead so tiny it looked like a grain of sand, could well believe it.

The aroma of sandalwood incense drifted into the room. "I'm sorry, Kate," Bonnie said from behind her. "I didn't hear the bell."

Kate turned and saw Bonnie with her hands clasped on the counter in front of her. Both arms were braceleted up to the elbow in silver, never repeating the same pattern twice, and large triangular earrings cut from mother of pearl and embellished with tiny leaves made from tinier beads swung from her ears.

Kate shrugged and smiled. "I just got here." She nodded her head at the earrings. "That's really nice work."

Bonnie inclined her head, accepting her due. "Thank you."

"I don't know anything about beadwork, traditional or otherwise. But I like your stuff."

"Thanks. I heard about your cabin. I'm so sorry. I can't imagine how you must feel. It must be horrible."

"It sucks green donkey dicks big-time," Kate agreed.

Bonnie didn't quite know how to take that, and took refuge in business. "Did you want your mail?"

"Sure." She accepted a handful of envelopes and a box from FATS Auto Parts in Anchorage, the new plugs she'd ordered for the pickup. Good thing her socket wrench set had survived the fire. Not to mention the pickup.

It occurred to her that she was taking the burning of her two-generations family home awfully well. She wondered how worried she should be about that, but right now her focus was on finding who did it and bringing him to justice. Her justice.

She became aware that her lips had thinned and her eyes had narrowed and that the back of her neck was heating up. Bonnie was regarding her with a puzzled and wary eye, and when Kate's eyes met hers she took an involuntary step back.

Kate pulled herself together. "Thanks, Bonnie." She tucked the envelopes into a hip pocket and the box under one arm. "Did you know Len Dreyer?"

Bonnie's face creased with concern. "Of course. I heard what happened to him. That's just awful."

"Yeah. Not a fun way to go. He pick up his mail here?"

Bonnie nodded. "He didn't get much, though."

"What did he get?"

Bonnie hesitated. "I'm not really supposed to give out any information about the United States mail, or any of the patrons."

"I'm helping the trooper investigate the events leading up to Len Dreyer's death."

Bonnie brightened. "Jim Chopin?" Her eyes behind their bright-rimmed glasses went dreamy and so did her voice. "Well, in that case, of course, Kate, I'm happy to help. Anything you need."

Mentally, Kate curled her lip. Some women went weak at the knees over any man to come down the pike. Any six-foot-ten, 240-pound blonde. Smart. Built. With blue eyes. And a deep voice. And a great grin. And a charm of manner Casanova would have envied.

She blew out a breath. "When was the last time you saw Mr. Dreyer?"

"I don't know, I guess that'd be the last time he came in to check his mail."

"How often did he come in?"

"I don't know. Maybe once a month." She thought. "Maybe not even that often."

"What kind of mail did he get?"

Again Bonnie was uncertain. "Packages mostly, I think. Tools, and parts. Stuff he needed for the work he did." She brightened. "And catalogues. Lots of catalogues."

There were probably more catalogues per Park rat than there were trees to make them from. The Park was an exclusively mail-order community. Kate remembered the session at Dinah's computer. Or it had been. "Is there anything in his box now?"

"Oh, he didn't have a box, Kate," Bonnie said, happy to be able to provide at least one definite answer. "He had his mail sent to General Delivery."

Of course he did, Kate thought glumly. Renting a post office box would require filling out a form. Filling out a form would require revealing personal information. And if there was one overriding characteristic Len Dreyer was revealing to her in this series of interviews, it was his determination to remain completely anonymous. "Any mail holding for him now?"

Bonnie shook her head. "Jim came and got it. It was only a couple of catalogues, and something from Spenard Builder's Supply."

"Almost everyone comes in here," Kate said. "Do a lot of them ask you where they can get work done?"

"Sure," Bonnie said.

"And did you send them to Dreyer?"

"Of course. He does—did good work. He put in my new toilet."

"Did he." A toilet was awfully uptown for the Park. Although Bobby and Dinah had one. Flushed and everything. "When was that?"

"The third weekend in August," Bonnie replied promptly.

"You're sure of the date?"

"Oh, yes. They were sending Brian Loy from Anchorage to talk to local businesses about the new services offered on USPS-dot-com. He always stays in my spare bedroom and I wanted the new toilet in before he got here."

"We have local businesses?" Kate said, momentarily diverted from her quest.

"The Association and the school, I guess." Bonnie leaned forward and dropped her voice. "I think Brian just wanted to go fishing."

Wouldn't be the first time an Anchorageite had manufactured an excuse to get out of town with a fishing pole in hand. "Do you happen to remember all the people you recommended Dreyer to beginning, oh, say early last summer?"

Kate emerged from the post office fifteen minutes later, a list jotted down on the back of one of her envelopes in which she admittedly had little faith. Bonnie's memory was fragmented at best, frequently interspersed with "I think that's when I was doing the poppy scarf, do you see over there, the silk one with all the bright orange on it" and "I remember, I was woofing in the blue to the green warp on the wool scarf I was making for my mother." Or Bonnie might have been warping the green into the blue woof, Kate wasn't sure.

She needed good coffee and a comfortable chair and someone whose memory was better than Bonnie's. So she went to Auntie Vi's.

"What was going on in the Park a year ago?" she said around a mouthful of fry bread. She could have waited until after she swallowed, but since she intended on filling her mouth again immediately, this way saved time. If the fry bread was nectar, then the coffee, rich and dark and strong enough to melt the bowl off a spoon, lightened with Carnation evaporated milk and sweetened with dark brown sugar, was positive ambrosia, and Kate was not silly enough to ignore offerings from the gods.

This particular god was a woman approximately the size of a walnut and much the same color and texture. Her still thick and defiantly black hair was caught in a heavy knot at the base of her neck, her brown eyes were clear and sharp and set in the middle of a sea of wrinkles, and her hands, small but sinewy, were sure and deft as they kneaded an immense mass of bread dough. She paused to sprinkle on a handful of white flour and proceeded to work it in with vigor. "Ayapu," Auntie Vi said, "you okay, Katya?"

"I'm okay, Auntie," Kate said. The fry bread and the coffee were soothing in a traditional sort of way. She could almost forget that she was homeless.

"Lucky you not there."

"Yes," Kate said. "Very lucky."

Sharp black eyes examined her shrewdly. "You mad?"

Kate took her time answering. "Yes, Auntie," she said, proud of how calm she sounded. "I'm mad."

She made the mistake of looking up. Auntie Vi nodded once, satisfied. "Good. But you be careful."

"I will."

"I mean it, Katya," Auntie Vi said sternly. "You have that boy looking to you now. You keep him safe. You build a cabin with more room, make it his cabin, too."

"I will." Although for the life of her she didn't know where the money was coming from. She'd earmarked last year's earnings to fight off Jane's custody suit. She wouldn't touch it. But the kid had to have a place to sleep.

"Good." Another sharp nod. "Good. Now. What you want to know?"

"You know I was gone last summer."

"Humph. I know." Auntie Vi waited, clearly not going to make it easy for Kate. She didn't approve of running; she was a stand-and-fight kind of woman, always had been. She had survived three husbands; nine children, two of whom had died of cancer, one in a car wreck on the Glenn, and one of drowning; thirty-two grandchildren; and a home that had changed hands from Native to federal to state and back to Native again, all in the span of her lifetime. She'd fought for the Alaska Native Claims Settlement Act and had sopped up oil on the beaches of Prince William Sound after the RPetCo oil spill. She served on the board of the Niniltna Native Association and on the board of their regional corporation, as well. She fished subsistence and owned and operated her own business, the bed-and-breakfast whose kitchen they were in now.

In fact, there wasn't much Auntie Vi couldn't have survived if she made up her mind to. In spite of every effort to ignore it, Kate felt a sense of shame at her headlong flight from the Park the year before. She remembered the conversation she'd had with Johnny. *I don't want you to learn that running away is an acceptable response to trouble.* He had shown up on her doorstep the day of her return, and she didn't know if he'd been told how long she'd been gone.

Well, he could just learn to do as she said and not as she did. She firmed up her jaw and said, "I'm trying to trace Len Dreyer's movements last year, Auntie. It's hard because he worked for everyone, all over the Park."

Auntie Vi grunted. "What you know so far?"

Kate produced her notebook, and Auntie Vi produced some reading glasses that when donned didn't make her look anything like Millicent Nebeker McClanahan.

An hour later Kate's head was reeling and she had the frustrated sense of having gone over the same ground for the third time in a row. Auntie Vi never missed a tangent when it presented itself. "You know those Drussells?"

"Gary and Fran? Sure."

"They move to town."

"I didn't know that."

She endured a less than tolerant glance her way. "You not here. How could you know?"

"Why are Gary and Fran selling their place?"

"Gary, he like everybody, not making a living with the fish. He go back to school, he say, learn computers, get a job in Anchorage."

Kate thought of the tall, raw-boned man with hair bleached blond by the sun and a perpetual sunburn, dressed eternally in ragged, oil-stained, scaly overalls, and tried to imagine him in a button-down shirt with a tie, sitting in front of a computer terminal in one of those little cubicles on the fourth floor of one of those office buildings in Anchorage where the closest you got to the outdoors was the view of Knik Arm through the window. She shuddered and looked back at her list. "Gary was on Bonnie's list, Auntie. He passed a message to Len Dreyer last May that he needed some work done on his homestead."

Auntie Vi nodded sagely. "Spruce the place up, get a better price for it."

"Who did Gary sell it to?"

"Not sold yet."

"How much is he asking for it?"

"Too much."

"Don't any of the girls want it?"

The Drussells had three daughters, all in high school, although the oldest one might be out by now. Maybe the two eldest, Kate couldn't remember. Auntie Vi shook her head. "Girls go to school in Anchorage, too."

Auntie Vi cut the bread into fourths and began shaping it into loaves. "Gary, he want to fix up his house before he put it on the market. To get a better price, you know."

"I know, Dandy already told me he and Dreyer worked on it together."

Auntie Vi glared at her. "If you already know everything, why ask?"

"Well, Auntie, I—" Sentences to Auntie Vi that began "Well, Auntie, I—" had an historic tendency to run on forever and end up with Kate apologizing for her own stupidity and for wasting her aunt's valuable time. Kate folded her lips down over her teeth and shut up.

Auntie Vi greased four loaf pans and patted the loaves into them. "You know this brother of Bobby's?"

"No. I haven't met him. Not yet."

Auntie Vi said something in Aleut that sounded highly uncomplimentary, but then Aleut spoken properly was full of a lot of rich, back-of-the-throat gutturals that just naturally lent themselves to insult. Kate caught a word here and there, enough to inspire a devout hope to see Jeffrey Clark coming so that she could head in the other direction. When she ran down, Auntie Vi switched back to English. "Len Dreyer put a new roof on Bobby's house in October."

This time Kate kept her mouth shut.

Auntie Vi gave her a sharp look. "You not writing this down?"

Kate snatched up her pencil. "Of course. Bobby's roof, you said? October? Very important, very important information indeed." A glance from Auntie Vi told her that she might be overdoing it. She picked another topic at random. "Johnny's made a friend."

"Boy or girl?"

That was Auntie Vi, cutting right to the chase. "Girl. But not like that."

Auntie Vi cast her eyes up to heaven, pleading for help in the face of this idiocy on the part of her niece. "It always like that between a boy and a girl."

"They're just kids."

Auntie Vi looked at her with a raised brow. "And you just a kid when Ethan come home from college."

Kate made a face. "I talked to him."

"Good." Auntie Vi slid the loaves into the oven and set the timer. "Which girl is Johnny's friend?"

"Vanessa Cox."

"Ah." Auntie Vi, wiping down the breadboard, nodded sadly. "Poor girl."

"Why poor?"

"She lose her parents in a car wreck Outside. That make anyone a poor girl."

Kate couldn't argue with that. "At least she had somewhere to go."

Auntie Vi made a face. "The Hagbergs."

"What's wrong with the Hagbergs?"

"Nothing," Auntie Vi said, "nothing. But she is young. They old. And that Virgil, he don't care nothing about nothing except Telma. And Telma, she care nothing about nothing, I don't think." She fixed a stern look on Kate. "You watch out for that girl, Katya. She start feeling lonely, she start being around your boy more, and you know what happen then."

"She's Johnny's friend," Kate said. "I'm not going to forbid her on the premises."

"Didn't say you should," Auntie Vi said promptly. "Who said I said you should do that? Maybe a good thing, that, with her and your boy. Both not from Park." She ruminated in silence for a moment. "I hear something about Virgil Hagberg," she said, her brows knit. "I think he selling the homestead."

"You're kidding. I was just out there yesterday, Auntie. He didn't say a word about it."

"Virgil thinking since they don't have kids they leave the homestead to that land conservancy Ruthe run."

"Really," Kate said. "I bet Ruthe loves that plan."

"They talking to her about it. Virgil, he anxious that the land stay as it is, and that they don't trade it down the line for something better."

"Ruthe wouldn't do that."

Auntie Vi gave her a look. "Ruthe Bauman do anything and

everything she can to carve out the biggest chunk of leave-it-alone in the state, Katya."

"Yes, Auntie," Kate said. "What else?"

What else was, Budd Davies getting collared by Dan O'Brian for taking too many beavers the winter before last. Kate winced. "Ouch. What'd Dan do to him?"

"Not too bad. Take the pelts, confiscate Budd's traps, and fine him five thousand dollars."

"No jail time?"

Auntie Vi shook her head. "No jail. Dan says that Budd get no lawyer, pay up without whining, Budd and him are good."

Kate had to laugh. Justice, Park style. "Is Budd pissed?"

Auntie Vi gave this judicious consideration, and shook her head. "No." A glimmer of a smile. "I see Harvey on my last trip into Ahtna. He say Budd has order for more traps."

What else was, the security guard who was patrolling the TransAlaska Pipeline on his snow machine getting caught in a whiteout February before last, flipping his machine, breaking his leg, and crawling two miles to the road for help, where he got run over by a vanload of college students taking the scenic route from the University of Alaska Fairbanks to a basketball game with perennial rival University of Alaska Anchorage. The guard had only recently recovered the ability to speak and to sit up. Opinion was divided in the Park as to whether his wife thought that was a good thing, since in the interim she had taken up with a freight handler for Frontier Airlines in Atka.

What else was all this and more, and Kate tried to correlate the inundation of information with what she had learned from Bonnie Jeppsen and what she had picked up from her previous interviews. Budd and the security guard didn't show up on Bonnie's list so she tentatively eliminated them, which reduced the list of people she was going to have to talk to, but not by much. She sighed.

"If it was easy, everybody do it," Auntie Vi said. She pulled the second bowl of dough off the back of the stove where it had been set to rise. "You want some more fry bread?"

There was never a time when Kate didn't.

9

It was a little after three when she emerged from Auntie Vi's bed-and-breakfast, stuffed full of fry bread and information. For the moment, Johnny was tucked safely away at Bobby's. She stood next to the truck, her hand on the door handle. Mutt watched her face with wise eyes. So many people to talk to, and she had to stay out of Jim Chopin's way while she did. She looked at the cross-referenced list of names and thought about the geography involved. She could start at the Roadhouse and work north. Or on the Step and work south. Or in Niniltna and work west.

Really, the first thing she ought to do was go back to Dreyer's cabin and investigate the scene more thoroughly.

She went back to her own instead.

It looked, if anything, even more forlorn than it had the day before. Her cabin, the place she had been born into this world, where she had spent most of what little time she'd had with her parents, the place to which she had retreated as a child when Emaa had tried to force her into living in Niniltna, the womb to which she had fled from the stifling, swarming confines of college, the place waiting for her on long weekends and vacations between time on the job in Anchorage, the one place in the world able to heal the wounds inflicted by five and a half years of casework featuring raped and beaten women and abused children, her home, her center, her sanctuary, her refuge.

It was all that and more, and now it was a pile of smoking rubble, too.

"It's only a cabin," she said out loud. Mutt, standing with her shoulder pressed to Kate's knee, looked up, gray plume of a tail waving ever so slightly. "Cabins can be rebuilt. All I need is some logs and some Sheetrock and some insulation. I could put in a flush toilet. I could even wire the place for electricity, finally hook it up to the generator like I've been threatening."

She could do all those things, but deep down she knew that this cabin could never be rebuilt. Her father was dead, the hands that had raised the cabin's walls long since crumbled to dust. Her mother, a good, kind, loving woman until the booze got hold of her, was no more. Emaa was gone, nevermore to darken the doorstep and blight Kate's life with the reminder of her bounden duty to her tribe. And Jack, with whom she'd spent so many nights making thunder roll out of the bed in the loft. Seventy years of laughter and tears and memories had been reduced to ashes by a malicious, anonymous hand, and there was no way ever to get them back.

Which was why when she heard the footstep behind her, she turned and without any greeting pretty much hurled herself into Jim's arms.

The angry words that had been ready to tumble out of his mouth since Bobby had run him to earth that morning and clued him into Kate's continued involvement in the investigation of Len Dreyer's murder were stilled when he looked down and saw that she was weeping.

She didn't just weep. She cried. She sobbed. She pounded his chest like it was a punching bag. She cursed and she cried some more and then she cursed some more. It took a long time, and somewhere along the way his anger faded. He held her gently until the flood began to ebb, wishing he could think of something of comfort to say, knowing there was nothing. He settled for rubbing her back, and felt like a lame-ass good-for-nothing as he did so.

Finally she looked up. Her eyes were swollen and her nose was red and running. She was not a pretty sight. "Sorry," she said in a husk of a voice. He winced inwardly when she wiped her nose on the sleeve of the blue shirt that looked familiar, just not on Kate. It didn't fit very well, or it fit very well, depending on your point of view, and then he damned himself for an insensitive bastard and put resolutely from his mind any thought of unfitting shirts. It helped to look over her shoulder at the ruin, so he did. "I just missed you at Auntie Vi's," he said.

"Oh," she said, on a shuddering sigh.

Any minute now she would start to be embarrassed at losing her self-control in front of him. And then she would be angry with herself, but of course she'd take it out on him because, hey, he was there. He braced himself.

She ran a hand through her hair, matted from being mashed up against his uniform shirt, which was itself looking rather the worse for wear. "Were you looking for me?"

He tried to get past the fact that she was still leaning against him, firm and resilient and vital, every inch of her alive, if a little more subdued than he was used to. Had he been looking for her? It was hard to remember. He waited for her to pull free and say something nasty, something designed to push him away, anything, and the sooner the better.

She laid her cheek against his chest and closed her eyes.

It was a trap. It had to be a trap. She was resting her full weight against him. He could feel her breasts, her thighs, oh my god, she was putting her arms around his waist. He worried about her knees and what she might decide to do with one of them.

She rubbed her check against his chest and gave a long, deep sigh.

Mutt, who had for some strange reason of her own not monopolized Jim's attention from the first moment of his appearance, gave the two of them a long, impenetrable look and vanished from the clearing.

The hell with it. Jim picked up Kate in one smooth, easy motion and walked over to sit down beneath a spruce tree with spreading branches overhead and fifty years' worth of needles piled beneath. He settled her in his lap and her head naturally found a place on his shoulder. He thought carefully about what to do with his hands, until one curved just as naturally around her waist and she relaxed into it with another long, deep sigh. The other he rested on her hip, the curve of which fit into his palm like it had been designed specifically for that purpose.

Time passed. The sun shone. A soft breeze teased the fat buds on the branches of the trees. Birds sang and cawed and called. A porcupine rattled out of the woods, looked them over, and rattled back in again. Jim thought he heard a moose stripping bark from a willow tree. There was a distant crashing of brush like a bear might be passing through, and he gave some thought to pulling his weapon, but it might have woken Kate and the danger wasn't clear and present enough to justify anything that drastic.

He'd never seen her sleeping before, not close up. Oh, she'd fallen asleep after they had made love last summer in Bering, but she'd been making love to someone else and he hadn't been able to get out of that bunk fast enough. Then there had been the encounter on the floor of Ruthe Bauman's cabin last January that had not involved any drowsiness at any moment on anyone's part. He watched her face and made a discovery. She frowned a little in her sleep, did Kate, as if even then there were jobs to be done, problems to be solved, disputes to be settled.

Her golden skin was smooth and unblemished. Her brows were as black as her hair and as straight. Closed, her eyes looked less Asian than they did when she was awake. A strand of hair lay across a high, flat cheek and the wide, full mouth that was unsmiling but relaxed. That hair, that thick cap of pure black that had once hung to her waist in a fat braid. He'd had fantasies about that braid, which had disappeared a year and a half ago during a guided big game hunt when a bunch of homicidal computer executives—geeks with guns; he still had a hard time with the concept—had opened up on each other instead of the moose and Kate had been caught in the crossfire.

Now he had fantasies about the cap.

What was it about this woman, this one woman, when his life had been filled, one might even say littered, with so many others?

She was smart, and he liked smart in a woman. When she forgot it was him in the room with her, she had a robust sense of humor. He didn't have a lot of empirical evidence, given the brevity and angst of their only two encounters, but he was fairly certain they were sexually compatible.

Fairly certain, hell. He knew beyond all shadow of doubt that he and Kate together would produce a fire that would make the burning down of Kate's cabin look tame by comparison.

Still. It wasn't like there hadn't been other women just as smart and just as fun and just as hot. Plenty of them.

He tried to remember the name or the face of just one.

She shifted in his arms, burrowing closer without opening her eyes. Any minute now she was going to wake up and remember whose lap she was in, and he could kiss his nuts good-bye.

He leaned his head back against the tree, gathered her in as close as he dared, and let himself drift.

He must have drifted all the way off to sleep because when he opened his eyes, she was kicking at the ruin that had been her cabin. The needles didn't feel as soft as they had when he had first sat down, and no doubt there was more pine sap leeching onto his uniform shirt with every passing second. He got to his feet and dusted off the seat of his jeans. His hat had fallen off at some point, and he picked it up and whacked it against his leg before pulling it on, tugging the bill as low down over his eyes as he could and still see.

She must have heard him, but she didn't turn when he came

up behind her. "I didn't say it before, Kate, but I'm sorry as hell about this. I know the place has been in your family since before you were born. I can't imagine how much seeing it like this must hurt."

It was the decent thing to say and he stopped himself before he could offer her house room. For one thing, he didn't have a house yet, and for another, just because she no longer had a home herself didn't mean she'd be moving in with him of all people.

Still. She had trusted him enough to let him hold her while she slept.

"I found the shotgun," she said, nodding at a blackened length of metal. The wooden stock was barely recognizable as such.

He winced. "Ouch. What's a new one run these days?"

"A good one? Starts about eight hundred, I'd guess. Lucky I had the rifle with me."

"Lucky," he agreed.

She picked her way to the water pump and tried to work the handle but it wouldn't budge. She tried again, a third time. "Damn it," she said, her voice tight. She'd have to plug this well and drill another. Would she even be able to rebuild on the same site?

"Did Bobby tell you about Hazen's RV? We called him, got a convoy set up for tomorrow. George did a flyover of the road in and he says it looks good. They should be here tomorrow night, the next morning at the latest."

"Yeah, he told me."

"It sleeps two." She looked at him and he said hastily, "Room enough for you and Johnny both, I mean. I've seen it, it's a big sucker."

She made an effort. "I take it you've been on one of Hazen's on-the-road-again parties to the Russian River?"

He shook his head. "Been invited. But something always came up."

She nodded. "You said you just missed me at Auntie Vi's."

When he looked blank she added, "When you first came down the trail. Were you looking for me?"

"Oh. Yeah. Right." He pulled off his cap and put it on again, screwing it down around his ears. "Bobby came looking for me this morning."

"Oh?" She had turned back to look at the cabin's remains.

"He tells me you're still working the case."

"Oh?"

Something in that single, disinterested syllable reminded him why he'd been angry. "I fired you, Kate."

"Ummm."

"I made your services available to the industry, as they say in the oil patch."

"Uh-huh."

He could feel the slow burn coming on, except that with Kate it was never slow, it was more like spontaneous combustion. This from a man who had not only a personal inclination but a professional obligation not to lose his cool.

He'd lost his temper with her yesterday morning. Full out, balls to the wall. It helped knowing that his rage was fueled mostly by fear, but not much.

It had felt good to yell at Kate Shugak. He was thinking he ought to do more of that. Starting now.

She looked at his face for a long time, her expression somber, her eyes unreadable. And then she surprised him again, picking her way out of the rubble to stand in front of him. She raised her hand and flattened it on his chest, right over his heart, just under his badge. "Jim," she said, her voice very soft, so soft he had to bend over to hear, so close to her that his breath stirred her hair.

He knew she was playing him, he just knew it. "What?" he said, and if it wasn't quite the growl he wanted it to be, at least it wasn't a whimper.

She raised her head and met his eyes. Mere inches and their lips would touch. His heart rate increased to a rapid, almost painful beat high up in his ears.

"I'm going to work this case," she murmured. "I'd rather it be with your permission than without it."

He closed his eyes and tried desperately to remember why he'd been angry. Something about a fire, and Kate and Johnny almost being killed, and Kate insisting on finding out who, in spite of the would-be murderer still being on the loose and for all they knew ready, willing, and able to kill again.

He started to rationalize. She was going to work the case if he let her or if he didn't. He had a full plate for the next week. He had to fly to Cordova that afternoon to take statements and file charges before a magistrate on the video/drug store case, and if the weather was as lousy as it often was in Cordova, he wouldn't be back tonight. The longer it took him to get to the Dreyer case, the less chance it had of being solved. Kate was a trained investigator. Better her poking around than Dandy Mike, who had found him even before Bobby had this morning and demanded to know when he was going to work.

Rationalization led to fantasy. If he let her work the case, maybe she'd—

No. Nope. Not going there. "Okay," he said, his voice thick. "You're rehired. Just watch your back, Shugak, okay? If you let somebody hurt you, I'll hurt you more."

An involuntary smile spread across her face, warm, almost loving, and just possibly entirely without guile. It wasn't an expression he'd ever had directed at him before, and truth to tell it made him a little dizzy. "Thank you." He couldn't remember her ever thanking him for anything before, either. A day of firsts. Between the smile and the thanks he was ready to run before the roof fell in.

"Okay," he said, taking a step back. "Good." What was he saying? "I mean, better if you kept your nose out of it like I wanted you to, but fine that you're going to investigate. What are you doing first?" He paused. "What have you done already?"

"Talked to Bernie and Bobby and Auntie Vi and Bonnie Jeppsen. Between them, Bernie and Bonnie have recommended Len Dreyer's services to just about everyone in the Park. I've got a list of who he worked for. It'll take me a couple of days to talk to them all, given the distance between sites."

"Good," he said, retreating another step. Kate was entirely too calm for his peace of mind. He wasn't comfortable when she wasn't yelling at him. He'd grown accustomed to her yelling; a day without Kate yelling was a day he obviously didn't know what the Sam Hill hell was going on.

"I want to go up to his cabin, too, look around some more."

"There's even less of it left than there is of yours," Jim said.

"I know. But I have to look."

"Yeah." He took another step back. "I've got to go. I'm heading out for Cordova."

"Will you be back this evening?"

"Sure. Well, maybe not. No. I don't think so. It's awfully late. Okay. Gotta go."

"Jim."

He stopped, his tongue clove to the roof of his mouth. She looked at the tree beneath which they had sat, and away. If he was not demented she was blushing. Probably his imagination. "Thank you," she said again, very softly.

He took a deep breath. His heart was thumping in his chest like the tuba in the high school orchestra, loud and off the beat and out of tune and unstoppable. "Sure. Whatever. Glad to help. Anybody would have—I gotta go." He sketched a shaky wave and headed out of the clearing at not quite a run, terrified that she was going to ruin what was probably the first civil conversation they'd ever had with a blast of invective as soon as the ground steadied beneath everyone's feet and Kate realized who was being civil to whom.

He was halfway up the trail when he felt a nip at his heel. "What the hell?" He turned and saw Mutt, her tail wagging furiously. As soon as she had his full and undivided attention, she jumped up, both paws on his chest, gave him a generous swipe of tongue, bounced back down, and trotted a few feet toward the homestead. She stopped and looked over her shoulder.

"Forget it," he told her, and kept walking.

Be damned if she didn't nip at his heels again. "Cut it out, Mutt!"

The third time she caught his pants leg in her teeth and gave a good strong yank. His feet flew out from beneath him, and the next thing he knew he was flat on his face.

"Son of a bitch!" He spit out a mouthful of new grass and got to his feet. "Jesus," he roared, "what is it with you Shugak women!"

She bounced a couple of steps down the trail and looked over her shoulder, giving an encouraging yip, tail wagging furiously. He could have sworn she was laughing at him.

He steamed into the clearing and back up to Kate, who was standing stock still and watching his battleship-like approach with her mouth open.

"What—" she started to say.

That was as far as she got. He was back in range in two steps and he had his hand knotted in that raven cap of hair in three. He had a glimpse of startled eyes before he kissed her. He took his time over it, poured everything he had into it, all the longing, the frustration, the need, everything he'd felt since that day in September when he'd found her crouched over her dead lover, keening a wordless lament.

Be honest with yourself at least, Chopin, he thought, Jack dying didn't make you want her. You've wanted her since the first time you saw her. And then all thought stopped.

She didn't exactly respond but she didn't resist, either. For a long moment he thought that was all he was going to get. Then something changed; she sort of woke up and suddenly he had himself an armful of woman, whole, alive, responsive, and oh my god, demanding of a return on that response in a take-no-prisoners onslaught that was likely to knock him off his feet. He heard bolts being thrown back and locks clicking open and doors swinging wide. There might even have been trumpets, although his ears were ringing so loudly he couldn't be sure.

He raised his head. Slowly her eyes opened. They looked at

each other. She was flushed again, and he had to get his breathing under control before he could speak. "Don't kid yourself, Shugak," he said, proud that his voice was steady. "Altruism had nothing to do with it."

And before she could say anything he turned and left. And this time, Mutt let him go.

Friday, May 9th

Kate's cabin got burned down. We're staying at Bobby and Dinah's until some guy in Ahtna brings his trailer down to Kate's homestead. It was supposed to be here Tuesday night but it got stuck on the road somewhere, and both escort trucks got stuck, too, and some construction crew that's coming to dig out the foundation of the new trooper post in Niniltna is bringing up a backhoe this weekend and on the way in will dig them all out. I like Bobby and Dinah and I love Katya but Bobby's brother is an asshole. I'll be glad to get back home.

Home. We've only been gone two days and I can't wait to get back. I'm turning into as much of a hermit as Kate. Only she says we're hobbits and gave me the book to read. Hobbits are cool, quick, nimble, when they throw at something they hit it. Mr. Koslowski could use Bilbo on the JV team. He'd be too short for varsity.

But I don't think that's what Kate meant.

She thinks that since Dinah ordered us replacement clothes on her computer and that she's still got her grandmother's album and her dad's guitar and that ivory otter and the cash can that she's fine, but she's not. When she doesn't know anyone's looking at her, she gets this look on her face, kind of angry but cold, too. Jim fired her and then they met up at the homestead and something happened and he rehired her, so now she's going all over the Park and talking to everyone that ever spoke to Dreyer in their whole lives. Bobby says she is obsessing and Dinah says she'll come out of it. They're both worried, I can tell. And Bobby's brother sure isn't helping. He called Katya a mongrel. She better not know what that means. She better not remember him saying it. If someday she asks me, I'll tell her it's the best kind of dog there is, like Mutt, the best of all different kinds mixed into one smarter and stronger than all the rest.

I didn't know black people could be prejudiced against white people.

I asked if I could ride along while she did her interviews and Kate said I had to go to school but that wasn't why. I'm not a baby. I could find out stuff, and nobody pays any attention to teenage boys unless they think we're drinking or doping or screwing around or stealing a car. I bet people would talk to me who wouldn't talk to Kate. Like Jim said, I picked up some stuff from Dad, I can handle myself.

I snuck a peek at her notebook and she's got a timeline drawn up of all the places Dreyer worked. One of the places was Van's uncle and aunt's. I asked her about him but she says she doesn't hardly remember him.

The Canadian geese have been flying in. I looked them up in the ADF&G wildlife notebook on Dinah's computer and there are six different species, including one called the cackling Canada geese which I really love the name of and I wished it nested here but the notebook says not. I think ours are dusky, six to eight pounds each.

I like the sound they make, they sound like spring. When I was living with Dad on Westchester Lagoon in Anchorage they used to come sliding in on the lagoon before the ice melted. Most of them took off as soon as they refueled (like jets) but some of them stayed and built nests. When the babies were born they'd hook up with other goose families that you could see sometimes in parks and on ball fields. Most of them were all head down in the grass, but there was always one adult with its head straight up, watching out for the others, and if you get too close it makes a noise and they all start moving away.

I was thinking about geese that day last fall that Mom showed up at Bobby's. Everybody in the Park was at his house that day, and almost every one of them got in her way when she was trying to catch up to me. Most of them didn't even know me.

But they knew Kate.

Geese mate for life, Ruthe says. Only if one of a pair dies, they change partners. There are so many in Anchorage that they let Alaska Natives harvest eggs from the nest and give them to elders to eat, but they've got to be sneaky about it because if they take the eggs too early the geese will lay more.

When Kate was with my dad, my dad never brought anyone else home and I'm pretty sure he never stayed over anywhere else. There were long times when they didn't see each other, too. Most people get married, like Bobby and Dinah. I figure since Dad married Mom that he would have liked to have married Kate, too, so she must not have wanted to.

I look at Kate and I see why my dad wanted her and why Jim wants her. A couple of times I looked up from the couch in the cabin and saw her getting dressed. I tried not to look but she is so beautiful, so strong and so smart and so tough. She can do anything. There's no one like her.

I bet she'd be surprised if I found out something about Dreyer that would help find out who killed him.

10

Dandy Mike's real name was Daniel. It was a good, solid name straight out of the Bible, like all of Billy and Annie Mike's kids' names were, but it hadn't taken, possibly because someone less likely to march into a lion's den it would be hard to find in all twenty million acres of Park land. Dandy was handsome, good-looking, and charming. He was also incurably lazy, and a confirmed rounder whose romantic exploits had livened up many an evening at the Roadhouse and provided a news-starved Park with many a tale. His only serious competition was Jim Chopin, who seemed recently to have hung up his zipper, at least temporarily, which brought even more public scrutiny to bear on Dandy's ongoing game of musical beds, especially in winter when there was nothing to do, if you didn't want to beat up on your wife and kids, that is.

Dandy earned just enough money fishing and odd-jobbing not to draw welfare, for which his mother would have laid into him big-time. She was already torqued enough at her youngest child for being caught growing a commercial crop of marijuana in his dorm room at UAF. He'd come home to serve out his sentence and had never gone back. As opposed to the three times he had. His personal best was three straight semesters without being suspended. The dean of students, a woman not without a sense of humor but whose patience Dandy had tried pretty far when he made a move on her, too, had told his parents that girls wasn't a recognized major.

He was also generous to a fault, buying drinks at the Roadhouse, buying beaded earrings from Bonnie Jeppson for all his girlfriends, buying wooden toys from Virgil Hagberg for the many children in his extended family, who it must be said all seemed to adore him.

He was thirty-four years old and he'd never held down a job that required filling out a W-2 form or onto a relationship that had lasted longer than a month. His employers found him to be reliable and reasonably skilled. "He's no ball of fire," Old Sam had been heard to say between beers, "but a slow simmer gets the job done, too, even if it does take a little longer." His ex-girlfriends, while legion inside and out of the Park never seemed to take the end of the affair to heart, were delighted to bask in the glow of his attention, even knowing that the end was near from the moment she took him to her bed. There was something so disarming about his affection for the opposite sex. He just flat out loved women, all women, of any size, shape, or age. He wasn't afraid of them, either, unlike most men, and he was more than willing to demonstrate that love to the red-shift limit.

He wasn't a cheater, he was a serial monogamist, remaining true to his current flame so long as she was current, which also worked well for him. "You look incredible, what have you been up to?" Bernie Koslowski heard one of Dandy's exes say to another woman on the other side of the bar. The second woman had smiled. "Dandy," she had said simply, and the first woman had actually laughed. "At least he listened," he'd heard a much-married woman and mother of five say on another occasion, "even if it was only for two weeks."

Which was why no one could understand why he wanted to go to work for trooper Jim Chopin. Jim was a devil with the ladies, no doubt, but not even his worst enemy had ever accused him of laziness. God, just look at this past week. He'd been in and out of Cordova three times, ensuring that that drug dealer wouldn't be selling no dope to no kids again anytime soon, inside video boxes or out of them. Apprehending that abusive husband hadn't been no picnic, neither, said the old farts in the Roadhouse, heads shaking over the black eye he'd brought back from Spirit Mountain, although there were still some amongst them who thought what went on between a man and his wife ought to stay private. "What," said Old Sam, "until she's dead?" and changed tables.

Along with the black eye, Jim had brought back a split lip and the husband, trussed like a calf for branding in the back of the Bell Jet Ranger, there being no level land worthy of the name anywhere near Spirit Mountain for a fixed-wing aircraft to land. Jim didn't look too upset at being whaled on, they had to admit, in fact was downright pleasant to one and all when he climbed out onto the Niniltna airstrip and hauled the husband out after him, like maybe he'd apprehended his suspect with a little extra enthusiasm that day and it had brought him some peace.

Which wasn't what he was going to get a lot of if he succeeded in his pursuit of Kate Shugak, if in fact that was what he was doing. It was a puzzle what was going on there. "Kate ain't easy," one old fart opined.

"If she was easy, everybody'd be doing her," someone else offered. There was a lot of snickering and Old Sam changed tables again.

In between, Jim was being run ragged, what with the notorious breakup blues winding down to a grand finale of wife beatings, child abuse, drunk driving, illegal hunting, theft, burglary, armed robbery, assault, rape, and now, for crissake, a murder, and if rumor were true, the attempted murder of Kate Shugak herself, resulting in the loss of her ancestral cabin. Jim would find out who did it; they had perfect faith in him. They just weren't sure Jim would get to the perpetrator first, and if he didn't, well, wasn't going to be much left to do except clean up the mess. "Whoever done it ought to just cut his own throat right now and be done with it," somebody said, and there was pretty much universal agreement at the sentiment. This time, Old Sam stayed where he was.

No, Jim wasn't lazy, and he didn't have a lazy man's job. It was a mystery why Dandy Mike would want to work for him, when it would surely to god have him out of bed far oftener than he would like.

In truth, Dandy Mike was in the unenviable position of being spoiled rotten from birth. Annie loved children, and the only reason she had stopped having them was that her obstetrician had spoken to her husband to such purpose that Billy had gotten a vasectomy the following day. It was the one time Annie had come anywhere near leaving him, and it didn't matter that the doctor had told Billy that her chances of carrying another child to full term were slim to none and the odds were in favor of it killing them both. "He said that last time and it was my easiest delivery ever!" she flashed. It a took a year of living on tiptoe for Billy to be forgiven, and another eighteen years, after the last child was grown and out of the house, for the full price to come due, which was the adoption of a baby from Korea, the product of a Korean mother and an American soldier, unwanted by either parent. Well, hell, Billy liked kids, too, and the house didn't feel right not smelling of dirty diapers and baby formula, and the little girl, whom Annie had named Mary for her mother, was the cutest thing he'd ever seen.

Between a new daughter in the house and his duties as tribal chief and president and chief operating officer of the Niniltna Native Association, which was negotiating some big-time contracts with a lumber company and a minerals exploration outfit for activities to take place on Association lands, Billy Mike didn't have a lot of time for any of his older children, most of whom had gone on to college and were now living in Anchorage, where they had indoor plumbing and cable. He had still less time for Dandy, his problem child, who seemed perfectly happy to spend as much of the rest of his life horizontal as he could.

It vexed Billy, but he did his best for Dandy, putting the screws to Jim Chopin to hire his son once the new trooper post was built. Jim wasn't notorious for bowing to pressure, and it wasn't like Billy was going to make life tough for someone who was opening a full-time, fully-staffed trooper office in Niniltna, either. There were less than three hundred troopers in the entire state of Alaska, and when most villages the size of Niniltna had trouble, they had to wait days and sometimes weeks for the law to respond. Oh no, while Billy Mike wasn't averse to exerting a little paternal coercion, no way was he going to screw up the stationing of a law enforcement professional in beautiful downtown Niniltna. Especially when he hadn't even had to lobby for it; this had all been Jim's idea.

Plus the Department of Public Safety had hired the contractor through the Niniltna Native Association, and was already sending out feelers for a cleaning staff. Plus Jim was going to need a place to stay, and so would any prisoners he apprehended in the course of his duty, and Billy was already preparing a bid to submit to the State Department of Corrections to house and feed the accused Jim brought in.

So the upshot was that Billy didn't know why Dandy wanted the job so badly, either, but in the best of all parental worlds his problem child would have realized the error of his ways, turned over a new leaf, and settled down to become a useful member of society. He might even take an interest in tribal affairs, Billy thought, allowing himself to dream.

In truth?

Dandy wanted the job because he wanted to wear a uniform.

He wanted to wear a uniform because his only competition for the ladies' favors had been a man in uniform named Jim Chopin, he of the blue and gold, with the Mountie hat and the shiny gold badge, and the big black nine-millimeter strapped to his side. If Dandy had heard one indrawn breath from whatever cozy bundle he had tucked into his arm whenever Jim walked in the Roadhouse door in full regalia, he'd heard a thousand.

Plus, he'd always liked John Wayne.

Plus, how hard could it be? He envisioned a comfortable chair behind a desk, where he would mostly answer the phone and send Jim out on calls.

Plus, there was that very nice state salary, and that even nicer package of state benefits, including retirement, which would add up even faster because they were so far out in the Bush. He could kick back and start drawing a paycheck for doing nothing by the time he was fifty.

Plus, who died and made Kate Shugak god? There was no rule of which Dandy was aware that just because Kate had once investigated sex crimes for the district attorney in Anchorage that she automatically got whatever extra job came with the new trooper post in Niniltna.

So it was with an impure and righteous sense of purpose that Dandy Mike was doing more or less the same thing that Kate Shugak was, albeit with little finesse and still less ability. His progress took him from ex to ex, interviewing girlfriends past and distant past, asking them if Len Dreyer had dropped by to fix anything lately. The amazing thing was, he wound up with a list that wasn't dissimilar to Kate's, though neither of them knew it at the time.

Len Dreyer had logged almost as many miles in pursuit of jobs as Dandy had of women.

He also wasn't quite the monk Kate had been led to believe. Really all that meant was that Dreyer had had nowhere near the action Dandy had, but that he had gotten laid occasionally. "It was kind of weird," Betsy Kvasnikof said. "He was kind of there, you know? And I was hurting from Dad going off right after I graduated, you know? Mom was mooning around like a lost soul and I was taking care of Rob and Sandy full-time. I guess I was looking for a little comfort, you know?"

"Did you get it?" was Dandy's tactful reply.

Betsy looked annoyed, at either Dandy or Dreyer or both. She was a slender, dark-haired woman in her mid-twenties with big, innocent brown eyes that made her look like she was still in her mid-teens. "No," she said shortly.

Dandy, usually so smooth at getting what he wanted out of women, backed up a little, but not all the way. "Did you, er—"

"Did I sleep with him? Yes. Did I have a good time? It was okay, I guess." She smiled at Dandy with a sweetness he remembered. "Not as good as some who came after."

Dandy grinned. "Naturally not."

She laughed. "Oh, you." She looked over her shoulder. "I think I hear my husband's truck. Best you leave now."

"I heard that." He kissed her good-bye, and then he kissed her again. The back door was closing on him at the same time the front door was opening on her husband, but it wasn't anything he wasn't used to. He trod noiselessly around the house and went to his truck, parked discreetly on the shady side of a turnoff down the road.

"When are you leaving?"

Dinah winced. Bobby had no tact. Still, it was a question worth asking.

"When you agree to come with me," Jeffrey Clark said.

That is, when the answer was something you wanted to hear, Dinah thought.

"Which will be a cold day in hell," his brother replied. Bobby's face wore the same expression it had for three days, angry and unyielding.

In that way alone were the brothers similar. Jeffrey was tall, slim, and elegant. His clothes looked freshly pressed, his hair was groomed to perfection, even his teeth, straight and white, looked tailored to fit his mouth.

Not that they'd seen much of them in the last three days, Dinah thought.

His cheekbones were high and sharp, supporting thickly lashed brown eyes. His brow was broad, his mouth firm-lipped, his jaw solid. He looked like something off the cover of *GQ*, and Dinah's fingers itched for her camera. She didn't dare, though. After the first shock of her overwhelming whiteness had faded, Jeffrey Clark had simply pretended that she didn't exist. She could live with that. She couldn't live with his attitude toward Katya, which was one of horrified disgust. If he called her daughter a mongrel again, she would rip his tongue out of his throat. She whacked viciously at the bread dough she was kneading on the kitchen counter and tried not to listen to Part 92 of the argument that had started Tuesday upon Jeffrey's arrival and showed no signs of abating three days later.

"I'm not going anywhere, Jeffie," Bobby said. "Least of all to Tennessee. I haven't been home since I joined the army and I'm sure as hell not going back now."

"It's Jeffrey."

"Sure, Jeffie," Bobby said.

"Dad's dying."

"The sooner the better."

"You don't mean that."

"The hell I don't."

"He wants to see you before he crosses over."

Bobby snorted. "I could give a shit what that bastard wants, dead or alive."

"You have to forgive him, Bobby, the way he's forgiven you."

Uh-oh, Dinah thought, almost sorry for Jeffie.

Almost. She kneaded bread and wondered where Kate was. For some reason Kate was the only one among them who didn't send Jeffrey Clark into pontifical orbit. Maybe he'd fallen into passionate, unreasoning, uncaring love with her. Maybe he'd marry her and whisk her home in lieu of his brother.

Maybe Kate would find whoever burned her cabin down and not hurt him.

Meanwhile, back at the front.

"Is he in pain?" Bobby said.

"Yes," Jeffrey said.

"Good," Bobby said, with a grim kind of relish.

"You don't mean that."

"The hell I don't!"

Katya, used to Daddy's bellows, was unacquainted with the tenor of this one. Her face puckered. Bobby plucked her from the middle of her toys and cuddled her. He dropped his voice but from fifteen feet Dinah could still hear the venom in it. "Lynnie is dead because of him."

Jeffrey's voice sharpened. "Lynnette Adams is dead because she committed a mortal sin, and when she was called to account for it, tried to wipe it out by committing another, and then the worst one of all. She was damned from the beginning."

Dinah froze, wrist-deep in dough. Where was the first-aid kit, exactly? Bathroom, that's right, above the sink.

After a moment of silence that positively sizzled, Bobby spoke in a tone that was a mixture of silk and razor wire that Dinah had never heard before. "Don't let me hear you say anything like that again, Jeffie. Not ever. Lynnie was a sweetheart, my sweetheart. We had plans, Lynnie and me. Because we got ahead of ourselves and she had an abortion doesn't make her a sinner."

"Dad didn't hold the razor to her wrists in that bathtub, Robert."

"And it wasn't Dad calling her a whore from the pulpit, either, I suppose?"

Dinah, chilled to the bone by the menacing purr issuing forth from the man previously known as her husband, found herself holding her breath. She looked over her shoulder at the gun case standing in one corner of the room. Still locked. Good.

The silence was broken by a tiny whimper. Dinah risked a look over her shoulder and saw her daughter hugging as much of her father's neck as she could get her arms around. "Daddy mad," she said in a tiny voice. "Daddy mad. Don't be mad, Daddy. Please."

Both men, glaring at each other, were recalled to the present. "It's okay, baby. Daddy's not mad at you. Daddy's never mad at you." Bobby rocked his chair back and forth with a hand on the wheel. Her arms relaxed and her head drooped to his shoulder. Dinah noticed she didn't let go of her father's neck.

In a more civil tone, Jeffrey said, "Mom needs you."

"Yeah, well, I needed her when I was sixteen and she was nowhere to be found."

A brief pause. "She gave you life."

"I didn't have a vote in that, Jeffie. That was their choice. This is mine."

"Robert—"

Dinah gave up the pretence of blissful ignorance and came around the corner, hands cupped so she wouldn't dribble flour all over the floor. "Give it a rest, Jeffrey, why don't you. Go on back to Auntie Vi's. Take a drive, see something of the Park while you're here." And give my man a break, she thought.

He turned his head and stared at a point somewhere above her left shoulder. In three days he had yet to look her in the face. She would never forget the shock in his when Bobby had introduced them, and the repugnance in his voice. "You married a *white* woman?"

"All right," he said now, still staring straight past her. "I'll be back this evening."

"Don't bother," Bobby said.

Jeffrey left without replying.

There was a whole lot of quiet going on following the muted slam of the door behind him. Everyone listened intently to the footsteps going down the steps, over the grass, the opening of the door to the battered blue Nissan truck Auntie Vi had rented to Jeffrey at a more extortionate rate than usual, the starting of the engine, the sound of it receding over the creek and down the road.

"So." Dinah blew out a breath. "That could have gone better."

Bobby cracked out a laugh. "You've said that every day since he came."

"I've meant it every day since he came."

He gave her an incredulous look. "For chrissake, woman! The man has yet to call you by name! Don't fucking tell me you're on his side!"

She went back to the kitchen and started kneading dough.

She heard the squeak of rubber on wood as he followed. "Dinah?"

"Jeffrey's right about one thing."

"Oh? And that would be what, exactly?"

Dinah took a deep breath and prepared for the storm. "He is your father. He gave you life. He wants to see you. You owe him."

She closed her eyes and braced herself. When he said nothing, she looked around.

He was weeping.

Katya raised her head from his shoulder and stared. She touched the track of one of his tears with a pudgy little finger. "Daddy sad?" she said. Her voice broke. "Daddy sad," she wailed, and started to sob, a horrible, heartbroken sound that struck both parents to the core.

Dinah gave her hands a quick wash, made up a bottle, and stashed Katya in her crib where, thankfully, for once Katya subsided without complaint and fell asleep with a milky face. Dinah marched back to her husband, shoved his chair into the living room, ordered him onto the couch, and curled up half in and half out of his lap. She put her arms around him and she hung on and that was all she did for about an hour, listening to the beat of his heart against her ear, feeling the intermittent shudder in his body when his breath caught. She hung on and she wouldn't let go and she wouldn't move. Slowly, steadily, he began to relax, one muscle group at a time. He rested his forehead against her shoulder. "I can't go back, Dinah."

She burrowed closer. "A day's travel, a day there, another day to get home. Three days you'll be gone, tops."

"I don't want to."

"He's your father." She raised her head and searched his face. "Bobby, don't you have one good memory of your father? Did he take you fishing, or hold you on your first bicycle, or cheer you on during a baseball game? Did he read you a story over and over again, or hold you when you were sick, or let you crawl in with him and your mother when you had a nightmare?"

He let his head fall back against the head of the couch and closed his eyes. "Maybe. One or two of those." He opened his eyes. "Maybe all. But Lynnie's dead because this supposedly good man called her a whore in front of her parents and her family and her friends. And me."

Dinah chose her words carefully. "They called you a fornicator, and a sinner."

He said nothing.

"And you didn't kill yourself."

His laugh was brief and bitter. "No, I let the Cong take care of that for me."

She straddled his lap and took his face between her hands. Never before had she noticed how white they were against the black of his face, and she could and would curse his brother loud and long for that. "Bobby, what if he dies? What if he dies and you don't say good-bye?"

"I said good-bye a long time ago, Dinah."

"What about your mother?"

He shook his head. "I always came second to Jeffie. He was the oldest, the smartest, the most gentlemanly. If she has Jeffie, she won't want me." He looked at her with a ghost of his old twinkle. "Jeffie got a full scholarship to MIT, did you know?"

"I think I heard him mention it twelve or fourteen times."

They both laughed a little.

Kate walked in, followed by Johnny with a full daypack over his shoulder. "Don't tell me, let me guess," she said. "The evil brother strikes again."

Bobby managed a smile. "And how was your day, dear?"

Johnny let the screen door slam behind him. "Kick him out, Bobby."

"I did, squirt."

"Good. Look at what we're studying in science, Bobby. Light is both a particle and a wave, did you know that?"

Bobby was more than glad to have the subject changed. "Explain it to me, squirt."

The men folk retired to the central console and bent over

Johnny's textbook. Bobby's voice eventually regained full volume.

Dinah poured Kate coffee and set about trying to salvage the bread dough. "Want some fry bread?" she said over her shoulder.

Kate moaned. "Auntie Vi stuffed me full earlier today."

"Does that mean you don't want any more?"

"Did I say that?" Kate pulled out a large skillet and poured in oil and set it over a medium flame. She took the plateful of round patties of bread dough and fried them until both sides were a golden brown. She set the first batch on the table along with butter, powdered sugar, honey, and three kinds of jams and said, "Come and get it!" stepping back quickly so she wasn't trampled in the rush.

She returned to the stove where the second batch was already in. "So?"

"Same old, same old." Dinah sighed and closed her eyes briefly. "He's only been here three days, Kate, and all I can think of is how nice it would be if our friendly neighborhood grizzly would just . . . kill him and serve him up for Sunday brunch to her cubs."

"Not much meat on the man," Kate observed.

"Not much incentive for a hungry bear," Dinah agreed. "Damn it."

"Want me to get rid of him?"

Dinah eyed her. "And how would you do that?"

Kate shrugged. "I'd figure it out." She saw Dinah's expression and choked on a piece of fry bread. "I didn't mean I'd kill him," she said, laughing out loud.

"What did you mean?"

"I don't know. Sneak up on him one dark night, throw a sack over his head, and trundle him out to the airstrip, where I'd have George standing by ready to fly his ass to Anchorage and dump it on the first plane south."

Dinah examined Kate carefully. It wasn't braggadocio she saw on her friend's face, it was sincerity and determination. "I believe you would."

"Say the word."

"You tempt me greatly," she said, and sighed again, wistful. "But no." She looked over her shoulder at their two men, one of whom was instructing the other in the fine art of pirating a little radio wave for the broadcast of Park Air. "There's a lot Bobby's been waiting to say to his family. I think he needs to."

Kate was surprised. "You sending him home?"

"This is his home," Dinah said firmly. "Katya and I are his home. But we are who our parents make us. His father's dying. If he doesn't say good-bye . . ." She let her voice trail off.

"Will he go?"

"He says not." Dinah looked at her husband.

"Want me to take Katya and Johnny and clear out for a while?"

Dinah shook her head. "No, I've already said all I'm going to." She gave a wan smile. "The rest is up to him." She shook herself. "Enough of that. How the hell *was* your day, dear?"

Before Kate could play along, there was a knock at the screen door and they looked up to see Jim Chopin standing there.

"Hey, Jim," Dinah said. She sounded less than friendly, which surprised Kate, because Dinah, while never having numbered among the legions of Jim's lovers, was not immune to his manifest charms, either.

"Hey, yourself." He looked at Kate.

Kate met his eyes without a trace of her usual discouraging scowl.

He looked confused, and then alarmed.

"Chopper Jim Chopin, long time no see," Bobby said. "Must be all of twelve hours."

Maybe it was the lower decibel level, maybe he didn't want to see what was on Kate's face, but Jim actually looked away from Kate. He frowned down at Bobby. "Who died?"

"My father," Bobby replied. "Or the son of a bitch is about to."

It was a toss-up who was more surprised at the words, Bobby or any of the rest of them.

"Screw it," he said. "Let's get drunk and go dancing."

They commandeered the big round table in the back corner, Bobby and Dinah and Jim and Kate. Katya had been dropped off with Auntie Vi, who had taken one look at Bobby and made plans for keeping the baby overnight, overriding all obligatory, if feeble, parental objections. Johnny had made a vigorous bid to stay alone at Bobby's—"I'm too old for a baby-sitter!"—which suggestion had been summarily squashed by Kate, and was also at Auntie Vi's.

Bernie brought over a round, took the temperature of the table, and departed at speed with the barest minimum allowable bonhomie.

"Drink up," Bobby said, and upended a bottle of Alaskan Amber like it was the last bottle in the last case Bernie had in stock.

Jim had left his cap, badge, and sidearm in his vehicle, which indicated that alcohol would be involved in whatever happened for the rest of the evening. He had a beer and a shot. He was out before Bobby was. Dinah was sipping at a double shot of Gran Marnier, warmed, in a snifter. Kate brooded over a sparkling water over ice, with lime.

The mood was not what you could call convivial.

As one might expect on a Friday night after breakup and before fishing season, the Roadhouse was jammed to the rafters. A gang of climbers stumbled in unshaven and smelly from a successful summit of Big Bump, and Bernie poured out Middle Fingers for all, the downing of which was accompanied by chanting and cheers from everyone else in the bar. Park rats admired insanity so long as it was sincere, and there was nothing more insane or sincere than the ambition of every mountain climber on the North American continent to summit the technically unchallenging but relatively high Angqaq Peak. Pastor Bill of the Jesus Loves You New Gospel Little Chapel in the Park and his congregation of four, down two since the wife of one had run off with the husband of another the year before, were singing hymns in the back room, although a rhythmic chinking sound accompanied by zither music indicated that they might be sharing space with the belly dancers that practiced at the Roadhouse once a month.

Jimmy Buffett was wasting away again in Margaritaville on the jukebox. "Come on, babe," Bobby said to Dinah. "Let's dance." He pulled her into his lap and rolled out into the middle of the floor, where they wove a complicated little spiral of wheels and feet to a calypso beat.

"This could be our first date," Jim said.

Kate closed her eyes and shook her head.

"A double date," he said. "We can hang out without you getting all stressed that I'm going to jump your bones."

Kate drank water.

"I am, of course, but that comes later. Me, too."

"Jim," Kate said.

"Kate," Jim said, and grinned.

She couldn't stop herself. She laughed.

"That's better," he said, and waved over another round. When Bernie had come and gone he said, "I haven't seen you since Tuesday. I see you're still living and uncharred, which I find to be a good thing. What have you got on Dreyer?"

"Nothing."

He looked skeptical. "Nothing?"

"Nothing." She shook her head and rolled the ice-filled glass back and forth across her forehead. "Jim, I was born and raised in this Park. I've howdied, as they say, with just about everyone who has lived or is living in it. I'm related by blood to at least a third of them, by marriage to at least another third, and the last third owes me one way or another. People talk to me because they know me and because they know I've been around forever."

"You got diddly."

"In the past three days, I've talked to anyone who ever said hi to Len Dreyer going into the post office, anyone who ever stood in line behind him at the Niniltna General Store, anyone who ever bumped into him in this bar. He did some kind of work for just about all of them, fixed roofs, laid floors, dug foundations, fixed boats, cars, snow machines, four-wheelers, hair dryers, irons, blenders, Skilsaws, and one 1994 Harley-Davidson two-tone blue and silver Fat Boy with twenty-four thousand miles on it that is apparently driving Archie Spring either into his second childhood or the sunset, depending on whether you talk to him or his wife."

"An all-purpose, super-duper utility handyman."

"With a work ethic that wouldn't quit. His mother must have been frightened by a slacker when she was pregnant. He always showed up when he said he would, he always stayed on the job till it was done, and he always got it right the first time."

"He could have gotten rich in a town like Anchorage."

"Why didn't he, then?" she said, frustrated. "And why didn't he live higher on the hog in the Park?"

"How did he live?"

"You know his cabin burned down?" He nodded, and she pulled out a photo and shoved it at him. "Got that from the Association files, you know that survey they did of every building in the Park and its history back when the ANCSA money started coming in?"

"Sort of like a Doomsday Book for the Park," he said, nodding.

"Yeah. Emaa wanted a starting place, an inventory for when she went looking for federal money to build housing."

They bent their heads over the photo. It showed a tumbledown shack made of weathered boards, with a roof that looked like it was about to slide in one direction and an outhouse in the background that looked like it was going to crumble in another.

"One man's hovel is another man's castle," Jim said, straightening. "What about family?"

"Did haven't any."

"Friends?"

"Didn't have any."

"Women?"

"Jim, I don't think this guy's been laid since he arrived in the Park."

"And when was that?"

"Near as I can figure, before I was born." She sat back, glum. "He may have shook hands with somebody between then and now, but that'd appear to be about the limit of Dreyer's human contact."

"You'd be wrong about that."

They looked up to find Dandy standing there with an insufferably smug look on his face.

"Dandy," Jim said.

"What are you talking about?" Kate said.

He pointedly ignored her. "I've been asking around."

"You've been what?" Kate said. She looked at Jim, who appeared less than thrilled.

"Conducting my own investigation, and it looks like I've been doing better than you." Without invitation, Dandy sat in Dinah's chair and pulled out a small spiral notepad that looked a lot like the one Kate carried when she was on a case. He flipped it open. "Len Dreyer's had five girlfriends. Susan Brainerd in the Park, Vicky Gordaoff down in Cordova, Cheryl Wright in the Park, Betsy Kvasnikof"—Dandy allowed himself a reminiscent smile—"and most recently Laurel Meganack."

"You're kidding me," Jim said, startled out of his disapproval into something like respect. "Laurel Meganack? Of the café Laurels?"

An arm snaked around Kate, startling her. It was only Bernie, removing her empty glass and replacing it with a full one. "Thanks," she said, squeezing the wedge of lime.

"Sure." He lingered until Jim gave him a look. "Oh, all right," he said, and moved on to Pastor Bill's table, at which service showed signs of ending. Kate's eyes followed him.

Jim noticed her thoughtful look. "What?"

"Nothing," Kate said. "Nothing at all." She looked at Dandy. "How sure are you about Dreyer's girlfriends?"

Dandy looked affronted. "They wouldn't lie to me," he said righteously.

He might even be right about that, she thought. "How long did they last?"

"According to them he was a hit and run kind a guy," Dandy said, smirking.

"One-night stands? Two? Be more specific."

Dandy looked at Jim, who raised an eyebrow. "I didn't ask," he said, on the defensive. "None of them sounded like it was very permanent. What does it matter?"

"You have dates?"

He showed her his notes. Jim took the pad and ripped out his notes. "Hey," Dandy said.

Kate looked at Jim. "Looking for love in all the wrong places?"

"Sounds more like scratching an itch," he said.

She nodded. "To me, too. Dandy, did he talk to any of these women, mention family, where he was from, anything like that?"

Fingering his depleted notepad, he looked relieved. "No. I did ask that. Vicky said it was one of the reasons she wasn't interested in it lasting. He didn't talk much."

She nodded. "Good work, Dandy."

Dandy looked gratified. "Even if no one asked you to do it," Jim said. "You've done enough, all right? Leave this to us now."

Dandy's face fell. "But I thought—"

"No," Jim said firmly. "Dandy, you don't have any training. We've got a six-month-old murder here, we can't afford to have amateurs messing up the evidence. Not to mention which, the murderer is most likely still in the Park. He's already demonstrated a willingness to kill not to get caught, twice. You heard what happened to Kate's cabin. Just luck she wasn't inside when it got torched."

Dandy's mouth set in a stubborn line. "I can handle myself."

"I don't doubt it. But you're done. I mean it, Dandy. Thanks for what you've accomplished so far, I appreciate it, I really do. But you're done now."

Dandy opened his mouth, recognized the implacability of Jim's expression, and closed it again. "Fine," he said tightly, and marched off.

Jim handed her the wad of notes and Kate stuffed them into a back pocket. "Why don't they have an ID on Dreyer yet?"

"His prints aren't in the system."

"Don't they have to be if you're in the military? Isn't that standard procedure?"

"We don't know that he was."

"Bobby thinks he was." She thought about the five women Dandy had found, and frowned into her drink. There was something about it, something about all five of the women, something she couldn't put her finger on.

Bobby and Dinah came back to the table then, Bobby roaring up in his chair and skidding to a halt that rose him up on one wheel. Dinah squealed and he kissed her, putting those patented Clark moves on her like she wasn't his wife.

"Jesus," Jim muttered, "take it outside."

Kate looked at him with such open-mouthed surprise that he had to laugh, albeit a little painfully. It was difficult to watch Bobby manhandle Dinah in precisely the way he'd like to manhandle Kate.

Bobby came up for air and dove into his beer, surfacing with a loud, satisfied smack of his lips. "Damn, this was a good idea. Bernie!" he bellowed. "More beer!"

From that point on there was a mutual unspoken agreement that no serious business would be discussed, no Dreyer, no Jeffrey, no Jane, no abusive husbands or dope-dealing video renters or arsonous murderers. There was flirting, between Bobby and Dinah and between Jim and Dinah and between Bobby and Kate. There might even have been a little between Kate and Jim. The stories started tall and got taller. Dinah danced with Bobby again, and then Jim, and then Old Sam, who had patented a kind of schottische-rhumba combination that was the dread of every woman in the Park.

After a while it got crowded enough that Bernie missed a

signal for another round and Kate went to the bar. Bernie was busy filling a tray, and while she was waiting she said hello to the man glowering into a glass of beer.

He nodded, a single, straight-up-and-down movement, his ill humor making his black face look like a thunderhead, ready to shoot lightning at any moment. "Ms. Shugak."

"Didn't see you come in," she said. She thought about asking him to join their table. She thought better of it.

"Robert did."

Ah. If so, Bobby had not mentioned it to the rest of them, which told its own story. She looked down the bar and caught Bernie's eye. He held up one finger, made a circular motion, raised his eyebrows. She nodded.

"You appear to have some influence with my brother," Jeffrey said stiffly.

Hating to ask favors of an inferior, Kate thought. "Nobody has influence on Bobby Clark," she said. "He's his own man. He does what he wants, when he wants."

She could tell he was resisting the impulse to glare. "Nevertheless," he said. "I'd appreciate it if you'd tell him you think it's a good idea to see his father alive one last time."

"I don't know that it is," Kate said.

This time he didn't resist. "He's his father. He wants to see his second son before he dies. That can't be too hard even for you to understand."

It was the "even for you" that did it. "You hate it that he's happy, don't you," she said, looking at him as if she were peering through a microscope. "You could have handled it better if he were broke, hungry, maybe homeless. Instead he's got a home and a wife—"

He snorted.

"—and a child, and a life. Your father made Tennessee so unliveable for him that he escaped into the army, and war, to get away from it. Just out of curiosity, did you know he'd left both legs in Vietnam before you came? Did your father know?

Did either of you bother to find out where he went and what he did when he left you?"

"He ran away."

"Which at this point only confirms my already high opinion of his intelligence," Kate said, and watched with interest as his face flushed red enough to be seen even given the already dark color of his skin and the dim light of the bar.

Fortunately, Bernie finally scooted down the counter to toss her a package of beef jerky. He felt the tension between her and Jeffrey Clark and gave her a quizzical look.

Kate tossed the jerky back. "Mutt's over at Auntie Vi's with Katya and Johnny," she said. "But thanks."

Bernie gave Jeffrey Clark one last look, decided it would be unwise to meddle with a volcano that close to eruption, and busied himself with filling glasses. "How's the hunt going?"

She gave him a long, considering look, and gave a nonanswer. "We're taking the night off."

"Oh. Ah. Well. Here you go." He shoved the tray at her and answered a call for another round at the opposite end of the bar, a look of barely suppressed relief on his face.

She delivered the drinks and stood for a moment, indecisive. "What, you're waiting for a fucking invitation!" Bobby roared.

She jerked her head. "Gotta flush," she said, but when she got to the back of the room she ignored the door into the rest room and went out onto the back porch instead. A set of stairs led down into the rest of Bernie's domain.

There were two neat rows of cabins, each big enough for a queen-sized bed and a bathroom, which could not, contrary to rumor, be rented by the hour. There were two covered picnic areas with brick barbecues, and tables and benches made of logs sawn in half. A neatly gravelled trail led through a stand of birch trees to a two-story house built of imported cedar, fronted with a large deck held down by a full suite of wrought-iron lawn furniture and an enormous gas grill. Kate went up a wide stair-

case laden with deep, square flower boxes at tastefully interspersed points and knocked gently on the French double doors.
After a few moments they opened. "Hello, Kate."

"Hi, Enid. Could I talk to you for a few minutes?"

11

Enid Elliot Koslowski was a Park rat, and a daughter and a granddaughter of more Park rats who were all now either working on the TransAlaska Pipeline or in Prudhoe Bay, or in the Pioneer Home in Anchorage, eating Doritos and watching Jerry Springer on cable. She was as white as you could get without bleach, her forebears having determined early on to retain racial purity insofar as that did not preclude amicable trading relations with the Alaska Natives who made up the majority of the customers who came into the general store.

The general store had been built by her grandfather, a Canadian of Scots descent whose ancestors had emigrated to America fleeing from the heavy hand of British tyranny. Her grandfather emigrated to Alaska fleeing what he perceived to be the Frenchization (his word) of the Canadian nation. "At least in Alaska," he opined famously, or infamously depending on the race of the listener, "a white man can be white."

He brought his wife with him, who quietly expired giving him his second son, who died shortly thereafter. He sent his one remaining son Outside to school, who returned eventually with a degree in history and an acceptably white wife. They had one child, Enid.

The store provided the Elliotts with a reasonably good living until it burned down one spring day in 1970. Enid's father, who had never cared much for living in the Bush, put the property up for sale and moved to Anchorage. There were no takers until Bernie Koslowski, fleeing the repercussions of burning his draft card on the steps of the U.S. Capitol that same year, came to the Park with a fistful of cash (the provenance of which no sensible Park rat inquired after) looking for a place to build a bar.

Enid flew into the Park to close the deal for her father. She didn't like living in Anchorage, and Bernie, if a draft-dodger, was white, thereby gaining her father's approval, so she married him. They had three children and appeared reasonably content.

Kate, however, knew a little about what went on beneath that placid Koslowski surface. Bernie wasn't a Cassanova on the order of Jim or Dandy but he did have an eye for the ladies, and there had been the occasional foray over the fence. He blithely imagined Enid knew nothing of these extramarital activities, but Kate had good cause to know that Enid was not as clueless as she made herself appear. Bernie was a good provider and a good father, though, and Enid had no wish to tend bar herself. She wasn't the first wife Kate had met who had decided to turn a blind eye to her husband's extracurricular activities. Didn't mean she liked it, though.

Enid made coffee, a welcome reprieve from the designer water Kate had been swilling in the bar. It was good coffee, too, dark and rich, and familiar. "I get it from Homer," Enid said.

"Captain's Roast," Kate said, and for an instant remembered the small bunkhouse in Bering, and rifling through Jim's duffle for clues as to why he was there, too.

"Yeah," Enid said, surprised. "How'd you know?"

"Lucky guess. Need to ask you some questions, Enid, if it's okay?"

Having Kate Shugak show up on your doorstep wasn't as bad as Dan Rather showing up with a camera crew, but it was a close second, and Enid had been nervous from the get-go. "Sure," she said apprehensively. "What about?"

"Len Dreyer." Kate watched as color receded from Enid's face. In a voice carefully devoid of any emotion, she said, "I imagine you've heard that his body was discovered in Grant Glacier."

Enid spoke through stiff lips. "I had heard."

Kate waited, and when Enid said nothing more, prodded her on. "He was shot at point-blank range."

If possible, Enid went even whiter. "Oh."

"With a shotgun. Messy."

"How . . . how awful," Enid said. Her eyes were fixed and staring right at Kate, as if she was afraid to look at anything else. "I don't know what I can tell you about him, Kate. I didn't know him that well."

Kate watched her from beneath lowered eyelids, and saw Enid look up and to her right. She snapped her gaze back immediately. Kate said, "Bernie says you had him do some work around the place last summer."

"Oh. Yes, I . . . I suppose we did."

"What did he do?"

"I don't know, I—oh, of course. He laid down some new gravel for the paths."

"I see." Kate lapsed into that time-honored investigator's trick, silence.

Enid was a good subject to practice it on: Innocent people usually are. She rushed to fill the silence with words. "He was only here a few days, I think. He did a good job, the paths are in great shape, even after the winter. Nice and level. I think he dug some of them out so they'd have a nice edge to them, so the gravel wouldn't scatter." Kate watched her realize she was babbling, watched her catch herself, and stop.

"When was he here?" Kate said. "What days?"

"I don't know, Kate, last summer sometime." Kate's unthreatening manner gave Enid courage. "Why do you need to know?"

Kate shrugged. "I'm helping Jim figure out what happened. Dreyer was probably killed last year, since no one reports seeing him after the end of October. I'm putting together a timeline of his activities, where he worked, who he talked to, like that, in case someone knows something that might help us finger the killer."

"Oh. Would you like some more coffee?"

Kate looked down at her mug, three-quarters full. "Sure." She waited until Enid was on her feet with her back turned before she looked around.

Through the doorway she could see the gun rack mounted on the wall. It had cradles for four weapons, all full. Two of the four were shotguns, a double and a single.

She faced forward just in time to hold out her mug for Enid to top off.

They were in the kitchen, a magnificent room of bleached wood and granite countertops and gleaming copper pots. Selling liquor had always been a profitable business. There was a corner bookcase filled with cookbooks, and a long table that seated twelve to serve dishes made from recipes in those books. Enid was the closest thing the Park had to a full-blown chef. Kate herself had sat down at this table to a chicken stew that Enid had called Sicilian and everyone else divine. Lots of garlic. Anything with a lot of garlic in it worked for Kate, who sometimes imagined she had something Mediterranean going on in her background. It was possible; there was everything else in there, including a Russian commissar and a Jewish tailor. There was also Uncle Dieter, whom everyone thought had been a Nazi in Germany sixty years before, but he was drooling away the rest of his life in the Sunset Apartments in Ahtna and nobody'd called Simon Wiesenthal, so they let it go.

Kate looked at Enid, who was fidgeting nicely. Blunt or oblique, she thought. Blunt. "You had an affair with Len Dreyer," she said.

Enid, taken totally off guard first by the long silence and then by the direct attack, burst into tears. Kate looked around, found a box of Kleenex on the counter, and fetched it over. It took a while, but Enid eventually sobbed her way through the entire box and the whole story. "It wasn't an affair," she said, hiccupping.

"What was it then, a one-night stand?"

"No! No. It wasn't anything like that. I just wanted—I just . . ." The words, backed up for a long time, flooded forth like a creek after breakup. "There's always someone. There's always been someone. It never lasts long but I know all the signs, I always know, and I always pretend I don't, and I just got tired of it, you know?" Her eyes, red and swollen, appealed to Kate for understanding.

Kate looked at her gravely.

There was a tense moment, broken only by the sound of broken breathing. "And then," Enid said, almost inaudibly, "and then there was Laurel."

"Laurel Meganack?" Kate said.

"Yes." Enid reached for more tissue. "I thought—he was more serious about her. It lasted a long time, longer than usual. I—I thought he might leave me for her." Enid blew her nose. "I didn't know what to do. I was afraid to talk to Bernie about it. I don't know. I think I thought if I said something I might make it happen."

If you don't look straight at it, Kate thought, it doesn't exist. "So along came Len."

"God, it wasn't like he was even that interested, I practically had to rape him. But he was right here, day after day. He had a nice body," she said wistfully. "Nice shoulders when he took his shirt off. Strong arms. I went out one day, took him a cold can of pop, and I, well, I guess you could say I propositioned him. We went into one of the cabins, and well, we did it. The next day he came back and I took him into a cabin again. Only . . ."

Kate, keeping to herself her opinion of someone who chose to sleep around on her husband in her husband's place of business, said, "Bernie walked in?"

Enid broke down again. "Yes," she said, sobbing. "He walked in." She raised tear-filled eyes. "He stood there looking at us."

"What did he say?"

"Nothing! He didn't say anything! He stood there, and then he walked out again, like it didn't mean a damn to him! He—" She started to sob again. "He even closed the door behind him. He closed it behind him, like he wanted to give us privacy! He wasn't even angry!"

Or, given his predilection for screwing around himself, he wasn't prepared to throw any stones, Kate thought. "Did you talk about it later?"

Enid, regaining some control, blew her nose and shook her head. "No. I tried, but he cut me off."

And it had been festering ever since. In both of them, probably.

Well, Kate didn't do therapy. She got to her feet. "Thanks for the coffee."

Enid trailed after her like a lost puppy. "Is that all?"

"Yeah, pretty much. You said Dreyer didn't mention any family or friends, or where he came from before he lived in the Park."

"I don't think Dreyer was his real name."

Kate halted. "Really? Why?"

"A letter fell out of his pocket. You know. That first day. It was addressed to a Leon Duffy."

Len Dreyer. Leon Duffy. Many people who assumed aliases chose names with the same initials. Easier to remember. "He say how old he was?"

Enid looked uncertain. "Uh, around my age, I think. Late forties, maybe? Maybe older."

That would fit, if Bobby was right about Dreyer serving in Vietnam. Kate wondered where he'd gotten the letter. Not through Bonnie at the local PO, that was sure. Maybe it was an old letter. A keepsake from a loved one, say! The killer could have gotten rid of it so as to delay identification of the body. "Did you happen to notice what he was driving?"

Enid shrugged. "Some beat-up old truck. With a canopy, maybe?" She thought. "Might have been gray."

"Yeah. Okay. Thanks, Enid. I'm sorry I had to ask you about it."

"It's okay." Enid drew a shaky breath. "You know what's the worst, Kate? The worst is it wasn't even that much fun. I made the pass. I took him to the cabin. I even undressed him, and me."

"Enid—"

"He had his eyes closed the whole time. Like he didn't even want to see what he was screwing." She tried to smile with trembling lips. "There's a name for that, isn't there? A mercy fuck, isn't that what they call it?" A tear slid from the corner of her eye.

"If it's that hard to take, why don't you leave?" Kate said.

Enid looked shocked. "I couldn't do that. There are the children. And besides . . ." She looked down at her hands, twisted together in a painful knot. Her voice dropped. "He didn't love me when we married. I thought, well, I thought that love, or maybe even just a little affection, would come in time. It didn't. I shouldn't have married him. It's my fault."

She stood in silence for a moment. When she raised her head the old Enid was back, armor in place. "Well," she said brightly, "thanks for stopping by, Kate." She opened the door and Kate, perforce, went through it.

She stood on the deck listening to Enid's footsteps recede.

She was thinking of the witches' coven in the woods she had stumbled onto a few years back, led by Enid and celebrating the death of Lisa Gette, who had slept with the husbands of every attending wicca-for-a-day. Even now, years later, the memory was strong enough to run a chill up her spine. Those women had been united in hatred, united in celebrating death.

It was too much of a cliché, but as Kate knew from long experience with the Anchorage D.A., that didn't make it untrue. Husband screws around, wife has a revenge fuck with the handyman, husband walks in, husband kills handyman. Certainly the white of Enid's face said that she was terrified that Bernie had in fact done just that. And there was that betraying glance at the gun rack.

The timing was off, though. Len Dreyer had laid gravel and Enid around Labor Day. He'd been seen elsewhere multiple times between Labor Day and the end of October.

Didn't mean Bernie couldn't have bided his time, planned it out. That's what a prosecuting attorney would say. A prosecuting attorney would also say that Bernie, by virtue of an everyone-comes-to-Bernie's Park practice, would be among the first to know about Grant Glacier advancing. According to Millicent and Dan, the glacier's subsequent retreat hadn't gotten the same kind of press. No immediate reason to believe it wouldn't be the perfect grave.

Enid had said that Bernie didn't care, but even the most indifferent husband had been known to react adversely to his wife sleeping with another man. And then, Laurel Meganack had slept with Len Dreyer and with Bernie Koslowski both last year, which was a whole other motive Kate didn't want to consider. Maybe Bernie was in love for the first time in his life. Maybe Dreyer had shouldered him out of Laurel's bed.

She shook her head. "Damn it," she said out loud. "Not Bernie. I know him, I've known him for years. He's not a killer."

Didn't mean she wasn't going to have to talk to him about it. She envisioned an unpleasant interrogation, followed by months of cold-shouldering. Great.

She wouldn't tell Jim, though. At least not yet. She headed down the steps and through the path back to the bar.

She was ambushed before she got to the door, a pair of very muscular arms scooping her off the step. She found herself pressed up against the wall, a knee between her legs and a large pair of firm hands investigating the scene of what was before much longer going to be a crime, if only a misdemeanor.

There was an undercurrent of laughter in Jim's voice when he left off nibbling on her ear and whispered into it instead. "Come on, Shugak, cuddle up, you know you want to." He kissed her, and since her feet were dangling a foot off the ground, she couldn't find enough leverage to fight him off.

Or that's what she told herself.

It had been a long time since she'd been the target of this much unrelenting male attention, and Jim hadn't had enough to drink to affect his moves. Her eyes went a little out of focus and then closed altogether.

No. There was nothing in the least reverential about Jim Chopin's kiss.

Her conscience was guilty at withholding information relevant to the case they were working together, that was what it was. So she'd let him grope her a little, kiss her a little, touch her a—oh my. The man certainly knew where all the parts were, and needed no instruction in how to get them running. Her arms came up of their own volition to circle his neck. Mostly to help support her weight, seeing as how she was hanging there in midair and all. She might have tilted her head to give him easier access to that spot just below her left ear. She might even have knotted her hand in his hair and brought his head back so she could kiss him for a change, but that wasn't very likely, now was it?

"Excuse me," a very dry voice said.

Jim, wallowing in the middle of what was the very first wholehearted, unconditional response he'd ever had from Kate Shugak, even if he had taken her by surprise, swore ripely and said "What!" in a tone of voice that had all by itself disarmed more than one frisky perp in its day.

Dinah, surveying them with a bleak eye, said, "Bobby's hungry. We were thinking of rodding on into town and grabbing a bite at the café."

"Sounds good," Kate said brightly, and eeled out of Jim's arms to hotfoot it around the corner and up the stairs into the bar.

Jim moved to follow her and was halted in his tracks by one upraised hand.

"What?" he said, exasperated, frustrated, horny, edgy, and embarrassed.

"What do you want with her?" Dinah said in a quiet voice.

Like it wasn't obvious. He tried to adjust the bulge behind his fly without her noticing. "What are you talking about?"

"With Kate," Dinah said, and this time her tone got through to him. "What do you want with her, Jim?"

"What?" he said again, this time bewildered.

"You want to lay her?"

This was so unlike Dinah's usual mostly ladylike self that he simply gaped at her.

She regarded him with palpable scorn. "Yeah, well, take a number. Here's the thing." She stepped forward and actually grabbed herself a handful of his shirtfront and pulled him down to an elevation where she could get in his face. "Kate's been a big girl for a long time now, and I don't expect she'd take kindly to my meddling in her business. But I'm her friend, and I don't want to see her hurt."

"Hurt?" Jim said. "Who's talking about hurting her?"

"You'll hurt her, given half the chance," Dinah said. "Kate's not one of your good-time girls, Jim. When there's someone in her life, it's serious, and it's monogamous. If you're not serious, stay the hell away from her."

He was angry now. He removed her hand. "You're right," he said, "it's none of your business."

He stalked around the corner.

Dinah stood where she was, staring after him. A smile that was one part mean spread slowly across her face.

If she was not mistaken, Jim Chopin, Alaska state trooper and sworn ladies' man, had just got his feelings hurt.

The four of them wound up at the Riverside Café, wolfing down sourdough pancakes and link sausage and eggs fried too hard. Laurel Meganack was there, cooking and serving and flirting with everyone in sight, particularly Jim Chopin, who in Dinah's opinion did not appear to be encouraging her, and who in Kate's opinion did not appear to be beating her off with a stick, either. All of this remained unspoken, of course, but the subtext lay heavily over the table.

They sat around drinking coffee after, Laurel making sure to keep Jim's cup in particular full to the brim. Before Laurel plopped herself down in his lap, Kate cornered her in the kitchen.

"Hey, Kate," Laurel said with a sunny smile, tending to the burgers on the grill, the dishes in the sink, and the coffee urn all at the same time. Watching her smooth efficiency in the compact kitchen made Kate feel like an underachiever.

"Got a minute?" Kate said.

Laurel flipped the burgers in three swift movements. "Now I do," she said, wiping her hands on her apron. "What's up?"

It was late and Kate had neither the time nor the inclination for diplomacy. "Rumor has it you had a thing with Bernie Koslowski last year."

Laurel's smile vanished. "I don't see where that's any of your business."

"It wouldn't be," Kate agreed, "except that some other stuff might have come out of it."

"Like what?"

"Like some stuff concerning Bernie's wife, Enid."

"She never knew."

"Yeah," Kate said, "she did. And she slept with Len Dreyer to get even."

Laurel didn't change expression. She was a striking young woman, maybe five feet ten with thick reddish brown hair clipped back from her face, large brown eyes, and dark arched brows. She had a high-bridged nose, handed down along with her height from the Yankee whaler rumored to have been her grandfather, and a small rosebud of a mouth. Her T-shirt was cropped and her jeans low-rider, both playing hide-and-seek with the gold ring piercing her navel. Kate winced away from the sight. "That," Laurel said, "would come under the heading of none of my business."

"Yeah," Kate said, "it is, because Len Dreyer's dead."

"I heard. You don't think—"

"I don't think anything, yet," Kate said, "I'm just gathering information. Which I have more of, by the way. I've heard that you had something going on with Len Dreyer, as well."

"What of it?"

Laurel was getting a little defensive, Kate was glad to see. Defensive people usually had to justify their actions, which meant they talked more. "Like I said, I'm just looking for information. I'm not accusing you of anything except sleeping with two different guys at the same time, which we could all plead guilty to at some point, right?"

"Or more," Laurel said, and then looked as if she wished she hadn't.

"I'm only interested in these two. How did things end with Bernie?"

Laurel shrugged. "Well, I think. It only lasted a couple of months. The wife and kids, his own business, not to mention the coaching job, they kind of cramp his style."

Kate took a guess. "He wasn't unhappy you called it off?"

"Well." Laurel thought it over. "He wasn't happy, exactly. Things were pretty good there for a while."

"So he was unhappy."

"No."

"Which is it?"

"We agreed together we should call it off," Laurel said, exasperated. "I wanted more than he could give, and no way was he leaving his family for me. He understood."

"You wanted marriage?"

"Good god, no!" Laurel said, and surprisingly, laughed. "I just wanted him around more, is all." She winked. "He's got some nice moves. Know what I mean?"

Bernie was a friend and this was not a visual Kate wanted. "What about Dreyer?"

Laurel noticed her arms folded tightly across her chest, and gave Kate a wry smile, inviting her to recognize the body language. The burgers were done and she flipped them to the buns, arranged lettuce, tomato, onions, and pickle on the plates, at which time the deep fryer alarm went off and she went for the basket of fries. "Len was a mistake," she said, shaking the basket.

"How so?"

"And my mistake, too," Laurel said, letting the fries drain. She looked up at Kate. "I thought he was interested." She shrugged and gave a self-deprecating smile. "Seemed like pretty much of a given. Let's face it, the ratio of men to women in the Park is pretty much in our favor."

That was one way of putting it, Kate thought, looking involuntarily through the pass-through at Jim, thick hair rumpled, laughing at something Bobby had said. He looked up suddenly and caught her staring at him.

Laurel was speaking again and Kate willed the sudden drumming from her ears so she could listen.

"I had him in here to do some fix-up stuff the contractor left behind."

"When?"

Laurel thought. "We opened the first week of school, the first Tuesday after Labor Day. Everybody's back from fishing by then, and Billy and I figured we'd get a boost from the teenagers coming in when classes let out." She shrugged. "They don't have anywhere else to go, and I make a pretty mean milkshake, if I do say so myself."

"What did you have Dreyer do?"

"Oh, you know, the linoleum wasn't completely glued down in one corner, they used flat paint instead of glossy on one wall of the bathroom, the garbage disposal wasn't hooked up right. Like that. So I asked around and somebody recommended Len." She sighed theatrically, hand on her heart. "There's just something about a guy with a pipe wrench that does it for me. He had his head under the sink and he'd stripped down to his T-shirt, and he was kinda buff, you know? I, well, I guess I jumped him." Her smile was a little shamefaced. "The troopers could probably run me in for assault."

"So it was a one-time thing?"

"Yeah. He wasn't that interested in more." Her brow creased. "Funny, you know? I mean, it's not like I'm Miss America or anything. But most Park rats wouldn't turn me down. It's supply and demand, you know?"

"I know," Kate said.

12

"ell, now," Brendan said, grim satisfaction rolling out of Bobby's receiver in waves, "amazing what a name change will do for the database."

"Why didn't his fingerprints pop up on search?" Kate said, leaning into mike range.

The satisfaction changed to disgust. "We're in the process of switching from paper fingerprint cards to electronic files, in order to sign on with the National Fingerprint File. I'm guessing your guy fell through the cracks." A pause, followed by a heavy sigh. "Plus it's the Feebs. I mean, jeeze, what're ya gonna do. Listen, Kate?"

"Yeah?"

"You said this guy kept his head down in the Park?"

"So down he didn't register on hardly anyone's radar."

Another pause. "Yeah. Well. His file ain't pretty. Tell Bobby to check his e-mail."

"Will do. And thanks, Brendan."

A rich chuckle. "I'm adding it to the tab, Shugak. You keep getting me up in the middle of the night. I'm telling you, it's costing you. Horizontally."

She laughed. "Ooooh, you big bully, I'm scared now," and knew enough to know that while 2 A.M. guaranteed few listeners there would always be at least one lonely trapper tuned in, and that the stories about Kate Shugak having radio sex with a member of the Anchorage law enforcement community would be circulating around the Park at first light and crossing the bar at the Roadhouse at opening time.

Brandon hung up and Bobby signed off. Fifteen minutes later, the file on one Leon Francis Duffy arrived in Bobby's in box as an attached file. Kate, too impatient to wait for it to print out, opened it and started scrolling.

Dinah, elbowed to one side, accepted a mug of coffee from Jim and went to sprawl next to her husband on a couch. He grabbed her, heedless of her mug, and whispered in a mock snarl, "When can we get rid of these yo-yos so's you and me can get horizontal?"

She made a token effort to save the coffee and an even more desultory effort to repel boarders before giving up.

Jim pulled up a chair to read over Kate's shoulder. He felt rather than saw her stiffen, and smiled to himself. The smile vanished when he realized that her reaction hadn't been caused by his proximity but by what she was reading.

"Leon Francis Duffy, born in Madison, Wisconsin, graduated Mendota High School in June 1968, joined the army what looks like the week after. Served one tour in Vietnam and received an honorable discharge, which he took in Anchorage, Alaska. Why Anchorage, do you think?"

"Keep reading," she said, tight-lipped.

He did so. "Oh. A year later he was working in the yard at Spenard Builder's Supply, pulling down a regular paycheck, to all intents and purposes a model citizen, and then he gets arrested for molesting a twelve-year-old girl on the way home from school. Charges dismissed. Oh, crap. Two more arrests, one ten-year-old, another twelve-year-old."

The printer spat out the last sheet and she thrust the bundle at him. "Here."

He shuffled the paper into order. Kate remained where she was, arms folded, glaring at the screen. Jim continued to read out loud. "The third charge stuck, and Leon Francis Duffy was sentenced to eight and a half." Jim flipped the page. "He was a model prisoner, served the minimum five and a half years for good behavior at Highland Mountain Correctional Facility, and . . . evidently disappeared from the public record after release." Jim flipped another page. "His probation officer never heard from him even once. Imagine."

"Imagine."

He squinted down at the page. "See the note from the corrections officer he was assigned to?"

"I couldn't read it on the screen," Kate said. "Is it any clearer printed out?"

" 'I regard Mr. Duffy as one of two of the most dangerous prisoners in this facility to be released this year. Mr. Duffy has refused treatment for his condition, refused to accept counseling of any kind, and has never accepted responsibility for the actions that brought him to be incarcerated. If he is released, I am convinced he will go on to commit the same offense again.' " Jim looked up. "And they let him go anyway. Imagine."

"Imagine. So he came to the Park."

He looked at the rigid set of her spine and wisely offered no sympathy. "So it seems."

"I never heard a hint, even a whisper that he was bent. I had him out on the homestead. He worked for me."

"He worked for everybody."

"I know." She closed her eyes and shook her head. "I've got good instincts, Jim."

"The best in the business," he said. "Listen, Kate. We've all got our blind spots. Mr. Fix-it was yours."

"How much damage did he do here?"

Jim was too smart and too experienced to give the obvious answer. "Not much. It's hard to hide that kind of thing in a small community. If he'd married, say a woman with children from a previous relationship, and if one of those children had been a girl, then I'd be seriously worried. But he didn't." He thought. "He could have been that one guy who was moving himself out of the reach of temptation."

She rubbed at the scar on her neck. "You read the report. You saw what the officer said about Duffy's attitude. It's the classic Who, me? response of the sexual predator. And they don't learn, and they don't grow, and they don't ever, ever change, and they never, never stop."

"You would have heard," he said. "I would have heard. Billy, Auntie Vi, Bernie, someone would have heard."

"I sure as hell would have heard!" Bobby roared, causing them both to jump. His chair skidded to a halt and he glared impartially at both of them. Dinah, outlined against the gathering light outside the big windows in the creek-facing wall, came soft-footed up behind him and put a hand on his shoulder.

"Yeah," Jim said, "we all would have." He looked at Kate. "And none of us did. Maybe he was that guy, Kate."

"No," she said. She moved finally, to save and close the file and swing around to face them. "Who was his corrections officer?"

Jim rifled through the stack. "Melinda Davis. You know her?"

"No. You?"

"No. We can call in the morning, see if she has anything to add."

"No." Kate got to her feet.

"No?" With him sitting and her standing she actually had the advantage of height on him. Not much, but a little. It made him want to pull her into his lap.

"No," she repeated. "I'm going to Anchorage."

"I'm not going to Anchorage," Johnny said. "My mother's in Anchorage. What if we run into her? What if she calls the cops? I'm staying here with Auntie Vi. I've got school."

That last remark showed how truly desperate he was to stay in the Park. She said, and despised herself for doing so, "Some nut burned us out of our house. You want him to do the same thing to Auntie Vi?"

"Oh." He flushed. "No."

"Okay, then."

George rolled the Cessna out of the hangar and they were in Anchorage in an hour and a half, and on the doorstep of Jack's town house on Westchester Lagoon fifteen minutes after that.

Johnny hung back. "I haven't been back here since she sent me away to Arizona to live with Gran. Do you think it's okay?"

"I changed all the locks. And she lives on the other side of town. She'll never know we're here, Johnny." Unless I tell her, she thought.

"Still." He stopped just inside the doorway and looked around like he'd never seen the place before. "How come we're here, anyway? I figured it would be sold. She wouldn't let me come back here and take anything with me."

Kate should have known that, and she should have taken steps to see that Johnny got his belongings following his father's death. She would have, if she hadn't been off wandering in a grief-induced fog of her own at the time. "He left it to me," she said. "It's part of your college fund. I suppose I should rent it out instead of letting it sit empty, but he had mortgage insurance and it's free and clear, with enough left over for taxes." She shrugged. "I'll get around to it one of these days. Find a manager or something."

She was as uncomfortable as he was, which, perversely, made him relax a little. "My stuff still there?"

"Everything's just like it was." One of the reasons she was finding it hard to move inside.

He took the decision from her hands, pushed the door open, and ran upstairs to what had been his bedroom. "It's all here, Kate! My Nintendo and everything!"

"Good," she said.

"What?"

"I said that's good, Johnny." She closed the door behind her.

The next thing she knew she was standing outside the door of Jack's bedroom.

A cold nose thrust into her hand, and she looked down to see Mutt looking up at her. "Yeah," she said, and went back downstairs to drop her bag in the sparsely furnished guest room. The bed had about as much give to it as bedrock, but the relief she felt was palpable. "Okay, let's go," she told Mutt. In the hallway she yelled, "Okay, we're outta here!" and Johnny came clattering down the stairs.

She went through the connecting door to the garage, where sat Jack's Subaru Forester. Johnny brightened. "This mine, too?"

She smiled. "You bet. But for now, I drive."

"Aw, Kate, come on, I can drive. I've driven your truck."

Kate opened a door and Mutt leaped into the back seat. "Get in the car, Morgan."

He was still arguing with her as they were backing out of the driveway.

Gary Drussell hadn't been in the phone book but he was listed. He wasn't exactly friendly when she called, Kate noted, but he did give her his street address and directions on how to get there.

He lived in Muldoon, in back of the Totem Theaters. This was way too close to Jane, who lived across Muldoon off Patterson. Johnny said nothing, but Kate noticed he slid down in his seat until his eyes were barely at dashboard level. She quelled a craven impulse to do the same. She wasn't afraid of Jane, but she was afraid of losing Johnny, and she was terrified of letting Jack down.

The Drussells were living in one of the zero-lot line homes that had gone up like weeds in Anchorage during the oil boom of the early '80s, most of them built on filled-in wetlands. This last made for either a damp basement or an unstable foundation or both, but by the time this was discovered the developers had long since decamped to Maui or Miami with their profits and their trophy blondes, leaving homeowners with a choice: bail or bail. Many more than Anchorage lenders were comfortable admitting to had simply turned in their keys and walked away. The rest invested in small pumps and garden hoses, and during especially rainy Augusts you could go into any one of these neighborhoods and count by tens the green plastic lines snaking from downstairs' windows, emptying the water out of basements as fast as it seeped back in again. Ear, nose, and throat specialists reported a radical increase in upper respiratory complaints during such seasons, mostly from the mold and mildew that resulted.

It made Kate proud that the Park had no such thing as a Planning and Zoning Commission. Not that she had anything left to plan or zone.

Gary Drussell answered the front door before the recollection had time to plunge her into remembered gloom.

It was Saturday, with weak sunlight filtering through a broken cloud cover. His hair had darkened and his skin lightened since the last time she'd seen him. Instead of overalls covered in fish scales, he was dressed in sweats, dark blue with white piping, clean and neat. "Hi, Kate," he said, and stepped back. "Come on in."

"Hi, Gary. This is Johnny Morgan. Mutt okay in your yard?"

Gary cast a wry look at the street. "I think the question is, is the neighborhood okay with Mutt on the loose?"

"Stay," Kate told Mutt, who gave a disgruntled sigh and plunked her butt down on the wooden porch.

"Morgan, huh?" Gary said, leading the way through a cluttered living room. A girl lay sprawled on the couch in front of a blaring television, remote in hand. She looked up, and Kate felt Johnny pause. She didn't blame him; the girl was lovely, with a rich fall of dark hair, dark blue eyes, and new breasts pushing out the front of her cherry red T-shirt in a way no adolescent boy could ignore.

Gary led them into the kitchen without introducing them. He nodded at Johnny. "Any relation to Jack?"

"His son."

"Nice to meet you. I liked your father, few times I met him. Not a lot of bullshit going on there, for a cop."

"Thanks," Johnny said.

"Heard he was dead. Hell of a thing. Want some coffee?"

"Sure." Kate settled herself at the kitchen table, covered with a faded print cloth and a small Christmas cactus, which was for some inexplicable reason best known to itself blooming in May. The refrigerator was covered with snapshots and honey-do lists. The counters were crowded with a toaster and canisters and a knife block and a little brown clay bowl with feet for legs holding three heads of garlic, one of which had begun to sprout.

A cat wandered in and did the shoulder-dive thing against Gary's leg. He reached a hand down and gave its head an absentminded scratch. The resulting purr nearly drowned out the sound of the television.

"What's this about, Kate?" Gary said, offering her a can of evaporated milk.

She took it and poured with a lavish hand. "It's about Leon Duffy." She looked around to offer the milk to Johnny, but he seemed to have vanished. She heard a murmur of voices from the living room.

"Don't believe I've had the pleasure."

"You knew him as Len Dreyer."

"Oh. Of course. Len. Sure. Best hired hand I've ever had." Gary cocked an eyebrow. "What about him?"

"You may not have heard. He's dead."

He raised both eyebrows this time. "Really?"

His surprise seemed minimal. "Yeah. Someone took out most of his chest with a shotgun."

"That's gotta smart." Gary drank coffee. "A shame."

Kate couldn't help but note that Gary's regret seemed even less than his surprise. "Why's that?"

"Well." Gary shrugged. "Like I said, he was first-class when it came to hired help. Never bid what he couldn't deliver. Never said he could do what he couldn't. Always showed up on time. Usually finished on schedule and on budget. Your basic home improvement dream team of one." He looked at her, face guile-less. "Why are you taking to me about him, by the way?"

It was Kate's turn to shrug. "You're a name on a list of people who had Dreyer do work for them in the days preceding his death. What'd he hire on for, anyway?"

If she hadn't been watching him so closely, she wouldn't have seen the infinitesimal relaxation of his guard. She did see it, noted it, drank coffee, and smiled an invitation for him to con-tinue.

He did, relief making him a little more loquacious. "I was putting the house up for sale, and I wanted to spruce it up a little before I did. Get the best price out of it. You know."

She nodded.

He became more expansive. "We remodeled the bathroom, ripped up that old linoleum and replaced it, stripped the kitchen cabinets and refinished them. That kind of stuff."

"Sure," Kate said, nodding some more. "Makes sense. What made you decide to move to Anchorage, anyway? I thought the Park had its hooks in you permanent."

"So did I." He watched coffee swirl around the inside of his cup for a moment before raising his eyes. "I been fishing the Sound since I could walk the deck of a boat. I inherited Dad's permit when he died. I didn't think I'd ever be doing anything else." He sighed. "I swear, Kate, there's more fish going up the river today than I've ever seen in thirty years of fishing, and at the same time the commercial catch is the lowest it's ever been. What the hell is up with that?"

He already knew but Kate answered him anyway. "Used to be the commercial fishermen had it all their own way, Gary. Now you've got subsistence fishers and sport fishers wanting their share, too."

"And then the market went to hell, what with the RPetCo oil spill and the farmed fish coming out of British Columbia and now Chile." He was silent for a moment. "You hear they caught an Atlantic salmon out of Southeast?"

"No."

"Fact." He nodded once. "Absolute fact. Before you know it, the escapees from the B.C. fish farms are going to be interbreeding with wild Alaska salmon stock, and then what'll happen?"

"I don't know."

"I'll tell you. We lose what market we do have because who the hell wants to eat that dry, diseased fish the farms produce? Fresh fish, my ass. I'll tell you what else will happen, too—more guys like me, who used to fish for a living, will be forced to move into the goddamn city and find a goddamn indoor job where we have to wear a goddamn tie."

They brooded together for a moment over the demise of commercial fishing in Alaska. The television was a steady drone from the living room.

Kate stirred. "Turns out Len Dreyer wasn't his real name."

He looked at her.

"His real name was Leon Duffy." She sat up straight in her chair and took a deep breath. "Gary, there's no easy way to say this, so I'll just come straight out with it. Before he moved to the Park, Leon Duffy was arrested and jailed for molesting an eleven-year-old girl here in Anchorage."

He stared at her without speaking. She couldn't read his expression.

"He served five and a half years of an eight-year sentence. He got time off for good behavior. He disappeared off everyone's radar screen after he was released." She paused. "His next known whereabouts were the Park."

The silence stretched out between them. The television was staying on one channel for a change, although the music, if you could call it that, resembled something between a pig squealing and fingernails on the blackboard. Kate winced. The barely discernable backbeat sounded like it needed a defibrillator. Maybe Bobby was right, maybe there had been no rock and roll recorded worth listening to since the '70s.

Gary stirred and she looked up. "He was never alone with my girls," he said. "That's what you're asking me, right? If he molested my girls."

The dogged way he said it nearly broke her heart. "Gary—"

"He didn't. He was never alone with any of them. He worked with me. I was always with him. You get it? You see?"

"Yes," Kate said gently, "I see." She paused, and closed her eyes momentarily, gathering the strength together to ask the next question. "Gary, when was the last time you saw Len Dreyer?"

He gave a mirthless laugh and drained his mug. "The last time I saw Len Dreyer was the day we finished putting the hardware on the kitchen cabinets."

"Can you remember what day it was?"

"Nope. Sometime last May, just before we packed up and moved." He rose to his feet. "If that's all, I've got things to do."

"Knock it off!" she heard Johnny exclaim, and walked into the living room to see him on his feet, an inch from the door, and if she was not mistaken caught in the act of zipping up his jeans. His face was beet red and he couldn't meet her eyes.

"Okay," she said, "gotta go. Gary, thanks for the coffee."

His expression when he looked at his daughter, flushed, rumpled, and defiant, was half in sorrow, half in anger. "Anytime, Kate. Good to see you again. My best to Billy and Annie, and Old Sam, and Auntie Vi."

"I'll tell them."

Fran and the two older daughters drove up as Kate and Johnny left the house. There were all slim and dark-eyed, with the same shiny dark hair and the same inimical expression when Gary reminded them who Kate was. "Good to see you, Fran," Kate said.

"You, too, Kate," Fran said, white to the lips.

The family stood watching as they backed out of the driveway and headed down the street.

They were stopped at the Bragaw light before she broke the silence. "What was going on back there, Johnny?" She glanced over at him.

He had his face turned to the passenger side window. His voice was choked. "I don't want to talk about it."

The light changed, and Kate put the Subaru into gear. She

drove slowly, while she searched out the right words to say. "I respect your privacy, Johnny, but what happened back there might have something to do with Len Dreyer."

They were caught again at the Lake Otis light. She admired the raven-stealing-the-sun-moon-and-stars sculpture on the southwest corner of the intersection, the only decent piece of public art in the entire city. A real raven perched on top of a light pole and directed traffic with a series of boisterous clicks, croaks, and caws.

"She made a move on me," Johnny said at last, face still turned away.

"Yeah," Kate said. "Tell me about it."

"I don't want to."

"Tell me anyway. I mean it, Johnny, this is important."

Johnny had gone into the living room and introduced himself to Tracy who had made room for him on the couch. "At first she seemed really nice. She's a senior at Bartlett, and we even know some of the same people from when I went to middle school when I was staying with Mom, kids who are at Bartlett now." He fell silent.

"Then what?"

His voice was muffled. "Then she—then she—she kind of scootched over next to me, and the next thing I know she's kissing me. Well, I kissed her back!" He whipped around and glared at her.

"Okay," Kate said. "Then what happened?"

He looked away again. "She started touching me. I mean really touching me, Kate. God, her father was right in the next room. And you, too!" His voice scaled up with his indignation.

Kate drove a while in silence. Sexual promiscuity was a classic symptom of an abused child. At last she sighed. "Johnny, I think maybe she might have been molested."

"Well, that doesn't give her the right to molest me!"

"No, it doesn't."

"I don't ever want to see her again. If you have to go over there again, you go without me."

"Understood."

They went the rest of the way downtown in silence. Kate pulled into a reserved space in back of the building.

Johnny cleared his throat and said, "Won't we get a ticket?"

Kate laughed.

13

"Did you manage to scare up Duffy's arresting officer?"

Brendan was a big-bellied man with thinning red hair he didn't bother to coerce into a comb-over. Shrewd blue eyes looked out over a fleshy nose and a mouth that was always kicked up on one side in something between a sneer and a smile, kind of like Elvis, only with more charm. His suit was rumpled, his loosened tie stained with what might have been breakfast, and his enormous feet, crossed on the desk between them, were clad in a pair of waffle-soled, lace-up leather boots that looked suitable for climbing Denali, if they'd had any heel left to them.

By contrast, his office was neat to the point of making your teeth ache. This was an office that would not tolerate any document misfiled, any folder mislabeled, any filing cabinet overcrowded. There wasn't so much as a speck of dust on any horizontal surface, and Kate got the feeling that if Brendan had the temerity to track mud into the room that a broom and a mop would follow immediately on his heels. His pencils were razor sharp, none of his pens were out of ink, and his telephone sat at a precise angle from his computer, with the fax, printer, and PDA cradle lined up like soldiers next to it. "Got a new secretary, Brendan," Kate said, and it wasn't a question.

He nodded, his expression of woe belied by the look of relief Kate glimpsed in his eyes. "Yeah, Janice, you saw her on the way in. I live in fear. About the arresting officer."

Kate didn't like the expression on his face. "What?"

"Well, he's kind of not around."

"Define not around. Is he retired?"

"Sort of."

"Oh, hell. Is he dead?"

"Might as well be."

"Brandon."

He flapped a hand. "Okay, all right. He's at Highland Mountain."

Kate's brows knit. "You mean he's a corrections officer now?"

"No, I mean he's an inmate."

"Oh, please. Say you're joking."

"Nope. He got fired from the force a while back."

"What for?"

"Making dirty movies with underage victims recruited from his case files."

"Ick," Johnny said.

"You said it, kid," Brendan said. "Still, I don't think we would have nailed him if he hadn't been selling tapes off the Internet from his office computer." He looked at Kate. "You know how it is sometimes. He was on the job too long, in sex crimes too long. Damn few can take it for more than five, six years. The smart ones get out before it gets to them."

Kate rubbed her hands over her face. "Oh, crap. Not only have I got a body that's six months old, now I've got an unreported child abuse and a cop in jail. This case just keeps getting better and better."

Brendan sat up, his lips pursed together in a silent whistle. "Oh. Don't believe I'd heard that. Okay, that's makes for a horse of a different color. How may I help you, Kate?"

For a fat man, Brendan McCord sure moved quick, Johnny thought. Observing the tight, even expression on the big face across from him, of the leashed power and authority that the big body radiated, Johnny also thought it might be a good idea to get on and stay on Brandon's good side. Like, for life.

"Can I talk to the officer?"

"I already did, made a phone call this morning. He says the girl was fortunate in her choice of relatives."

"Oh yeah?"

"She was Harold Elwell Bannister's granddaughter. You never heard me say that, of course, the record is naturally sealed as she was a juvenile."

"Oh." Harold Elwell Bannister was an old-time Alaskan, a stampeder who had stayed on after the gold rush to found a chain of grocery stores and subsequently to guide the footsteps of first territorial and then state governors. The Bannisters were a wealthy and historic Alaskan family, and Kate doubted there was a cop or a prosecutor, or more importantly a judge, in the state who wouldn't have done their utmost to see that a crime against any relative of his did not go unavenged. "I see."

"Yeah. It wasn't like there was any doubt, though. There was semen residue, and they tested it for blood type. And there was an eyewitness who saw him make the snatch. She was out walking her dog. She was eighty-three and you know how dark it is winter mornings, but she ID'd him in a lineup. Girl was waiting for the school bus. Duffy had staked her out, and grabbed her up the one morning she was standing there alone."

"Did he admit that?"

"Not to staking her out, but the cop is pretty sure that's what happened. Still, the prosecutor had to fight for it, blood tests back then were pre-DNA, there was plenty of room for the defense to maneuver, and our eighty-three-year-old witness wore Coke-bottle glasses and failed to identify her own daughter in the courtroom."

"But Duffy was found guilty anyway."

Brendan shrugged and grinned. "The judge was a regular guest at Einar Bannister's duck shack out on the Beluga flats every September."

"Collusion," Kate said. "Conspiracy. Also," she added, "justice."

Brendan sobered. "As close to it as the girl was going to get, I reckon." He smiled, and Johnny felt a chill run up his spine. "Myself, I'm of the opinion that castration without benefit of anesthesia, followed by hanging, drawing, and quartering at high noon in the town square, televised live on all local stations with viewing made mandatory by all citizens either live or in living color, would be a more effective deterrent."

Kate thought of Gary Drussell's youngest daughter putting the moves on a boy she had met for the first time half an hour before, and said, "Sounds about right to me."

Johnny's eyes went wide. "Jeeze, you guys."

"Sorry, kid," Brendan said, but the smile didn't reach his eyes.

"Thanks, Brendan," Kate said. "I appreciate you coming in on your day off to help."

"I have no days off. My pleasure." He found a leer somewhere and produced it to effect. "Your tab's piling up, Shugak."

She batted her eyelashes. "I can hardly wait until the bill comes due, McCord."

"Really," said a dry voice from the doorway.

They turned and Jim Chopin was standing there.

They all wound up at the Lucky Wishbone for a late lunch. Jim was jealous of Kate's easy camaraderie with Brendan, trying like hell not to show it, and not succeeding very well. Brendan was hugely enjoying the resulting spectacle and losing no opportunity to flirt with Kate by word, glance, and touch.

Kate was doing her best to ignore them both, which wasn't easy, because the only other person there to talk to was Johnny, and Johnny wasn't speaking to any of them because before Kate had left Brendan's office, she had called his mother and set up a meeting for later that afternoon. He'd stared at her, speechless in betrayal, and had refused to listen to any explanation she had tried to give between Third and L and Fifth and Karluk. She'd given up, finally, saying the one thing she'd never expected to hear out of her own mouth: "I'm older than you are, I'm smarter than you are, and I'm tougher than you are. You're going to have to trust me that this is the right thing to do."

They were pulling into the parking lot as she spoke, and his eyes grew to the size of saucers. "Look! Look at that!"

"What?" She looked where he was pointing with an accusing finger.

"There're cops all over the place!"

Three blue-and-whites were parked in front of the row of windows that separated booths from the parking lot. "So cops like fried chicken. That a problem for you?"

He'd slammed out of the Subaru without replying and stamped over to where Brendan and Jim were waiting. He'd made his displeasure known in a few curt sentences and been further outraged by Brandon saying, "Better to get it over with, kid," and Jim saying, "He's right, Johnny." So he sat in a corner of the booth, face like a thundercloud, studiously ignoring the gang of men in black and badges sitting in the next booth and shoveling in fried chicken and French fries in a mechanical manner that wrung the heart of Heidi, their ebullient, redheaded server. She kept topping up his Coke and adding to his fries with a hopeful smile, which he ignored until Jim pulled his cap off and smacked Johnny with it. Even then all Heidi got was a stiff nod of the head and a gruff "thanks." Kate longed to send him out to wait in the Subaru, but she was restrained by the fear that he would take off, and by the knowledge that his anger was caused by fear.

Brendan burped and patted his belly, of a size that barely fit between booth and table. "That was great." He smiled at Heidi as she came to the table, and repeated the remark. She beamed at him and topped off his coffee and put a little extra into the process of walking away, which Brendan greatly appreciated and which Kate was sure added substantially to her tip. "I gotta go, I gotta girl waiting on me," he said. "Kate, always a pleasure. Jim, likewise. Kid? Get that lower lip of yours off the floor, you're in good hands that I don't see letting go of you any time soon."

With a genial wave, he was off. "I flew in a perp," Jim said. "Brendan told me he'd be in so I figured I'd drop off the file in person."

"Did I ask?" Kate said.

It made him nervous that the question wasn't pugnacious. In fact, she was smiling, which made him even more nervous. Things had been so relaxed between them the night before, there was no reason for him to be nervous now. But he was. Dinah's voice kept coming back to him. *What do you want with her?* He'd never asked himself that question; it seemed obvious to him what he wanted. He'd never thought about what happened after he got what he wanted.

He was thinking about it now. He cleared his throat. "So you're going to meet with Jane."

"Yes."

"Want me along?"

"I appreciate the offer," Kate said, "but let's not make her any more insane than she is already by showing up with a trooper in tow."

"If you need me . . ."

"I'll yell for help."

That was so out of character that he stumbled getting out of the booth. It didn't help that she caught his arm and helped him regain his balance. "Are you in town overnight?"

She nodded. "Yeah."

"Got a ride home?"

"George."

"Oh. Ah. Well. I'm in overnight, too. I'm picking up the autopsy report on Duffy in the morning." His eyes searched the heavens for inspiration. "You could cancel George, ride with me. Save yourself some money."

"I was planning on billing the state for the trip," she said.

"Oh. Right. Sure. Of course. You're here on the Duffy case. So I'll see you back at—"

"But, okay."

"Sorry?"

She thoroughly enjoyed his moment of blank incomprehension. She wasn't sure she, or anyone else for that matter, had seen Jim Chopin unsure of how to act around a woman. It gave her, she admitted, if only to herself, a feeling of power. Not to mention satisfaction. Jim Chopin, the father of the Park, the cause of many a feminine flutter of heart, at her beck and call. She decided to push it, just a little. As her grandmother would have said, if you had power and didn't use it, then you'd be giving it away to someone else, and they surely would. Kate didn't like the idea of giving away any power she had over Jim Chopin. He'd bedeviled her long enough, he with the too-knowing eyes and the predatory grin. And the unquestioning comfort of his embrace, and the quick understanding of her loss, and—well. It was time and more than time for some payback. "Okay, we'll ride home with you. Save the state some money."

"Oh. Okay. Sure. Fine. Um, say around ten?"

"Plane at the trooper hangar at Lake Hood?"

He nodded.

"See you there."

"Okay. Ten. Tomorrow. Right, see you then."

She smiled.

He turned and blundered out of the door. His palms hadn't been that sweaty since he was seventeen and asked Beverly Dobbyn to the prom.

Kate watched him run into the door frame, apologize to it, walk into a man on his way inside, apologize to him, and trip over the edge of the sidewalk.

Sometimes it was just too easy.

Kate had arranged to meet Jane at another restaurant, hoping that everyone would be less inclined toward making a scene in a public place. She'd picked Denny's on Northern Lights. She'd never been there and it had a large and rapid customer turnover, which meant that the odds were good she wouldn't see anyone she knew and that if she did see them, they wouldn't be there for long. There were in addition two ways out of the parking lot if it so happened that she needed them. She circled the block twice but saw no evidence of massive SWAT team deployment. Maybe Jane hadn't called the cops. She parked in the space closest to the driveway leading onto Denali Street. If they had to make a getaway and they made it as far as the car, she could duck across Denali into the Sears Mall parking lot, do a little bobbing and weaving, jump across Northern Lights onto a side street, hit Fireweed and grab the New Seward north. Of course, that wouldn't help if they went back to Jack's town house, where everyone in the law enforcement community knew he had lived, and it wasn't like there were more than two roads out of town anyway. "Hot pursuit" didn't have quite the same ring to it in Alaska as it did elsewhere.

At this point she pulled herself together and gave herself a mental scolding. There would be no question of hot pursuit because there would be no need to escape. She and Jane and Johnny were going to sit down and discuss the situation like two civilized adults and one marginally civilized adolescent. She closed her eyes to Mutt's pleading expression, locked her into the Subaru, and followed Johnny into the restaurant.

"You *bitch*," Jane hissed as Kate sat down opposite her.

"I'm out of here," Johnny said.

"Like hell you are," Kate said, grabbing his arm and forcing him into the seat next to her.

"You stole my son!"

It was a light between-lunch-and-dinner crowd but heads were turning in their direction. "Please keep your voice down, Jane," Kate said.

"Or what? You'll call the cops? Here's a thought. Let's call the cops!"

Jane was a tall, slim woman with white blond hair, skin color that was almost albino, and dark blue eyes with the lids weighted down with thick eyeliner and thicker mascara. She was dressed in blazer, slacks, and a soft white roll-neck sweater. She looked like she'd just stepped out of Nordstrom. Kate, remembering the inside of Jane's closet, thought it was a good chance that she had. "Okay, Jane, let's call the cops," she said.

"What!" Johnny said.

"Why not?" Kate said, holding Jane's angry gaze. "They'll come. You'll accuse me of kidnapping. Johnny will accuse you of abuse. You'll tell your story, he'll tell his story, I'll tell my story, and after a while we'll all wind up in front of a judge. Until we do, Johnny'll probably be stuck into some foster care home with people he doesn't know and other fostered kids who have already graduated from B&E 101 and are ready to move on to bigger and better things. Johnny'll find it educational."

"At least they'll put you in jail where you belong!"

The waitress, a woman in her seventies with bright eyes buried in a sea of wrinkles and a wisp of gray hair confined neatly beneath a cap, said brightly, "Take your order, please?"

"Coffee all around," Kate said with a smile, "thanks."

"You bet, sweetie." Granny moved on to the next table.

Kate considered Jane's last remark with a judicial impartiality that wasn't wholly assumed. "No," she said at last, giving her head a shake, "I don't think they'll put me in jail, Jane. For one thing, I was a part of the law enforcement community in Anchorage for five and a half years. If they don't know me, they've heard of me. No, I don't think I'll be put in jail."

"You're a kidnapper." Jane smiled. It wasn't a pleasant smile, and her voice dropped to an even less pleasant purr. "And who knows what else you've been doing to him, stuck on that homestead out in the middle of nowhere." She ignored Johnny's gasp. "An older woman, a young boy. It's not like it hasn't happened before."

Johnny went white to the lips. "You wouldn't," he said with difficulty. "You—you *couldn't.*"

Jane had yet even to look at her son. She was watching Kate like a cat watched a mouse.

Kate displayed neither shock nor anger. She'd been expecting this, or something like it. Her only surprise was that Jane had waited this long. "When you look back on this later, I want you to remember that you started this," she told Jane. She looked at Johnny. "Johnny, I'm going to say some stuff about your mother you might not like to hear. You want to go out and keep Mutt company?"

"You've got that goddamn wolf with you?" Jane's voice scaled up with indignation.

This time all heads turned their way. Kate waited until everyone went back to their own business. "Johnny?"

"No." His jaw came out and he folded his arms. "I'll hear it all."

"Okay." She looked back at Jane, whose eyes were sparkling with malice. "People who live in glass houses shouldn't throw stones."

The smirk didn't lessen. "I don't know what the hell you're talking about." She pulled a cell phone from her purse. "I'm calling 911."

Kate waited until Jane had completed the dialing sequence. In an almost lazy voice she said, "How's the bidding process for capital projects for the federal government going in the state?"

Jane's hand froze in the act of raising the phone to her ear. She stared at Kate.

"I've always thought the blind bid process was a good one," Kate said, still in that lazy, disinterested voice. "Fair, or at least as fair as it can be, human nature being what it is. Gives all the contractors a level playing field. They all want a slice of the big fat government pie, which means they work at keeping their bids low in hopes that they'll get the winning bid on the new courthouse in Bering or the new jail in Newenham or upgrading the airport in Niniltna."

Jane didn't move.

"It would, of course, entirely subvert the blind bid process if one of the contractors knew in advance what their competition was bidding on the same project they were bidding on." She paused, and added, "Not that it hasn't been known to happen."

She shook her head, and smiled sadly. "Human nature being what it is."

An increasingly irritated voice was coming out of Jane's phone. "I'm sorry," she said jerkily into it. "I misdialed." She hung up and put the phone back in her bag. Her face, Kate noted with interest, was even whiter than usual.

"If you were that one, bent contractor, you'd need someone on the inside of the bid process, someone who had access to the bid file and the ability to sign them or smuggle them out of the building. Someone with a long record of stellar service in the bureaucracy, someone absolutely trustworthy. Hard to find, because believe it or not I've found most government employees to be dedicated, hard-working, and professional." She paused, and added, "Not that it hasn't been known to happen. Human nature being what it is, and all."

It had been a very long time since anyone had looked at Kate with that kind of malevolence. Kate was almost enjoying it. "The government worker would need a copy machine to copy the relevant documents for those bidders who might want an advance peek before they put their bids in," she said thoughtfully. "Pretty expensive item, a copy machine."

Something in the quality of the silence that followed this remark made the hair prickle on the back of Johnny's neck. His mother's eyes had narrowed into dark slits and her lips had thinned into a single, straight line. If they opened, he wasn't altogether sure that a forked tongue might not flicker out.

In contrast, Kate's expression was amiable, even benevolent. She looked, Johnny thought suddenly, a little like he'd seen Old Sam Dementieff look when Old Sam was bluffing Alexei Grutoff and Earnie Swenson out of a cutthroat pinochle bid. Patient, resolute, and very, very Aleut.

Granny bustled up with coffee. "There you are, dears. Anything else? No? You wave me down if you think of anything." She beamed at them.

"You," Jane breathed as Granny bustled off again. "It was you who broke into my house that time."

Kate waved a dismissing hand. "But really, a decent copy machine would be a legitimate operating expense, seeing as how government copy machines need access codes to operate, which makes it easy to track who's copying what."

Johnny, without knowing why or how it had happened, recognized in a dim way that the balance of power had shifted, and began to breathe again. Everything was going to be all right.

At that point Jane's language deteriorated. The only good news was that she was keeping her voice down. Johnny listened with strict attention. The next time Lyle Paine put Van's Carhartts down, Johnny was going to melt down his eardrums.

Eventually even Jane ran out of new and interesting ways to describe Kate's relationship with her ancestors and had to fall back on the tried and true. "You fucking bitch," she whispered, the words coming out in a long hiss. "Do you know how long it took for me to get my credit straightened out? And all that stuff you ordered on my Visa card! And the money you took out of my bank account! You're nothing more than a common thief!"

At that Kate did wince. "Surely not common," she said.

Johnny almost laughed.

"I won't pay you a dime in child support," Jane said.

Johnny wanted to shout in triumph. He felt a warning kick beneath the table and swallowed it.

"No one's asking you to," Kate replied evenly.

Jane turned on Johnny. "I won't pay for you to go to college, either."

He met his mother's eyes with a flinty composure that surprised and pleased Kate. "Dad had a college fund set aside for me. Don't worry, I'm not asking you for a dime."

"We're heading back to the Park tomorrow," Kate said. "If you like, Johnny could write a few times a year, letting you know how he's getting on."

"Like hell I could," Johnny said, feeling his oats.

"I don't care if I never hear from the ungrateful little bastard ever again," Jane said. Seriously stung, she was eager to hurt back.

Johnny, now that he knew he was safe, tried to imitate Kate's composure. "If I had anything to be grateful for, I'd be hurt by that remark," he said.

"Okay," Kate said, getting to her feet before the blood on the table was more real than imagined. "We're done here. Good-bye, Jane."

She hustled the boy out of the restaurant and into the Subaru, and they were out of the parking lot and speeding down Northern Lights Boulevard before she realized she'd stuck Jane with the bill.

Johnny would never know how relieved she had been that it had not been necessary to reveal what else she had found in that burglary of Jane's house. There were some things a son should not know about his mother.

"Home tomorrow," she said out loud, and felt good about it for the first time since the cabin burned down.

After Johnny had gone to bed and Kate was alone in the living room, *Terminator* playing on Jack's VCR, she muted the television, picked up the phone, and dialed a number from memory, keeping mental fingers crossed. When a woman answered, she breathed a sigh of relief. "Fran, it's Kate Shugak. Please don't hang up, and please don't let Gary know it's me."

There was a long silence, but no click and no dial tone. Background noise included voices and the inevitable television. Kate said, "If you can, get to a paper and pencil." There was another long silence, followed by scrabbling sounds. "I know a counselor who works with kids who have been sexually abused. Her name's Colleen Diemer." She recited the number once, waited, and repeated it. "She's very good. If you and Gary need to talk, she can refer you to someone who counsels adults. But whether you two do or not, get your daughter to her, or to someone like her." She paused, and continued with difficulty. "There are things she just can't say to you or to Gary. Things that need to be said. Colleen Diemer. Her office is in one of the medical buildings on Lake Otis, just north of Tudor. Her staff is really good about working out payment. There are all kinds of state and federal programs to subsidize the fees."

Fran said nothing.

Kate took a deep breath and let it out, slowly. "Colleen is very trustworthy, Fran. She'll understand about Gary. She won't call the house, she won't send you a bill there."

"Who's that, honey?" Gary's voice said in the background.

"No, thank you," Fran said, "we're happy with our long distance service as it is. Good-bye."

There might have been a whisper of a "thank you" as Kate hung up the phone, but it might also have been her imagination. She went back to *Terminator,* which was a positive haven of peace and nonviolence compared to some of the homes she'd been into on the job.

She only hoped she had not visited one of them this afternoon.

14

Dandy was still torqued at what he saw as Jim Chopin's patronizing dismissal of Dandy's services. He was so torqued that he had slept alone the night before in spite of overtures on the parts of two different women.

His bed was located in the apartment he'd fitted up over the warehouse that sat on the five acres of land he'd received as a result of the Alaska Native Claims Settlement Act of 1972 back when he was all of nine years old. The five acres sat on the river, and his father had built the warehouse as a place to park his fishing boat during the winter. Dandy's apartment had started life as a net loft, but then the Native Association had begun paying dividends and Billy had started paying someone else to mend his gear, and Dandy had asked for the space. Billy shrugged. It was Dandy's land, after all.

Dandy hadn't done much beyond installing a bathroom and enough of a kitchen to allow his girlfriends to cook for him. The floor was hardwood with a couple of thick sheepskins scattered around for effect. A king-sized bed dominated one corner, with nightstands on either side with drawers big enough to accommodate condoms in bargain-size boxes and a weekend's worth of clean clothes for sleepovers. In another corner there was a wide, long brown leather couch next to a Barcalounger, which sat in front of a 32-inch television. There was also a combination VHS/DVD player, and a set of shelves with an extensive selection of movies, most of them starring Meg Ryan and Tom Hanks. Dandy didn't bother with satellite television, as he wasn't into any sport you couldn't play from a horizontal position and everything else was blood and gore. Women didn't like blood and gore, as a rule. Dandy was willing to watch anything that got women into the mood, and he was continually expanding his movie library with that end in view. Audrey Hepburn was a recent discovery. The scene with Peter O'Toole under the museum stairs in *How to Steal a Million* had in recent testing proven itself to be fail-safe. He was hoping it would come out on DVD before his VHS copy was completely worn through.

Hands behind his head, he frowned at the ceiling. He was still annoyed with Jim for blowing off his efforts in the Len Dreyer case, but he was willing to forgive him because he knew what it was like to be led around by his cock, and he sympathized.

He was more annoyed with Kate, and he couldn't decide if it was because she was the one leading Jim around, or if it was because she'd never tried to lead him, Dandy, around.

Easily sidetracked, he wondered about that. It wasn't like Kate was a nun, she'd had her share. There was Ethan Int-Hout, and that doofus Anchorage investigator with more and blonder hair than Farrah Fawcett, and then there was Jack Morgan. The Kate-and-Jack thing went way back. Jeeze, Jack had been an okay guy, but sticking to one partner for, well, hell, he guessed it had been years. Years, for crissake. Dandy's mind boggled. A real man wanted a little variety in his life. Sleeping with the same woman for years, *years*, that wasn't variety, that was monotony, that was boredom. Dandy loved undressing a woman for the first time, loved the small discoveries that came with the act, the placement of a mole, the bony knees, the pillowy thighs. He loved finding out that a natural blonde wasn't. Was she or wasn't she? Only Dandy and her hairdresser knew for sure.

The trouble was, you could only undress a woman for the first time once. Fortunately, there were many, many women out there, and equally fortunately, many of them were happy to take a month's romp at face value. Dandy Mike scorned to break hearts; he wanted whatever woman was in his life to have as good a time as he was, until it was time for both of them to move on. He prided himself that they almost always did. Oh, he'd had his failures, including one horrific experience when the girl of the month introduced herself to his mother and asked for help in planning the wedding, but on the whole he was fairly pleased with life in general. He attended the marriages of his classmates and friends with a smiling face, but privately he couldn't imagine why any sane man would feel it necessary to settle on just one woman. It wasn't natural, he thought, and just look at nature, while we're on the subject. Why, he was reading an article just the other day, all about how new DNA studies were showing biologists that geese weren't as monogamous as had been previously thought. The male of every species was designed to spread his seed as far and wide as possible. It strengthened the gene pool, insured the survival of the species. Dandy hadn't finished college, but even he knew that.

Not that Dandy ever wanted to have children. He shuddered at the thought. He didn't know how Bobby and Dinah were going to manage, always supposing for some unfathomable reason they still wanted to sleep together at all, in that big open house with a rug rat crawling all over it.

Nope, no question about it, old Jack must have been half a bubble off, as they said in the contracting business.

Where had he heard that saying? Oh, yeah. Len Dreyer. On the deck of the *Freya* last September.

Which reminded him of his grievance. Kate had old Chopper Jim on the hook, no doubt about that, she was just waiting until it was good and set before reeling it in. Thought she had the job landed at the same time, probably.

No two ways about it, Dandy was going to have to solve this Dreyer thing on his own just to get Jim's attention. Once he had it, why, Jim would just naturally see what an asset Dandy would be to the local constabulary. And hopefully Dandy would never have to work this hard again.

The information he'd collected from his ex-girlfriends hadn't made much of an impression. His face screwed up in thought. Well. He'd done a lot of jobs with Dreyer. Maybe he could put together the list of names he'd scrounged from his girlfriends, and maybe put in dates when he'd worked with Dreyer. Then maybe he could go talk to the people who had employed the two of them. They'd call that something on television—constructing a timeline, that was it. He'd construct a timeline for old Len Dreyer, was what he'd do, charting all old Len's activities leading up until the day he died. Dandy didn't know what day Len had died, but he dismissed that as a minor problem.

He swung out of bed, refreshed, and took a quick shower. He was scrambling some eggs when there was a knock at his door. He opened it to find Stacy Shumagin on his doorstep.

Well, shoot. Len Dreyer was dead, wasn't he? He could wait.

The white Cessna with the gold shield on the side touched down neatly in a perfect three-point landing. It rolled to a halt in front of George Perry's hangar, who waited for the prop to stop turning before ambling over to open the door. "Hey, Kate." He looked across Kate at Jim. "Hey, Chopin. Taking business away from me, taking the food out of the mouths of my children."

Since George had no children, this was taken for the jest it was.

"Hey, George," Johnny piped up.

"Hey, squirt. How was Anchorage?"

"Educational," Johnny said promptly, without the trace of a smile.

Kate grinned. "Think I can get out of this flying tin can, Perry?"

George stepped back and she hopped out. "Well. From the expression on your faces I'd say it was a successful trip. So, who did kill Len Dreyer?"

Jim paused, one foot in the plane, one foot on the ground. "Oh, shit." And it had been such a nice ride home.

Kate turned to him. "That's right, you said you were picking up the autopsy report."

He frowned at her. "Not in front of the civilians."

"You people are just no fun at all," George said, and ambled back into the hangar, where his Super Cub could be seen, cowling peeled back and engine exposed. Even from where they were standing, it gleamed with the care George lavished upon it.

The airstrip was dark with overnight rain, but not enough to be muddy. A low, thin layer of cotton-puff clouds was dissolving beneath the noon sun. There was a flash of white in the brush across the strip and Mutt gave a joyous bark and shot off in pursuit. Johnny gave a sigh of pure joy and headed for the post office. They'd only been gone overnight, and on a weekend at that, but like every other Bush dweller Johnny lived for the mail, and he had new clothes coming. If there was a package slip he could always go round to Mrs. Jeppsen's house in back of the post office and talk her into opening up long enough to get it for him.

"So?" Kate said to Jim.

"ME says Dreyer's been dead about six months, give or take three in either direction. She's going to do some more tests, but that's her best guess and she's thinking her final one. She says the deep-freeze effect delayed rigor and lividity and she doesn't know if he was sitting, standing, or lying down when he caught it. Death resulted from massive trauma caused by a direct hit from a shotgun. From the stippling, she thinks the perp was less than four feet away."

"Did you have a chance to talk to ballistics?"

"From the pattern, they think it might be one of the older models, maybe a Remington, maybe a Winchester, maybe old enough to be one of the discontinued models."

"That might help. Might be fewer of them around."

He shrugged. "You're dreaming and we both know it. Who in the Park doesn't have an old shotgun his father left him?"

"Me," Kate said.

"Oh. Right. Forgot. Sorry."

"Yeah, well." Her turn to shrug. "So nothing we didn't know before, or not much."

"Nope."

"Mind if I say this totally sucks?"

"Nope." The sun broke through the clouds and he watched her lift her face into it and close her eyes. He wondered what she would look like naked in the sun, if she would turn her whole body into the light and warmth the way she did her face. He wanted to find out. He did most sincerely want to find out, preferably before his need robbed him of independent mobility. He cleared his throat. "Rein in that hairy Bigfoot of yours and we'll drop her and the kid at Auntie Vi's and go see if the café is open. Talk it out over coffee."

She had been about to suggest Auntie Vi's, but Auntie Vi would insist on sitting in on the deliberations. "I keep forgetting there's a café now. A café in Niniltna. What's next, a Wal-Mart?"

"Bite your tongue."

She loitered deliberately until he had driven off. Before she whistled up Johnny and Mutt, she walked over to the hangar. "Looking good, George," she said, circumnavigating the Super Cub.

He didn't preen, but it was close. "Thanks."

"Nice to see a well-maintained aircraft. Gives you faith in the airline, and the man who flies it."

His head came up like an animal scenting a predator. "Gee, thanks, Kate. Nice of you to say." He turned his head and looked at her. "Was there something else?"

"You used to hang with Gary Drussell, didn't you? Do some hunting together every year?"

A brief pause. "Sure. What of it?"

"I was wondering," she said in a casual tone that fooled nobody. "When was the last time you saw him?"

"Last time I saw Gary?" he said thoughtfully, wiping down an open-end box wrench that didn't need it.

"Yeah." She waited.

"Gosh, I'm not sure, Kate." Minute attention was paid to the wrench. "I guess when he moved out last summer. Actually, I guess it was closer to spring, right after breakup."

"Really," Kate said.

The face he presented to her was wide-eyed. "Yeah, right around breakup, I figure."

"Long time," Kate said. "He didn't even come back to go hunting in the fall?"

"Nope." George hunched over the engine. "Hell of a thing, what moving to Anchorage will do to your priorities."

"Yeah, hell of a thing," Kate said.

The café was still enough of a novelty to be crowded at noon on Sunday, although Laurel Meganack behind the counter was all by herself enough of a draw for most Park rats. Jeffrey Clark sat alone in a corner, scrupulously polite to Laurel, ignoring everyone else. Jim jerked his head. "What's with Lord High Everything Else?"

Kate laughed. Jeffrey Clark's eyes snapped up and narrowed suspiciously. He was sure they were laughing at him, mostly because he didn't see anything else they could be laughing about.

There were two stools available at the end of the counter. Kate copped the one against the wall and leaned against it so she could face Jim. He ordered their coffee and turned his back on the rest of the room so as to face her. It gave them the illusion of privacy. "I can't wait till the post gets built," he said.

She smiled faintly. "Make it easier on the interviews."

"No kidding." The coffee came. "Talk."

She doctored her mug liberally with sugar and evaporated milk, which an intelligent Laurel ordered in by the case and for a serving of which she added fifty cents onto the price. "Okay," she said, sitting back. "Some of this will be new to you."

He raised an eyebrow. "Talk, Shugak."

She told him about Enid Koslowski.

He whistled. "Bernie caught them in the act?"

"Yes."

"There's motive for murder enough right there."

She was silent.

"What else?" he said.

She looked over his shoulder at Laurel, carrying five plates in two hands to a table where Old Sam and four of his cronies were waiting. "Seems Bernie and Len both shared the favors of Miss Meganack, here."

"No kidding?" He hung his chin on his shoulder for a moment. "Can't say as I blame them." He looked back at her and noticed no trace of jealousy. That could be either a good thing or a bad thing. "Did she dump one for the other?"

"She says not. She says she was overcome by Len's tool belt, it was a one-time thing on the floor of the kitchen when he was doing some fix-up stuff for her before the café opened. She was surprised when he didn't try to turn it into more."

"So am I."

"I'm not," she said, "but I'll get to that in a minute."

"Take your time, I'm still on the kitchen floor."

"Yeah, yeah," she said without heat. "Enid says it was pretty much the same for her."

"Enid made the first move?"

"Yeah."

"Seems a little out of character."

"It is. It was when Bernie was sleeping with Laurel. Enid found out."

"Ah," he said, understanding. "A revenge fuck."

"Two of them, to be exact."

"The second one being when Bernie walked in."

"She seduced Dreyer aka Duffy in one of the cabins. I'm just going to call him Dreyer if you don't mind," she added. "Main reason I hate aliases, just gets too damn confusing."

He considered. "Enid wanted Bernie to catch them at it. Catch her at it."

"Yeah."

"Nice little quadrangle, if that's the right word. Bernie sleeps with Laurel, Enid finds out and sleeps with Dreyer, Dreyer sleeps with Laurel." He straightened. "Wait a minute. How serious was Bernie about Laurel?"

"Not enough to leave Enid," Kate said sharply. "And not enough to kill Dreyer, either, even if he knew about Dreyer and Laurel. Which he probably didn't."

"Enid can talk," Jim said.

"I know. But I don't think she did about this. The less conversation she had with Bernie about Laurel, the better."

Jim wasn't slow. "He didn't care, did he?"

"Who?"

"Bernie. He didn't care when he caught Enid with Dreyer." She said nothing.

"Ouch," he said. "That had to sting."

"Not enough to murder."

He gave her a thoughtful look, and left it alone for now. "What else?" She met his eyes and he said, "Come on, Kate. You're holding out on me. You found something out in Anchorage. What?"

Laurel came over and topped off their mugs. Kate barely registered on her peripheral vision, but she gave Jim a wide, warm, one might even say inviting smile, and underlined it by putting a little extra into the sway of her hips as she walked away. Waitresses. He watched her go with pure male appreciation. When he turned back he found Kate looking at him, one eyebrow raised. "Don't change the subject," he said firmly.

She thought about it, but he was right. She took a deep breath. "Remember Gary Drussell?"

He frowned. "Can't say as I do."

"He was a fisherman out of Cordova. Had a homestead about ten miles out of Niniltna. Married. Three daughters."

About to drink, Jim put his mug down heavily.

"Gary'd had one lousy season after another, going on ten years now. Commercial fishing in Alaska isn't what it once was. The two oldest daughters were college age or about to be. He decided to sell out, move to Anchorage, and go back to school, learn a new trade. So he put his homestead up for sale. And of course, like every other homestead staked out a hundred years ago, it needed work."

"And he hired Len Dreyer to do it."

"Yes."

"Which daughter?"

"The youngest. I think. Nobody admitted anything. But I'm pretty sure." Kate shook her head. "I don't know, the vibes I got from the mom and the other two daughters . . . well, they were pretty intense. Dreyer might have given them a pass because they were too old, but I'd bet money the youngest girl's been talking. Gary himself is in total denial."

With studied casualness, Jim said, "Did you ask him the last time he was in the Park?"

Kate remained silent.

Couldn't, he thought. Couldn't bring herself to open that wound any wider. "Does Gary fly?"

"I don't think so, but I don't know for sure." The quickness of her answer told him she'd given it some thought.

"I'll check for a license. In the meantime, you ask George if he remembers ferrying Drussell in or out last fall."

She muttered assent.

"Has to be done, Kate. No matter how much it's starting to look like justifiable homicide."

"I know. I know. I just . . . I know."

"Yeah," he said. "Me, too."

They were sitting in glum silence when Kate looked up to see Jeffrey Clark standing at Jim's shoulder. "I talk to you?" he said.

She was almost glad to see him. "Sure," she said.

He jerked his head. "Not here."

She followed him outside.

He pulled the collar of his jacket together. "I want my brother to come home with me."

"You've made that pretty clear," she said.

"He won't come."

"Like I said before," Kate said, displaying for her a remarkable amount of patience, "that's pretty much his decision to make."

He spoke with a kind of dogged persistence that she had to admire. "I want you to help me to convince him that it's the right thing for him to do."

Kate did sigh this time. She hated having to repeat herself. "First of all, Bobby is a grown man. He's kind of already got his pass/fail in Living 101. Second, he's my best friend, and the surest way I know to screw that up is to start telling him how to live his life. Third? I don't know that his going home is the right thing to do."

He glared at her. "Our father is dying."

"I know the story," she said, holding up a hand to stem the tide. "Spare me the lecture. Tell me something. Why do you really want Bobby to go home again?" Again, she held up a hand. "No. I want the real reason. From anything Bobby's told me, your father has been pretty hard-nosed all his life, with fixed notions about right and wrong. Bobby screwed up and your father didn't just turn his back on him, he condemned him out of hand at Sunday-go-to-meeting in front of all your neighbors and friends. You were there, weren't you? You saw and heard it?"

He looked away, face set in stubborn lines. "Yes."

"Well, then."

"He has to forgive him."

"Why?"

"Because my father's not dying easy," Jeffrey said heavily. "I've been calling home every day. He's calling for Robert. It's all he can think about. He wants him to come home. He needs him to come home."

She examined him long enough for him to begin to look un-comfortable. He might even have squirmed.

"What?" he said, defensive now.

"That's the first time I've heard you sound like a human being, with all our faults and frailties," she said.

He stiffened.

"Oh, lose the attitude," she said, exasperated. "Swear to Christ, if I didn't believe my own eyes I wouldn't think you were in any way related to Bobby."

Taken aback, he said, "I beg your pardon?"

"So Bobby married a white woman," she said, "so what? So he's best buds with a Native woman, and he's friendly with more, and a bunch of white folks besides. I don't know that you've noticed, Jeffrey, but this ain't Tennessee. It's a lot bigger, and with way fewer people. It gives us a lot of freedom and a lot of autonomy, and at the same time draws us closer together, no matter who we are or where we come from."

She paused for breath, and went on in a milder tone. "The Park has a way of weeding out the unfit. Bobby fits. He always has. Because it's not what you're used to doesn't make it not his home. Okay," she added, "I know there's like a triple negative in there somewhere, but you've been here what, a week now? You've had time to see that — well, hell." She turned to go back inside. Over her shoulder she said, "Bobby's found a place he loves that loves him back. Near as I can make out, he's been looking for that place ever since your father booted him out."

"He didn't boot him out! Robert ran away!"

She thought of Johnny. "In this case, Jeffrey, I don't see the difference."

"Everything okay?" Jim said as she slid back onto her stool.

"No," she said.

"You think Bobby should go home?"

She curved her hand around a now cool mug. "I keep thinking about Emaa," she said.

"Your grandmother?"

"Yeah. I was angry at her for a long time. We were just starting to work things out when she died. I have some regrets."

" 'Remorse is the ultimate in self-abuse,' " Jim said.

"Who said that?"

"Travis McGee."

She couldn't help the grin. "And a better detective than you or I'll ever be, Chopin."

"One of your greater twentieth-century philosophers," he agreed. "You know what they say about hindsight."

He was trying to comfort her in that ham-handed way men do, and she was a little touched. "It's okay, really. But Bobby, at the very least, needs to say good-bye. From what Jeffrey says, it doesn't sound like he's got a lot of time left to get it done."

"Not your problem," he said tentatively.

She fixed him with a steady look. "Like hell it isn't. What kind of friend am I if I see him in trouble and I don't try to help?"

"Depends on if he wants you to, I would think."

"And you would think wrong."

"Okay," he said, "obviously not an argument I'm destined to win. Besides, I think you're probably right. There'll be an unsaid good-bye hanging out there until the end of his life if he doesn't."

"If it was your father?" Kate said.

"I'd go home, make my obeisance. I don't know that my father would notice, but I'd be doing it more for me than for him anyway."

And Kate had thought her relationship with her grandmother was complicated. Men and their fathers raised an appreciation of the word dysfunctional to a whole new level.

For a long time she'd felt suffocated by Emaa's expectations. The bloodlines that tied her to the Park were tenacious to the point of strangulation. You can't choose your relatives, as the old saw went, but she wondered now, why not? Why not walk away, as Bobby had, and build your own from scratch in a place where no one knew you and you had no history? Why not start a family the same way, from the ground up, gathering together people you liked and respected and learned to cherish? What was so awful goddamned special about blood, anyway?

"Kate," Jim said, waving a hand in front of her face.

"Huh?" She recollected herself. "Oh. Sorry. What?"

"Want to take a look at the site?"

He was referring to the acre of ground next to the Niniltna Native Association building that the state had acquired at an almost but not quite extortionate price, upon which the ground was even then being prepared for Jim's new post.

"Sure." She'd stayed as far away from the whole trooper post thing as she could get all winter long, but Jim was going to be in a good position to throw work her way. The homestead was hers outright, along with the buildings and tools and vehicles. She owed no one any money, and she'd always been able to feed and clothe herself off the money she made from odd jobs in the Park, from fishing to mining to guiding. But she had Johnny to think of now, and the memory of Jane's words. *I won't pay you a dime in child support.* Personal angle aside, she had good cause to stay on Trooper Chopin's good side.

The trouble was, she had a sinking feeling she wasn't going to be able to leave out the personal angle anytime soon. Kate Shugak's life's work was spent searching for truth, and it was therefore folly for her to ignore a home truth staring her in the face. Something was going on between her and the big trooper. She didn't know what, exactly, and she didn't know if it was bad or good, but it was past time she admitted it was there.

She followed the white Chevy Crew Cab up the hill and parked behind it. They walked across the road and looked at the site, which to his faint surprise showed signs of industry in the form of a completed cinder block foundation. "All you need is some lumber and the framers," Kate said, "and you'll have yourself a post." She looked at him. "Know where you're going to live yet?"

"Figured I'd build."

"Got your eye on some land?"

"I talked to Billy, and Ruthe. She says she might carve off a slice along the river edge of John Letourneau's place for me. So long as it reverts back to the Kanuyaq Land Trust upon my death."

Kate grinned. "I love Ruthe Bauman. You always know where you stand with Ruthe."

"Yeah, dead last," he said, laughing a little. "Way behind the land, that's for damn sure."

"You going to do it?"

He shrugged. "It's a prime piece of land, great view, all cleared and ready. It'd amount to taking out a lifetime lease, with no buildup of equity. But hell, I'll have all I need on retirement. Yeah, I'll probably take her up on it." His eyes glinted. "Build me a comfy little house where I can entertain."

"Or not," she said.

"Not an option," he said, and smiled.

"What?" she said.

The smile widened. She'd never trusted that grin; it always made her think of the first pass of gray fins in deep blue water.

"What?" she said again.

"This dance we do," he said. "See Kate. See Kate run. See Jim chase Kate. We going to get tired of this anytime soon?"

It was kind of silly, now she came to think of it. "Habit, I guess," she said.

"My problem is I'm competing with a ghost," Jim said.

She stiffened. "I beg your pardon?"

"It's true," he said, almost in despair, or as close to it as proper macho feeling would permit. "Tell me something. Isn't there one thing Jack did that drove you insane? Did he flush spit between his teeth instead of floss? Did he fart in public? Did he sing outside the shower? Anything?"

She thought about it, really hard, for a few moments. Finally, she said, "He couldn't drive a stick shift."

"What?"

"He couldn't drive a stick shift to save his life," she said. "First gear, we'd jerk down the street like the car had Parkinson's."

Jim started to smile.

"Second gear, the jolt would throw me against the seat belt so hard I'd bruise my breastbone. Getting into third was a little easier, although he always went there before he had enough revs and we'd slow way down and everybody in back of us would honk. And he never, not once did he ever find reverse on the first try."

Jim was grinning now.

It was odd, but she had the feeling that Jack was grinning right along with him. Kate was not usually a creature of impulse, but then she'd hate to be called predictable, either. She stepped forward and was pleased to see that the shark's grin had faded. "What?" he said, not without apprehension.

She stood on tiptoe and slid a hand around his neck, enjoying the surprise in his eyes. With her other hand she pulled off his cap and tossed it behind her. "Shut up and kiss me," she said.

He did, to such purpose that neither of them heard the vehicle pull to a stop behind them.

"Excuse me," Billy Mike said apologetically, "but really, guys. You might want to take it indoors."

They looked over his shoulder and found the entire staff of the Niniltna Native Association crowded into Billy's Ford Explorer, faces peering inquisitively out the windows. Auntie Joy even waved.

Monday, May 12

The RV's okay, I guess. It's got a shower, but since the pump burned down with the cabin we have to haul water up from the creek. I never want a shower that bad, but Kate's awful picky that way. Man.

The RV isn't level, either. I'm sleeping in the bunk over the steering wheel and this morning I woke up mashed against the far wall. All you have to do is inhale and the whole thing shakes.

But it's got a roof. Plus it's free.

I don't know if Kate has enough money to build a new cabin. I know Dad had an insurance policy and I was the beneficiary, but Kate would never let a dime of that go for anything here. I bet we could sell the town house in Anchorage and use that money for anything we wanted here, but she won't touch that, either. And I'm not even going to college. Man. Women.

As long as I live I will never forget Kate facing down Mom across that table. Kate is—she's—I don't know how to describe her. I remember Dad said once, "Trust me, kid, it's always better to have Kate Shugak on your side than on somebody else's." Boy, was he right. She always knows the right thing to do, and then she does it. How many people are like that? She even scares me sometimes, she's so fearless. And smart. And beautiful.

Jim Chopin thinks so, too. I can't tell if she likes him, too, or not. I hope not. He's not good enough for her. Nobody is.

There are a bunch of snowshoe hares living on the other side of the creek behind the big stand of cottonwoods. *Lepus americanus*, according to the ADF&G Wildlife Notebook. They can grow up to twenty inches long and get as big as four pounds. I was up early this morning (Kate was tossing and turning and the whole RV was shaking so I couldn't sleep) and I went outside to write in my journal and I could see them from where I was sitting on the rock. There's an open space that is kind of sandy and they were running around and into each other and chasing each other and I think their tails. This afternoon after school I went to Dinah's and looked them up on the Internet and the notebook says they're most active at dusk and dawn. I'll say. If Mutt had been there she wouldn't have to eat again for weeks. The Wildlife Notebook says that the hare is a primary food source of the lynx. Man, I'd love to see a lynx. It also says that the hare competes with the moose for forage. I'd love to see a snowshoe hare go up against a moose for a willow twig, too.

I told Kate about how crazy they were acting and I asked her if they maybe had hydrophobia or something. She laughed and said no. I think she's spent a lot of time on that rock herself, watching the bunny rabbits go berserk.

Only two more weeks of school. Yay. I asked Van if she could remember anything more about Len Dreyer but she clammed up on me. I wonder if Kate missed something up at his cabin. We've been finding stuff around here that didn't burn all the way up, even some books that were in the loft and only smell like smoke, you can still read them and everything.

Somebody ought to go look.

15

It was a big RV, a Winnebago, with a bunk over the cab and a double bed in back. There was a toilet, sink, and shower in the bathroom, a refrigerator beneath the counter, a propane stove, a small sink with running water, and a fixed table between two padded booths that would let down into a third bed if they needed it.

That was the good news. The bad news was that the window next to the table looked out on the charred ruin that had been her cabin.

It was Tuesday morning and Johnny had just headed out to school on Kate's four-wheeler, after a spirited attempt to talk her into letting him take the pickup. "You're fourteen," she'd told him. "I'm just guessing on this, but I think the state would like you to wait a couple of years before you start rodding around alone in my truck."

"Roger Corley drives his father's truck to school," Johnny said pugnaciously.

In a perverse way she was enjoying the argument. Now that he had seen her fight dirty for him, now that he knew she was going to stick by him, he was testing her the way any ordinary teenager pushed the envelope with the most convenient adult. "One, you aren't Roger Corley. Two, I'm not Ken Corley. Three, the Corleys live half a mile from the school, not twenty-five miles. Four, you're fourteen. You haven't even got your permit yet."

"But—"

"No," she said, and smiled. She'd watched friends who were parents deal with adolescents, and it appeared to her that in these kinds of situations a cheerful, uncomplicated, and definitive "no" had the most chance of success.

It worked, this time anyway. He sulked all the way out to the four-wheeler and yanked on the helmet she insisted he wear. She noticed he took a spare. Probably for Vanessa Cox. She wondered how the girl was getting along with the Hagbergs. Well, she looked clean, even if her clothes were Early American Depression, and well fed, even if Johnny did say that Vanessa ate a lot of PB&J. Telma might be dotty but she was still capable of adequate childcare. Still, Kate made a mental note to invite Vanessa over on a Saturday when she would be making her justly famous moose stew.

Except, of course, that she had no pots and pans left, no spices, and no canned goods with which to cook a meal. The RV had camping gear, suitable for freeze-dried food bought in foil envelopes from REI, but not much else. She looked down at the list she was making. Pots and pans. Dishes. She wondered if anyone even made the heavy ceramic fisherman's mugs anymore. Flatware. Utensils.

Music. Her tape player was a lump of melted plastic, and her tapes were literally toast. She'd rescued the rifle, the guitar, and the photo album, but her books, oh, her books. Gone, almost all of them, gone. She'd stopped briefly into Twice Told Tales Saturday afternoon and grabbed up a bag full of books, but they wouldn't last her long. A lot of the science fiction, like F.M. Busby's Bran and Rissa series and Zenna Henderson's People stories, was long out of print. Not to mention *Little Fuzzy*, *Rite of Passage*, and anything written by Georgette Heyer. Rachel thought that the Heinlein juveniles were still available and had promised to start looking in Anchorage and on the Internet for those and other titles, but some of Kate's books had been with her since she'd discovered recreational reading in college, and she didn't know if they could be replaced.

Still. Thanks to the kindness of their friends, they weren't homeless, they weren't hungry, and they weren't by any means destitute. They had clothes, courtesy of Dinah's computer and the United States Postal Service. Her tools and vehicles were unharmed. The good weather was holding, fair and dry. She supposed she should get a shovel out of the garage and start digging out the rubble and pegging out a floor plan for a new foundation. She'd never built a house before, and she was a lot better with engines than she was with cabinetry, but there was no way she could afford to hire a contractor out of Ahtna or Anchorage, and since Len Dreyer's death there was no one else in the Park. She supposed she could rent Mac Devlin's D-6 and just push the remains on out to her dump in the woods, but the trail to the dump was just wide enough for a four-wheeler in summer and a snow machine in winter and a blade would take out a lot of the trees on either side. She hated the thought of widening the path and taking out trees for no good reason.

She had to get a move on. Summer days were long but the season was short, and she and Johnny ought to be under a roof of their own before cold weather set in again.

She pushed the list to one side and took up another. It seemed the more she investigated the events leading up to Len Dreyer's death, the more suspects she had. Detection was usually a process of elimination, not accretion, and she couldn't shake the feeling that she was spinning her wheels. "Okay, Shugak," she muttered to herself, "think it out."

On the floor Mutt stirred.

"Listen up," Kate told her. "Maybe you'll catch something I missed." She drew a fresh sheet toward her and began a timeline, starting at the bottom with Dreyer's death and working up, on the theory that if she looked at the facts upside down they might reveal something new. "Means we've got. Dreyer was killed by a single blast from a shotgun fired at point-blank range. Ballistics thinks it might have been an older shotgun, which is just peachy, since every shotgun I've ever seen in the Park dates back to the gold rush."

Mutt made a valiant attempt at interest.

"Don't try so hard," Kate told her. "We know from the ME that Dreyer's been dead since fall, best guess late September, although there is leeway in both directions because he wintered under a glacier and that tends to affect the preservation-slash-deterioration of human tissue. He could have been left outside a night or two before he got stashed, or he could have been stuffed under the glacier the day he was shot. With me so far?"

Mutt cocked an ear.

"That, of course, is going to be the main problem in narrowing down opportunity. If we don't know exactly when Dreyer was killed, it doesn't matter who was doing what where and when in the Park last fall."

Mutt cocked an eyebrow.

"I know what you're thinking," Kate told her, "you're thinking all we have to do is find a good, convincing motive strong enough to push someone into murder. Well, let me tell you, missy, there's motive so thick on the ground I'm needing to get out my shovel." She began to list names.

"In May, Dreyer did some remodeling on Gary Drussell's house so Gary could sell his homestead and move to Anchorage. While he was there, Dreyer molested Gary's youngest daughter. Gary knows it. So does Fran. I don't know about the other two daughters, but sisters tend to talk to each other, and even if these sisters didn't, I'm betting the first thing Gary did when he found out was ask the other two if Dreyer had molested them, too. All five Drussells have motive." She tapped the pencil on the table. "I wonder when Gary found out. Right away, do you think? Or after they moved to Anchorage? Or sometime in between?"

She looked at Mutt. "I ask because I can see Gary catching Dreyer in the act and blasting him with a shotgun. Hell, I can see myself doing that. But what if he found out after the fact, like maybe not until fall, oh, say, September. Would he take his shotgun and get on a plane and come to the Park, kill Dreyer, hide his body beneath Grant Glacier, and leave? It argues a certain amount of cold-bloodedness that I'm not sure Gary Drussell is capable of."

Mutt bared her teeth ever so slightly.

"Yeah, yeah," Kate told her. "He could have hired you."

Mutt yawned.

"But he didn't." She thought. "I'm not a father, but if Dreyer had gone for boys, and if he'd even looked at Johnny . . . Okay. Let's move on." She examined her notes. "Now we come to Bernie my-idiot-friend Koslowski, full-time and well-respected Park businessman, bartender, hotelier, and basketball coach, and part-time fool-arounder. He had what I think was a fairly serious affair—serious for Bernie, anyway—with Laurel Meganack. Laurel broke up with him because his marriage kept him from spending time with her. Shortly thereafter, she slept with Len Dreyer."

Mutt sneezed.

"Let's not quibble," Kate told her. "She seduced him on the floor of the café kitchen, all right? My question is, is that enough to drive Bernie to murder? Of course not. But then along about—surprise!—September, Bernie hires Dreyer to regravel the paths between the cabins and the Roadhouse, at which time Enid, Bernie's wife, seduces Dreyer, not once but twice."

Mutt wore an expression of worldly wisdom.

"You're right, of course," Kate said. "Enid probably only slept with him the second time because Bernie didn't catch them at it the first time. Not to be crude, but I wonder that Dreyer, with a record in very young things, could even get it up for Enid. Enid is tubby, gray-haired, and wrinkled. She looks sixty-five if she looks a day." More tapping of the pencil. "Okay, Bernie catches him in the act, and the only surprise there is that Enid is more upset that Bernie isn't upset than she is that Bernie caught her cheating."

She bent a stern look upon her four-footed friend. "My question to you is this: Was Bernie's lack of emotion when he caught Enid a put-on? Was he hiding how he really felt just to hurt back, and was he even then plotting a revenge involving the business end of a shotgun? Or"—Kate raised an admonitory finger—"was he still angry that his ex-girlfriend, one Ms. Laurel Meganack, slept with Len Dreyer? Did he perhaps feel a tad more proprietary toward the new café wench than he did his own wife? Did that feeling surpass any feeling he had about catching Enid in the act with Len, thus explaining his non-reaction reaction? Perhaps finding Enid with Len put the finishing touch on what he knew about Len and Laurel; perhaps finding Enid and Len together brought it all back and moved him finally to act. He knew all about the glacier from the bar talk every night, it would have been an obvious place to hide a body. Especially in the late fall, when you can't count on the bears to clean up after you."

Bernie was the source of many good, shrink-wrapped things to eat and Mutt wasn't about to rat him out. She pretended to fall asleep.

"My feelings exactly," Kate said. "Still. Have to keep him on the list." She considered. "How about Enid? No. There's no motive there. Dreyer had served his purpose when Bernie caught them, she was done with him, and it wasn't like killing Dreyer would hide their, what, affair is too strong a word. Two-night stand."

Mutt's ear twitched.

Kate considered her notes. "And lest we forget," she said, "there are the two strangers in our midst, Mr. Keith Gette and Mr. Oscar Jimenez, who urgently needed their greenhouse repaired first thing last spring. We have been to the old Gette homestead, Mutt. I think we both know what they're growing in that greenhouse."

Mutt looked up and wrinkled her nose.

"Exactly." Kate brooded. "Here this slob inherits a perfectly good homestead from his deceased cousins and the first thing he and his buddy do is start a commercial dope farm. I mean, really. He might have done a little market research first, there's no way he's going to move that much weed in the Park, and if he decides to wholesale it in Alaska, it's not like he can sell it out of the back of a pickup truck. I mean you can do that with Avon's Skin-So-Soft, but there's a market for Skin-So-Soft in mosquito season."

Mutt looked patient.

Kate held up a hand, palm out. "I know, I know, I'm getting off the subject. My point is that if Dreyer saw what they were planting in that greenhouse, he could have blackmailed them to keep quiet about it. He probably wouldn't have called it black-mail, of course, maybe just a small loan from time to time to keep him in beer. But they could have gotten tired of it."

Mutt emitted a noise somewhere between a snort and a yip.

"You think it would have taken more than a summer's worth of floating him loans for them to get tired enough of it to shoot him? May I remind you who held a shotgun on whom when we went up to the Gette place?"

Mutt lifted her lip in a sneer.

"True," Kate admitted. "I don't think that shotgun of Ji-menez's has been fired since the Eisenhower administration, ei-ther. Still. They had motive, damn it. I'm putting them on the list."

Mutt laid her head back down, apparently defeated, but Kate knew better. She sat back and gazed out of the window, for the first time not seeing the burnt ruin that had been her home, which was at least one good thing to put to Dreyer's credit. From high overhead an eagle called, a haunting, high-pitched sound, just before she plummeted down to snatch up a leveret from one of the snowshoe hares' broods across the creek. The baby hare hadn't lived long enough to learn caution in the open. He would never learn it now.

"You know," Kate said, "it occurs to me that Len Dreyer had the perfect job for a predator. He ran tame in and out of every home in the Park. He saw us all in our jammies and bunny slippers and bed hair. He saw husbands fighting with their wives and kids beating up on their siblings. He knew who was having trouble paying the bills and who was drinking too much. A perfect opportunity for a predator. He could watch and wait and strike when it best suited him, because he would know when he was least likely to be caught."

She looked at Mutt, who had sat up and fixed her with a steady yellow gaze. "He targeted young girls, prepubescent, slight of build. The women he slept with were of a similar physical type. I think we can rule out Enid and Laurel as contributory to his standard, as they seduced him." The news about Dreyer's real identity and past conviction would, given the reality of the Bush telegraph, soon be known across the Park. She didn't want to be anywhere near Enid or Laurel when they heard it. "We should concentrate on the places we know he worked, where girls and women of that general description lived. There could be other parents besides Gary Drussell with a motive for murder."

She shuffled through her notes and read down the list she had compiled that morning, combining what she had discovered from Bernie and Bonnie and the information that Dandy had culled from his ex-girlfriends.

In May, Dreyer/Duffy worked for the Drussells, during which time Kate was certain he had assaulted the youngest daughter. Early June saw him rototilling the Hagbergs' garden, a yearly chore, and he was back a month later putting in a foundation for an outbuilding, in company with Dandy Mike. In July he also repaired the Gette greenhouse.

In August he did some work on George's hangar, and installed Bonnie Jeppsen's new toilet.

The week before Labor Day he had worked a day for Laurel Meganack, down at the café. Kate wondered if he'd billed for a full eight hours or if he'd knocked off an hour for when Laurel had jumped him.

He seen some action that week, because that was the same week he worked on the paths around the Roadhouse, at which time he slept with Enid Koslowski twice, or at least Enid slept with him. Bernie had been forthcoming with the former information if not the latter, but however indifferent he was to the event, it was not a story he had cared to repeat to Kate. Possibly because he knew that he had triggered it by getting a little too serious about his affair with Laurel Meganack.

Later that month Old Sam had flown Dreyer/Duffy and Dandy Mike to Cordova to do some maintenance on the *Freya*. Kate knew a moment's annoyance that Old Sam hadn't hired her on instead, and then she remembered that she had only just returned from a summer in Bering, and had arrived to find Johnny Morgan on her doorstep to boot. In a rare moment of compassion Old Sam must have decided that she had enough on her plate.

In October Dreyer/Duffy had reshingled Bobby's roof, finishing up on October 22nd.

Neither she nor Jim nor Dandy had been able to find anyone who had seen Dreyer/Duffy alive after that date.

She thought for a while about the girlfriends. In the Park there was Susie Brainerd, Cheryl Wright, Betsy Kvasnikof, and Laurel Meganack. Vicky Gordaoff in Cordova.

She thought about Vicky Gordaoff. She was one of those eighteen-year-olds who looked like they'd just started the seventh grade, or at least that was Kate's recollection of her. Kate remembered Dreyer/Duffy as being well-spoken, not unintelligent, with a certain dry humor. And a lot of women had a thing for guys with tools; there was just something so capable about them, it led women to wonder what else they were good at. Vicky was young and impressionable, and there was the added coup of an older man noticing her, especially if her friends were watching.

It might behoove Kate to check into Vicky's life a little, see if there had been a jealous boyfriend or a disapproving father. But then she could say that about all the women he'd slept with.

There was a gingerly sort of knock on the door that caused the whole RV to shake slightly. A look through the window found George Perry standing on the chunk of twelve-by-twelve doorstep someone had thoughtfully placed there. "Hey, George," she said, opening the door.

"Woof!" Mutt said, on her feet and tail wagging vigorously.

"You didn't even see me coming," he said. "Shouldn't you be on the lookout? Didn't somebody just try to barbecue you recently?"

"Woof!" Mutt said again, emphatically.

"Even the dog knows," George told Kate, and gave Mutt a thorough scratching behind the ears.

"Who do you think you are, Jim Chopin? Sit. Coffee?"

"Sure." He wedged himself into the opposite booth and looked at the pile of paperwork covering the table. "You about got it all figured out?"

He sounded hopeful. "Why do you care?" she said, bringing pot and mug to the table and refilling her own. She set out Oreos and milk and sugar and he helped himself to all three.

"Well, hell, Kate, you're one of my best customers. Gotta keep the seats full if I'm going to stay in business." He stirred his coffee absorbedly.

"Uh-huh," Kate said. She doctored her own coffee and waited. He didn't say anything and she sipped coffee and waited some more.

Silence, as Kate had noted before, was the most underrated tool in the investigator's toolbox. It had a way of creating a vacuum into which words were irresistibly sucked, and so long as the investigator kept her mouth shut, the words would perforce come from the witness. And unless Kate was very much mistaken, George Perry had just become a witness in the Leon Duffy murder investigation. So she sipped her coffee and let her eyes drift to the window and her mind drift to the scene outside. As an additional precaution she also kept her mouth full of Oreos. No sacrifice was too great for the investigation.

This year, May in the Park was looking a lot like Camelot in the song. It was only raining after sundown and then only in brief showers, just enough to help the ground thaw and the plants to raise eager heads to the sun, which so far had been remarkably reliable about showing its face every morning. Canada geese were arriving by the squadron and settling in for the summer on the Kanuyaq River delta, along with flights of every duck ever identified by the Audubon Society and a few Kate suspected were not. She hoped so, at any rate. There was far too little mystery left in the world as it was, and deep in her bones she knew that nature was not done with them yet.

She wondered if the sandhill cranes had arrived. Unknown to anyone, she kept an acre of ground mowed where her property line met the creek, not for a garden but for the sandhill cranes to land and feed. She might even have been not known to spread a few sackfuls of grain around the acre from time to time. She liked sandhill cranes, with their red foreheads and their long ungraceful legs. The Yupik called them the "Sunday turkey" and they were in fact Alaska's largest game bird, but Kate never hunted them, at least not the ones who landed on her property. One of the few memories she had of her mother was of sitting in her mother's lap at the edge of the mowed circle, hidden in a tangle of alder, listening to the cranes sing their rolling, rattling song and watching the awkward passion of their mating dance. Her father had grumbled, but Kate noticed that even after her mother died he kept the patch mowed.

The last thing she did before the first snowfall every year was mow the crane patch. Come to think of it, it was probably time to service the mower. It was always a little sluggish from having sat around all winter. There might even be some dried corn left over from last year, if the mice hadn't eaten it all.

George, who had begun to fidget, cleared his throat. "So."

Kate turned and smiled at him, giving him the full treatment. "So," she said.

He shifted in his seat, uneasy beneath all that wattage. "So you asked me Sunday if Gary Drussell flew into the Park last fall."

Everything inside Kate went still. "No, I just asked you when the last time was you had seen him in the Park."

"Yeah. Well. I told you I hadn't seen him since last breakup."

"Yes."

"I lied."

Kate was silent.

George was examining the contents of his mug as if he could divine in which valley in Sumatra the beans had been picked. "Don't even start with me," he said.

Kate was silent.

"I mean it, I don't want to hear it."

Kate was silent.

"The last thing I need is a lecture on my civic duty."

Kate was silent.

George shoved his mug away. "He's a friend, okay? We've hunted together every fall going back, what, fifteen, sixteen years now. I know his wife, and I watched his daughters grow up. I mean from the time they were tiny babies, Kate." He sat back and looked out the window. "I'm not much of a kid person. Never wanted marriage or anything that came with it. So I wasn't thrilled when Gary asked if it'd be okay if we brought Alicia along on a caribou hunt."

"Which one is that?"

"The oldest daughter. The smart one. Well, they're all smart, but Alicia, well, she's special. Regardless of the way things happened, I don't think Gary's sorry to have moved into town. Cheaper for her to live at home while she goes to college, and he really wanted college for Alicia."

Kate waited.

"Anyway. Alicia was all of ten years old when Gary decides he's going to make a hunter out of her. I tried to talk him out of taking her, but he was determined. So we did, and I'm here to tell you, that little girl hiked me right into the ground. I mean, she kept up, Kate, and she carried her own pack the whole time. She damn near outshot us, she like to use up her dad's tags and then she started in on mine." He shook his head at the memory. "That was one tough little girl. Shirley, now, she was the same, smart, even tougher than Alicia, bagged her a moose on her first hunt. Of course, it was a cow, but what can you do. We butchered her out without Dan nailing us, for a change. Those were good kids, Kate. Good company on the trail, too, knew when to talk and when to shut up, and when they talked they had something to say. I liked them both."

"What about the youngest daughter?"

"Tracy?" George's face darkened. "I don't know what happened with Tracy. I don't know her as well as I do Alicia and Shirley. She never came on the hunt with us. I think maybe . . ."

"What? Come on, George, I need to know it all."

"There isn't any all," he said. "Goddamn it. Gary Drussell is no murderer. Even if he was . . ."

"What about Tracy?" Kate said, inexorably.

His face creased with what looked like pain. "Tracy . . . she's the baby, you know? I think the last kid in any family is spoiled, mostly I think because the parents are tired of laying down the law to the other kids by then and they slack off. Also because it's their last kid and they want to. Anyway, she was pretty and she knew it, especially when she hit her teens. Fran used to worry about her flirting; Gary mostly shrugged it off." He leaned forward again, anxious to explain all of it so that there would be no misunderstanding, so Kate would think only good thoughts of his friend and his friend's family. "She wasn't obnoxious about it, Kate. Tracy, I mean. She wasn't as bright as the other two and she knew it."

"So she tried to make up for it with her looks?"

"Yes," George said. "I mean, no. Oh, hell. I guess so. It doesn't mean she deserved what happened."

"No, it doesn't," Kate said. "What did happen?"

"Shit," George said wretchedly. "I promised Gary I wouldn't tell anyone."

Mutt let out a soft whine. "Tell me," Kate said gently. "It won't go any further than it has to."

What had happened, as near as anyone could figure from what Tracy said, which wasn't much, was that overnight Tracy Drussell had changed from a pretty, ordinary teenaged girl into Linda Blair. "It was like a nightmare, Gary said," George said, voice so low Kate had to lean forward to catch the words. "She wouldn't talk, wouldn't eat, shut herself up in her room. Then Fran noticed she, uh, she, well, you know."

"She missed her period," Kate said.

He nodded.

There had been no signs of a baby at the Drussells' Anchorage home. "Oh, crap," she said. And how inadequate was that?

He nodded again. "They were in Anchorage by then. She was only eleven weeks along, so it was fairly easy, although Fran said Gary like to kill some guy with a sign outside the clinic. Tracy told them then, of course. Said it was her fault, she'd been flirting with Dreyer, and he took her up on her offer."

Kate thought of little Vicky Gordaoff in Cordova.

"Only it wasn't an offer," George said. His hands had become fists during the telling. He looked down and noticed, and straightened them out again.

"Why did it take Gary so long to come looking for Dreyer?" Kate said.

George looked blank.

"You said she was eleven weeks along when she told them. Dreyer worked for them in May. I'm guessing that's when he raped Tracy."

George winced away from the word but he nodded.

"School let out the first week of June, Gary and family moved to Anchorage the day after high school graduation. They must have found out about the middle to end of July." She looked at him for confirmation. He nodded again. "So how is it that Gary didn't come looking for Dreyer until over two months later?"

"Because she didn't tell them who the man was," he said, snapping the words off. "Otherwise he and his shotgun would have been on the next plane."

"He was traveling with a shotgun, was he?" Kate said.

George looked at her. She wasn't used to being looked at with that expression by people she considered her friends. I have to ask, she told him silently, you know I do.

"Yes," George said, his voice icily precise, "he was traveling with his shotgun."

"I see. And what day in October would that have been?"

His hand was shaking slightly when he thrust it into the pocket of his begrimed overalls. It was still shaking when he brought out the yellow slip of paper. He shoved it across the table and wriggled out of the booth.

She looked down. It was a copy of a ticket for Chugach Air Taxi Service, roundtrip Anchorage-Niniltna-Anchorage, in the name of Gary Drussell, and it was dated October 24th.

The day after the first snowfall of last winter, according to Bobby's NOAA records. The date after which they had determined Leon Duffy aka Len Dreyer had never been seen again in the Park.

She became aware that George had not left. She looked up to see him standing in the open doorway.

He was staring at the burned pile of lumber that had been her cabin, and her father's cabin before that, and what could have been her grave. As if he could feel her eyes on him, he said without turning around, "I'm sorry, Kate."

"So am I, George." She hesitated, and then spoke. "Did Gary come back to the Park again?"

He nodded, still without turning around.

"Last week?"

He nodded again. "He said it was to clear up some paperwork with the guy who bought the homestead. He was in and out in a day."

"Which day?"

"The day your cabin burned. But he was gone," George said desperately, "he was gone by then."

"Did you fly him out?"

He hesitated, and then shook his head. "No," he said in a whisper. "He flew Spernak that time."

He looked at her, his expression miserable. He started to speak, and then shook his head again.

The door swung shut gently behind him.

After a while she got up and washed out the mugs.

So there it was. She thought of Tracy Drussell sprawled on that couch in Anchorage, convinced that she had invited the assault inflicted upon her, when all she had been doing was testing her wings. It wasn't her fault that the sky had opened up and swallowed her whole. Kate hoped like hell that Fran had called Colleen.

And she hoped like hell no one else needed Colleen's services before this was over.

She needed to find Jim and fill him in, but whenever she thought about getting up, she sat back down again. If it were left up to her she'd have given Drussell a medal. At least she would have before he tried to burn her cabin down with her and Johnny in it.

She was sitting on the other side of the booth this time, the one that faced away from the rubble pile. Something dug into her hip. It was a loose-leaf binder, Johnny's. He must have forgotten it when he left for school that morning. Not surprising, as he'd been in quite the snit, or pretended to be. Not for lack of something better to do, because any minute now she was going to get up and climb into her truck and go looking for Jim, tell him she'd solved his case for him, she flipped open the notebook and began to read. Johnny's writing was cramped but legible. She smiled at the first paragraph, and then she laughed out loud.

She was deep into it before she realized it was more of a diary than it was the journal his teacher had assigned them, and that the teacher would probably never see it, and that neither should she.

But about halfway in something started to niggle at the back of her brain. She flipped back to the beginning and began again. "Oh shit," she whispered, "shit, shit, shit."

She slammed the binder shut and leaped to her feet. Mutt was at the door a second later. Kate grabbed keys and windbreaker and they were gone.

16

"Are you sure about this?" Vanessa yelled over Johnny's shoulder.

"Sure," he replied the same way. "You always start with the scene of the crime."

"But you say Kate doesn't think he was killed there."

"You know what I mean."

They hit a bump and she was almost bounced off. Four-wheelers were notoriously rough rides, and the road up to the Step was a notoriously rough road, if you could call something that was essentially two ruts with a grassy ridge between a road.

"I thought Betty Freedman was going to climb on behind me before we got out of there," she yelled.

"No kidding. Did you tell her what we were doing?"

"No!" she said, indignantly.

"Sorry," he said. "She was just so determined to come with. I thought maybe you said something."

She had been hanging on to his waist. Now she removed her hands, and he felt her body, a pleasant warmth against his back, lean away from him. "You told me not to say anything. I didn't say anything. I don't go around blabbing our business to everyone."

What he thought was the correct turnoff came up on their right and he took it. The road deteriorated into a six-foot-wide game trail choked with tree roots, between which someone had dropped round smooth rocks that looked as if they'd been hauled up from the bed of the Kanuyaq River. It was a jolting and extremely uncomfortable ride, and he was glad when Vanessa grabbed hold again.

It ended in a small clearing, at the center of which was a not large pile of charred timbers. He killed the engine. Vanessa climbed off. He followed. She wouldn't meet his eyes. He touched her shoulder. "Hey."

She wouldn't look up. He put a hand under her chin and pushed. "Come on, Van. Talk to me. I'm sorry, I shouldn't have said that, it was stupid. I know you wouldn't tell anyone what we were doing."

"I know how to keep a secret," she muttered.

"I know you do."

She sniffed, more an expression of disdain than distress. "No, you don't."

"Okay, I don't. I'm sorry."

She kicked a rock across the clearing. "Okay."

Her hair was all messy from the helmet, but he liked it anyway. He liked most of what he saw about Vanessa Cox. She was smart, but unlike Betty Freedman she didn't spend all day every day proving it. Johnny liked smart. She didn't talk a lot, but then he couldn't abide a chatterer—Andrea Kvasnikof drove him up the wall and sometimes out of the school. And when she did talk, Vanessa was absolutely honest.

Honesty was big with Johnny, maybe even bigger than smart. His mother wasn't honest. She would have lied about Kate molesting him without turning a hair. She would have put Kate in jail if she could have. Johnny hated a liar. Vanessa didn't play games, either, like he saw the other girls at school play with the other boys. He liked that, too.

Johnny Morgan knew enough to know he wasn't your typical teenager. He looked around at his thirteen- and fourteen- and fifteen-year-old classmates, and knew that he was a hundred years older in experience and maturity by comparison. Most teenagers thought they were immortal, that nothing could ever hurt them, and that they were going to live forever. Johnny knew better. His parents had split up and he got stuck with his mother for too long, and then his father got her to let Johnny live with him, Johnny still didn't know how and wasn't sure he wanted to know. He'd been living with his father, who had been big and strong and smart and way cool, at least as cool as fathers could get. And then he was gone.

Johnny saw his classmates screwing around with booze or dope or huffing, or even just not doing their homework. Why did they bother with school, if they weren't going to do the work? Admittedly all too often boring to the point of inducing narcolepsy, nevertheless the work would pay off with a high school diploma in the end, and that diploma got you into places like trade school or college or even just a job. Not having one kept you out.

The fact that he planned on taking the GED when he was sixteen and getting an early out of high school so he could apprentice with Kate Shugak didn't detract from this opinion.

He looked at Vanessa. There was one thing he would be sorry to leave behind with high school. In addition to her other virtues, Vanessa was kinda cute, too, with that dark hair and those big dark eyes looking gravely out at the world. His hand was still beneath her chin. On impulse he leaned forward and kissed her.

He never would have done it if he'd thought about it, and then it was too late. Her lips were soft and cool beneath his. It felt good, it even felt wonderful, but in spite of prolonged study of the tongue scene in *Top Gun*, he didn't really know what to do next and he wasn't sure he was ready for next anyway, so he pulled back and looked at her. "Are we okay?"

"I guess so," she said slowly. A lovely wild rose of a blush colored her face. She touched her mouth with tentative fingers.

He'd thought he was in love with Kate, but in his heart of hearts he'd always known that Kate was unattainable, a goddess who would always be out of his reach. Vanessa was here and now. He wanted to kiss her again and see what happened, but they had come there on business. He reminded himself of that, several times, and cleared his throat. "Okay. Let's look around and see what we can see."

She followed him to the remainder of Len Dreyer's cabin. "What are we looking for?"

He said, and hoped it sounded like he knew what he was talking about, "Clues. Something that will give us a lead on who killed Len Dreyer."

"I thought you said his name was really Leon Duffy."

"I did. It was. But everyone in the Park knew him by Dreyer, so let's stick with that."

"Hasn't Kate already been here? And her boyfriend, that trooper guy?"

"He's not her boyfriend," he said curtly. Kate might not be destined for him, but that didn't mean she was destined for Chopper Jim Chopin, either.

"Oh. I thought—well, the way they acted that morning at your place and all. I thought they were, well, you know."

"Well, they aren't."

"Oh."

He bent over to pull at a piece of what might once have been a two-by-four. "Sometimes people just kiss. Sometimes it doesn't mean anything."

There was a brief silence. "You mean like when we just kissed?" she said. "Did that mean anything?"

He straightened right up and looked at her. She looked as grave as ever, but he could see the hurt in her eyes. "It meant something."

"What?"

Sometimes honesty and directness were overrated. "I don't know," he said testily, "it's the first time I ever kissed anybody."

"Oh." Her voice was much softer this time. "Me, too."

He dared to look at her again. "You didn't mind, did you?"

She shook her head. Her hair fell across her face so he couldn't see her expression.

He summoned up all the Achillean courage it takes for a fourteen-year-old boy to admit his interest to a specific girl, and to her face at that. "I liked it."

She was motionless, her hair still hiding her face.

Somewhere between bold and desperate, he said, "Could we, you know, do it again sometime?"

She looked at him then. The blush was back. "Yes," she said, and smiled.

He felt a wave of relief, quickly followed by a wave of anticipation, as quickly succeeded by another wave of apprehension. His tongue felt suddenly too large for his mouth and his feet too heavy for his ankles. The sun, already brighter, took on a particularly golden hue, the sky seemed bluer, and birdsong sounded especially harmonious. Except for the magpies. A bunch of them, quiet until Johnny and Vanessa had proven themselves no threat, were yak-yakking and chittering and squalling off in the brush. "God, they're noisy," he said, mostly as a way to lift a silence that seemed to suddenly weigh a ton.

"Yeah," she said. She stooped to pick up a warped saucepan blackened by fire and knocked it free of ash. "I didn't like him."

"Who?"

"Len Dreyer."

"I thought you said you couldn't remember him," he said, surprised.

She was silent for a moment. "He did some work out on the place for Uncle Virgil, like I told you," she said finally, "with one of those machines with a claw on the back of it."

"A backhoe?"

"That's it. He was breaking sod to make the garden bigger. It was big enough already, I thought, especially since I have to weed it."

"You do?"

She nodded. "And it's like an acre."

"With vegetables, I bet."

She nodded again.

"That you have to eat later?"

"Yeah."

"That totally bites."

"No kidding. And then later that summer he and Dandy Mike came out to build a greenhouse for Uncle Virgil. Anyway, I didn't like him."

"Why not?"

Another magpie flew overhead in a flash of ink blue and white, and there was a temporary increase in caw-cawing volume.

"He looked at me funny."

Johnny was looking at a shard of mirror, the mercury almost all gone. This looked too much like Kate's cabin for comfort. Then Vanessa's words registered. He dropped the sliver of glass. "What?" he said.

She shrugged, uncomfortable. "He looked at me funny. And he touched me."

"What do you mean, touched you?" Johnny heard his voice getting louder, saw her flinch, and made a conscious effort to lower it. "Vanessa, Len Dreyer didn't do anything to hurt you, did he?"

"No." But she avoided his eyes.

The rage surprised him with its immediacy and strength. "Vanessa?"

"He wanted to," she said, her voice almost a whisper. "One time when we were out in the garden alone, he offered to teach me how to run the backhoe. He pulled me up in front of him on the seat. And while we were moving and my hands were on the controls, he, well, he touched me, or he tried to." She made a vague motion toward her chest. "Here. And, you know. There."

The rage was so strong it was making Johnny sick to his stomach. "Didn't your uncle and aunt see?"

"There's trees between the house and the garden. Besides, I don't think Aunt Telma ever looks out a window. And Uncle Virgil was in his shop."

"God, Vanessa, I'm so sorry," he said. "What did you do?"

"I jumped off."

"You jumped off? While the backhoe was still moving?" She nodded, and he fought to repress a smile. "Good for you. What did you do next? Did you tell your Uncle Virgil?"

She hesitated.

"You didn't tell him? Vanessa, why not?"

"I just—I didn't want to talk about it. It was so—ugly. And I don't talk to them anyway, and they don't talk to me. I just made sure I was never around when he was there. Uncle Virgil got mad when I skipped the weeding, but I didn't care."

"Vanessa," Johnny said, his voice very stern—did he know it sounded very much like his father?—"you don't understand. Guys like that, they do that kind of stuff all the time. I heard Dad and Kate talking about it once when they didn't know I was listening. Those people, they're sick and they can't be cured, they can only be locked up. And they can only be locked up when somebody like you steps forward and makes a complaint."

"He's dead now, isn't he?"

"Oh yeah, he's dead, and whoever killed him tried to kill Kate."

"And you," she said in a very small voice.

"And me," he said.

A couple of jays flew overhead, toward the noise the magpies were making. Moments later, a raven glided by, high and graceful. It lit in the topmost branch of a spruce tree and let loose with a series of caws and clicks. Soon after, another raven showed up, and then three more.

"I'm sorry," Vanessa said. "I'm sorry I didn't tell."

"I'm sorry, too," he said, still angry. He'd like to roast Len Dreyer over an open fire, but since Dreyer was dead and Vanessa was alive, she made a better target.

She swallowed. "I'd just got here. I didn't want people to

meet me and think, oh yeah, that's the girl who got molested."

A tear slid down her cheek, and it destroyed him. "Oh, hey," he said, all anger gone. "I'm sorry, Vanessa, I'm so sorry." He put his arms around her and patted her awkwardly on the shoulder. "I'm sorry I was mad. I'm sorry you had to go through it, and I'm sorry you didn't have anyone to tell. I wish Len Dreyer was alive so I could shoot him again."

Her voice was muffled against his jacket. "It's okay. I was mad, too. I still am."

"Good. It's good to be angry. And you did the right thing, running away. Smart. And he never caught you again."

"No. Never came close."

"Good. Good." They stood together in silence.

The magpies were squabbling again, interspersed by the harsh call of the jays and the clicks and croaks of the raven. A high raptorial shriek pierced the air, silencing them all. A moment later, they started up again.

"What's going on with those birds?" Johnny said. He pulled away from Vanessa and walked into the brush, following the bird sounds, which got louder and more frantic as she aproached.

Vanessa stood where she was, a little forlorn. She wiped her nose on her sleeve and began to follow him, only to halt in her tracks when he came barreling out again, nearly trampling her in his haste. His eyes were wide and his face was white. "What?" she said. "What's wrong?"

"Another body," he said, breathing hard.

"What?" She didn't understand. "What do you mean, another body?"

"Somebody else dead. Another man."

"What? How?"

He swallowed convulsively. "The birds have been — the birds — he's pretty messed up. But I think he died the same way Dreyer did. There's a big hole in his chest."

Her knees began to shake, and with an effort of will she steadied them. "Do you know who it is?"

He shook his head. "I think so, but like I said, the birds have been—" He swallowed again.

She stared at him, her lips parting.

He took her hand and pulled. "Come on. We've got to find Kate. Or Jim."

Four of the six-man construction crew was beavering away at the framing, while the other two were unloading more two-by-fours from the back of the flatbed truck that had followed the backhoe into the Park. As fast as they could unload it, the framers were able to keep up, and kept the unloaders hopping.

Looked like progress to Jim, and he turned and looked down the hill. Spruce, birch, and alder interrupted now and then by a cluster of mammoth cottonwood crowded the hillside. The dark green roof of the Niniltna Native Association offices was about a thousand feet down on the left, and after that it was pretty much all trees for half a mile until they ended abruptly in the airstrip, a jumble of Niniltna rooftops, and the Kanuyaq River. It was a bright, clear day, the sky washed clean by a morning shower, and everything looked as bright and shiny and inviting as a king salmon hitting fresh water for the first time.

The foreman came up to him, a thickset man in his middle thirties with big, calloused hands and brown skin that was half race and half making his living outdoors in all weather. He removed his hard hat, revealing a head shaved down to the skin, and wiped his arm across his forehead. "If the weather holds I don't know why you can't be in by this time next month. It's not that big a project." He spat. "You say something about a house?"

"Yeah, Jim," a voice said, "you say something about a house?"

He looked around to see Dinah standing next to him, a smile that was a little more nasty than it was nice on her face. "Haven't got a site for the house yet," he told the foreman.

"Really?" Dinah said innocently. "What about that acre you bought from Ruthe, down on the river? Plenty of room for a decent size house, I'd've thought. You'll want three bedrooms, of course, one for you and the missus, one for your office, one for hers."

"Missus?" the foreman said. He was from Ahtna, and Ahtna knew all about Chopper Jim Chopin. The foreman was married with three children, and like many such had given the occasional wistful thought to the freedom of his bachelor days. It comforted him to know that Chopper Jim was out there living them for him, and he was caught between amazement and a slight sense of betrayal at the thought that his idol might have fallen from his pedestal. He couldn't prevent a look of deep reproach.

Jim set his teeth. "Is there something I can help you with, Dinah?"

She gave him a sunny smile. "Now that you mention it, yes." She motioned him to one side. "It's about Kate."

He was immediately wary and it showed.

She flapped a hand. "Calm down. This is about her cabin." Her voice sunk to a confidential murmur. He listened, his suspicions gradually fading. At one point he held up a hand. "Wait a minute," he said, and went to talk to the foreman. "Okay with him," he said, coming back a few moments later. "Turns out a while back Kate helped find his sister when she ran off to Anchorage."

"We'll get a lot of that," Dinah said. "Good, great. I'll talk to Auntie Vi and Bernie. How about you?"

"How about me? How about I get back to work?"

"How's it coming? Any breaking news on the Len Dreyer/ Leon Duffy front?"

He sighed deeply. "So, you've heard."

She gave him a look of total scorn.

"Yeah, yeah," he said.

"A lot of people are upset about his record."

"They worried about their kids?"

"I was just up at the school. I did a video for the freshman health class and I took it up for the teachers and the principal to preview. They're all talking about Duffy."

"Maybe that should be my next stop."

"Maybe it should. I would think a pissed-off parent would have the best motivation for murder in the world." She added, "And there have already been a few parents up there, banging around, wanting to know what's being done."

"Great," he said.

"They're scared," she said, somber, "and I don't blame them. They're terrified what horrible things might have been done to their children, what they might have allowed to happen. And when you live in the Park, this kind of thing is such a shock. There are so few of us in such an enormous space, we depend so heavily on each other. You just don't think the neighbor who repairs your roof at cost plus a cord of wood is going to attack your child when your back is turned. No, I don't blame them," she repeated. "If Katya—he was on our roof for four days straight, Jim. If Dreyer had touched Katya, if he had even looked at her the wrong way, I would have burned down the house with him on top of it. And that's only if Bobby hadn't gotten to him first."

She spoke with an intensity and conviction that demanded both belief and respect. He touched her shoulder, a gesture of comfort. After a moment she was able to smile. "Sorry. It just gets to me."

"Which parents were up to the school?"

Dinah thought back. "Cindy and Ben Bingley. Demetri Totemoff. Arlene and Gerald Kompkoff. Billy and Annie Mike. The Kvasnikofs."

"Which Kvasnikofs?"

Her brow creased. "All three couples, I think, and Eknaty Sr. and Dorothy, as well." She counted mentally. "And a few I don't know."

He wrote the names down on a list. She watched him. When he was done, she said, "Jim, what if one of them did it? What if one of them killed Dreyer?"

"I know, Dinah. You have to remember that whoever killed Dreyer tried to kill Kate, too. And would have gotten Johnny as a bonus if he'd succeeded."

"But he didn't."

"No. And he won't." He tucked the notebook away.

"Jim—"

She might have said more but for the four-wheeler roaring up, Johnny Morgan on board with Vanessa Cox clinging on behind. They veered off the road so abruptly that Jim and Dinah leapt back out of the way. The four-wheeler locked up and skidded sideways, sliding to a halt just inches away.

"Watch it, damn it!" Jim started to say, and then he got a good look at Johnny's face. "What's wrong?" he said instead.

Johnny swallowed hard, an agonized expression on his face. He opened his mouth and nothing came out.

Without knowing how it had happened, Jim found Johnny's shoulders between his hands, Johnny's feet dangling a good foot above the ground, and Johnny's face, even whiter than it had been, two inches from his nose. "What. Is. Wrong," he heard someone say from very far off. The hands gripping Johnny's shoulders gave him a shake. It didn't look like much of a shake, but Johnny's head jogged back and forward again. "Where. Is. Kate," he heard that other person's voice say, louder now.

"Jim. Jim, let the boy go. Let him go now. Jim! Let the boy down, damn it! Jim!"

He felt a sharp pain in his knee and looked down with some astonishment to see Dinah pulling back to kick him again. "I'll do it!" she said fiercely. "Put the boy down!"

He looked back at Johnny and realized it was his own hands holding Johnny in the air. "Oh," that other voice said. "I'm sorry."

He lowered Johnny to the ground without letting go of him. "I'm sorry, Johnny." It hardly seemed adequate, especially when he looked over Johnny's shoulder to see the Cox girl, her face as white as Johnny's, still on the seat of the four-wheeler with her arms wrapped around her middle looking like she was going to vomit. "Christ," he said. His hearing came back suddenly. "Christ," he said again. "I'm sorry, Johnny."

Some of the color returned to the boy's face and he looked

at Jim like he was seeing a human being instead of a monster. Jim knew a keen and sudden shame. "I'm sorry as hell, kid," he told him. "What's wrong?" He tried not to cringe while waiting for the answer, and didn't question the wave of relief that threatened to swamp him when Johnny did.

"There's a body," Johnny said, "a man."

"Dead?"

Johnny nodded.

"Where?"

"Up at Len Dreyer's cabin. In back, in the woods. The magpies . . . the ravens . . ." He turned and took two steps and threw up neatly onto a currant bush just leafing out from the bud.

Jim waited until he was done and produced a handkerchief that he kept in reserve for moments like these. Johnny wiped his mouth and blew his nose and held it out. "Keep it," Jim said. "Do you know who the man is?"

Johnny nodded. "At least I think so. Like I said, the birds . . . I think it's the chief's son."

A cold knot grew in the base of Jim's stomach. "Which one?"

Johnny looked confused. "I don't know. The one who's always around. The one who wanted to work Len Dreyer's case with you. The one with all the girlfriends."

"Dandy," Jim said.

Johnny nodded. "He's been there a while. Long enough for the . . ."

Jim put a hand on his shoulder. "I got it."

Johnny took a wavering breath. "I think . . ."

"What?"

"I think he was killed the same way Dreyer was killed. He had a hole in his chest. A big hole. He . . ." He shook his head and went over to the four-wheeler and sat down. The Cox girl hid her face against his shoulder.

"Son of a bitch," Jim said. He wheeled for his vehicle.

Dinah trotted next to him. "Jim—"

He had the door open and one foot in the Blazer. "Want to

tell me again why I shouldn't be looking for Dreyer's killer, Dinah?"

She flushed. "No," she said tightly. "I wanted to know who was going to tell Billy and Annie."

He was shamed, and rightly so. "Ah, shit," he said. "Okay, look. Take those two kids home to Bobby. Tell him and no one else. No one, Dinah, you hear?" He pulled himself inside the cab and reached for the keys. "If it really is Dandy, I'll tell Billy and Annie myself."

And then he stamped on the gas pedal and got away from the devastating sympathy in her big blue eyes.

17

Kate knocked and the door opened. "Hi, Virgil," she said.

"Kate Shugak," Virgil said, inclining his head with that inbred old-world courteousness displayed by male Park rats who had spent their formative years on a continent other than North America. "Won't you come in? Telma," he called out, "Kate Shugak is here."

There were immediate sounds of industry in the kitchen, and she had coffee poured by the time they got there. As Kate sat down, Telma brought out a plate of cookies. She smiled at Kate.

"Thanks." Kate munched and drank without appetite. Virgil sat down across from her. Telma took a sponge and Comet to what looked to Kate like an already spotless counter. Virgil watched her, touching her hand when she came within reach. "You should sit down, Telma," he told her. "I do not want you to be tired out."

"Good cookies," Kate said, washing down the last bite.

Virgil smiled. "It is a special recipe my Telma makes, pumpkin and chocolate chip."

"Really," Kate said. "You'll have to give me the recipe."

Virgil's smile broadened. "My woman, she does not give out

the recipes, Kate Shugak. They are family recipes, meant to be handed down from mother to daughter."

Telma paused in her scrubbing to shake out more Comet.

"I'll have to bribe Vanessa, then," Kate said with her own smile. "Actually, I came to talk to Vanessa. Is she here?"

"She is not back from school yet," Virgil said. "Is something wrong with the girl?"

"No, no," Kate said, hoping it was true and reluctant to alarm the Hagbergs over what might be nothing.

Virgil examined her with shrewd eyes.

"How has your breakup been?" Kate said brightly.

"Fine, fine," he said. "I service the vehicles, you know, like always they are slow to start after a winter's sitting in the garage. And I have the few projects I am doing." He cocked an inquisitive eye. "You would have the more to do this breakup, I am thinking."

She gave a glum nod. "That I would, Virgil."

"You will be building a new cabin, I am thinking."

She nodded.

"Something bigger, now that you have the boy with you."

She nodded again. "I don't know when, but yes, something bigger."

"You are sleeping in the RV now? The one they got stuck on this side of the Lost Chance Creek bridge?"

She smiled a little. "That's the one."

"That is a very sharp turn, that turn coming off of the east end of that bridge. The gravel they put there keeps sliding down the bank. It is always muddy."

"It is that," Kate said.

"It is good that you have a place to sleep out of the wet, Kate Shugak, but I am thinking you will not be happy in that RV for very long. Nor the boy."

"No," she said, a little mournfully.

"So you will build again. You need the help, I am good with the woodworking," he said.

She was touched. "That's a wonderful offer, Virgil. Thank you."

Telma finally finished with the counter, sat down next to Virgil, folded her hands on her lap, and smiled at Kate. Virgil put his hand on hers and squeezed. "My Telma," he said fondly.

Kate helped herself to another cookie even though she didn't want one. "I'll need all the expert help I can get, especially with Len Dreyer dead."

Virgil's smile didn't change. "A man cut down in his prime," he said piously. "A sad thing, that."

Not necessarily, Kate thought.

"You will catch the terrible person who shot him," Virgil stated.

"That I will," she said. "And more to the point, the person who burned down my cabin." She looked at Telma. "These really are wonderful cookies, Telma. You're an amazing baker. I hope you're passing some of that skill along to Vanessa."

Telma smiled. "She is a fine girl. My cousin's child."

"Vanessa is not interested in the cooking yet," Virgil said.

"Oh," Kate said. "What is she interested in?"

"The reading. She would read all day of every day if we let her. And she likes that boy of yours, that Johnny."

"She has good taste then," Kate said easily. "He's a good kid. How long has Vanessa been with you now?"

Virgil frowned in thought. "She comes to us last May, so almost a year now."

"Must be nice, having a girl," Kate said, with feeling.

"She is a quiet little thing," Virgil said, "no trouble at all in the house."

Kate wondered about that. One of the first signs of abuse was a retreat into oneself. "Was she always this quiet?"

"Oh, yes," Virgil said. "From when she first came to us, she is always quiet."

"I like children," Telma said unexpectedly.

Kate didn't know what to say to that, although she was glad of the sentiment. She ought to just come right out with it, like she had with Gary Drussell, but this was an older couple with no experience of children and certainly none of child abuse, and from Virgil's attitude, the news about Len Dreyer's past history had not permeated to the Hagberg homestead.

"But helpful," Virgil said, "very, very helpful, at least out of doors and away from her books. She is good with the wood chopping, after I show her how. She helps me with the weeding of the garden all summer. And she is interested in the tanning of the caribou hide I bring home in the fall."

Kate smiled and nodded. "Have you been teaching her how to drive?"

He shrugged. "The four-wheeler she already uses to go back and forth to school after the snow melts. Before, I teach her the snow machine. It is not difficult, and the girl is quick."

"My boy is the same," she said. "I was thinking of teaching him how to run the tractor, too. He wants to drive the truck."

Virgil smiled. "At fourteen, all boys want to drive the truck."

"Nice to have help down on the farm," Kate said.

"It is that," Virgil said.

"Especially now that it looks like we won't be able to hire any, so far as we know."

"Neighbors will help," Virgil said. "I will help."

"I appreciate that, Virgil, but I was thinking more along the lines of fixing roofs and replacing glass and rototilling gardens. It was nice to have help you could hire. Dreyer crossed a lot of items off a lot of peoples' lists."

"He did," Virgil said. "Have another cookie, Kate Shugak."

"A good worker, everyone said so," Kate said.

"A sad thing," Virgil said, shaking his head. "He did a fine job in the garden last spring. You should come see." He got to his feet.

"Huh? I mean, okay." Kate rose. Telma smiled impartially upon them both as Virgil led Kate out of the house.

Virgil paused on the porch. "Your dog. Where is she?"

Kate nodded toward the woods. "Either chasing rabbits or asleep in the sun."

"Ah. That is good. I have too many rabbits on my land. Come see my garden, Kate Shugak."

She followed him around the house. Maybe he'd be easier to talk to away from Telma. He was more of this world than his wife. If Dreyer had hurt Vanessa, he might actually have noticed something.

They walked through a copse of evenly spaced trees, all neatly pruned. There were squares of raspberries, blueberries, and currants. The garden was impressive, orderly rows of rich soil thirty feet in length in a plot fifty feet wide.

Every five feet there was a line of flat rocks, providing access to the produce without harming any of it. "Wow," she said, impressed and envious. She turned. "Where did you—"

The last thing she saw was the bottom of a spade coming straight for her head.

"Ah, shit," Jim said.

Johnny had been right, it was Dandy Mike. Johnny had also been right about the birds. Something else, maybe a fox or even a wolverine, had been at Dandy, too. The magpies and the ravens had fluttered away at his approach, but not far, and they scolded him from their perches in the trees for interrupting their meal.

"You dumb bastard," Jim said to the corpse, "you dumb bastard! I told you to stay away from this case. I told you you didn't have the training for this. Goddamn you anyway!"

He whipped off his cap and slapped it against his leg. It stung, even through his jeans. "Shit," he said again, and went for the crime-scene kit he had in the crew cab. He shot two rolls of film, and made a drawing of the crime scene with measurements before he brought out a body bag and muscled Dandy into it and the bag into the back, scolded all the while by the magpies and the ravens. He thought about fetching the shotgun clipped to the dash of the pickup and letting it loose on them, and then he got his temper under better control.

Dandy had caught a blast in the chest from a shotgun held on him at short range, just like Len Dreyer/Leon Duffy, which meant he either knew his murderer well enough to allow him to get that close even with a weapon in his hand, or his murderer had surprised him.

Jim surveyed the clearing. He didn't know what the hell Dandy Mike was looking for here, but with the cabin burned there wasn't a hell of a lot of cover. What with the rain and the tracks from Johnny's four-wheeler and the footprints of Johnny and Vanessa, there wasn't a lot to read from the ground. The bushes and shrubs looked as though Dandy had been pulled from the clearing through the brush. He followed it, bent in half, eyes straining for anything the killer might have dropped. There wasn't so much as a shell casing.

He quartered the clearing, nose to the ground. Although the rain had washed most of it away, he thought he could see a darker patch of ground that might once have been blood. A very faint trail that might have been dragging boot heels led to the bushes. He went to the truck and opened the body bag. Yes, Dandy had mud built up on the heels of his boots. He zipped the bag back up, avoiding another clear look at what was left of Dandy's face.

Rigor mortis had set in and had yet to go off, but Dandy had been lying outside and it was still only early May. Jim juggled numbers in his head. He'd probably been shot the day before, Monday afternoon, say anywhere between six P.M. and, oh hell, it could be as late as midnight. Shit squared.

At least he hadn't been stored in a glacier.

So Dandy had returned to the site of Len Dreyer's cabin, and had had the monumental bad luck of meeting Len Dreyer's murderer doing the same thing. Or had the murderer been following him? He'd certainly followed Kate.

He had a teeth-grinding need to find Kate, to make sure she was all right. The strength of the need, the urgency of it, annoyed him. Kate Shugak was the last person in the world to need a baby-sitter. Which he was not, by the way.

And he had more pressing business. He climbed in the pickup and drove to Niniltna as fast as he could without bouncing Dandy's body out of the back. He made the airstrip in time to see George Perry preflighting the Cessna.

George looked alarmed at Jim's precipitous approach, or that was what Jim thought. Jim didn't bother to reassure him. "Got a body, it has to go to the medical examiner in Anchorage right now."

"You're kidding me," George said. He looked at the body bag. "Who is it?"

"Dandy Mike."

George looked thunderstruck. "You're kidding me," he said again.

"No."

George was beginning to get it. "He hasn't been . . . nobody killed *Dandy*," he said.

"Shotgun, close range, right in the chest."

"Jesus H. Christ," George said. "You mean like Dreyer?"

"Exactly like Dreyer," Jim said grimly.

"When?"

"Yesterday, sometime between six P.M. and midnight, near as I can figure. The lab'll narrow it down."

The oddest expression flashed across George's face. In any other situation Jim would have called it relief, but that made no sense at all. "Get him into Anchorage," Jim said.

George all but saluted, and was in the air by the time Jim was at the river, making the turn for Bobby's house.

"I've got to get home," Vanessa said.

Dinah looked at the girl. She was sitting in the middle of the living room, playing with Katya. There was a bowl of magnetic fish between them, and the two were engaged in catching them with miniature fishing poles with magnetic lures. Katya kept nudging Vanessa's hook out of the bowl but Vanessa kept sneaking it back in again. Both of them were giggling. Dinah didn't think she'd ever seen Vanessa Cox with a smile on her face before.

"They'll be worried about me, Mrs. Clark," Vanessa said, and hooked a pink fluorescent fish with purple lips and fins.

"Dinah," Dinah said automatically. She looked out the window. It was five o'clock, and there was still plenty of daylight to go. "Why don't you stay for supper? Johnny can drive you back after."

Vanessa hesitated. Johnny, engrossed in some electronic mystery posed by the jumble of equipment at the central console, looked up. "Stay," he said. "You go home late a lot. They know you're probably with me. They won't really be worried, will they?"

Vanessa thought about it. "I guess not."

Dinah made a mental note to know where Katya was every waking moment of her life until she was eighteen, and after that to enjoin Katya to call in every day until she, Dinah, was dead.

She thought of Billy and Annie Mike and she closed her eyes for a moment. Billy and Annie had six other children, plus a tiny American-Korean baby they had adopted the year before, and at least nine grandchildren that Dinah knew of. There would be comfort in that. But not much. Suddenly she crossed the room to scoop Katya up in her arms and hug her fiercely.

Katya's protest was immediate and loud, and went out to everyone in the Park, because Park Air was up and running, Bobby on the mike broadcasting a bunch of want ads from around and about the Park. "Okay, you yo-yos, the principal down at the school, yeah, Mr. Oltersdorf, he needs a new battery for his truck. This is because the old one disappeared last night right outta his truck when he had it parked in back of the school while he was working late." Bobby paused for effect. "He says for me to tell you that unless he gets his battery back, he'll see to it that nothing is played at the prom but Beethoven. I told him to throw in a little Wagner while he was at it, but he seems to think that might be a little harsh. Me, harsh is my middle name. You done been warned. Let's see, what's next." He balled up the handwritten note and tossed it over his shoulder, where it joined a dozen others scattered on the floor. "Here's somebody else needing a carpenter, Fred Van Zyle out at Mile thirteen, wants to add on a floor. He'll pay actual cash money, he says, but he wants to see something you've done first before he hires you on. Untrusting bastard, that Fred." Another crumpled note went flying. "Auntie Vi will be hosting a quilting bee at the Roadhouse on Wednesday, starting at six P.M. Bring fabric, needles, and thread, but don't think you'll get the finished product until you convince them you have reproduced. Lessee, what else. A bake sale on Saturday to earn the senior class money to help pay off the tickets for their senior trip to Seattle in December. If Nelda Kvasnikof donates one of her death-by-chocolate cakes, I personally will be in the front row, and I advise you not to bid against me if you ever want to broadcast an ad over this station again. Okay, enough of that, here's some soul sisters coming atcha, and why wouldn't you be their baby if you had the chance?" The Ronettes rolled out of the speakers at full volume and Bobby rolled his chair over the hardwood floor to Dinah and swept her off her feet.

Katya, who had wriggled free, laughed and clapped her hands and trotted over to join in. A dancing family, the Clarks, Vanessa thought. She wished there was more music in her home. But she was lucky she had a home, she told herself. The Hagbergs, neither one of them ever said so, but she knew she could have easily wound up in foster care with strangers and probably even stranger kids. It was just so quiet on the Hagbergs' homestead. Virgil didn't talk much and Telma didn't talk at all.

She looked at the tousled head of thick brown hair bent with intent over what looked like a nest of tiny, colorful snakes, and her heart did that crazy somersault thing again. She thought of him kissing her that afternoon. She wondered when it could happen again.

"Goddamn, woman," Bobby roared, "not in front of the children!" Vanessa looked up to see Dinah, flushed and laughing, hop from the chair.

A happy family, she thought, and wished with all her heart that she was part of it.

The door was open to admit the balmy breeze that had been blowing in zephyr-like fashion all day, which was why Bobby Clark's ugly brother could walk right in without knocking. That's what Vanessa called him, the ugly brother. There were ugly stepsisters, weren't there? So Jeffrey Clark was the ugly brother. Although he wasn't that ugly. In fact, he and Bobby looked a lot alike, and Bobby was a good-looking man. Kind of like Denzel Washington in *The Pelican Brief*, only thicker through the shoulders and arms, and with more hair, and, of course, no legs below the knee. And his jaw was wider, and his eyelashes longer and thicker. But otherwise a dead ringer.

"Ah, Jesus," Bobby said, unaware of the fantasy being woven about his person, "and it's been such a fine day up until now."

"I'm still here," Jeffrey Clark said.

"I see that," Bobby said. "Go home, Jeffie. Just go the hell on home."

The ugly brother's face hardened into a stubbornness whose implacability could only be mirrored on the face he was currently staring into.

"Would you like to stay to dinner, Jeffrey?" Dinah said cheerfully.

Bobby glared at her. "No, he would not like to stay to dinner, Dinah. Jesus. Women." He almost turned to Jeffrey for support and thought better of it just in time. "Don't let the door hit you in the ass on the way out," he told his brother.

Jeffrey looked over Bobby's head and met Dinah's eyes straight on for the first time. "I'd love to stay to dinner," he said.

It was an interesting evening, Vanessa thought later, as she washed and Johnny dried. Jeffrey was determined to be pleasant and Bobby was determined to be obnoxious. They were both successful. Dinah kept the pork chops and applesauce and mashed potatoes and mixed vegetables moving briskly around the table, as if she thought that if she kept people's mouths filled they wouldn't be able to spew venom at each other. She was only partially successful, hampered by having to feed Katya at the same time. Johnny had grabbed the seat next to Vanessa, and partway through the meal she felt his foot sidle up to hers. He'd looked at her sideways and given her a small smile. She'd smiled back, a little shy.

When the last fork was dry, Vanessa hung up the dish towel and said to Johnny, "I really better get home."

"I know." He looked toward the door.

"What?" she said.

He hesitated. "I'm just wondering about Jim. You know, the trooper. What he's doing."

She was silent for a moment. "Was it awful?" she said. "The body?"

His lips compressed into a thin line. "It was awful," he said. "I hope you never have to see anything like that." He shuddered. "I hope I don't ever have to see anything like that ever again."

"What will the trooper do?"

"He'll find the murderer," Johnny said sturdily.

"But he's killed two people now, and the trooper didn't find him after he killed the first one."

"There's more evidence now," Johnny said with an authority that secretly impressed her, which had, of course, been the point. "The killer got away with it the first time, so he got careless. He left something behind that'll help Jim catch him, you watch."

"You think so?"

"I know so." He smiled at her, and she was reassured.

In the living room Jeffrey had enthroned himself in the middle of the couch that had its back to the window. Katya trotted over to him with a copy of *The Monster at the End of this Book* and pushed her way onto his lap regardless of the cup of coffee and slice of lemon cake he held. "Read," she commanded.

He looked up to find Bobby ready to explode, and the expression on his face was all too obvious. "Why, sure, sugar, I'll read to you," he said, his voice as smooth as honey.

Dinah put a restraining hand on Bobby's arm, a gesture she had perfected during the evening, and indeed during the past week. "She's going to go right off," she whispered, and sure enough, Katya was asleep long before Jeffrey got to the monster. Sleeping babies gain ten degrees in body temperature and ten pounds in body weight, and it was amusing to watch Jeffrey cope with both. Amusing for a while, anyway, and Dinah went to rescue Katya before she slid completely out of her uncle's arms.

Jeffrey thanked her for the meal, said to Bobby, "I'll be back in the morning," accepted a terse "Don't bother" in reply with seeming equanimity, and took his leave.

Bobby blew out a breath and let loose with a colorful commentary on Jeffrey, Dinah, dinner, and life in general. It was a restrained performance, for Bobby, and it didn't wake up Katya, so Dinah let it go. She sat down next to him on the sofa and he pulled her to him in a tight embrace. "I wish he'd go home," he said. "Just go on home."

"He's a man on a mission," Dinah said.

He was silent for a moment, unusual for Bobby. "Dandy keeps wandering into my mind," he said, surprising her.

"Mine, too," she said, looking over her shoulder. Johnny and Vanessa were engaged in a whispered conversation next to the sink.

"Worthless bastard," Bobby said.

"Harmless, though," Dinah said.

"Somebody didn't think so," Bobby said. He kissed her suddenly, hard enough to hurt her lip.

"Ouch," she said mildly when free again.

Her husband's hands roamed, touching, fondling, caressing, possessing. "He was only ever interested in one thing. If he was going to get shot by an irate husband, it would have happened years ago."

"I don't think Jim thinks it was an irate husband. I think he thinks it was the same person who killed Len Dreyer."

Bobby's eyes narrowed. "Dreyer I could see killing, now that we know who he was and what he did. But Dandy?"

"He must have gotten close to Dreyer's murderer."

Bobby looked skeptical. "I wouldn't have thought he was that bright."

"I'm going to take Vanessa home now," Johnny announced, standing a safe distance away from the living room. After six months in the Park he'd had experience of the Clarks' lack of inhibitions, and he'd seen enough to horrify him for one day.

"Thanks for dinner, Mrs. Clark," Vanessa said. "And Mr. Clark."

Dinah disentangled herself from her husband and stood up. "Come back anytime, honey. Johnny? You got everything? Helmets?" She looked out the window. The sun was a long way from going down. "You guys watch for bears, now." She recollected that there appeared to be a madman with a shotgun loose in the Park and said, brows creased, "Maybe you better follow them home, Bobby."

"I'll take 'em," Jim said, standing in the doorway.

He had his cap pulled so low it was hard to see his expression, but there was a harsh line to his mouth.

"You told them," Dinah said.

He gave a sharp nod.

"I'll go over."

He made a negating motion with his hand. "Don't. I sent Auntie Vi up to their house. She's calling their kids. I sent George into town with the body, so the kids in Anchorage can meet the plane and at least some of them can fly back out with him. They don't want to see anyone but family, not yet."

"All right. Have you had anything to eat? There are leftover pork chops, and a little mashed potatoes."

"Anything's fine."

Dinah fixed him a plate. He ate standing up. "Thanks, Dinah."

As if she couldn't restrain herself one moment longer, Dinah turned and went straight for Katya's crib. Bobby followed her.

"Come on," Jim said to Johnny. "Kate at home?"

"She was when I left this morning. I have to take Vanessa home first."

Jim nodded. "I'll follow you."

18

His teeth were clenched so tightly together he was starting to get a headache. He made a conscious effort to unclamp them but it was like chipping at cement.

There had never been any question of what Jim Chopin would do with his life. He couldn't remember a time when he had wanted to be anything else but a cop. The job had never let him down, either; it kept him busy, interested and amused, and the Smoky the Bear hat was an unbelievable babe magnet. There were those times when he had to look at men he had known when they were alive, dead men now, dead men who'd been shot, stabbed, beaten, messed about by animals even, but he could handle that. He could handle the occasional drunken pipe-liner putting a gun to his head at Bernie's Roadhouse; he could handle a twenty-car pileup with jackknifed semis at Glenallen the day of the first snowfall; he could handle abusive fathers and drunken husbands and vengeful wives and embezzling cannery owners and dope-dealing video store rental clerks. And, hell, the pay was even good, he was putting away a hell of a chunk for retirement, always supposing he ever did retire.

The times he did think about retirement were when he was

walking up to the front door of someone's home to deliver the worst possible news to the people inside. He couldn't handle being the goddamn grim reaper, was what he couldn't handle. Billy and Annie hadn't believed him at first, a common reaction. He'd had to repeat himself, and then repeat himself again, and then Annie had slid down the side of the wall as if all the bones in her body had dissolved, and Billy had begun to weep.

And then he'd had to ask them when was the last time they'd seen Dandy, and who was his latest girlfriend, and had he told them anything about trying to find Len Dreyer's killer. He hadn't got much sense out of either one, big surprise, but he'd done his duty, by god. The academy would be proud of him; his probationary officer would have nodded approvingly; Lieutenant Gene Brooks, his boss in Anchorage, would find nothing about which to complain.

He felt his gorge rise, and for a moment thought he was going to have to pull over to puke. He fought it back, winding down the window and inhaling large gulps of cool spring air. He'd slowed down a bit and the four-wheeler ahead of him pulled away. He stepped on the gas and caught up again.

Leon Duffy aka Len Dreyer was no loss to the Park. If Dreyer's death resulted in a open file growing steadily colder over the coming weeks and even years, that was pretty much okay with him. Duffy was a child abuser. Jim would not have connived at his murder, and he would have tried to stop it had he been present at the event, but after the fact his personal opinion was that a quick shotgun blast to the chest was far too short an ending. Something involving large amounts of pain and suffering would have been more appropriate, but at least Duffy had been removed from the general population, to its far greater good.

However. Jim had every reason to believe that the murderer had tried to burn down Kate's cabin and Kate with it, and that was not allowed, whether he was sleeping with the prospective flambé or not.

And now Dandy. Dandy, that charmer of women, that guiltless slacker, that cop wanna-be for who knew what reason, hell, maybe he liked the hat, too. Dandy, who was just stubborn enough, just stupid enough not to back off the investigation when told to, little Dandy Mike, stumbling around the Park, poking his nose into what didn't concern him, asking questions of all the wrong people, causing enough talk so that someone would decide to shut him up for good.

"Fuck!" Jim yelled.

He pounded on the ceiling of the cab until his knuckles split.

"Fuck!" he yelled again.

It didn't make him feel any better.

Right now what he wanted most in the world was to talk to Kate Shugak. He was going to sit down with Kate and discuss this case from the beginning of last summer and the attack of Tracy Drussell to the discovery of Duffy's body, the burning of Kate's cabin, and the murder of Dandy Mike. They were going to lay out a timeline, they were going to put names and places next to the dates, and they were "fucking going to find this asshole with the shotgun and the firestarter!" he bellowed, and pounded on the ceiling again.

His knuckles hurt. He sucked on them, watching the four-wheeler ahead with a fierce gaze. No way was anything going to happen to Johnny Morgan on his watch. And the girl, what was her name? Van, Vanessa something. Right, Vanessa Cox. The Norwegian bachelor farmer's daughter, only she wasn't his daughter and he wasn't a bachelor. Jim had met Virgil Hagberg at a town meeting in the high school gym once. He didn't remember a wife, but he remembered someone saying there was one, but she seldom left the homestead.

He never should have let Dandy Mike imagine for one moment that he might have a chance at a job at the Niniltna trooper post. He never for one moment should have allowed Dandy's father, Billy, to believe that he had influenced Jim into giving Dandy a job. There was such a thing as being too goddamn diplomatic. Screw diplomacy from now on, diplomacy got the wrong people killed.

He blinked. For one heart-stopping moment the four-wheeler disappeared, and then he drew level with the lane they had turned on and spotted the telltale dust hanging in the air. With a curse, he floored the gas pedal and dove down it after them. Tree limbs caught at the rearview mirrors and deadwood cracked beneath his tires, but he caught up with them as they pulled up to the house.

It was a nice house, trim; somebody had already raked the square patch of lawn free of dead leaves and new grass was poking its head up. The outbuildings were neat, too, well maintained, a shed for everything and everything in its shed.

Kate's truck was parked in front of the house. Good. He'd by god hijack the woman and they'd pull an all-nighter and figure out who the murderer was. Almost calm, he pulled up on her rear bumper—just in case she had any ideas about getting away from him—and killed the engine and got out.

Johnny eyed him. "You got a lot of room to park out here, you had to park it right behind Kate's truck?"

"Yes," Jim said, and something in the tone of his voice shut Johnny down cold.

He was Jack Morgan's son, though, so only for a moment. "It's your funeral," he said, and turned to Vanessa. He was too manly to try anything with Jim watching, but she had no such qualms. She kissed his cheek, a swift, shy gesture, and murmured something that Jim didn't catch. Johnny blushed, and with a quick glance over his shoulder murmured something back. With a little wave, Vanessa went up the steps and in the door.

Jim followed her. "Hold on," he said before she vanished. "Find Kate for me, will you? Tell her I need to talk to her."

She nodded. He stood in the doorway and waited.

"Hi, Aunt Telma. I'm home."

"So I see, dear," a pleasant voice said.

"Where's Kate Shugak?"

"Why, I don't know, dear. Kate who?"

"Kate Shugak, Aunt Telma. Her truck is parked out front."

"Oh." A brief silence. "Did I give her cookies?"

"You might have. You give everyone cookies. Was she here?"

"Someone was here."

"When?"

"Oh, I don't know, dear. A while ago." A pause. "Would you like some cookies?"

"No, thank you, Aunt Telma."

Vanessa came back down the hall. "She's not in the kitchen or the living room."

"Your aunt seems—"

"Yes. She is." Vanessa stood very straight and looked him directly in the eye.

"Yes. Well." Jim respected loyalty, deserving or not. "Maybe Kate's with Virgil outside somewhere. I'll go look." He went back outside.

"Where's Kate?" Johnny said.

"I don't know." A faint unease whispered around the edges of his mind. After a moment he identified it. Where was Mutt? Generally speaking, he couldn't set foot within a mile radius of Mutt without being instantly attacked. She never strayed far from Kate's side, except when Kate was tucked in for the night. So where was she?

Maybe Kate had left her at home. But Kate seldom did so, and would Mutt allow that anyway? Unlikely.

Without thinking, he reached down to unsnap his holster.

Johnny's eyes got big. "What's wrong?"

He tried for a reassuring smile. "Nothing. Stay here, okay? In fact, get in my truck and lock the doors. If Kate or Mutt show up, beep the horn."

"Okay." The boy looked up at the house. Rapunzel, Rapunzel, let down your long hair. Ain't love grand. Young love, anyway. Grown-up love was a colossal pain in the ass.

Jim walked around the house, not tiptoeing exactly, but not announcing his presence, either. He walked between the house and the garage, a neat pathway paved with irregular stones with a flat surface, worn by much use and bordered with neat beds of raked soil, ready for planting.

He heard a sound and followed the path to it, around a stand of paper birch and through a tiny grove of what he thought might be apple trees, although he didn't know how fruit trees could survive either the cold or the moose in the Park.

He came out of them onto a large plot of turned earth. Virgil was digging in it with a number two shovel, taking earth from a pile of dirt and tossing it into a hole.

Jim walked forward, his footsteps muffled in the grass. "Hey, Virgil," he said.

As uneasy as he was, he was still unprepared for the other man's reaction.

Virgil dropped the shovel and lunged for a shotgun that Jim only just then noticed propped upright by its butt in the dirt. He tried to grab it before Virgil got hold of it, but Virgil was closer and quick for an old man. He swung it around, both barrels pointing at Jim.

There was nothing more mesmerizing in this world than the twin barrels of a .12-gauge shotgun staring down at you. Jim could hardly take his eyes off them. He kept his voice soft. "What seems to be the problem here, Virgil?"

Virgil squinted at him. His thin cheeks were sunken, his eyes hollow. "Jim Chopin?" The shotgun began to lower.

"That's right," Jim said, risking a step forward and halting when the barrel jerked back up again. He grabbed a quick look over Virgil's shoulder and what he thought he saw made his blood run cold. "Virgil," he said urgently, "put the gun down. Now."

Virgil shook his head. "I am very sorry to disobey an officer of the law, but I cannot to do that, Jim Chopin. My Telma, she would not like that."

"Put it down, Virgil." Jim saw Virgil's knuckle tighten on the trigger and felt sweat pop out on his forehead. "At least tell me why," he said. "Why, Virgil?"

Virgil looked behind Jim, and Jim dared a glance backward. Virgil was looking at the house, at the second floor, where the light was on and a woman, Jim guessed Telma, was brushing

her hair. "Because, Jim Chopin, love doth make fools of us all."
And he fired.

Involuntarily Jim closed his eyes.

There was no blast.

He opened his eyes again.

Virgil fired the other barrel. Jim flinched, but again no shot.

The shotgun was empty.

Virgil sighed. "I guess I forgot to reload."

Jim had the shotgun out of his hands and Virgil on the
ground with his hands cuffed behind his back in thirty seconds.
In the next second he was up and running for the hole in the
garden. "Oh god," he said in an agonized whisper, "no, no, no,
no."

He stumbled into the hole and began digging at the dirt with
both hands. Flesh and fur both showed. His heart was beating
so hard in his ears that he couldn't hear and he couldn't get
enough air into his lungs. "No," was all he could say, over and
over again, "no, no no no."

He got Kate out first, so covered in dirt and blood he hardly
recognized her. He shoved her out of the pit and scrambled up
beside her. She was warm to the touch, thank god she was warm.
He put his ear to her mouth and remembered to count to five.
Nothing. He beat back panic and tried for a pulse in her neck,
forced himself to count off ten seconds. Nothing.

"*No,*" he said. He forced his thumbs into her cheeks, opening
her mouth, and sucked out the dirt and spat, once, twice. He
pulled her head back to create an airway and started CPR. Fifteen and two, fifteen and two, fifteen and two. Not too hard,
don't want to break any ribs. Get air into the lungs, into the
brain. Fifteen and two, fifteen and two, fifteen and two.

He looked up once and saw Johnny standing in front of them,
a stricken look on his face. "Get Mutt," he said, jerking his head,
and went back to breathing for Kate.

He seemed to have been doing CPR forever, he had nearly
given up hope, when her breast rose and fell on its own. She
choked, and then she coughed, and then she puked, a gory mass

of coffee and cookie chunk with plenty of dirt in it. He turned her to her side and then he puked, too, right next to her, on his hands and knees like a dog.

Like a dog. He turned and saw that Johnny had somehow managed to muscle Mutt out of the pit. She looked as bad as Kate did, but she was breathing on her own. "Stay with them," Jim said, and got to his feet.

The boy, dumb, kneeled between woman and dog, his face wet with tears, as Jim jumped over Virgil and ran for the crew cab.

"Why?" Jim said. He was too tired and too angry for subtlety. If Virgil gave him the slightest excuse, he was going to knock him flat on his back. He didn't care that Virgil was twenty years older than he was. He didn't care that Virgil was seated, with his wrists cuffed. He was tired from being up all night and if Virgil didn't answer all of his questions straight out and straight up, he might kill him and use the hole Virgil had dug for Kate and Mutt to bury the body.

"So fuck diplomacy, and fuck technique," he said out loud, earning a curious glance from Bobby.

They were in the conference room at the Niniltna Native Association. Bobby had gotten the keys from Auntie Vi, who had gotten them from Billy Mike, and Jim was in mortal fear that Billy and Annie were going to show up at any moment, another of the reasons he wanted this interview in the bag.

Kate and Mutt were in the back of George's Cessna on their way to Ahtna. Bobby had already alerted the hospital and the vet. They were both suffering from severe head trauma, resulting from a single blow to the head. Jim had the shovel in the back of the crew cab. It wasn't the blood on the shovel that got to him, it was the short, silky black hairs. He'd almost used it on Virgil then and there.

"Why did you kill them?" he said. "I want answers, Virgil, and I want them now."

Virgil looked as serene as ever. No force had been necessary in subduing him. "I have to get back to Telma now, she will be worried."

Jim noticed Virgil wasn't worried about Vanessa, shell-shocked and speechless, currently in the capable hands of Auntie Vi. "You should have thought of that before you killed two people and tried to kill a third. To say nothing of the dog." Jim caught himself choking back a laugh. He wondered if he was hysterical. He knew the signs. He took a deep breath. "Let's take it from the top, Virgil. Why did you kill Len Dreyer?"

Virgil focused on him and said gently, "Would you please see to my Telma, Jim Chopin? She should not be left alone, way out there by herself."

"I'll get hold of Bernie," Bobby said. "He'll find the Grosdidier brothers, send them out after her. We'll bring her back to town, Virgil, and I'll have Auntie Vi look after her. She'll be all right."

"I thank you, Bobby," Virgil said, smiling at him.

"You're welcome," Bobby said. *"Now fucking answer Jim's questions!"*

Virgil's smile didn't falter. He looked at Jim.

Jim sat down across the table from him. "Why did you kill Len Dreyer?"

"Because he found them," Virgil said simply.

"Found who?" Jim said.

"The babies."

"What babies?" Jim looked at Bobby, who pointed a finger at his ear and made a circle.

"Our babies," Virgil said, closing his eyes, his voice dreamy. "Four boys, and a little girl."

Jim took a deep breath, let it out. "You don't have any children, Virgil."

Virgil opened his eyes. "No," he said. "None living. It is the sickness, you see."

"The what?"

"After the babies are born. Telma . . ." Virgil's face creased with sorrow. "I would try to watch, to keep them safe. But I am only one man, and I must work to make our living, so we do not go hungry, so we have a roof over our heads and clothes to wear upon our backs. I would have to go out, to do these things, and when I would come back . . ." He made a helpless gesture. "They would be dead."

Jim stared at him incredulously. He felt rather than saw Bobby's jaw drop. "Are you telling me that you and your wife had five children, and that Telma murdered every one of them?"

"Not murdered," Virgil said vehemently. "She loves the children, does my Telma. She loves the babies. I read up on this, I know what I am talking about. It is the sickness that mothers sometimes get after the birth of their babies. It makes the mothers do strange things."

"Jesus Christ," Bobby said blankly.

Virgil smiled, misty-eyed. "My Telma, she is so beautiful when the babies are born. She holds them close to her. She will not let go."

"She smothered them?" Jim said. He'd heard of similar cases, but five?

"She loved them!" Virgil said. "She loved them," he said in a quieter voice.

"And after she killed them, you buried them on the homestead," Jim said.

"I bury them," Virgil said, nodding. "I make their little coffins—so tiny, they are—and I dress them in the white clothes that Telma has made for them, the little innocents. They are so sweet, our babies."

"Five? You buried five babies?" Jim said. "For crissake, Virgil, why didn't you try to get Telma some help after the first one?"

Virgil looked at him, surprised. "They would have taken her from me, my beautiful Telma," he said in a gentle voice, as if explaining the matter to a child. "I cannot live without my Telma, Jim Chopin."

"You'll have to learn how now," Bobby said.

"Why did you kill Len Dreyer, Virgil?" Jim said, although he thought he already knew.

Virgil's words confirmed his suspicion. "I hire him to rototill my garden in May, but he does not dig where I tell him to."

"He dug up the bodies instead."

Virgil nodded. "My babies," he said sadly, "he digs up our babies. I do not know this at first, of course, only when he comes back the next month, when I have hired him and Dandy Mike to build my greenhouse."

His face darkened. "And then this Len Dreyer asks me for money, and I know if I do not give it to him that he will tell. He comes back every month for the money. I wait until fall, when the snow is going to fall and keep everyone home so they won't see me, and when he comes in October—"

"You shoot him with your shotgun," Jim said. "And then you took his body up to the glacier because you'd heard it was advancing and you figured his body would never be found."

Virgil shrugged. "And if it were, it would be a long time, and nothing to do with me."

"And then," Jim said grimly, "I had the brilliant idea of hiring Kate Shugak to ask around about him. And that frightened you."

"My Telma was upset when she came to the house, asking after Len Dreyer," Virgil said.

"So you set fire to her cabin," Jim said. Bobby, his face dark and his eyes narrow, sat next to him, simmering with a palpable rage.

"I set fire to her cabin," Virgil said. "But she does not die. And then I think I should leave it alone, that Dreyer is dead, that there is nothing to connect him to me, that if I say nothing no one ever will, and me and my Telma will be left alone."

"What about Dandy Mike?" Jim said tightly. "Why did you have to kill him?"

Virgil looked sorrowful. "I went to where Dreyer lived, to make sure there was nothing to find. He came. He wondered that I was there. He said nothing, but I could tell. I had my shotgun with me." He patted the air next to him. "My shotgun," he said, and looked around in some bewilderment when it didn't materialize beneath his hand.

Bobby snapped his fingers. "That's why you wanted to sell your property to Ruthe Bauman for the Kanuyaq Land Trust. You figured if it was designated wilderness, no one would ever find the babies' bodies!"

Virgil looked at him. "Could you see to my Telma now, please? You said that you would, and I am thinking she is very lonely, out there on our homestead, all by her herself. It is only the babies with her now, you see."

And he smiled.

19

"Oh good, you're awake."

Kate's eyeballs felt like they'd been sandpapered.

"You're getting to be a regular customer, Ms. Shugak." A round figure beneath a starched white coat, the inevitable stethoscope draped around her neck, Adrienne Giroux had a soft voice and a gentle touch. "If we had frequent flyer miles, you'd be eligible for a first-class upgrade by now."

"My dog—" Kate said.

"Is fine," Giroux said firmly. She tucked a strand of brown hair back into its twist. "The vet says she had a concussion, like you." She shook her head. "I don't understand how but neither of you were badly hurt." She smiled. "Born lucky, I think is the phrase. Both of you."

Kate blinked up at her. "Mutt's all right?"

"Yes."

"She's not dead?"

"No. She's not even hurt that badly." Giroux smiled. "I imagine that hunky trooper of yours will bring her in at some point during your stay, violating hospital protocols right, left, and center."

"He's not my hunky trooper."

"Really," Dr. Giroux said. "My mistake."

Kate thought back. "Dirt," she said. "I could hardly breathe."

"Yes," the doctor said, "apparently—" but there was no apparently because Kate's eyes closed and she slid gratefully back into sleep.

The second time she opened her eyes Auntie Vi was there, sewing something, her half-glasses slipping down her nose, looking impossibly dear. Kate watched, saying nothing, until Auntie Vi looked up and said, "Katya! You awake!"

"Hi, Auntie," Kate said with what she knew must be a very weak smile.

Auntie Vi smiled back. "You want some water?"

Kate nodded, and sipped at the cup held to her lips, and slipped back into sleep.

The third time she woke up Mutt was there, sitting next to the bed, just tall enough to rest her nose on its edge. Big yellow eyes blinked at Kate, one eyebrow raised, and Kate heard the thumping of a tail against the floor. The area beneath her right ear had been shaved and there were stitches. She looked like Dr. Frankenstein had been using her for experimentation.

"Mutt," Kate said. Tears blurred her eyes. "Mutt," she said again, and reached out. A rending pain beneath her forehead blinded her. Her gasp caused a flurry of movement beyond her vision. She didn't slide into sleep this time, she plummeted.

The fourth time she woke Mutt was still there. Johnny was sitting in Auntie Vi's chair, bent over a book.

When Kate moved, a long rasping tongue came out and washed her face. She half-smiled and tried to clear her throat. "What are you reading?" she said.

Johnny looked up. "You're awake!" he said.

"Everybody says that, and every time they do I fall back asleep. What are you reading?" He held it up, mute. *"Have Spacesuit, Will Travel.* One of my favorites." Wait a minute. Memory came back, painful and painfully. Someone had burned down her cabin, and all her books with it, and all Johnny's, too. "Where did you get it?"

"We got a box of books from Rachel yesterday," he said.

"Good old Rachel," Kate said, closing her eyes and smiling. "Read to me."

Johnny was doubtful. "You want me to start at the beginning?"

"Anywhere."

Kip and Peewee were on their way to Tombaugh Station and Pluto when Kate drifted off this time.

The fifth time she woke she was alone, and hungry, and she had to pee. The catheter was out, thank god, and so was her IV. She sat up carefully, and discovered Mutt asleep on the floor next to the bed. The hair was starting to grow back through her stitches. "Don't we make a pair," Kate said.

Mutt's ears twitched but she didn't move. Kate stepped over her and negotiated the distance between bed and bathroom successfully. She made a fairly praiseworthy attempt at a spit bath, found a comb and wetted down her hair, carefully avoiding the lump that had somehow missed being shaved, and came out looking for her clothes.

"Get the hell back in that bed," Jim said from the door.

She glared at him, swaying a little, the draft coming in through the open back of her hospital gown. It made her feel vulnerable. She hated feeling vulnerable, especially in front of Jim. "Where are my clothes?"

"If I knew I wouldn't tell you. Get back in that bed now, or I'll put you in it."

He looked like he meant it. Grumbling, she obeyed, keeping her back turned away from him. "I'm hungry."

"Yeah, like that's a surprise," he said, and deposited a Styrofoam container on her lap.

She opened it and found country-fried steak, no gravy, eggs scrambled soft, and home fries with onions and green peppers. She blinked. She might even have sniffled.

"Don't you dare cry."

She looked at him, misty-eyed.

"I mean it," he said, sitting on the extreme edge of a chair.

"Where's the coffee?"

He handed her an Americano tall, with cream.

She couldn't help it; one lone tear escaped to run down her cheek. He looked away, glaring at a potted plant sitting on her nightstand. She swiped at the tear with her hand while he wasn't looking. A small brown bag held a side of sausage gravy, plastic flatware, and salt and pepper. "Could you push the table over here?"

He pushed.

"Could you raise the bed, please?"

He raised.

"What day is it?"

"Friday. May sixteenth."

"Thanks." She waded in. Mutt woke up, noticed Jim Chopin was in the room, and padded over to welcome him with a lavish tongue. Her head wound must have slowed her down some, at least temporarily, because she was less effusive than usual. He could be grateful for that while abhorring the cause. He was silent, sipping his own coffee as he waited for Kate to eat. Nothing got in the way of Kate Shugak and a meal, not even a double homicide and two, three if you counted Mutt, attempted ones.

Mutt subsided, lying back down and resting her head on his right foot. He'd been tapping it nervously, so he took that as a hint.

Kate finished the last bite with a positively voluptuous sigh and leaned back, uncapping the coffee and sniffing it ecstatically. She sipped, and made a sound that sounded appropriate coming from a bed. Jim gritted his teeth.

"I'm going to live," she said, smiling at him.

"Good," he said briskly. "Now tell me what happened. You went out to the Hagbergs' place. Why?"

Right to business. She searched her memory, and to her relief the fragments came together. "Because I got to looking at the list of people who'd had contact with Dreyer prior to his murder, and after what Gary Drussell said, I wondered if there were minor girl children in any of the other homes. And then of course I remembered Vanessa."

"Of course."

"So I went over there to talk to Virgil and Telma about Vanessa. I wanted to make sure she was all right, that Dreyer hadn't gotten to her the way he had Tracy Drussell, and that if he had that we got her some help."

"I see." He sat still for a moment. "And Virgil thought you were there because you'd figured out that he had killed Dreyer."

She looked up. "Virgil killed Len Dreyer?"

He nodded. "And Dandy Mike."

She stared. "What?"

"He shot Dandy Mike," Jim said stonily. "Dandy was just like you, he wouldn't stay fired. He kept asking questions, and Virgil got to hear about it, and last Monday he followed Dandy up to Dreyer's cabin and shot him with the same shotgun he used to kill Dreyer."

Kate closed her eyes. "Dandy's dead?"

"Yes," Jim said, snapping the words out. "Dandy is most definitely dead. They're releasing his body today, so you'll be home in time for the potlatch. Billy and Annie are planning one hell of a potlatch."

There was silence for a long time in the room. "I was so sure," Kate said at last in a faraway voice, "I was so sure after we found out about Duffy serving time for a child abuse conviction that the killer would be some outraged parent. I was even prepared maybe to let it slide."

"I wouldn't have let you."

"You wouldn't have known," she said. "Did you talk to George?"

"No. George? Why?"

She told him. "And then he came out to my place the next day and said that he'd lied to me, that Gary Drussell had flown into the Park last fall, looking for Len Dreyer, and that he'd had a shotgun with him. He told George he hadn't found him, but we both figured he was lying. So I was sure Gary had done it, had killed Dreyer."

"And it turns out," Jim said after a moment, "that instead it was something that Dreyer/Duffy found during one of his jobs." He told her the rest of the story.

"Five?" she said. "Five babies? All dead?"

He nodded. "And buried out back. Dreyer dug in the wrong place. You've got to wonder if he meant it to happen, letting Dreyer dig so close to where they were buried."

Another silence. Kate said, "I was thinking before what a perfect position Len Dreyer was in to ferret out Park dirt." She gave a humorless laugh. "In the end that's exactly what he did. He was rototilling the garden and up come the bodies." Her brow wrinkled. "He was out there twice, though."

"Out where?"

"Out to Virgil's, last summer. Once for the rototilling, and once to help Virgil dig the foundation to a new greenhouse."

He nodded. "Yeah, he didn't tell Virgil right away that he'd found Virgil and Telma's little cemetery. He waited until he had a plan, and when Virgil hired him back to help on the greenhouse, he laid it out for him."

"Blackmail?"

"Yeah. Not a lot of money, but steady. What Dreyer didn't know was that Virgil had a plan, too. I'm not sure he decided to kill Dreyer until the glacier offered him a place to hide the body."

She pushed her coffee away. "Where is Telma?"

"She's in API, undergoing a psych eval."

"And Virgil?

"At Cook Inlet Pre-Trial. He's not crazy, he's just homicidal. Which reminds me. How the hell did he get both you and Mutt?"

They both looked at the big gray half-husky, half-malamute, chin resting on her god's shoe, eyes closed in an expression of perfect bliss. "I don't know, exactly. I turned Mutt loose to forage. The next thing I remember was looking at the side of a shovel coming at me, and that's all I remember until I woke up here."

"It was a miracle he didn't shoot you both," Jim said savagely.

"Why didn't he?"

"Beats the hell out of me. I would have." He glared at her. "I think it was because he forgot to load the shotgun after he killed Dandy. Wasn't used to killing people, I don't think, although we haven't dug up his whole homestead—who knows, there might be a dozen more bodies out there."

Kate shifted beneath the sheet that was all she could bear in the way of covers. It was too hot in this damn hospital. She longed for the cool, the peace, and the solitude of her cabin. The easy tears came back when she remembered it no longer existed. She battled them back. "Thanks, by the way."

"For what?"

"You did the CPR. Johnny told me."

He shrugged. "And then you puked all over me."

"Sorry about that," she said, a little nettled.

"Yeah, well. You brought yourself back, really. Were you conscious when he dumped you in the ground?"

"Barely. Enough to pretend to be dead. I managed to scoop out a little breathing space beneath my nose without him seeing, before I passed out."

"So you'll be able to testify at trial."

"Bet your ass," she said.

"Good. Although it may not come to trial."

"Did Virgil confess?"

"Oh hell yes," Jim said, mouth compressed in a firm line. "He's confessed to burying the babies after his wife had them and then smothered them in her arms. He's confessed to killing Len Dreyer aka Leon Duffy and hiding his body in Grant Glacier. He's confessed to running Dreyer aka Duffy's truck into a lake on his property, from where we have now recovered it. He's confessed to burning down your cabin, and he's confessed how much of a shock it was to see you alive the next morning. He's confessed to killing Dandy Mike because Dandy just got too darn nosy, poking his nose into other people's business, and he's confessed to trying to kill you. And Mutt. He's real sorry about Mutt, by the way. He wanted me to make sure you knew."

"Are you okay?" she said.

"Oh, I'm fine. I'm peachy keen, I'm jim—you should pardon the expression—dandy, I'm good to go. Why do you ask?"

"No reason," she said, wary now.

"I'm sorry," he said.

"Okay," she said.

"No, I'm not." He rose to pace. Mutt, dislodged, uttered a protest, which was ignored.

There wasn't much room for more than two strides, so he turned a lot. Mutt and Kate watched him, heads swiveling like they were at a tennis match. "Virgil has also confessed to loving his wife. That's it, that's his sole reason for two murders and three attempts. He loved his wife and he didn't want her to go to jail for murdering her babies. The thing is, they were his babies, too. And they wanted children, he told me so."

"There is something called postpartum depression," Kate said.

He waved an impatient hand. "Yeah, yeah, I've read the cases, there have been enough of them in the news lately, and I've responded to more than one SIDS death. I could understand Telma having postpartum depression, what I can't understand is her having it five times with five babies and her husband standing by for burial detail every time without turning a hair."

"You think he didn't want them? You think he maybe killed them?"

He shook his head and came to rest in front of the window. Looking down at the parking lot, he said in a quieter tone, "No. I think she killed them and I think he buried them. You know, Kate, I have seen some shit in my time. Cops get their faces rubbed in the worst of human nature every goddamn day of our working lives, and I am sorry as hell to report that a lot of the time it has something to do with somebody loving somebody else. Hell of a testament to the power of love, don't you think?" He turned to face her. "I asked him. Why, Virgil, I said. Why did you do it? I love my Telma, he says back to me. Jesus. *He loved his wife*, was all he could say. Well, the hell with that. Kate?"

"Jim?" she said, still wary.

"I've been chasing you."

"I've noticed," she said cautiously.

"Lately, it hasn't seemed all that one-sided."

"Lately, it hasn't been," she said.

"It's over," he said.

"I beg your pardon?"

"I'm getting off this ride," he told her. He picked up his ball cap and yanked it down over his eyes. "If this is what love's all about, I don't want any part of it." He paused. "I'm sorry if I led you on, made you imagine there was any more to it than a good time."

She looked at him with eyes a little wider than normal but otherwise with no expression.

"I take full responsibility," he said doggedly. "I don't know, maybe I just wanted you because Jack had you and I couldn't. And then Jack was gone and I could. I've always wanted you, hell, you have to know that. But you're a serious woman, and you tend to be with one man at a time. That's not me. I'm not that man."

He looked at her, clearly bracing himself for an attack. She took a long, slow, careful breath, inhale, exhale, and felt a triumph so fierce well up inside her breast that it was hard to speak around it. She made the effort, and managed a mild, neutral, "If that's how you feel."

"That's how I feel." He would make it be how he felt if it was the last thing he ever did.

"Okay," she said, praying he was out of the room before she burst out laughing.

"Love doth make fools of us all," he added.

"Huh?" Kate said.

"Yip?" Mutt said.

"Dothn't it," he said, and the door swung shut behind him.

She waited until she heard his footsteps recede down the hall before lying back on the bed. She stared at the ceiling, and the laughter that welled up was so loud and lasted so long that the nurse came down from her station to see what was causing Kate's heart rate to speed up on the monitor. When she saw the tears on Kate's face, she rushed forward, all concern.

Kate waved her off. "I'm fine, believe me, I've never been better." She beamed and scrubbed her cheeks. Her head still hurt but otherwise she felt fine, just fine. "All men are morons."

The nurse's face cleared, but she remained cautious. "That would be a given. Still. Can't live with 'em, can't live without 'em."

Kate felt that it had been worth getting hit on the head with a shovel just to hear those words. "Where's my pants?" she said.

"So I go out there, all concerned, thinking that Vanessa might have been raped by Dreyer," Kate said, "and it turns out he was moving on up to blackmail."

"Fucking insane," Bobby said.

"Hagberg or Dreyer?"

"Over the fucking rainbow, both of them."

"Can't argue with that," Kate said. She was at Bobby's house, a pit stop between the plane ride from Ahtna to Niniltna and the long drive home. "It's funny, too. Before I went out there I was thinking about Dreyer and all the opportunities he'd have for blackmail. He was in and out of our homes every day, not to mention the post office, the café, the Roadhouse. The opportunities for picking up information were endless. Hell, I don't know why he didn't hit Keith Gette up for a few bucks."

Bobby smiled smugly. "And why would he think he could do that?"

"They're growing dope in the Gettes' old greenhouse, Bobby," Kate said. "What, you didn't know?"

The smug smile vanished. "They are not," he said indignantly. "They're growing herbs."

"Herbs?" she said with heavy sarcasm. "Herbs? Is that what we're calling marijuana these days?"

"No, it's what we call parsley, sage, rosemary, and thyme," he said with equal sarcasm. "They're gonna dry 'em and sell them on their website."

"Website?"

"Yeah, the one Dinah's helping them build, www-dot-praiseofcooks-dot-com. Or dot-org. Dot-something, anyway. That 'praise of cooks' thing comes from the Charlemagne quote," he added parenthetically, "you know the one."

"No," Kate said, and wondered if perhaps she had left the hospital before she should have. "Can't say as I do."

" 'What is an herb?' Alcuin his tutor asked him," Bobby declaimed, with gestures. "And Charlemagne answered, 'The friend of physicians and the praise of cooks.' "

"Herbs," Kate said. She was skeptical, not necessarily of the quotation but certainly of what Keith and Oscar were really growing up on the old Gette homestead. A cop's instinct to expect the worst died hard. "And you know this how?"

"Bonnie down at the post office in Niniltna sent them to me when they asked her who knew how to set up a computer and a satellite dish."

Kate digested this for a moment. "Have you actually seen this alleged parsley, sage, rosemary, and thyme growing?"

"No, but they gave me some, and a couple of recipes." Bobby assumed a virtuous expression. "Really, Kate, I don't think you should go around assuming the worst of people. Just because—" And then he had to duck when she threw a pillow at him.

"Besides," he said, recovering his dignity, as well as rolling strategically out of range, "if Dreyer was going to blackmail them, he'd think of something much better."

"Something better than growing marijuana?"

"Yeah," Bobby said, and started laughing. "They're gay, Kate."

"Gay?"

"Gay," Bobby said, nodding, a broad grin on his face. "Jesus

Christ, how naïve are you, Shugak? They're a couple."

"A couple?"

He lay back in his chair, helpless with laughter. Dinah was laughing, too. Even Katya was getting in on the act.

"Yeah, yeah, so my gaydar isn't as good as some other people's," Kate said when the laughter finally died down to a couple of hiccups and the odd tear.

"Jesus, you don't need gaydar when they're practically necking right in front of you," Bobby said. He rubbed the heel of his hand across his face. "Man, I haven't laughed like that in I don't know how long. Thanks, Kate."

"Anytime," Kate said dryly.

"Seen Jim lately?" Dinah said.

Kate's face went opaque. "He came to the hospital to clear up some questions about the case."

"Oh." Something going on there, Dinah thought, and exchanged a look with her husband. Turning back she caught a very small, very odd smile on Kate's face. She would have pursued it to its source, but Kate was talking again. "So Jeffrey went home."

"Yes, finally, the prick did go home," Bobby said.

"Alone," Kate said.

"I don't believe what I'm hearing," Bobby said. "You actually think I should have gone with him?"

"Oh, man." Kate sighed and shook her head. She got to her feet and went to the window, looking at the Quilaks for inspiration. She stretched a little, wincing as new skin rubbed against her shirt. "I ever tell you how Emaa died?"

She heard the whisper of rubber tires as he wheeled up next to her. "No."

"It was in the middle of AFN. She wasn't feeling well, kept rubbing her left arm. For crissake, I trained as an EMT when I worked in Anchorage, I even went on a few runs. I know the signs, but I didn't see them on my grandmother." She closed her eyes. "She was supposed to make a speech on subsistence in front of the whole convention, in front of Alaska Natives from

Metlakatla to Point Lay. Hundreds of people in the room, and she was such a giant, they all wanted to hear what she had to say. It would define the issue for a lot of them, they'd go home quoting her."

She took a deep breath. "So she's feeling lousy, and she hands it off to me." She looked down at him, her smile wavering. "Just walks away, and leaves me standing there with no speech and no track record and no profile to speak of, not compared to hers."

She was wrong about that last, but Bobby held his peace.

"So I told them some yarn about shooting a moose in my front yard that year. They held still for it, they even put their hands together for it."

Bobby somehow managed to hide his amazement.

"Right after, a woman I know, she's—well." Kate gave up on trying to describe Cindy Sovalik. "Someone I met when I was doing that job for Jack in Prudhoe Bay. She said I should check on Emaa. Well, that was what she meant, anyway. So I did."

She took a long, shaky breath. "I got the maid to let me into her hotel room, and she was just lying there, kind of frowning. And already cool to the touch."

She shoved her hands in her pockets and turned to look at Bobby. "She handed off to me, did it in public so everyone could see that she expected me to take up where she left off, and then marched off to die."

There followed a bleak silence, broken when Bobby cleared his throat. "I don't see that you could have done anything but what you did."

"No." A ghost of a laugh. "Emaa called the shots in her death, the same way she called the shots in her life."

"Then I don't get it," Bobby said. "My father's calling the shots here, too."

"You're letting him."

He looked at her, angry. "I'm not letting him dictate to me, if that's what you mean."

"Sure you are. You let him push you out of your own home,

let him push you into the army, let him push you all the way to Vietnam. I don't think it's a coincidence that you chose to re-build your life in Alaska, about as far away from Tennessee as you could get and still be in the same country."

"But he wants me to come home."

"Don't go home for him. Go home for yourself. He helped make you what you are, Bobby, like it or not. Go home and say good-bye." She paused, and said slowly, "I didn't get the chance to say good-bye to Emaa. I'll regret it for the rest of my life."

There was another long silence. From her seat on the couch, cradling a sleeping Katya, Dinah looked from one stubborn face to the other, biding her time.

"I just hate the thought of doing anything Jeffie wants me to," Bobby said at last.

And there it was. "This is a guy who's never been out of the state of Tennessee before, right?" Dinah said.

Bobby snorted. "I'd be surprised if he's ever been fifty miles from his own front doorstep."

"Until now," Dinah said. "He was here, though. Humbling himself to you, begging you to come home."

"Ordering," Bobby said, "ordering. There's a difference."

"Whatever it sounded like, he was begging. His father, your father is dying. He could even be dead by now."

There was a brief silence. Finally Bobby said, "Dad always did like him best."

Relieved, Dinah laughed a little harder than the jest deserved.

Bobby looked at her. "So you think I ought to go home, too?"

Dinah chose her words carefully, knowing they would live to haunt her marriage if she got them wrong. "I want a life with you, Bobby, a long one. You brought a lot of baggage with you. I don't care, it's who you are." She smiled a little. "It's part of why I love you. But I also think it's time to get rid of some of it, so it doesn't weigh us down."

"Why, Dinah," Bobby said, "that's fucking poetry."

Dinah reddened. "I mean it, Clark."

Bobby, sober now, said, "I know you do, Dinah." He rolled

over to her and lifted both her and the baby into his lap.

Kate walked past them. "You'll think about it?" she heard Dinah say.

"No," Bobby said, jaw coming out. "I'll go. If I think about it, I won't."

20

The morning Bobby left, Dinah decided she needed something to occupy her time, otherwise she'd sit around waiting for Bobby to call and say they were moving back to Nutbush, Tennessee. It wasn't the call she feared so much as the move. She had fallen in love at first sight with Alaska, and she didn't want to leave it. Not to mention which, Jeffrey's reaction to the undeniable fact of her overwhelming whiteness had been somewhat daunting. She could deal with that, and with any hundred other people who reacted that way, too, but how would those same people treat Katya?

She looked down at her daughter, a hot heavy sprawl in her arms, a little milky drool coming from one corner of her mouth. Love pierced her like a knife. If anyone in Nutbush, Tennessee dared, if they dared to say something hurtful to Katya, if anyone dared to call her half-and-half or half-breed or mongrel, Katya's mother would . . .

"What would Katya's mother do?" she said out loud. Katya stirred, and Dinah gathered in her child's rambling limbs and tucked her into her own bed. Then she went for a pad and paper and started making a list. She liked making lists as much as Kate

Shugak, and this one was a list Kate would get behind.

At least she hoped so.

She spent the next week on the Internet and the phone, talking to suppliers in Anchorage and a trucking firm in Ahtna that boasted enough vehicles for her purposes. The following week she strapped Katya into the children's seat, strapped the seat into the truck, and drove around the Park knocking on doors. Her plan was met with enthusiasm and near universal approval, mostly under the heading of "Jeeze, I wish I'd thought of that."

She stopped by the trooper post to touch base with Jim Chopin. He listened courteously and agreed to everything she suggested. She came away with a crease between her brows. Something was seriously wrong there. Jim was a pretty even keel kind of a guy. The only time she'd seem him angry was with Kate Shugak, who seemed to know where every button on his control panel was located and exactly when to push which one. At the moment, he had his guard up. Dinah wondered if he had his guard up with Kate. She wondered about that little smile she'd seen on Kate's face.

She hesitated before knocking on Billy Mike's door, but he received her idea with hosannahs, and he and Annie convened the Native Association's board of directors and essentially made her plan happen. Afterward she realized that she'd done them a favor. Anything was better than sitting around grieving. Billy even managed to pull some string that connected to the manufacturer Outside that bumped their order to the top of the list. It came into the Port of Anchorage on board the *CSX Anchorage* the following week, and the shipping firm, mindful of maintaining good community relations in a place as small as Alaska, took care to see that the shipment was first out of the hold and first off the dock. A day later it was in Ahtna, and by then the road into the Park had dried out enough to grade. This time Old Sam pulled a string—Dinah suspected the driver was an old drinking buddy of his—and the grader stationed at the state highway maintenance facility outside Ahtna led the parade, and a parade it was. First the grader, then a fleet of flatbeds and a couple of semis, followed by a dozen rigs of varying age and shape, all riding very low on their axels.

Dinah and Billy and nearly everyone else in the Park met them at the trailhead. "Does she know we're coming?" Billy said.

"She doesn't know anything about this," Dinah said. "I'm terrified she's going to kill me."

Billy Mike looked a little older and a little more tired, but the grin that split his round moon face was still broad. "But not very," he said.

She laughed. "No, not very," she said.

He squinted at the sky, clear and blue and filled with the beginning of a long summer day. "Picked a good day for it."

"Yeah," she said. "The long-term forecast looks good, too. I think the gods are backing us up on this one, Billy."

"God," he said, staring at the horizon. "One's enough."

The grader ground by, continued a hundred feet down the road, and pulled to a halt. The driver swung out and down and trotted back.

"Need to finish that road, don'tcha Bud?" Billy said, quizzical.

Bud Riley grinned. "No way am I missing out on this. Kate helped a friend of mine out of a thing in Anchorage one time."

The parade ground to a halt, dust rising, but not so much as anybody sneezed, and the driver of the lead flatbed jumped to the ground. "Dinah Cookman? Jake Bradley, Ahtna Fast Freight. Got a delivery for you." He made an elaborate show of producing a clipboard. "Sign here, please."

A shout of laughter started in the crowd behind Dinah and spread down the line of vehicles. Billy showed Jake the road in. Jake scratched his head. "Well, hell, could be worse, I expect." He spat and shifted a wad of chewing tobacco from one cheek to the other. "We've all got come-alongs, so we won't get stuck and stay stuck. And it ain't like we ain't done this kind of thing before. Probably should take out a few of those trees. Think she'll go for that?"

"Probably, but it don't have to be that hard," someone said, and Dinah turned to see Mac Devlin puffing up. She looked beyond him and saw his D-6 Caterpillar tractor idling up the road, the sound of its approach hidden only by the convoy. He looked at Dinah and raised a brow.

"Why not," she said, and stood back. If Kate was going to kill her, let it be for more than one reason. Besides, Bobby's truck had been stuck on that damn game trail down to Kate's cabin more than once.

Mac hustled back to the D-6 and put it in gear, and they made room for him to start down the trail.

She'd spent most of the night like she had most nights recently, wide awake and staring at the ceiling. It was bothering her, how she'd missed Dreyer's predilection for children. After five and a half years working sex crimes in Anchorage, many of them involving children, she should have spotted him out of the gate. Why hadn't she?

And then there was Virgil. She'd waltzed right on into the lion's den, riding to the rescue of a girl who didn't need one, and was cold-cocked by a shovel—a number two shovel!—for her pains. It was downright embarassing.

At four A.M. Mutt got tired of listening to her thrash around and sat up to give Kate a look. "Are we losing it, girl?" Kate asked her. "Are we slowing up? Do we just not have the stuff anymore?"

Mutt raised an eyebrow and lay down with her back turned pointedly to Kate. Evidently she wasn't past her prime.

And Dandy, that harmless, ambitionless rounder, dead. She shouldn't have warned him off so firmly. She should have pulled him into the investigation instead of pushing him out. She'd probably offended every molecule of his testosterone by shutting him down so hard. He'd found real information for them. True, none of it had helped solve the case, but still, he'd hustled for them and she'd flicked him off like a bug.

Conveniently, she forgot that Jim had been sitting right next to her and had done his own share of flicking.

Of course Dandy's pride had kicked in. Her attitude had been nothing less than a challenge to him. Her attitude had gotten him killed. Hubris, she thought Sophocles had called it. Whatever it was, she had it and it had gotten Dandy killed.

She had just given up on sleep and was rolling out of bed, the RV shuddering beneath the shifting weight of her 120 pounds, the movement causing Johnny to slide even further down in his bunk than he had been, when she heard the muted roar of an engine, a big one. Mutt, whose nose had been pressed to the door for some time, with attendant whining, gave a short, sharp yelp. "What the hell's going on, girl?" Kate said, shrugging into a shirt and jamming her feet into her shoes. "Go get 'em." If someone was mowing down trees on her property with the blade of a Caterpillar tractor and without her permission, she would know the reason why before she was very much older. If she was lucky, she might get to shoot somebody.

Mutt shot out of the open door and across the clearing like a bullet out of a gun. She vanished up the trail, and shortly thereafter there was a loud yell of alarm followed by a lot of barking.

"What's going on?" Johnny said, raising his head, his face flushed and his hair mashed to a conehead point.

"I don't know," Kate said grimly. "Someone's got a Cat going. That can't be good." She reached for the .30-06 leaning against the door. "Better go back up Mutt."

His eyes widened, all trace of sleepiness banished, and dove out of his bunk and into his clothes in the same moment. She thought about telling him to stay put, and she thought about how effective that would be, and said only, "Stay behind me. Especially stay behind the rifle."

He gave her a look and she grinned at him. "Gotta say that. It's part of the job."

"Yeah, yeah." He stayed close behind her up the trail, from the top of which there seemed to be coming a lot of noise of one kind or another.

They met Mac Devlin halfway down. Mutt was standing directly in front of the blade. She was barking and wagging her tail at the same time.

Kate felt as confused as Mutt looked. Behind Mac on his Cat there was quite a crowd: Dinah looking nervous, Billy Mike grinning, Annie Mike dispensing coffee and what looked like a mountain of fresh doughnuts, Auntie Vi and the other three aunties unloading coolers and boxes and grocery bags, Bernie and Enid unloading cases of pop and beer and bags of ice, Dan O'Brian with the whole gang down from the Step, including Dr. Millicent Nebeker McClanahan. Laurel Meganack had baked up a dozen pies, apple and cherry and pumpkin, and Auntie Balasha had a whole salmon carton of fry bread, fresh out of the frying pan if the steam rising off them was any indication.

"What are you all doing here?" Kate said. She caught a glimpse of vehicles lined up down the road and stepped forward. Yep, all the way down to the curve, where she had confronted Roger McAniffe years ago.

"Well, Kate," Dinah said, shifting from foot to foot, "it's like this."

She paused.

"Like what?" Kate said. Next to her Johnny was starting to grin. "What's going on?" she asked him.

"It's like this, Kate," Billy Mike said, taking pity on Dinah's agony. "We're going to build you a house today."

"I beg your pardon?"

"You can help," he told her, "but don't get in our way."

She was so staggered that she let him push her gently but firmly to one side of the track.

Mac put the Cat in gear and finished carving out a track, finishing in a neat little circle that would be nice for parking. He roared backward up the trail, dragging the blade to smooth out the tracks, and someone Kate didn't know pulled up in a dump truck loaded with gravel. Mac packed that down in about thirty minutes and then things really got lively.

Kate had had the well redug and a septic tank put in. The foundation was in over them by that evening. They let the cement cure overnight. Tents sprung up like mushrooms all the way back to the road, and some slept in their trucks, but they all stayed.

"It's a Lindel Cedar home, Kate," Dinah told her the next morning. She was still nervous, still unsure. "It's got two bedrooms and two bathrooms, one full, one three-quarter."

"Bathrooms?" Kate said.

"And it's got a loft, just like your old cabin," Dinah said. "Well, okay, maybe not just like it, but it's a loft. There's a covered porch in back that we're going to extend all the way around to a deck in front."

"A deck?" Kate said.

"It's twenty-five by forty-one, only sixteen feet longer than your cabin, which makes it thirteen hundred seventy-one square feet total," Dinah said. "Four hundred forty-five up and nine hundred twenty-six down." She saw Kate's expression and added hurriedly, "I know it's big, especially compared to the cabin, but you need the extra room now that you've got Johnny living with you. You'll get used to it, I know you will, and pretty soon you won't even notice—"

"Dinah."

"Yes, Kate." With a valiant effort Dinah stilled the trembling in her knees.

"Thank you." Kate kissed her on both cheeks and hugged her. "Thank you very much."

"Oh." Dinah blushed. "Ah. Okay. Good. You're happy."

"Tell me how I'm paying for this and I'll be even happier."

"Oh." Dinah's eyes slid to one side. "Well, you'd have to talk to Billy Mike about that."

Billy Mike said, "Well, you'd have to talk to Auntie Vi about that."

Auntie Vi said, "Well, you'd have to talk to Pete Heiman about that."

"Pete Heiman isn't here," Kate said, and then realized the implication. "Wait. Wait just a damn minute here. You mean to tell me you're putting my new house up with *federal money*? For crissake, Auntie! What if they find out?"

Auntie Vi gave her niece a pitying look. "Katya, for such a bright girl you are not very smart."

The frame was up by noon, the trusses, with the help of the cherry picker, four hours later. All they would let Kate do was bring people drinks, so she did. "Thanks, Kate," Bill Bingley said, laying down a screw gun and flat-footing the Coke she handed him. He wiped his mouth and grinned at her. "Thirsty work, this."

His wife Cindy was working next to him, and smiled her thanks.

Mac Devlin, now at the controls of the cherry picker, paused in the act of raising a load of shingles to the roof to take a drink. "Fine day," he said, red face shining with sweat. He might even have smiled.

Auntie Joy scurried by with a nail gun and plucked up two cans of Diet Sprite on the run, tossing one to George Perry, who paused in the countersinking of Sheetrock screws for a cold drink. "God, how I hate Sheetrock dust," he said cheerfully, and went back to work. Dan O'Brian and Millicent Nebeker McClanahan were stapling electrical cable to the studs right in front of him, and right behind him—"Anne!" Kate said. "Anne Flanagan! What are you doing here?"

"Cutting holes for the outlets," the minister said, laughing. "Did you think I would miss out on this?"

Bernie and Enid Koslowski were mudding and taping one wall, working together smoothly, like a team who had done this before. On the opposite wall two older women were doing the same thing, one climbing a ladder to work on the open area above the living room, the other holding the ladder. Kate took a second look, unable to believe her first. "Cindy? Olga?"

Olga Shapsnikoff and Cindy Sovalik paid her no attention. "Old woman, you are not using enough mud on that seam," Olga said.

From the top of the ladder Cindy Sovalik said, "Old woman,

how can I put enough mud on the seam when this ladder shakes like there is an earthquake underfoot?"

Old Sam Dementieff was on the roof, skipping nimbly from rafter to rafter, accompanied by the rat-a-tat of a staple gun. Kate handed up a can of pop. "I can't believe this," she told him. "I just—I can't—" Speech failed her.

He grinned down at her, sweat dripping from his nose. "Believe it," he said.

And if Kate had been worried as to how to fill up all this achingly empty new space, her fears would have been allayed by the appearance of two beds and a couch big enough to fill up the living room all by itself and a dining table with four chairs handcarved from some kind of pine. There were pillows and sets of sheets to fit both beds, with blankets to spare, and kitchen utensils, and Costco packs of Ivory soap and toilet paper and paper towels. Keith and Oscar brought her a flat full of herb starters. "It's not for the house exactly," Oscar said, a little shy.

"They're exactly right," Kate told him.

"Here," Old Sam growled, shoving a book at her, and damning the duo with a suspicious glare. "Get your library kickstarted."

Kate had to blink several times before she could focus on the page she opened at random. " 'There's the picture—and it isn't exaggerated,' " she read.

> We find them everywhere. Slowly, but surely, our male citizenry is becoming emasculated to the point of utter helplessness. Sliding along, content in their weakness, glorying in their inability to do things. Proud of the fact that they've never been taught to use their hands—and blind also, to the fact that they know mighty little about using their heads.

A laugh was surprised out of her, and she looked at the cover. "*Modern Gunsmithing,*" she said. It had been published in 1933. She looked up at Old Sam, whose name was written on the flyleaf in round, careful boyish letters. "Thank you, Uncle."

He nodded, satisfied, and stumped off.

But it was the gift from the four aunties that rendered Kate speechless. It was a handmade quilt embroidered and appliquéd with Alaskan wildflowers, so colorfully and painstakingly made that they were even more glorious than the real thing. It was a solid piece of work, thick and soft and heavy.

"You have a son now," Auntie Balasha said.

"So you get a quilt," Auntie Joy said.

"You sleep warm under it," Auntie Edna said.

"You watch that boy," Auntie Vi said, "he get too skinny, you send him to me, I fatten him up."

The expression on Kate's face must have been enough, because they, too, stumped away with satisfied expressions.

Dinah said softly, "Everyone I talked to wanted to help, Kate. The people who couldn't make it to the house-raising contributed materials or phone minutes or ran around for me in Anchorage or sent gifts. This wasn't just the Park, this was pretty damn near the whole state. Brandan says hi, by the way. So does Andy Pence." She smiled a little. "Bobby may never speak to me again, however. He's so pissed he missed this."

"He's okay?"

Dinah nodded. "He's okay. He's staying for the funeral at Jeffrey's request, but he'll be back on Sunday."

Kate smiled at her. "Is he glad he went?"

"Yeah. It was tough, he said, but his father was glad to see him, and his mother was glad because his father was glad." She grinned. "He showed them a picture of me and Dinah, and Jeffrey was afraid it was going to push the dad into the great beyond then and there."

Kate laughed. "Bring him out right away so I can show him the new house."

Dinah's eyes glinted. "Well, maybe not right away."

By midnight it was done, right down to the plumbing and the wiring. Kate wandered around the inside, half dazed. The heavy wooden door fit solidly into its frame, weather-stripped within an inch of its life and snug behind a glass storm door. There were wall plates over the light switches and the electrical outlets. There were toilets in the bathrooms. There was a refrigerator and a stove in the kitchen, both propane-powered. A brand new woodstove big enough to heat the whole house stood in one corner of the living room, with pipe ascending to the ceiling and emerging outside in a capped chimney.

Oh, she still had to paint, and get a fuel tank for the furnace, and they'd left the choice and installation of floor covering up to her, but the windows were all in and they opened with little cranks and they had screens on them, even up in the loft. There was a deck—a deck, she couldn't believe it.

The whole house smelled sweetly of cedar. In the morning, light would pour into the house from the windows that started at the floor and ended just beneath the eaves. Through them, the Quilak Mountains curved south and diminished into the west, and she could almost imagine that she could see a blue shine off the surface of Prince William Sound. She would wake up to that view every morning of her life.

She took a deep breath, blinked back tears, and walked out the door of the kitchen onto the deck and up to the brand-new railing, looking at the people sprawled around her front yard.

Jim Chopin was squatting at the edge of the crowd over a toolbox, wiping tools with an oily rag and stowing them away. He was responsible for some of the kitchen; she had seen him working in it. He felt her gaze and looked up.

She held it for a moment, and then let her eyes drop down over his body. She raised them again just as slowly, loitering here and there, a long, lingering, and from the expression on his face, almost palpable look. She met his eyes again, and smiled, a smile that told him she knew exactly what changes her look had wrought. He flushed right up to the roots of his hair, definitely a first in Park history, slammed the toolbox shut, and took off out of the clearing as if the hounds of hell were at his heels.

She looked back at the rest of them, her relatives, her friends, her fellow Park rats—yes, her family. No less than three barbecues were broiling hamburgers and hot dogs. Folding tables had been set edge to edge with buns and condiments and salads and desserts and a tower of paper plates and a bucket full of plastic flatware. Now that the work was done, tubs of beer packed in ice appeared. Someone was strumming a guitar and a few voices were beginning to sing along.

"Hey," she said. Nobody heard her. "Hey," she said, more loudly this time. Heads turned and voices stilled. She felt movement beside her and turned to see Johnny. Vanessa watched both of them through the window.

Kate held out an arm, and Johnny came to stand within its curve. "The kid and I want to say thanks for our new house. Thanks." She laughed a little and shook her head. "There are no words."

Her eyes filled with tears. There was nothing she could say that would express the fullness of her heart. Johnny gave her an awkward boy's hug, and she hugged him right back.

People rose up, one by one, until everyone was on their feet. "Here's to Kate's new house," Billy Mike said.

"Hear, hear," someone else said.

"Here's to Kate," a third person said. There were cheers and whoops and whistles, and a growing, deafening sound of applause that thundered up into the perpetual twilight of an Arctic spring, spreading across the Park to Niniltna and the Step and the foothills and the Quilaks and the coast and the Gulf and— who knew? Perhaps even beyond.

Kate held up a hand for silence. She got it, eventually. She looked around for her glass and Johnny thrust his pop can into her hand.

"No," she said, and raised the pop can like it was a crystal chalice filled with only the best champagne.

"Here's to you."

Sunday, June 1

I don't believe this house we've got, this is nicer than Mom's house in Anchorage, it's as nice as Dad's house on Westchester Lagoon. Everything is so new, I'm afraid to touch anything. Kate says that's what a house is for, to live in, and that dirt happens and she's bound to track in as much or more than me. And I have my own room, and there is an indoor toilet and Kate says maybe we'll even get a hot water heater and be able to have showers!

I know Kate's a little sad still about the cabin being gone. I mean, her father built it and she was born in it, so I can understand. But the new house is so cool, and the way it got built is even cooler. Ms. Doogan said it was positively Amish.

Van is living with Mr. and Mrs. Mike. She says it seems kind of funny to be living with the parents of the guy her uncle murdered, but she says they love kids and that seems to include her. They've got a little baby they adopted from Korea and sometimes she baby-sits and she likes that, too, especially since they pay her. There might be some trouble with DYFS when they find out that Billy and Annie just took her in, Kate says, and I'm quoting, "but it's not like we haven't bearded that lion in his den and whupped his ass before." Sheesh.

Van says they talk at the Mikes, and you can play music and make as much noise as you want, Annie doesn't mind. I'm letting Van settle in and then I'll go visit. Mrs. Mike makes fry bread almost as good as Auntie Vi's.

Jim hasn't been around much lately, but we heard that Virgil Hagberg pled guilty to all charges. Auntie Vi says the stuffing went out of him when Telma was put into care, whatever that means. Hard to feel sorry for him. I mean, he killed two people and he would have killed Kate if we hadn't shown up in time. And me, when he burned down the cabin. And Mutt. Still, it's sad. Those poor dead babies. Mrs. Hagberg must really be crazy.

I've been reading up on the corvis family of birds, magpies, crows, jays, and ravens. I was having a hard time dealing with what they did to Mr. Mike's son. I know it's just nature but it was really ugly. I told Ruthe about it and she gave me a couple of books and I've been reading them. This Bernd Heinrich guy has spent a whole lot of time with birds, I'll say that much for him.

I think I saw a wolverine the other day. I didn't tell Kate because she hates them, which is kind of funny because she's kind of like a wolverine. They're pretty solitary and so is she. They defend what's theirs and so does she. They need a lot of territory, a lot of space, and so does she. They stay off by themselves except in mating season. No way I'm going near that one. The wolverine I saw was beautiful, almost black with two lighter stripes down its sides, real shiny coat, shiny as Kate's hair. It looked very tough and muscular, able to take care of itself. That's like Kate, too.

Kate's got her bedroom in the loft and I can hear her moving around up there. She's already scrounging for some Blazo boxes so she can have shelves. I tell her she ought to break down and buy a dresser, but she say that an old Blazo box is probably better made than any new piece of furniture. I don't know, my new bed is kinda comfortable. I like it.

The other day I asked Kate a question. "Why don't you carry a gun?" I said. I mean, if she carried a gun, no way would Mr. Hagberg have been able to take her out with a shovel. Dad had a gun. Jim Chopin has a gun. Kate gets into it with bad guys all the time. I can't figure why she doesn't carry one. And then when she does, like when she grabbed the rifle when we heard Mac Devlin's Cat up the trail, she never even took the safety off.

She got this funny look on her face. "Guns are too easy," she said. And that's all she said.

So now I'm wondering. Too easy for what? Too easy to shoot? But if someone's trying to kill you you've got a right to defend yourself, and why should you have to work at it, why shouldn't it be easy?

I'll never understand Kate. Van says maybe I'm not supposed to, and maybe I'm not. She's got a lot to teach me, though, Kate does, and I want to learn it all.

I'm home.